"MASTER OF THE LEGAL THRILLER."
—*Abilene Reporter-News*

"Excellent . . . Bernhardt, an attorney, handles a complicated two–tier story well, and the court scenes are exciting and surprisingly informative."
—*Orlando Sentinel*

"The trial preparation and actual courtroom scenes are intense and fresh and will put you on the edge of your seat."
—*Alfred Hitchcock Mystery Magazine*

"Superb storytelling, a masterful plot, edge–of–the–seat suspense, and a hero to die for make *Silent Justice* a one–of–a–kind reading experience. William Bernhardt is unsurpassed at creating tension ridden plots and *Silent Justice* shows him at the height of his abilities. As a bonus, Ben is the sort of hero daydreams are made of."
—*Romantic Times Magazine*
(A "Top Pick" selection)

"[A] riveting courtroom drama . . . Plenty of thrills . . . [Bernhardt] injects suspenseful subplots, which serve to propel the non–stop action."
—*Record-Chronicle* (Denton, Texas)

"A great book . . . Might have inspired the hit movie *Erin Brockovich*."
—*Winnipeg Free Press*

By William Bernhardt
Published by The Ballantine Publishing Group:

PRIMARY JUSTICE
BLIND JUSTICE
DEADLY JUSTICE
PERFECT JUSTICE
CRUEL JUSTICE
NAKED JUSTICE
EXTREME JUSTICE
DARK JUSTICE
SILENT JUSTICE

THE CODE OF BUDDYHOOD
DOUBLE JEOPARDY
THE MIDNIGHT BEFORE CHRISTMAS

SILENT JUSTICE

William Bernhardt

BALLANTINE BOOKS • NEW YORK

This book contains an excerpt from the forthcoming hardcover edition of *Murder One* by William Bernhardt. This excerpt has been set for this edition and may not reflect the final content of the forthcoming edition.

A Ballantine Book
Published by The Ballantine Publishing Group
Copyright © 2000 by William Bernhardt
Excerpt from *Murder One* by William Bernhardt copyright © 2001 by William Bernhardt

All rights reserved under International and Pan-American Copyright Conventions. Published in the United States by The Ballantine Publishing Group, a division of Random House, Inc., New York, and simultaneously in Canada by Random House of Canada Limited, Toronto.

Ballantine and colophon are trademarks of Random House, Inc.

www.randomhouse.com/BB/

Library of Congress Catalog Card Number: 00-193278

ISBN 0-345-42813-7

Manufactured in the United States of America

First Hardcover Edition: February 2000
First Mass Market Edition: March 2001

10 9 8 7 6 5 4 3 2 1

Dedicated to F. W. "Steve" Stephenson,
bookseller for more than fifty years,
and a treasured friend to anyone who ever wrote a book

A good person once said, that where mystery begins,
religion ends.
Cannot I say, as truly at least, of human laws,
that where mystery
begins, justice ends?

—Edmund Burke (1729–1797)

PROLOGUE

* *

* Six Months Before *

Who let him in here? Ben Kincaid wondered.

He peered across the study quad at the scruffy-looking older man hovering near the front double doors to the University of Tulsa College of Law. Ben's attention was drawn by the fact that the man was wearing a long overcoat; it was ill-fitting, wrinkled, and stained. The man's chin was covered with salt-and-pepper stubble. His eyes were red and ringed, as if he hadn't had a good night's sleep in weeks. He was looking for something, or someone.

Ben couldn't imagine who or what that might be. The man did not look as if he belonged here. Even the lawyers-to-be with the most rudimentary grasp of personal hygiene did not rise to this level of dishevelment. Ben wondered if maybe the man had gotten lost on his way to . . .

To what? The homeless shelter? Come to think of it, there wasn't anyone or anything anywhere on the TU campus that was likely to welcome this visitor. Ben wondered if he should ask the man what he wanted. Or perhaps whisper a word into the ear of Stanley Robinson, the security guard he'd just seen outside the dean's office.

Ben was distracted by a petite, attractive woman making her way toward him. She had a creamy complexion perfectly accented by two tiny patches of freckles on either side of her aquiline nose. Her engaging gait not only spoke of extreme self-confidence but, as an added bonus, did remarkable things to the curly strawberry-blond hair dancing just above her shoulders. As she sidled up to Ben, he admired her crazy-quilt miniskirt, which had more colors than a jumbo box of Crayolas.

Ben arched an eyebrow. "Is that a dress or a cry for help?"

Christina McCall didn't bridle. "It's ethnic chic. I'll have you know this pattern is all the rage in Mozambique."

"Is that a fact?"

"It is."

"I haven't kept up with Mozambiquii fashion trends the way I used to."

"More's the pity." Christina tilted her head back, sending her hair bouncing behind her shoulders. "I hear you're teaching The Tiger's class this afternoon."

"True." Although Ben had been practicing law for years, only recently had he begun teaching classes at the local law school as an adjunct professor. As he had quickly learned, The Tiger was Professor Joseph Canino, a curmudgeonly Ichabod Crane who'd been teaching Civil Procedure since the dawn of time. "Apparently he was called away at the last moment. Some kind of emergency."

"Probably heard of a law student somewhere he hadn't publicly humiliated and rushed off to remedy the omission."

"Quite possible."

"I don't know where such a student might be, though. Mozambique, perhaps."

Ben smiled. Professor Canino was of the old school; he used the Socratic method like a dagger to slit the throats of the unwary or unwitting. "I gather you're in this class?"

Christina had worked as Ben's legal assistant for as long as he'd been in solo practice in Tulsa. Two years before, she'd decided to expand her horizons and start law school. Since they worked together and knew each other personally, they both agreed it was best that she not be in any of Ben's regular classes. But it looked like this morning they were going to be in the same classroom whether they liked it or not.

"I am," she replied. "So don't be cruel."

"I'll try to restrain myself."

Christina scampered off toward class, leaving Ben to admire once again her seemingly inexhaustible high spirits. It had been almost ten years since Ben finished law school, but it hadn't been so long that he'd forgotten how much he'd hated it. Egomaniacal professors, arbitrary subjective grading, unrelenting pressure to succeed, unrestrained favoritism—a hideous gauntlet one was required to run in order to practice the world's least respected profession. What a deal.

As Ben crossed the study quad, he observed that most of the students' sentiments were aligned with his own, not Christina's. The sweaty brows and twisted grimaces of those purporting to study told him that law school had not changed much over the past decade.

In a carrel just off the main hallway, Ben spotted the grizzled man in the overcoat he'd seen near the front doors. What was he doing? Certainly not studying; he wasn't even carrying a book. His eyes were still roaming about. Who was he expecting to see?

Or maybe he had it wrong, Ben reasoned. Maybe his first impression had been correct. Perhaps the man was homeless and he was just looking for a place to lie down where security guards wouldn't hassle him. Ben considered recommending one of the cushioned sofas in the library. It was quiet in there, and if he covered his face with his hands, the staff would take him for another student who had fallen asleep while reading the rapturous words of the distinguished Learned Hand.

"Which class did you draw this time?"

Ben turned and saw Professor John Matthews, the leading tort law expert in the state of Oklahoma. He'd written texts and hornbooks on the subject; he was the unquestioned authority.

"I'm filling in for The Tiger."

Matthews stroked his beard and smiled. "Ah. Lucky man."

"How do you figure?"

"If those kids are expecting to see The Tiger walk through that door, they'll be virtually orgasmic when they see anyone else. Even you."

"You sure know how to flatter a guy, John."

Matthews laughed and headed down the corridor.

Ben entered the classroom. All at once, the students fell silent, shifted around, and turned their eyes front and center.

What a marvelous ego trip, Ben thought, not for the first time. This must be how judges feel when they enter the courtroom.

The classroom was designed in the Greek theater style: three tiers of elevated seats and continuous tabletops formed a semicircle around the podium, which was on the lowest level. Ben took his place in the center, opened his teacher's edition of the textbook, and started.

"My name's Ben Kincaid, and I'm filling in for Professor Canino this morning, as I expect most of you already know. So let's get to it. Who can tell me what a JNOV is?" He glanced at his seating chart. "Mr. Brunner?"

A middle-sized man in his early twenties pushed himself unhappily to his feet. "Uh . . . what were those letters again?"

"JNOV," Ben repeated, enunciating clearly.

"JNOV," Brunner repeated thoughtfully. "Is that a rock band?"

There was a tittering of laughter throughout the classroom. This would never happen if The Tiger were present, Ben knew. Apparently Ben had a less imposing reputation. He wondered what his nickname was. The Titmouse, perhaps.

"No, Mr. Brunner, you must be thinking of Run-DMC. Or perhaps, ELO, if you're as old as I am." He turned his attention to the rest of the classroom. "Who can tell me what a JNOV is?"

The first hand up rose above a very familiar head of red hair. Ben supposed he was obliged to call on her. She shouldn't be penalized for knowing the substitute prof. "Ms. McCall?"

Christina bounced to her feet. "A JNOV is a judgment notwithstanding the verdict."

"Excellent." Ben put a little check mark beneath her name on the seating chart. He had no idea what, if anything, The Tiger planned to do with these check marks, but Christina had certainly earned hers. "And what does that mean?"

"It means that after the jury delivers its verdict, the judge may set it aside."

"You're two for two, Ms. McCall. On what grounds may the judge disregard the jury's verdict?"

"Well . . . it looks to me like the judge can do it on just about any legal grounds he wants. Anything the judge believes calls the verdict into question."

"That's exactly right." Ben's eyes swept across the three raised tiers of seats. "There's a lesson to be learned here, future advocates—one you must never forget. In the courtroom, the judge is King of the Forest. So try not to cross him or her." He glanced down at his notes. "Ms. McCall, could you give me the facts of *Conrad versus Richmond Pharmaceuticals*?"

To his surprise, Ben saw that she was no longer looking at him. Her eyes had diverted toward the door.

He glanced over his shoulder. It was that shabby man in the overcoat—the homeless man, or whatever he was. He was peering through the glass in the door, the expression in his eyes strange and intense.

What was his problem? Ben wondered. He was definitely beginning to regret not reporting the man to Security. Something about the sight of him lurking outside the door was unsettling.

Ben turned back around and cleared his throat. "The case, Ms. McCall?"

"Oh. Right. Sorry." She glanced down at her textbook. "Conrad was a woman who had been advised to use a new sedative manufactured by Richmond while she was pregnant. Turned out the drug had serious side effects, although that did not become apparent for—"

Ben heard the click of the door behind him. The man in the overcoat was entering the classroom.

"Can I help you?" Ben said, not doing a very good job of masking his irritation. Somehow he knew The Tiger would never tolerate such an intrusion.

The man kept walking until he was far too close to Ben for comfort. His breath reeked; Ben detected traces of several diverse meals and perhaps some alcohol as well. His body was not much better; the smell rising from beneath that coat was so pronounced Ben almost winced.

The stranger spoke in a quiet, hushed voice. "You the professor?"

"I'm trying to be," Ben said, with an edge that could cut butter. "What is it you want?"

"You know what I want." The man stepped even closer and whispered in Ben's ear. "Is the merchandise secure?"

"What?"

"You heard me. Is it?"

"I'm afraid I must ask you to leave."

"Not until you tell me what I want to know."

Ben's irritation was augmented by the feeling that he was losing control of the classroom. "Sir, once again, I must insist that you leave."

"Answer me!" The hush was gone; the man's voice swelled. "Is the merchandise secure?"

"I don't know what you're talking about." Ben looked at Christina, then jerked his head toward the door. Intuitive as ever, she received the message and started for help.

"Is it *secure*?" The man's breathing accelerated. Sweat trickled down the sides of his grimy face. "Is it?"

Out of the corner of his eye, the man saw Christina making her way toward the door. "Stop!" he shouted.

Christina did not stop. On the contrary, she picked up the pace.

In the blink of an eye, the man reached beneath his wrinkled overcoat. Less than a blink later, he was holding a sawed-off shotgun in his hands, cocked and ready to fire. "I said, *stop!*"

Christina froze in place, obviously unsure what to do next.

Shrieks pealed out of the gallery. Some of the students rose; some of them ducked under the desks.

"He's got a gun!" someone cried.

"He's crazy!" shouted someone else. Frenzied confusion followed.

Damn! Ben thought. Where had that shotgun come from? This man was crazier than he'd thought—and more dangerous, too.

Ben took a hesitant step forward. "Now, look, let's stay calm."

The man whipped the sawed-off around so it was pointed at Ben's face. "Stay back! Stay away from me!"

Someone in the rear of the classroom screamed, a loud, ear-piercing cry that sent chills down Ben's spine. The stranger faded back till he was pressed against the chalkboard. He panned back and forth with the weapon, assuring everyone present that they were within his line of sight.

Ben felt his knees beginning to tremble, but he tried to block that out of his mind. He was in charge in here—in theory, anyway. If anyone had a chance of bringing this maniac around, it was him.

He took a cautious step toward the man. "Please stay calm. I'm sure we can find out whatever it is you want—"

"Stay back, I said!" The man pressed forward, his eyes wild and crazed. "Don't think I won't fire. I will! I got nothing left to lose!"

Behind him, Ben saw Christina quietly roll back into action. She was trying to take advantage of the momentary diversion of the stranger's attention to slip out the door.

No! Ben tried to send her an unspoken message with his eyes. But it was no use. Christina kept edging toward the door.

"I warned you!" the man bellowed as he whirled around with his shotgun—and fired.

Ben's heart stopped at the report of the shotgun, like a sonic boom in the small classroom. The shot hit the wall just above Christina's head, spewing plaster and chalky dust all over her.

Christina threw up her hands. "All right! I'm not moving! I'm not moving!"

The intruder rushed toward her, gun still at the ready. He grabbed her by the hair, wrapped it around his fist, then shoved her back against the wall, hard.

More of the students shrieked as Christina's head slammed against the wall. Her eyes batted rapidly as she struggled to maintain consciousness.

"Don't hurt her!" Ben shouted.

The man with the gun stepped back, bringing Ben into his line of sight. "I can hurt all of you. I *will* hurt all of you. If you don't tell me what I want to know!"

He fired the gun again, this time into the ceiling. Ben ducked behind the podium. This man was insane, Ben thought grimly. He had to be. And he couldn't count on reasoning with a man who had no reason. They were all in deadly danger.

"Fine," Ben said, choking on the plaster dust that filled the air. "Fine. I'll tell you anything. Anything. Just ask."

The man's teeth were clenched tightly together. "I already did! Is the merchandise secure?"

Ben stretched out his hands. "I don't know what you're talking about!"

The man fired the gun again, this time near Ben's feet. *"Is the merchandise secure?"*

"Yes!" Ben shouted. "Yes! It is! It's so secure—you wouldn't believe how secure it is."

The man rushed toward him. He grabbed Ben's lapel and shook him. "You're lying to me!"

"I'm not! I don't know anything about your . . . merchandise!"

There was a momentary flicker in the man's steely gaze, as if a new thought was being processed for the first time. "Isn't this your classroom?"

"Yes, but . . ." Ben's lips parted. "Do you think I'm Professor Canino? Because I'm not."

"You're not? But you said—"

"I'm filling in for him. I'm a substitute teacher."

The man stepped away from Ben, slowly and cautiously, keeping his wild eyes on the entire classroom, daring anyone to move.

His retreat was interrupted by the clattering of footsteps just outside the door. Security, Ben saw through the window. Thank God. Stanley must've heard the shots.

Three security officers started through the doors, including Stanley. As soon as Stanley saw the man holding the shotgun, he drew his own weapon. Ben feared there would be a shoot-out—and then he realized it was going to be something else, something far worse.

The man with the shotgun grabbed the back of Christina's head and shoved her forward, using her as a human shield. "Stand back! I'll shoot her! I will!"

The three security officers froze.

"Drop your guns!"

Ben could well imagine what was going through Stanley's mind. Normally, cops were taught never to relinquish their weapons. But Stanley wasn't a cop. What's more, the man with the shotgun was acting crazy. They might be able to talk him down, prevent him from doing anything brutal. But if they continued to threaten the man now, he would probably explode—and Christina would be caught in the fallout.

With evident reluctance, Stanley laid his pistol on the floor. The other security officers did the same. The man with the shotgun rushed forward, pushing Christina ahead all the way, till he had recovered the weapons and shoved them into one of his outer coat pockets. "Now, get out of here! Now!"

Stanley tried to maintain a calm demeanor. "Couldn't I stay and talk? I know you don't really want to hurt anyone. Why don't we—"

The gun exploded in Stanley's face. The shot struck just over and behind him, splattering the wall. Stanley ducked, horrified, clutching the side of his face. The shot had come so close it had singed his cheek.

"Now get out of here!" the man screamed. "Now! Now! Now!"

This time the security guards left, including Stanley. After the door closed, the man with the shotgun whipped around. He shoved Christina down to the floor.

"Nobody moves! Nobody goes anywhere! We're all staying right here until I get what I want!"

Ben rushed to Christina's side. He took her hand and helped her up. "How are you?"

Christina shrugged. "I'm fine, damn it." She gazed at the maniac with the shotgun. "Wish I'd moved a little faster."

"You and me both." Ben helped her to an empty seat in the front row. He had a sinking feeling they were both going to be here for a good long while.

Eight hours later, Ben and the rest of the captives were sweaty, hungry, and even more worried for their lives than when this siege began. Ben had hoped that in time the man with the shotgun would calm down. Instead, just the opposite seemed to be happening. He was disintegrating, becoming progressively less rational. Every few minutes he would start raving again, babbling on about the "merchandise." No one knew what to tell him.

"I see what you're trying to do," the man ranted, swinging his shotgun erratically from one side to the other. "I see! You're trying to cheat me. Cheat me out of what's rightly mine!"

The police had managed to get a cell phone in, but so far, all attempts at negotiating had proved worthless. Ben wondered what poor soul had drawn the thankless task of acting as chief negotiator. Someone from the local Tulsa PD, he suspected, perhaps even Mike, his friend and former brother-in-law. Or by this time, perhaps the FBI had moved in, a development that would really chap Mike off. Whoever it was, they weren't getting anywhere. The man brandishing the shotgun was simply too paranoid, too suspicious of every suggestion. He wouldn't let them send in pizza for the students; he was afraid they might do something to it, or smuggle something in with it. They couldn't even negotiate safe passage out of the classroom. He didn't want it, he kept insisting. All he wanted was the "merchandise."

"It's mine!" he screamed into the cell phone. "I earned it! I deserve it!"

About four hours into their captivity, Ben had tried to reason with him, had attempted a little negotiation of his own.

"Look," Ben said quietly when he had the man's attention, "you don't need all these students for hostages. Having so many people around only increases the chances that something unfortunate will happen."

The man glared at him with a steely eye. "Like what?"

"I don't know. Anything. My point is, why don't you let the kids go? Keep me. I'll be your hostage. I'll do whatever you want. And I won't try to escape."

"Why are you trying to get them out of here?"

Ben chose his words carefully. "I want to help you. One manageable hostage is better than twenty-seven unmanageable ones."

"You don't want to help me." He took a step closer, his gun poised between them. "Why are you so anxious for them to leave?"

"I'm just—"

"They've got it, don't they? The merchandise. You're trying to smuggle it out with one of them."

"No, no, I'm just trying to—"

"Or maybe they're going to get it. They're going to take it away and hide it so I can never find it."

"No. I'm telling you—it's nothing like that—"

"Nobody leaves!" the man screamed. "Nobody leaves till I say so! Nobody leaves till I have my merchandise!"

And so, eight hours after it began, the grim hostage scenario was still not resolved. And Ben was beginning to worry that it never would be. At least not without serious bloodshed.

Ben and Christina, along with the others trapped in the room, were hot, tired, and terrified. Ben's former foil, Mr. Brunner, seemed to be in particularly bad shape. His forehead dripped with sweat; he was muttering desperate nonsense to himself. Ben was afraid he might snap at any moment. And then they'd have two irrational people in the room—except Brunner wasn't packing a gun.

A few of the students were holding up with admirable stoicism. Some had even approached Ben about trying to wrestle the gun away from the maniac. Ben did his best to put an end to any wild notions of heroism under fire. He didn't want anyone maimed or killed. The best plan was simply to wait it out—until the authorities were able to resolve the crisis.

He knew they were trying. A few hours before, Ben had taken a walk behind the highest rear tier of seats, just to stretch his legs. A row of narrow, rectangular windows lined the back wall, and through them, Ben had spotted men in green quickly scurrying into positions. SOT—what the world outside Tulsa called a SWAT team—unless he was very mistaken.

Maybe the man with the shotgun knew it, too, or at least suspected. He had covered the window in the front door, and he never went near the windows in the back. He was not going to give them a shot. If they wanted him, they were going to have to come in after him. In which case he could probably kill half a dozen students before they brought him down.

"I know they're out there!" the man shouted. His arms trembled as his hands clutched the shotgun, the barrel pointing every which way at once. "I know what I know. Why doesn't anyone believe me? All I want is what's mine!"

"Psst!" Ben whispered, trying to get Christina's attention. She seemed to have recovered from her manhandling earlier. She didn't look good, but then, at the moment, no one did. "Any idea what he's babbling about?"

Christina cautiously scooted closer. She knew the man with the gun became paranoid whenever he saw people talking, and he didn't need to be made any more paranoid than he was already. "I haven't understood what he was babbling about from the moment he walked into the classroom."

"If he would just give me an opening," Ben said quietly. "Get distracted for a moment."

"Ben, please promise you won't try anything stupid. I don't want you to get hurt."

"Like I do?"

She ignored him. "Has Mike still got you taking kung fu lessons?"

"Yes. Every week at the Chinese Boxing Institute. Lately we've been practicing dropkicks and back flips."

"Are you any good?"

"Better than I was."

"Fast?"

Ben frowned. "Not faster than a shotgun." He watched as the crazed man paced the length of the classroom. "I wish I could get him to calm down and just tell us what it is he wants."

"Don't even try, Ben. It's too dangerous. And you wouldn't learn anything. He's delusional."

"Maybe. But if I could at least find out what he's after, then maybe—"

Christina clamped down on his arm. "Ben, please. It would be suicide."

"We can't just sit here and—"

"What are you two whispering about?"

Ben leapt back—because he suddenly found the business end of the shotgun shoved between them.

"Answer me! What were you saying? Were you plotting against me?" Sweat flew from the man's brow as he whipped his head back and forth. "Is that what it was?"

"N-no, of course not," Ben answered, trying to remain as calm as possible. "We're just . . . hungry, that's all."

"You've got the merchandise, don't you? You're the one keeping what's mine."

"That's not true. I just—"

The man shoved the shotgun barrel directly under Ben's nose. "Don't lie to me! Don't you lie to me!"

Ben threw up his hands. "I didn't. I wouldn't."

"Don't you ever lie to me!"

"I won't. I promise."

The man's face flushed with crazed desperation. "All I want is what's coming to me."

"I know that. I know it."

His voice boomed. *All I want is what's mine!*

"Stop it!" This shout came from behind the man with the gun. Mr. Brunner. "Stop shouting at him! Just stop!"

My God, Ben thought, Brunner's expression is almost as demented as the gunman's. He's cracked. He's gone over the edge.

"I'm tired of this!" Brunner shouted. "I want out of here! I want out *now*!" He turned his back to the shotgun and started toward the door.

"Stop!" the man with the gun warned. "Don't do it!"

"I can't take this anymore!" Brunner bellowed. "Don't you understand? I can't take it!"

"I'm warning you." The man drew the shotgun up to his eye, sighting carefully. "Come back."

"Well . . . if you insist." Brunner turned, seemingly resigned, and then, all at once, he sprang forward. Moving like quicksilver, he flew across the classroom on a line drive toward the man with the gun.

He was fast . . . but not fast enough. The shotgun blast hit Brunner in the chest, knocking him to the ground. He cried out in pain, then curled up like a fetus, clutching his abdomen.

Screams and shouts pierced the air. A new level of panic swept through the classroom. Most of the students ran in terror to the opposite corner.

Christina knelt down beside Brunner, oblivious to the shotgun tracking her every move.

"How is he?" Ben asked.

She didn't answer. She didn't have to. The gaping hole and the blood-soaked shirt said more than enough.

Brunner was still breathing, but just barely. He was still bleeding, too.

The hostage negotiators had been working the cell phone doubletime, trying to get the man with the gun to allow a medic in to treat Brunner. No luck. Ben remembered attending a seminar with Mike Morelli where he had learned about the FBI's four touchstones for successful hostage negotiation: honesty, conciliation, containment, and resolution. Unfortunately, even after ten hours, these negotiators couldn't get past honesty. Their standard scripts weren't working. They were trained to deal with men who were desperate—but still fundamentally rational. With this crazed paranoid, the standard operating procedures were useless.

More than once, Ben had managed to take a slow stroll behind the third tier of seats, glancing out the windows. He no longer saw the fleeting figures in green. But he was certain they were there. He thought he had heard a muffled drilling sound earlier; possibly they were poking a hole through one of the walls, making an opening for a fiber-optic camera, or even a high-powered rifle. Meanwhile, there were probably half a dozen sights trained on those rear windows, just waiting for the man to show himself. But the man with the shotgun stayed out of sight, safely tucked away on the lowest level of the classroom.

The students' spirits were dwindling. The attack on Brunner had sucked the life out of the best of them. Several simply lay prostrate, not moving, waiting for the end they feared was inevitable. Others were praying, had been praying nonstop for hours. And a few still managed to maintain a stiff upper lip. But Ben knew that was just for show. They couldn't last forever. None of them.

Ben wiped his brow, then stared at the profuse sweat that dampened his hand. None of *us*, that is.

"Damn you! Damn you all! You will give me what I want!"

Ben watched in horror as their captor threw the cell phone across the room. It hit the wall, shattering into pieces. Apparently that wasn't enough for him. He fired a shot after it, breaking the phone into still more pieces and leaving a sizable indentation in the wall.

"I know what you think!" the man shouted, to no one in particular. "You think you can cheat me and get away with it. But you can't. You *can't*!"

Another blast went into the ceiling, knocking out several

panels and shattering a fluorescent light. Bits of glass and neon tubing flew across the room.

That's it, Ben thought, biting down on his lower lip. What little hope we had was on the other end of that cell phone. And now even that is gone.

Ben walked down to the lowest level of the classroom, where Christina was huddled over Brunner's agonized body. She had been nursing him since his injury, holding his hand, talking to him, trying to keep him alive.

"I know you're in pain," Ben heard her whisper to him. "I know it must be excruciating. But you've got to hold on. Please. Help is on its way."

Ben placed his hand on her shoulder and squeezed. "You're worn out. Want me to spell you for a bit?"

"No. I'm fine." She tossed her head back, trying to knock the hair out of her eyes, but the hair was wet with sweat and stuck tenaciously to her forehead and cheeks.

Ben reached down and brushed it back. "Don't exhaust yourself."

If she heard him, she gave no indication of it. Her eyes were focused on Brunner. "Don't give up. Please don't give up."

But even as she said it, Brunner's eyelids slowly closed.

"No!" Christina cried. "Please, no!"

Ben felt his teeth grinding together. This had gone on too long. He didn't want anyone to get hurt—not even the man with the shotgun. But Brunner was fading fast—maybe gone already. If he didn't get medical attention quickly, there would be no hope. And after Brunner, who would be next? One of the other students? Christina?

Ben closed his eyes, forming his resolve. If he started this, he would have to stick with it to the end—no matter what the consequences.

He made up his mind. "I'm leaving," he said. His voice was oddly flat, but definitely audible.

The man with the shotgun looked up abruptly. "What?"

"I'm leaving." Ben turned slowly and started toward the back of the classroom.

"Ben?" Christina said. "What are you doing?"

"I'm leaving."

Their captor raised his gun. "You're not."

"I am." Ben continued moving, with the same slow but steady pace. "I'm leaving."

"You're not!" The man ran toward the first-tier table and cocked his shotgun. "I'll stop you!"

"You can kill me," Ben whispered eerily. "But you can't stop me." He reached the third level of the classroom, then stood on the tabletop, his back facing the windows.

"Don't try to cheat me!" the man shouted. He jumped up on the first-tier table. "You can't leave till I have what's mine!"

"I can. And there's nothing you can do to stop me."

"I will! I will stop you!" The man giant-stepped to the second-tier tabletop. He and Ben were now barely three feet apart. "I'll kill you!"

"No, you won't. You're not a killer. You're just a poor pathetic wretch. I don't know what happened to you. I know you lost something you cared about very much. I don't know what it was, but I know it was something important to you. So important you think you have to get it back. You can't go on without it." Ben paused. "But you won't get it by killing me. That's why you won't do it."

"I will!" the man screamed, rushing forward. Ben grabbed the man's free hand as soon as it came within reach and, heaving with all his strength, flipped the man backward. He thudded against the back wall, his head level with the back windows.

Two seconds was all the sharpshooters outside needed to identify their target and take action. Six high-powered bullets crashed through the glass. All of them hit their mark. The man with the shotgun fell, half on a chair, half on the floor. His blood-soaked head hit the desktop with a sickening thud.

Barely a second later, people began swarming through the front door of the classroom, paramedics at the forefront. They carefully rolled Brunner onto a stretcher and carried him to an ambulance waiting outside. Other medics began talking with and helping the students, gingerly escorting them to freedom.

After a few minutes had passed, a police sergeant approached Ben. "The man who held you hostage is dead."

Ben nodded silently. He wasn't surprised.

"Do you have any idea what it was he wanted?"

"No. But I know who you should ask. The Tiger. Professor Canino. That's who the man came to see."

The sergeant's eyes widened slightly. "Haven't you heard?" He shook his head. "No, of course you haven't. You've been trapped in here for ten hours."

"What?" Christina appeared behind him, listening intently. "What is it?"

The sergeant turned slightly toward her. "We've been looking for Professor Canino since that lunatic first mentioned him. We can't find him. He's not in his office, he's not at home. He's not anywhere. He's vanished. Without a trace."

* Six Years Before *

Tony Montague watched the gaily colored hexagons swirling above his head like a kaleidoscopic whirlwind. A breeze rippled across his face, a pleasant refreshment in the midst of this 102-degree Oklahoma heat. The cool air allowed his brain to settle into a more tranquil, reserved state, like the nirvana that usually followed the second shot of tequila, except without the booze. He found himself mesmerized, hypnotized even, by the multicolored pageant. The red, the blue, the yellow, the speed, the repetition, the endless cycle, over and over again—all of it made him . . .

All of it made him sick, actually. Nauseated. Rarely had he managed to acquire motion sickness when he wasn't moving, but that's what was happening now.

"Are you going up?" He felt a slap on his shoulder and realized it was Bobby Hendricks, chief supervising accountant for his division. "The line is short."

Tony shook his head. "I'm not much of one for Ferris wheels."

Bobby smirked. "Getting too old, huh?"

"When I was six, I didn't like Ferris wheels."

"Then why did you come?"

Tony hesitated. He wasn't sure he knew the answer to that question himself. Why had he come on this company outing, a bus ride down the turnpike to Frontier City? He hated amusement parks. He saw quite enough of his colleagues at the office, thank you, and he never socialized with them. So why was he here?

"I don't know," he said. "Guess I thought if I cozied up to the boss, I might get a little more than the usual six percent annual raise."

Bobby laughed, then slapped him again on the shoulder. "You were wrong. So, are you coming or not?"

"Not." He watched as Bobby and some of the other faces from the office raced toward the gigantic spinning contraption. He had to get away from here, and quick. It was making him ill. The Ferris wheel—and everything else. Everything about this. Everything about his life. Everything.

Tony spotted her near the concession stand—the Double D Cowpoke Corral, to be precise. He'd gone in to get a Coke to settle his stomach. She was sitting at one of the picnic tables nursing some kind of drink. She was tall and thin and looked to him like someone you'd expect to see smiling down from the cover of *Elle* magazine. But there she was, sitting at a chipped and faded picnic table at Frontier City—alone.

He knew it was stupid, but he couldn't help himself. Maybe it was the intoxicating swirl of the Ferris wheel still working on his brain, undermining his common sense. Maybe it was the sad truth that he had nothing to lose, because his present life was so empty. Whatever the cause, he found himself walking toward her, eventually taking a seat on the opposite side of her table.

To his surprise, she did not appear annoyed. Not particularly pleased, but not annoyed, either.

"Waiting for someone?" he asked.

Her head turned slowly toward his, but her eyes did not leave her cup. "No. Why?"

"I—thought maybe you were waiting for your kids."

"No. I don't have children."

"Boyfriend?"

"No."

"You're here . . . by yourself?"

"Is there something wrong with that?"

"No. I just . . ." He shifted awkwardly, knocking into his Coke in the process. He caught it at the last possible moment before it spilled. He felt like an idiot. Who did he think he was? Casanova? Casanova was never such a klutz. "Most people don't come to amusement parks alone."

Her eyes rose slightly. "Are you here alone?"

"No. Well . . . no. Feels like it, though."

She responded with a barely perceptible nod. "I just wanted to be someplace where . . . where people are happy."

Tony fell silent. He didn't understand. And then again, he did.

"Where will you go next?" he asked.

Her eyes were strangely vacant. "I don't know. I have no idea."

He stretched his arm impulsively across the table. "You should come back with me."

Again he feared she would be annoyed, but she wasn't. A tiny smile played on her lips. For the first time, her eyes met his. "Is that so?"

"Yes. Come with me. Please."

"Why should I?"

"I'd make you happy. I want to make you happy."

"Where would we go? Another amusement park?"

"No. This is no place for someone like you. A woman like you—you deserve to be . . . I don't know. You deserve to be on some island in the South Pacific, relaxing on a lounge chair on the beach, maybe a couple of servants to bring you drinks served in the shell of a coconut."

Her smile increased. "My, my. You do think big, don't you?"

"Oh, I've barely begun. After you spend a leisurely afternoon on the beach, you retire to our beach house—no, our hacienda. A big spread, with fountains, and an Olympic-size pool, and . . . and . . . our own personal tennis court. Ours would be the biggest spread on the island. In fact, I think we'd own the island."

"Stop me if I'm wrong, but this fantasy you're spinning might be somewhat expensive. Should I assume you're a billionaire?"

"Well . . ."

"What do you do for a living?"

He stared into her dark hazel eyes. Somehow, he couldn't lie to this woman. It would be wrong. Worse than wrong—it would be . . . like a sin. "I work for a big corporation not far from Tulsa. I'm an accountant."

"That doesn't sound like a job that brings in private South Sea island–type income."

"No, it isn't." A shadow fell over his face. "But I know where I could get money. A lot of money."

"Oh?" Her eyes widened, large and watery. "Then why haven't you?"

"I don't know. I suppose . . . I never had any reason to. Before now."

She looked at him carefully. His hand was touching hers now, just barely. But she did not move away. "Why would you do this for me? You don't know anything about me."

"I do. I mean, I don't, but . . ." He gazed into her lovely endless eyes. "I know enough. I know you lost something you cared about very much. Or someone. I don't know who or what it was, but I know it was important to you, so important you feel like you can't go on without it." He took her hand and squeezed it. "But you can. *We* can."

Her fingers tightened around his hand, like a drowning person gasping for air. "I wish I could believe you."

"You can," he said, and he was never so sure of anything in his entire life. "You can."

"Brace yourselves!" the bus driver shouted.

Tony lurched forward, trying to see what was happening. He was sitting in the back, but he could still observe the on-coming headlights whiting out the windshield. The bus began to skid, and it seemed like it skidded forever, on and on . . .

Until they crashed. The impact flung Tony forward, almost over the next row of seats. His head banged down on the hard plastic seat back, cutting a deep gash across his forehead. Backpacks, cups, broken glass flew everywhere. The screams from his fellow passengers pierced his ears.

And the bus was still moving. Not forward this time, but sideways, teetering, losing its grip on the highway.

Dear God, don't let us turn over, he thought, but it was much too late for prayer. The bus pitched to one side, hitting the highway with a shattering impact.

"No!" Tony wasn't sure who was screaming now. There were dozens of them, scrambling, fighting their way to their feet, trying to quell their panic.

"Get off the bus! Everyone off the bus!" The bus driver was shouting at them. At first, no one moved. Many of them had been sleeping; all had been resting before the crash. Everyone was too dazed, too stunned by the double impacts.

Then the driver added the kicker: "I think we pierced the fuel tank."

The driver was silhouetted by an eerie orange glow. Tony pulled himself up from the rubble and saw that it was true. A furious fuel-fed fire engulfed the front of the bus . . . and was slowly making its way toward the rear.

They screamed. Everyone still conscious scrambled, moving all ways at once. Tony fought his way downstream, back toward his original seat, back to the beautiful woman who had been sitting beside him.

Her eyes were closed. Tony took her shoulders and shook her, first gently, then much less so. He didn't know what to say. He didn't even know her name. But she had to wake up. She had to.

She did not rouse. Fine, he thought, clenching his teeth. Then I'll drag you out. He threw her arm over his shoulder and started toward the rear of the bus.

Before he had moved two feet, he ran into Bobby Hendricks. "There's no exit!" he shouted in Tony's ear.

"But—there must be—the back—the emergency exit—"

"There isn't one!"

Tony looked over his shoulder. He saw three of his

colleagues pounding their fists against the rear window, futilely trying to escape.

There was no emergency exit on the left side of the bus. The only rear exit was on the right side, which was now pressed flat against the concrete.

He turned back toward the front of the bus. The flames were still there, burning a steady path through the bus. The blaze licked the ceiling, obscuring everything behind it. It was as if someone were standing at the front of the bus with a flamethrower. The fire was coming straight toward them. All of them.

Tony tried to block the panicked shrieks out of his mind. He released the woman, then started toward the back. Three panicked men were pounding on the rear window, but it wasn't giving.

We need a tool, he thought. Anything. He saw a picnic basket at his feet and scooped it up. There was a large thermos inside. He raised it like a hammer and began pounding at the window. He pounded again and again, but the window didn't break. Didn't even crack.

He turned and saw the flames were still coming, even closer than before. The fire had reached the eighth row of the bus—only twelve more to go. Already the heat on Tony's face was scalding; it was as if he had dipped his face into the sun.

He had to get the woman away from the fire. He owed it to her; she was only here because of him. As he scanned the bus, all around him, he saw a solid mass of desperate, screaming, flailing figures, all pressed together in an increasingly smaller space.

Tony crawled over the tops of the seats, swearing with each step. It was so hot he could barely breathe. The seats were so hot they scalded his fingers. Don't think about it, he kept telling himself. Put it out of your mind. You can complain later. Right now you have to move.

Something exploded. The boom split his eardrums as he was buffeted backward. The explosion rocked the bus, though not enough to clear an exit. They were still trapped—those who hadn't burned already.

He saw the beautiful brunette woman near the fifteenth

row, now very close to the fire. Her eyes were still not open. He had to get to her.

Most of the survivors had been thrown together in a huge pileup, fighting their way toward the rear of the bus. Tony had to get past them. He saw a six-inch space at the top and dove for it. Someone else saw him coming and tried to protect his place at the top. It was Bobby. He jabbed his elbow into Tony's eye.

Tony screamed, then tumbled off the pileup. He landed face first against a window. And as soon as he regained his bearings, he noticed that some of the windows were broken—but since they were pressed against the highway, he could not escape through them.

He fought his way to the beautiful woman, who was still unconscious. He pulled her up and tucked her in a corner, so she would be safe from his crazed, panicked coworkers. She was so lovely, he thought, even now. She deserved so much better.

It was difficult to breathe, even more difficult to move. He propelled himself forward through the broken and lifeless bodies that surrounded him. They were weighing down on him, choking him. Straining with all his might, he forced himself through. He had to get away from the encroaching flames. He grabbed the back of a seat, then screamed. It was like touching a frying pan. The seats were so hot they literally melted between his fingers.

Steeling himself, he placed his hands on the seat again and this time he held fast. The pain was excruciating, but he had to do it.

"I want to get out! Please let me out!"

Tony's heart sank as he heard the tiny voice behind him. It was a little girl—Bobby's nine-year-old daughter. Damn! Why had he brought her? Why had he brought any of them?

The girl's blouse was on fire. Tony reached across and ripped the blouse off her. He scooped her up, then shoved her toward the back of the bus. "Go as far back as you can, sweetheart, then wait," he told the terrified girl. "Wait for an opening. A door, a window, anything. As soon as you see one, you run for it as quickly as you can."

The girl nodded and obeyed. Tony had no idea whether

there ever would be such an opening, but at least he had given her something to hope for. Something to do other than watch the flames draw closer.

The smoke was so dense now he could hardly see. He could sense his attention waning. Smoke inhalation was getting to him, poisoning his system, robbing him of his final moments of unclouded thought.

The sea of bodies had become too dense, the flames too intense. He could move backward no farther. He pushed himself toward what was once the left side of the bus, toward the only unobstructed windows. Flames were everywhere. The screams and shrieks of terror were becoming less frequent—for the worst of all possible reasons.

He glanced behind him and saw the still-slumbering face of the woman he had invited onto the bus. Her eyes were still closed; her face was caked with blood and soot. But she was still beautiful.

"Forgive me," he whispered, and all at once, tears filled his eyes.

He turned toward the windows above him, suddenly consumed with rage. He tried to lower the sash, but the buttons were unbearably hot, and even when he forced himself to keep trying, they didn't work. Clutching the back of a seat with each hand, he swung himself upward, kicking the windows with all his strength.

"Safety windows," he muttered under his breath. They were supposed to be safety windows. Kick them and they pop out. But as hard as he kicked, nothing happened.

"Break, damn you!" he screamed. *"Break!"*

Five minutes later, the police and firefighters arrived at the scene—less than ten minutes after the crash. But by that time, there was nothing they could do. The fire had consumed the bus to such a degree that the policemen could not initially tell what it was. Flames were everywhere, radiating from all points, surging twenty feet into the sky.

* Now *

Billy's mommy figured he probably had the flu. There wasn't that much to it at first—just coughs, runny nose, congestion. She went through the usual drill: rest, lots of liquids, and occasional doses of Tylenol. After a week, though, he still wasn't any better, and his fever was climbing. His appetite had disappeared; he had to be forced to eat and even then ate precious little. He seemed pale, and this was a twelve-year-old boy in the midst of an Oklahoma summer. He moved more slowly, although he still wasn't willing to curtail his social life.

"Gee, Mom, I gotta go out. Gavin's got a new computer game. They say it makes Doom 2 look like sissy stuff."

Cecily Elkins, Billy's mother, checked the reading on the thermometer. "You're not going anywhere until your temperature comes down."

"But Mo-om—"

"Don't Mom me. You're staying in bed."

"Oh, all right. Great." He glanced back at her. "What about you?"

"What do you mean, what about me?"

"You look kinda tired yourself. You've been workin' too hard."

Come to think of it, she was rather tired. Having a sick child at home for a week was a major strain, no two ways about it. But how many twelve-year-olds would've noticed?

"Tell you what, pardner," she said, fluffing his pillow. "If you'll stay in bed, I'll go take a short nap."

"Make it a long one, Mom. You need your rest."

She put her hands on her hips. "Now wait a minute. Who's the parent here?"

Billy laughed.

"I think I'm supposed to be in charge, buster, remember?"

"I think we should take care of each other, now that it's just the two of us." Billy's expression was innocent and without guile. "Isn't that right?"

She wanted to hug him, but she resisted, since she knew he would complain about it.

More days passed, and Billy still did not get well. Cecily became most concerned, however, when she noticed the bruises. There were several of them up and down his arms. When she removed his shirt, she found them on his chest as well. That was when she began to suspect they might be dealing with something other than the flu. She made an appointment for Billy to see his pediatrician that afternoon.

Dr. Harlan Freidrich tried to mask his concern, but it was obvious to Cecily that he was alarmed by Billy's appearance. He said words that were calming and reassuring, but Cecily ignored the words and focused on the doctor's eyes. The eyes were worried.

Yes, he had some upper respiratory congestion. Yes, there must be an infection of some sort. The bruises might be an indicator of some sort of anemia, he explained, a deficiency of blood platelets. Billy's lymph nodes were also slightly swollen. Eventually, in his calm, there's-nothing-to-worry-about voice, Dr. Freidrich told Cecily that he suspected Billy had some sort of blood disorder. That hit her hard, but what struck even stronger was the creeping sensation she got from peering into the doctor's eyes. What he had told her was horrible. But she sensed there was something more, something he suspected but dared not tell her—yet.

If Cecily had not looked at the chart left behind in Billy's hospital room, two weeks later, she might not have been prepared for the worst. But she had looked—and why shouldn't she? She knew it shouldn't have been left on that desk, that it was an accident that resulted when the nurse tried to do too many things at once. But Billy was her son, damn it. She had a right to know anything there was to know. Even things the doctors were not yet prepared to tell her.

Much of the gibberish on the chart meant little or nothing to her. "Underweight, lethargic, twelve-year-old. Normally active, but not of late. Easy bruisability." She skipped to the analysis of the now dozens of blood tests that had been performed. "Results indicate generalized lymphadenopathy, although no petechiae. The spleen was not palpable." It didn't sound good, but she didn't really know what it meant.

She continued flipping through the pages. The day before, the doctors had performed what they called a bone marrow aspiration. Decoding the doctor's atrocious handwriting, she read the results. "Thirty-eight percent blast cells." Next to the results, the doctor had drawn an arrow and written in: "Definite signs of leukemogenesis."

That afternoon, Dr. Freidrich called Cecily into his office. He had also wanted Billy's father to be present, but when Cecily called him, he said he was in the middle of an important project at work and couldn't get away. So Cecily was alone when she received the bad news she already knew was coming.

"Your son has leukemia," the doctor said. He cleared his throat, then walked around his desk and sat in the chair beside her. "There's no doubt in our minds. It's acute lymphocytic leukemia."

Cecily steeled herself, tried not to react. After all, she had known it was coming. She was proud of herself, in a strange way, proud that she wasn't behaving like a typical weak-kneed mother. She would show the doctor that she had strength. That she had what it took to weather this crisis.

"The next few weeks will be critical for Billy," the doctor continued. "We're going to try to induce a remission through a combination of radiation and drug therapy. I believe the chances of remission in this case are good. But I have to be honest with you. There's also about a ten percent chance that Billy will . . . pass away. In the next few weeks."

Cecily heard his words, but she felt oddly distant, as if she wasn't really there at all. Her eyes focused on the window behind the doctor's desk. She watched the cars racing up and down Maple, shoppers headed for Wal-Mart, diners going to the Blackwood Bar-B-Q. She focused on the glints of sunlight that streamed through the window, refracted, and formed miniature rainbows on the wall. She wasn't really there. She wasn't really there.

"The greatest potential hazard we face in the upcoming weeks is not from the leukemia itself but from the risk of infection. The chemo will kill the cancer cells in Billy's blood and bone marrow, but it will also damage his immune system. The simplest infection—a cold, even—could cause him to . . . pass away."

There it was again, that evil phrase. Pass away. What was this man, a priest or something? Why didn't he just say what he meant? Why didn't he just tell her that the boy she had carried in her womb and nurtured for twelve years might die?

"I know there must be a thousand thoughts running through your mind at this time," Dr. Freidrich continued. "Let me put some of them to rest. This is not your fault. No one knows what causes leukemia. There's nothing you could've done to prevent this." He placed his hand on the edge of her chair. "I want you to know we're going to do everything we can to help your Billy."

Damn right, she thought silently. Damn straight you'll do everything you can. And more important, so will I. I will not let my baby boy die. I will not allow it.

The initial treatment of chemo and radiation took about a month. Billy received several blood transfusions, as the doctors worked to increase his platelet count. Cecily spent every night with Billy throughout his hospital stay. Every night. Billy's hair began to fall out and he was constantly nauseated. His platelet count remained low, but it did not drop further, and no new bruises appeared on his skin. At the end of the month, the doctors could find no traces of leukemic cells in his blood or bone marrow. They declared him to be officially in remission. The treatment had been a success.

After he was discharged, Billy had to visit the hospital twice a week on an outpatient basis to complete an extended maintenance program, which included more chemo. He obviously didn't enjoy it. He was tired of throwing up all the time and he wanted his hair to grow back. But for a twelve-year-old who had been through what he had, he remained remarkably chipper.

"Mom, I think next summer I'm gonna want to play baseball," Billy announced one evening during dinner.

Cecily raised an eyebrow. This was an interesting development. She'd been trying to get him to go out for baseball for three years, but he'd never shown any interest. He preferred soccer. Baseball was a sissy game. Or used to be, anyway.

"What brought on this about-face?"

"Well . . . I think the kids at school are startin' to get suspicious."

"Suspicious? Of what?"

"Of me. Wearin' this baseball cap every day." Billy wore a baseball cap at school to hide the fact that most of his hair had fallen out. Everyone knew this, but Billy preferred to imagine everyone thought it was just a fashion statement. "I was thinkin' maybe if I was actually playing baseball, it might seem more natural."

Cecily couldn't resist a smile. She was so proud of her son. He had been through so much, but still had not lost his spirit. "Tomorrow we'll go to Wal-Mart and buy you a baseball mitt. What d'ya say?"

"All right!"

Billy did not play baseball the following summer. Five months later, during a routine visit, Dr. Freidrich noticed that Billy's blood platelet count had decreased. He immediately ordered a bone marrow aspiration, and when that proved inconclusive, he ordered a second and a third. By this time Billy was experiencing constant nosebleeds, and the bruising had returned with a vengeance. The fourth aspiration revealed 46 percent blasts.

Dr. Freidrich met Cecily in the hospital corridor outside Billy's room. He instinctively clasped her hand, something he had never done before with a patient or their relatives.

"Tell me," she said, her lips pressed together to prevent them from quivering. "Just tell me."

"He's relapsed," the doctor said quietly. "The leukemia is back."

"Can we restart the full-time treatment? Induce another remission?"

"Probably." The doctor drew in his breath slowly. "But even if we do, it will only be temporary. We have to look at this realistically. The chances of an absolute cure in this case are . . . remote."

"This isn't a case," Cecily said, struggling to maintain control. "This is my son."

"I know that, but—"

"I want him to start back with the radiation. And the chemo. Immediately."

The doctor nodded, holding his private thoughts in reserve. "As you wish." He hesitated a moment, then added, "Cecily, I'd like to give you some names." He pulled a scrap of paper out of his white lab coat. "These are parents of some of my other patients."

"I'm not going to some soapy support group," Cecily said firmly. "I'm too busy to spend my time sitting in a circle whining."

"Cecily . . . these parents also have sons. And their boys also have leukemia. Some of them . . . even more advanced than Billy's."

Wordlessly, Cecily took the list he proffered. Her eyes scanned the names. "Colin Stewart? He lives on the same block we do."

The doctor nodded.

"Ed Conrad. Jim Foley. These boys go to the same school as Billy. How can this be?"

"There's no explaining cancer, Cecily."

"But didn't you tell me leukemia was very rare?"

"Yes. Fewer than four children out of one hundred thousand each year."

"But—these are four children who live within a mile of one another!"

"And there are others besides. I'm not the only pediatrician in Blackwood. Do yourself a favor, Cecily. Talk to some of the other mothers."

She shook her head, then crumpled the paper in her hand. "I've got a boy to take care of."

*   *   *

Dr. Freidrich reinstituted a program of full-time radiation and chemotherapy, and by the end of the month, the disease was once again in remission. But by April Billy's platelet and white–blood cell counts were falling again. Dr. Freidrich performed several bone marrow biopsies. It seemed the number of cells in Billy's blood marrow was now decreasing altogether. He recognized this as a condition called aplastic anemia. It was not leukemia, but it could be just as deadly. And there was no reliable treatment for it. After considerable thought, he decided to send Billy home. He feared the worst, but there was nothing he could do about it.

Three weeks later, on Mother's Day, Billy did not wake up in the morning at his usual time. When Cecily went in to check on him, his breathing was shallow and raspy. Hard as she tried, she could not wake him.

My God, she thought silently. This is it. It's happening.

Straining with all her might, she lifted him out of bed. He roused slightly, but was still too weak to walk.

"Mommy," he said quietly.

She clenched her teeth, fighting back her emotions. He hadn't called her Mommy for years.

"Mommy, I don't feel so good."

"It's all right, baby," she said, running toward the car as fast as she could. "I'm going to take you to the doctor."

The prospect made him wince. "Mommy." His voice was so soft she had to bend her ear toward his mouth to hear. "I think I'm going to go now."

"You are not going anywhere," Cecily said firmly. "I will not allow it."

She tossed him into the front seat and started the car. She hadn't dressed yet, but that wasn't important. She only stopped long enough to snatch her purse, because she knew if she didn't bring her health insurance card the hospital probably wouldn't even let her through the door. She started the car and blazed down Park toward the hospital.

As she approached Maple, she noticed that Billy's eyes were closed and his chest wasn't moving. Breathe, she thought, as she pulled the car over and climbed across the seat. Breathe, she commanded, as she pounded on his fragile chest. Breathe, she pleaded, as she pressed her lips against his. Please, God. Just let him breathe!

A roving police officer spotted Cecily's car on the side of the road, saw what was happening, and called for an ambulance. But by the time it arrived, Billy was long gone.

Cecily forced herself to retain her fixed, impassive expression. She would not break down, she told herself. She would not be typical. She would not give them what they wanted.

As the paramedics loaded Billy's body into the ambulance, one of them spoke to her. "Is your boy one of Dr. Freidrich's patients?"

She stared at him, at first not comprehending. His voice was pulling her to the present, tugging her back to earth. "Yes. How did you know?"

"My boy Jim had leukemia, too. I'm Ralph Foley."

Ralph Foley, she thought. Of course. She remembered seeing Jim Foley's name on the list Dr. Freidrich had given her.

"I know what you must be going through right now," Foley said. "Me and some of the others have a group that gets together once a week. If you ever need someone to talk to . . ."

"I'm not a talker," Cecily said. She climbed into the back of the ambulance and accompanied her boy to the hospital.

Once the formalities were over, Cecily knew she was free to leave. But somehow, she couldn't make herself do it. Her feet refused to take the first step. To leave the hospital would be to acknowledge that it was all over, that Billy was gone, truly gone, never to return again. She had sworn to herself that she would not let her son die. She had sworn to him that she would not let him die. She had failed them both.

All at once, tears flowed like floodwater. The dam had burst. Everything she had resisted, everything she had been holding back for months, came gushing out.

She was racked with pain, gasping for air with great heaving breaths. Her whole body trembled. She hurriedly found a chair in the waiting room and sat in it before she collapsed. The aching was like an electric current radiating through every part of her body. She was so tired, tired of fighting, tired of losing. Exhausted. And her baby boy was gone.

"Can I be of help?"

She turned and saw a priest, dog collar and all, sitting behind her, his hand outstretched. She did not know him, but she thought he belonged to that Episcopal church on West Elm.

She wiped her face clear. "Not unless you can perform miracles."

The priest was not offended. "That is not within my power. But I can listen."

"Talk, talk, talk." She realized her voice was louder than it needed to be. It sounded shrill, awful, even to her own ears. "Why is everyone so goddamn anxious to talk?" She turned her back on him.

"Listen to me," the priest said gently. "You're going through a difficult time. You've lost someone you cared about very much. I don't know who he was, but I know he was important to you. So important that maybe you don't think you can go on without him."

"Of course I can go on," she said, once again wiping her eyes. "Don't you see? This isn't about me. It's about *Billy*. What happened to him isn't right. It isn't fair."

"The world is unfair, at times. We don't understand what happens, or why."

"I understand perfectly what happened," Cecily said, forcing herself to her feet. "But this is what I don't understand. This is what I have no answer for. How could God let this happen? And *why*?"

The priest placed his arm around her shoulder, but he did not attempt to answer her question. Cecily thought that was probably wise. There were no answers. Not with him, not with anyone else. No answers. No answers at all.

In the weeks and months that followed Billy's death, Cecily became obsessed with the question she had raised that night in the hospital: Why had this happened? She had always believed in a rational, logical world. She had studied science before she married, hoping to become a biologist. She had been taught to believe in cause and effect, trial and error. Nothing happened without a reason. Anything could be explained, if one only had the analytical tools to comprehend it.

But no matter how she tried, what she read, or whom she talked to, she was unable to uncover a solution to the enigma she most wanted resolved: why her precious boy died.

Until one morning she read a story on the front page of the *Blackwood Gazette*. And then she knew.

ONE

* *

This Be the Verse You Grave for Me

* 1 *

"You were digging around in the man's trash?"

Ben Kincaid tugged at his collar. "Uhh . . . yes . . . but only in the most respectful way."

Judge Lemke did not appear amused. "In the man's trash?"

"It was part of my . . . legal . . . investigation."

"The man's *trash*?"

Ben glanced back at Christina. She just shrugged. No help from that quarter. "I try to be thorough."

"Thorough? Thorough?" Lemke was becoming mildly apoplectic. "That's not thorough. That's . . . disgusting."

"The trash had been moved to the street corner for pickup, your honor. I can assure you there was no privacy violation."

"And you did this for a week?"

Ben's eyes averted. "Well . . . two, actually. I wanted to be . . . um . . ."

"Thorough. Yes, I know." Judge Lemke was well into his sixties, but had been gray for the last thirty years, at least. Ben suspected Lemke thought a crest of white gave him an air of distinction, sort of like a halo. And he might be right. He wore wide black glasses that framed his jowly face and also contributed to the overall owlish appearance.

Judge Lemke was a kindly man, as judges went, but in the last decade or so his mind had begun to wander and his memory wasn't what it once was. Still, he was a judge from the old school. He expected the formalities to be observed and wouldn't brook any foolishness. Unfortunately, the present case seemed to be nothing but foolishness. "Could we possibly proceed with the examination of this witness, Mr. Kincaid?"

"Yes. Of course, your honor." The witness at hand was the defendant, Michael Zyzak, who was being sued by Ben's client, Rodney Coe, for breach of contract.

Coe tugged at Ben's sleeve. "How're we doin'?" Coe owned a comic book and collectibles store in town called Starfleet Emporium. He was a baby-faced entrepreneur, barely twenty-one. He was still inexperienced enough with the legal system to assume that those in the right always prevailed—which created a huge problem for Ben, who knew better.

When this case had first come through Ben's office door, he had leapt upon it with great alacrity. It looked like a rare opportunity to escape the grit and grime of criminal law for the more tony, genteel world of civil disputes. Wrong. At the moment, Ben would've given a great deal to be out of here and in the middle of a nice triple homicide.

Ben addressed the witness. "Mr. Zyzak, when did you and Mr. Coe enter into the contract?"

Opposing counsel, one Darrel Snider, rose to his feet. "Objection, your honor. Assumes facts not in evidence."

Judge Lemke nodded. "Sustained."

"All right," Ben said, drawing in his breath. "Let me try again. Mr. Zyzak, did you enter into a sales contract with Mr. Coe?"

"No." Zyzak, a professional collectibles dealer, was thirtyish and extremely overweight. His face was covered with fuzzy stubble, which Ben took as evidence of either laziness or a total absence of fashion sense. Possibly both. He wore a rumpled, stained T-shirt that read SPOCK FOR PRESIDENT and wore jeans that were several sizes too small. "We never did. There was no meeting of minds."

Ben resisted the temptation to roll his eyes. Zyzak had obviously been well coached by his lawyer. "Well then, when did you discuss the possibility of entering into a contract?"

"That would be August fifteenth of last year."

"Fine. And a written sales contract was drawn up, was it not?"

"Sure. Coe had the thing in his back pocket when he showed up. All we needed to do was fill in the dollar amounts and sign."

"And you did sign, didn't you? But afterward, you learned that the market prices had risen. So barely an hour after the contract was signed, you called my client and tried to welsh on the deal."

"Excuse me," Judge Lemke said. "I'm a bit confused."

Ben sighed quietly. Anytime the judge decided to insert himself into your witness examination, it was bad news.

"I've heard no discussion of the subject matter of the contract. The res gestae, if you will."

Swell. Now he was hauling out his Latin. Probably looked that one up in *Black's* before he came out of chambers.

"Mr. Kincaid, I can't very well understand the nature of the proceedings if I don't know what was being bought and sold."

Ben nodded. He had hoped to avoid this. Should've known better. "Mr. Zyzak, could you please explain to the court what you were selling?"

Zyzak shifted slightly to face the judge. "Pez dispensers."

The judge blinked. "Excuse me?"

"Pez dispensers. You know. For Pez."

The judge stared back blank-faced. "I'm sorry. It sounds like you're saying pez."

"I am saying Pez. Pez. P-E-Z. Pez."

"If I may, your honor," Ben said, reentering the fray. "Pez is the brand name of a candy. Small rectangular sugary treats. Sort of like Sweetarts."

"Sweetarts?" the judge replied. "Are we dealing with pastries now?"

Ben smiled wearily. Just his luck to have a bench trial before a judge whose cultural knowledge ended with the Andrews Sisters. Or wanted people to believe it did, anyway. "Your honor, I'm afraid Sweetarts is also a brand name. For another candy."

"Oh. I see," he said, although the expression on his face suggested that he did not. "And you say this man was selling Pez . . . dispensers?"

"Yes, your honor. Little plastic gizmos designed to . . . well, dispense the candy. They have heads."

"The candy?"

"No. The dispensers. The heads are made to resemble

popular culture icons. Comic book characters. Cartoon characters. Santa Claus. That sort of thing."

"Oh. I see." Again the surefire indicator that he was clueless. "Excuse me, counselor, but I'm still confused about something." The judge rustled through his papers for a moment. "I believe I read somewhere that the sales contract at issue was in the amount of eighteen thousand dollars."

"Yes, your honor. You see, as I explained in the pretrial order"—hint, hint—"some of the older Pez dispensers are treasured by collectors and sell for large sums of money. Like baseball cards. Or comic books."

"Comic books." Judge Lemke clapped his hands together. "I used to read those when I was just a boy. I reveled in them."

That's lovely, your honor. But what does it have to do with this case?

"There was one of which I was particularly fond. What was it?—oh, yes. Captain Marvel. He was just a little boy, you see, but when he said the magic word, he became a huge strapping hero."

Ben glanced at Christina, but once again, all she offered was a shrug. Was there an objection for the addled judge's taking an irrelevant stroll down memory lane?

"I remember there used to be a little worm Captain Marvel fought. What was his name? Why, Mr. Worm, of course. No—Mr. Mind. That was it. Yes. Spoke through a little radio transmitter hung around his neck." He paused for a moment, then sighed. "Don't see how those comics could become valuable, though. They only cost a dime."

Ben cleared his throat. "Your honor . . . if I may."

Judge Lemke looked up abruptly, shaken from his reverie. "Oh, yes. Of course. Proceed, counselor."

Ben turned his attention back to the witness. "Didn't you agree with my client that eighteen thousand was a fair price for the dispensers?"

Zyzak shook his head vigorously. "I did not."

"You wrote that amount on the contract."

"He wrote that amount on the contract. I would never have sold my dispensers that cheaply. Especially not the Wonder Woman."

Judge Lemke looked down again from the bench. "Excuse me?"

"Wonder Woman. The 1965 version, in mint condition. That's before she lost her eagle."

Lemke removed his glasses and massaged the bridge of his nose. "I'm sorry. I don't quite follow."

Zyzak was happy to explain. "Everyone knows that, originally, Wonder Woman had the emblem of an eagle across her . . . um . . ."—he waved his hand vaguely around his chest area—"you know. On her bodice. But in the Sixties, her corporate masters, DC Comics, now part of the Time-Warner megamonster, changed the emblem to a stylized double *W*. They wanted a trademark they could register and market, and you can't claim dibs to the American eagle. So they changed it. The 1965 dispenser, however, was made before the change; hence its heightened value. Some people think it's the 1969 Wonder Woman dispenser that's so hot, but that's incorrect. The 1969 dispenser was of the short-lived superpowerless karate-chopping Wonder Woman written by the legendary Dennis O'Neil. She was modeled after Diana Rigg's Emma Peel character on *The Avengers*, which, by the way, was itself a steal from Frances Gifford in *Nyoka and the Tigermen*. Of course, the Nyoka character was taken from the serial movie adaptation of Edgar Rice Burroughs's book *Jungle Girl*, but the Hollywood slime changed her around so they wouldn't have to—"

"Excuse me," Ben said, coughing into his hand. "This is fascinating, but could we return our focus to this case?"

Zyzak shrugged. "Sure. Whatever."

"Mr. Zyzak, you claim that there was never a meeting of minds between you and Mr. Coe?"

"That's correct."

"But the fact remains—you did sign the contract."

"Yeah. . . ." He adjusted his bulk from one side of the chair to the other. "But I didn't know what I was doing."

"I beg your pardon?"

"You heard me. I was . . . uh . . . what's the phrase? Not of sound mind."

"Are you saying you were temporarily insane?"

"Nah. Nothing like that."

"Are you claiming you signed the contract under duress?"

"What, like I was threatened by a wimp like Coe? Nah."

"I gather you're not a minor."

"Only in the eyes of the cosmos."

"Then I'm afraid I don't understand why—"

"I was drunk."

Ben lowered his chin. "Drunk?"

"Yeah. Smashed. Blown. Snockered. Get my drift?"

"I certainly do. You said the same thing at your deposition. You're claiming you were intoxicated at the time you signed the contract, and therefore didn't know what you were doing."

"Yeah. That's it exactly. And that guy, Coe"—he pointed across the courtroom—"he knew I was plastered. He took advantage of me."

"Mr. Zyzak, that's about the lamest excuse I've—"

"Now, now, Mr. Kincaid." Judge Lemke rapped his desk with his water glass. "Let's remember our manners."

"Your honor, this is ridic—"

"Counsel, we must take this defense seriously."

"Why? He's just trying to weasel out—"

"I'm afraid I'm in complete agreement with the witness, Mr. Kincaid. If he was drunk, and your client knew he was drunk, I will not enforce the contract."

"But your honor, he's just—"

"You heard what I said, Mr. Kincaid."

"Yes, your honor." He shifted his attention back to the witness. "All right, then. We'll play it your way, Mr. Zyzak. If you were drunk, what had you been drinking?"

"Beer. The staff of life."

"I assume that was three point two beer. This being Oklahoma, after all."

"Well . . ."

"You'd have to drink a hell of a lot of three point two to get so drunk you didn't know what you were signing."

"Oh, I did. Put down a whole six-pack and a half in about ten minutes. I was grieving, see. I had just found out the Sci-Fi Channel was removing *Earth II* from its lineup."

"So you had about nine beers, then."

"I did. Man, I was reeling. Could barely stand up straight."

"Tell me this, then, Mr. Zyzak. After you finished those nine beers . . . what did you do with them?"

"What did I do with them? What do you mean? I didn't do anything with them, 'cept maybe when I went to the john."

"The cans, Mr. Zyzak. What did you do with the beer cans?"

"Oh. Why didn't you say so? I just threw them in the—"

All at once, Zyzak's face froze.

Ben smiled. He held up a typed piece of paper. "I have here a signed and notarized affidavit listing the complete itemized contents of Mr. Zyzak's trash, on August fifteenth, the next day, and the next two weeks. There were no beer cans, Mr. Zyzak. Not one, much less nine."

"Oh." Zyzak stared down at his hands for a long moment. Finally, he looked up. "Judge, is it too late for me to settle?"

Judge Lemke smiled beatifically. "I think that would be very wise." He leaned forward a bit. "Tell me, son. Was there ever a Captain Marvel . . . uh . . . um . . ."

"Pez dispenser?"

"Yes. That."

Zyzak nodded. "Oh, yeah. But it'll cost you."

* 2 *

Jones passed the files and documents and photographs back to the woman in the gray coat. "Look, I'm sympathetic. I know this must've been horrible for you. But we can't help you."

The woman didn't budge. "Why not? What happened to us was wrong. Very wrong."

"I don't dispute that. But you have to understand—every

wrong does not have a legal remedy. There's only so much the courts can do."

"What these people did was unconscionable. They should be made accountable." She paused. "I've done a lot of reading about this. We could sue for wrongful death."

"And you would lose. You've got a causation hole big enough to fly a 747 through."

The woman did not relent. Obviously, this was important to her. "We could get some experts—"

"Do you have any idea how much it costs to hire an expert witness, ma'am? Because I do. As the office manager for this firm, I have to. They're expensive. You wouldn't believe how expensive. And that would just be the tip of the iceberg. A case like this would cost thousands to try. Hundreds of thousands. Do you have that kind of money?"

For the first time, the woman hesitated. "No. But I thought perhaps some sort of contingency fee arrangement—"

"Meaning we would have to pay all the bills up front. Let me tell you something, ma'am, speaking as the man most intimately aware of this firm's feeble financial status. We can't afford your case. Perhaps some other firm."

"I've tried other firms. They all say the same thing. They won't take the case because they don't think they can make any money off it. The reason I came here is that I heard Mr. Kincaid was a lawyer who actually cared about something other than the thickness of his wallet."

"I'm sorry," Jones said insistently. "It's simply impossible."

"How can you know that? At least let me talk to him."

"Mr. Kincaid is very busy. As the office manager, it's my job to screen potential clients."

"All I need is ten minutes of his time."

"I'm sorry, no." Jones rose, obviously suggesting that she should do the same.

The woman in gray gathered her materials and grudgingly prepared to leave. "Could you at least explain why you're hustling me out the door like this? Are you so certain Mr. Kincaid wouldn't be interested?"

Jones shook his head. "I'm certain he would."

* * *

Jones almost had the woman out of the office when Fate intervened to spoil his plan. Ben Kincaid walked through the front door.

Ben glanced at the woman he didn't know, then over to Jones. "Well, we're back."

Christina came in a few steps behind him. "And back triumphant, I might add."

Jones beamed. "You won? Excellent."

"We were fortunate," Ben said. "Had a good day. The client was very happy."

"So happy he paid you on the spot?"

Ben tilted his head to one side. "Well . . . no. Actually, there's a bit of a problem with that."

Jones slapped his hand against his forehead. "Dear God," he murmured, "don't let this mean what I think it means."

"Seems our friend Mr. Coe has had a turn of bad business luck. . . ."

Jones pinched the bridge of his nose. "I knew it. I just knew it."

"His profits are way down," Christina explained. "His store hasn't recovered from the loss of those Pez dispensers."

"Let me guess," Jones said. "He can't pay you."

"Not in cash," Ben said. "But he did give me a lovely near-mint-condition copy of Aquaman number eighteen."

"Why would we want that?"

"Are you kidding? That's the one where Aquaman marries Mera the merwoman."

Jones shook his head. "I can't take it. I just can't take it anymore."

The woman in gray stepped forward. She had large doe eyes, vivid blue and unblinking. "Are you Ben Kincaid?"

Ben extended his hand. "Guilty as charged."

"I'm Cecily Elkins. I'd like to talk to you about a possible lawsuit."

"Would you be the plaintiff?"

"One of them. I believe it would be a class action suit."

"Really?" Ben raised his eyebrows. "Cool. Did you talk to my office manager?"

A tiny frown spoiled her face. "Yes. He assured me you wouldn't want to talk to me."

"Nonsense. Of course I want to talk to you."

Jones tried to step between them. "Boss—if I may—I think this is a mistake—"

"Don't be such a wet blanket, Jones. We're just going to chat. Why don't you put on some coffee?"

Jones drew himself up indignantly. "I do not do coffee. I'm the office manager."

"Fine. Then go manage something." He pointed toward his private office at the end of the hallway. "Ms. Elkins, would you join me?"

Ben escorted the woman down the hall. Christina started after them, but Jones grabbed her arm. "I want it recorded for posterity that I tried to prevent her from talking to him. That I was against this from the get-go."

Christina shrugged off his hand. "Jones, why are you getting so worked up? It's just another case."

"Yeah, just another case," he echoed grimly. "But it could well be our last."

Half an hour later, Ben had scanned all the papers the woman had brought with her, and worse, had seen all the photographs. He'd heard the woman's story, at least in miniature. It had been one of the most emotionally wrenching half-hours of his life.

"I'm beginning to understand why my office manager didn't want me to talk to you."

"I understand the difficulties," Cecily said. "But I think it's important. We can't let something like this happen."

"I agree," Ben said, "but you have to realize that the odds against us are staggering."

"I'm not going to back off just because it won't be easy."

"There are other concerns as well. Important ones. I've spent most of my career working in the criminal courts. Sure, I've done some civil work along the way, but with a case of this magnitude . . . you might be better off with a different firm. A bigger firm."

"I've been to all the big firms," she explained. "In Tulsa and in Oklahoma City. They all said no, because—"

"I know why they said no." Ben gingerly laid the photos down on his desk.

"If you'll agree to take us on, I'll help in any way I can. I'll do anything you want."

"I know."

"So?" She leaned forward eagerly. "Will you do it?"

Ben drew in a deep breath, then slowly released it. It seemed like an eternity before he answered, both to Cecily and to Ben himself.

"I want to meet the other parents."

He had waited long enough. The lights in the house had been out for more than an hour now. There had been no sounds, no movement, not the slightest indication that anyone was awake. True, it might be safer to wait another hour or so; it was only eleven o'clock. But he was ready now, and when he was ready, he was ready. It was difficult to explain. It was a tingling at the base of his spine, an itching at the back of his eyeballs. A sixth sense, if you will. It was like that passage in the Bible, in Ecclesiastes: There was a time for everything.

This was the time to kill.

Quietly, using maximum stealth, he crept out of the alleyway between houses toward the front door of a large two-story Tudor-style home. He kept to the shadows; only his piercing green eyes shone in the darkness. He tiptoed up the steps to the front door.

Which was locked. As he had known it would be. He had learned some time ago that the key to success in this world was advance research. He had planned this outing well, well enough to know that the door would be locked. He also knew how to get around that.

From an inside coat pocket he withdrew a palm-size glass cutter. He attached the suction cup to the window panel on the left side of the door, close to the lock. He extended the string to its full length, then carefully drew a circle with the diamond stylus. He repeated the motion, again and again, cutting a smooth, round section of glass. When that was finished, he grasped the handle on the suction cup and removed the circular section of glass.

Voilà! Smooth as a baby's bottom.

He reached through the new opening in the glass and slid

out the chain lock. He gave the doorknob a little twist, popping open the lock.

There was still the matter of the dead bolt. Reaching inside his coat once more, he removed a stainless steel lock pick. He had acquired this baby during his last trip to D.C. He loved it. It resembled a Swiss army knife, except the various blades were all picks designed for a variety of different locks. He chose the two most appropriate for this door and started to work.

Two minutes later, he was inside. The lights were out, but moonlight streamed through the bay windows, making it easy to find his way around. He located the staircase almost immediately. As he knew, all the bedrooms were upstairs.

There were three people in the house, not counting himself: Harvey, Harvey's wife, and their fifteen-year-old son, the junior high track star. At the top of the stairs, he quietly crossed over to the first bedroom, carefully creeping, to use Sandburg's phrase, on tiny cat feet. He soundlessly pushed open the door.

The boy was asleep in bed, on top of the covers, wearing nothing but a ratty pair of gym shorts. He had no grudge against this boy, and there was nothing the boy could tell him. Unfortunately, the kid was young and strong, and if he awoke during the subsequent proceedings, there was a tremendous possibility that he could create problems. It was an unacceptable risk.

The man reached into his overcoat pocket and this time withdrew a Sig Sauer .357. He walked to the edge of the bed, aimed it at the boy's head, and fired.

Bang-bang, he thought, adding the sounds his silencer-equipped gun did not. You're dead.

The boy twitched spasmodically as the bullet hit his skull, like a laboratory frog touched by an electrode. After that, he settled down, never to move again.

The man stood for a moment, admiring his handiwork. There was very little blood, since the boy had died immediately. The only suggestion of how he had met his demise came from the almost perfectly round red circle in the center of his forehead. It was a rather attractive addition, in its own way. Ornamental. Like something that might be required by an Eastern religion or something.

But enough ruminating. He had more work to do. He turned and moved rapidly out of the boy's bedroom.

Too rapidly, as it happened. His right leg caught on a metal trash can, knocking it over. It clattered down on the hardwood floor. Not a huge noise, but in this absolutely tranquil house, it seemed deafening.

He heard a rustling sound at the other end of the hallway, in the other bedroom. Someone was awake, which was unfortunate.

He raced down the hallway, caution to the wind. It didn't matter whether they heard him now; they knew he was coming. He flung open the bedroom door, his gun raised and poised, ready to go.

There was a woman sitting in the bed, slightly upright, her head resting against several large pillows. She had dark hair and a hard set to her jaw. Her eyes were open.

The man knew that she was Harvey's wife. He also knew that she was an invalid, that she could only move slowly, and barely that. She wasn't going anywhere.

He approached the bed, keeping his gun pointed at her brain. He didn't stop until he stood directly in front of her at the foot of the bed.

"Where's Harvey?" he said, gun still at the ready.

The woman stared back at him with cold eyes. "He's out of town."

He could still see the slight depression on the other side of the bed. A hand to the sheets told him they were still warm. "Tell me where he is."

"Cincinnati," she replied. "He's staying at a hotel. I can't think of the name. Saint Something or other."

He shot her in the kneecap. After the initial shock subsided and her cries of pain diminished enough that he could be heard, he aimed his gun at her other kneecap and asked her again. "Where's Harvey?"

Needless to say, she told him.

* 3 *

The other parents gathered in Ben Kincaid's office shortly after noon. Their hometown, Blackwood, was in Tulsa County, a thirty-minute drive from downtown Tulsa, and they all agreed to come when Cecily called them.

"There were eleven?" Ben said, as he studied the faces before him. Cecily had told him there were others, but he never dreamed there could be so many. "Eleven."

It was true. Eleven sets of parents, all of whom had recently lost a child between the ages of eight and fifteen to leukemia. For more than two hours, Ben listened to their stories, all told simply and undramatically, and all of them heart-wrenching just the same.

Cecily told Ben about her son, Billy, how he had been diagnosed with leukemia when he was twelve, how they'd fought it with drugs and radiation and chemotherapy, twice pushing the cancer into remission, only to lose finally at the end of a struggle that took more than two years. She told him about her last frenzied race to the hospital, how Billy had died during the drive, how she had attempted to revive him, crying and pleading, all to no avail.

"I tried everything I knew to bring him back. Everything. I would have gladly changed places with him, given my life for his. But it didn't help. My baby boy was gone. And there was nothing I could do about it."

Margaret Swanson told Ben about her son Donald, who was a star soccer player at Will Rogers Elementary. When the bruises first began to appear, Margaret assumed they were sports injuries; after all, soccer was a rough-and-tumble sport. When they didn't go away, she began to suspect other causes. Their ordeal lasted almost three years. Donald endured more than a hundred blood tests, more than two dozen bone marrow aspirations. He spent the entire last year of his life in the hospital. But the end result was the same.

"Donald begged me to let him go home, to let him play soccer again, but I always said no. I still held out hope, you see. I still pretended to myself that he might recover. So I made him stay in the hospital, where he was miserable. Now I'd give anything to turn the hands of the clock back, to let him go out and kick the ball, even just once. To give him one tiny moment of happiness before he was gone."

Ralph Foley had a simpler tale to tell. He and his wife hadn't been put through the protracted series of treatments and therapies, advances and setbacks, that the other parents had endured. The first warning sign they received that Jim was in danger came when he developed a persistent cough. Three months later, Jim was dead.

"People kept telling me I was lucky—lucky that the inevitable end had come so mercifully fast. I don't feel lucky. Even now, I can't believe Jimmy is gone. It was all too quick, too unreal. One day, you have a healthy ten-year-old boy, and the next, he's buried in a hole in Meadowland Cemetery. Things don't really happen like that, do they?" There was a tremble in his voice, the advance guard for the tears that began streaming down his face. "It can't be over so fast, can it? They can't take the most precious thing in your life and just . . . and just . . ."

He never managed to finish his sentence.

Ben listened to those stories and all the others. Each time he thought he had heard the worst, he found out he was wrong. Rarely in his life had he sat in a room in which the sense of tragedy was so palpable. These were grieving parents, mothers and fathers who had poured their hearts and souls into raising their children, only to lose them due to something entirely outside their control. There could be nothing worse than that, Ben thought. Nothing at all.

When the stories were done, Ben asked a few simple questions. "How did you all come together?"

Cecily answered first. Ben gathered she was their unofficial leader. "I got some names from Billy's pediatrician, after his first relapse. He wanted us to form a support group, but I never called the others. I was too busy trying to save my boy's life. After Billy was gone, I met a priest from the local Episcopal church. Father Richard Daniels. I wasn't Episcopalian, or even particularly religious. In fact, at that point in time I probably felt less religious than at any time in my life. But he was a comfort. He knew what I needed to hear—in part because he had been through this before. He told me about some of the other parents in town who had lost their children. Before long, we started getting together regularly to talk about what had happened—and what we were going to do about it."

"Cecily's been the ramrod behind this since day one," Ralph Foley explained. "She's the one who refused to just take it. She kept saying all these leukemia deaths in the same area couldn't be a coincidence. Something had to be causing it."

"What do your doctors say caused it?" Ben asked.

"They all say the same thing," Jim answered. "That no one knows what causes leukemia."

"But I wasn't prepared to accept that," Cecily said. "It was just too coincidental. Look at this."

She unfolded a map of the small city of Blackwood. On the map, she had pencilled an *X* where each of the deceased children had lived. They were all congregated at the north end of the city, all within about five square miles of one another.

"Leukemia is a very rare disease," Cecily continued. "And yet here were eleven cases, all clustered together at the north end of a small town. And you want to tell me that's just a coincidence? A statistical anomaly? No way."

"Then what caused it?"

"That's what I didn't know. At first, I thought maybe there was some kind of virus going around. I had read that there was a type of leukemia cats got that was transmitted by a virus. But that wasn't the kind of leukemia Billy had. So then I tried to think of something all the boys and girls who died shared. Most of them went to the same school—but not all. Most of them played sports—but not all. Then I tried to think of things that were universal, that everyone shared. Like the air." She paused significantly. "Or water."

"Did you share your theories with the rest of the group?"

Margaret Swanson answered that one. "She certainly did. We all thought she was crackers." She glanced quickly at Cecily. "Nothing personal. But we did. We knew she was struggling to accept her son's death. We all were. But this seemed a strange way to go about it. She was talking about hiring scientists, suing the city. We didn't want any part of it."

Christina leaned forward. "What changed your mind?"

"This." Cecily reached into her oversized purse and retrieved a folded newspaper. "This is the front page of the *Blackwood Gazette* from about four months ago. See for yourself."

Ben took the paper from her. The headline story, in bold black letters, proclaimed: POISON POOL FOUND IN BLACKWOOD AQUIFER.

Ben quickly scanned the article. A reporter named David Daugherty had discovered a half-buried pool, half an acre in size and about four feet deep, of contaminated water. The pool was connected to a ravine, which in turn fed the Blackwood water aquifer. In the water, the reporter found traces of arsenic, chromium, lead, and other heavy metals. The pool was uncovered by a construction crew in the process of laying the foundation for a new apartment complex. Ben also saw a line toward the end of the article that Cecily had underlined in red. *Arsenic is believed to be a carcinogen,* it said, *even in small doses.*

"Okay," Ben said, "that's frightening. But how does it link up to your stories?"

"Here's another paper," Cecily said, "from a week later." This time she didn't wait for Ben to read it. "The first article kicked up quite a stink in little Blackwood. The city council ordered the city engineer, one John Schultz, to test the city's water supply. As the article explains, the city of Blackwood is serviced by four water wells. Three of them tested fine. But one of them was contaminated due to underground seepage from the poison pool. That was Well B. And guess where the water from Well B goes." She paused, her jaw set. "North Blackwood. Our neighborhood."

Ben scanned the article now in his hands. Everything Cecily had said seemed to be correct. The city engineer determined that the well's water was tainted by several undesirable chemicals, including trichloroethylene, also known as TCE, an industrial solvent used principally to dissolve oil and grease. He had ordered the well shut down immediately.

"Wow," Ben said quietly. He knew it sounded stupid, but it was all he could think to say. "That's amazing. And . . . horrifying."

"I always thought the water tasted funny," Barry said. "But what can you do about it? Water's water."

"I thought it was gross," Margaret said. "We bought bottled water for drinking. But you can't use bottled water for everything. We couldn't afford it."

"All our children were exposed to this water," Cecily said. "They drank it, they bathed and showered in it. It was unavoidable."

"You may have grounds for a suit against the city," Ben said. "The city engineer may have been negligent in the performance of his duties. But what would it get you? I can guarantee you the city coffers aren't large enough to pay off any big judgment. A town that size probably doesn't even have insurance."

"We don't want the city," Cecily answered. "We want the bastards who poisoned the water in the first place." Once more her hand dipped into her oversized purse, this time retrieving a report bound in a clear binder. "I started researching this as soon as I read the first article in the paper. I studied to be a biologist, back at OU, so I wasn't totally in the dark on this. I started reading about TCE and how it's been linked to tumors in laboratory animals. I also found out I wasn't the only person concerned about the Blackwood aquifer."

What Cecily handed Ben was a report by the Environmental Protection Agency. After the preliminary discovery of the poison pool, they had placed the Blackwood aquifer on the National Priorities List—which put it in line for cleanup via Superfund dollars. The EPA ranked all the sites on its list, based upon the chemicals involved, their concentrations, and the proximity to residential areas. The EPA ranked the Blackwood aquifer seventh out of over five hundred sites. Like the city engineer, they found TCE in Well B—280 parts per billion, an extremely significant contamination. They also found lesser amounts of other foreign substances, including tetrachloroethylene, better known as perc, another industrial solvent. The EPA considered both TCE and perc to be "possible carcinogens."

Ben flipped the pages, passing quickly over dense paragraphs of jargon which he frankly didn't understand, long academic sentences, and charts and graphs dealing with groundwater contours and well logs and such. But there was a short paragraph at the end of the report that he definitely understood.

It was in a section labeled Contaminant Origination. It explained that Well B had been polluted by the underwater pool recently discovered in Blackwood. And it explained that the most likely cause of the contamination was dumping by the H. P. Blaylock Industrial Machinery Corporation, which owned the land and operated a manufacturing plant and headquarters not far from the poisoned pool.

Ben closed the report. "You want to go after Blaylock Industrial?"

"Of course," Cecily responded. "They're the ones responsible for this. Isn't it obvious?"

Ben and Christina exchanged a sharp look.

"So," Cecily said eagerly. "What do you think?"

Ben bit down on his lower lip. "I think we should take a break."

Ben called for a fifteen-minute recess before the meeting proceeded. He needed to think about what he was going to say, and how he was going to say it. He wanted to be honest with these people, and that meant telling them many things they would not want to hear.

Christina followed him to the kitchen while he poured himself a restorative Coke. "What are you going to do?"

Ben shrugged. "Tell them the truth."

Christina nodded. "So you're not going to take the case?"

"It would be suicide, Christina. You know that."

She did not disagree. "These people have been through an awful lot, Ben. More than you or I can imagine."

"I understand that. But encouraging them to file a kamikaze lawsuit wouldn't be doing them any favors."

Ben returned to his office early. He found all the parents

waiting for him. They had never left. They were too anxious to hear what he had to say.

"First of all," Ben began, "I want you to understand that you have my utmost sympathy. I really mean that. What you've been through was a living nightmare, something no one—no parent—should have to endure. But you also have to understand one simple reality. The courts cannot right all wrongs. In fact, I would say they can't right most wrongs. They can handle locking up crooks, and they're pretty good at resolving disputes that are simply squabbles over money. But this case is about more than money. A lot more. And frankly, I don't think the courts can help you."

He saw Cecily stiffen. "Couldn't we file a lawsuit for negligence? Or for wrongful death?"

"Yeah," Ben answered, "you could file it. The question is, could you win it?"

"But the EPA report says that—"

"The EPA report won't get you anywhere," Ben said flatly. "It probably isn't admissible, but even if it is, it won't help. It's full of the usual cautious academic language. Possibly this. Most likely that. When you're in court, you have to be able to prove your case. To *prove* it. By a preponderance of the evidence."

"But surely when the jury sees the map—when they see all the leukemia victims clustered together in one neighborhood—"

"I admit, the map is very compelling. Common sense tells us this cancer cluster can't be just a coincidence. But common sense isn't evidence. In court, we have to be able to prove that Blaylock poisoned the water, and moreover, that the water caused the cancer. If we can't do that, we won't even get to the jury. The judge will shut us down before it ever goes to trial."

Ben scanned the circle of sober, unhappy faces surrounding him. He was not telling them what they wanted to hear; he knew that. But it was what needed to be said.

"To even attempt to prove a case like this, we would need expert testimony—by the barrelful. And that is very expensive. We'll need geologists, toxicologists, engineers, hydrologists, not to mention doctors. They'll all be billing hundreds of dollars an hour for their time—plus expenses. We'll have to conduct studies of our own, with our own researchers, so we can get them in as evidence. And we'll need to somehow prove that Blaylock contaminated the site, something I can guarantee they won't admit."

Ralph Foley cleared his throat. "Isn't it possible Blaylock might agree to settle? You know, to avoid the expense and bad publicity of a trial."

"Is that what you were hoping for? Well, you can put that pipe dream to rest. Blaylock will never settle. Because if they did, every citizen of north Blackwood would turn around and sue them. They can't afford to let that happen. They'll fight this tooth and nail."

"That's fine," Cecily said defiantly. "We'll fight back. Hard."

"With what?" Ben asked. "Let me tell you something. I know for a fact that the Blaylock Corporation is represented by Raven, Tucker & Tubb, the largest firm in Tulsa. I know this because I used to work there. I also know the Raven litigators are some of the best in the business. They know all the tricks. They'll try to delay, to protract this and make it as miserable and expensive for us as possible. They'll file frivolous motions, ask for hearings, demand pointless discovery, all to run down the clock—and run up the tab. This litigation will cost thousands of dollars—probably hundreds of thousands of dollars. Who's got that kind of money? I certainly don't. Do you?"

Again Ben peered out at the sea of faces. No one was nodding. He didn't need to be a financial whiz to know there were no billionaires in the room. None was rich to begin with—and all had just suffered debilitating medical expenses.

"So basically, what you're asking me to do is file a high-profile lawsuit that we can't afford and can't win. To run up expenses with no hope of recovering them. That's why you haven't been able to get anyone to represent you." He paused, drawing in his breath. "And that's why I can't represent you, either."

The room was blanketed with silence. None of the parents spoke, or even moved. They all looked as if they'd been hit in the face by a baseball bat.

Christina had a pensive expression on her face. She was

biting her knuckle, a sure sign that she was troubled. But she, too, held her tongue.

At last Cecily broke the silence. "May I ask you a question, Mr. Kincaid?"

He shrugged. "Sure."

"Have you raised any children?"

"No." He frowned. "Well, I helped raise my nephew for several months, but—"

"Did you love your nephew?"

"Of course I did. Do. But—"

"How do you suppose you'd feel about this if your nephew had been one of the youngsters who died?"

"Ms. Elkins—"

"For that matter, you're still young. You might have children of your own. How would you feel if your own flesh and blood had died—for no reason? Because some corporation didn't have the decency to keep their poison out of the water well?"

Ben drew in his breath. "I'm sure I'd feel just as you do. Devastated. But these are all emotional appeals. They won't get us past a summary judgment motion."

One last time Cecily's hand dipped inside her purse. "This is a picture of my boy. Billy. He was such an angel. He never did anything wrong. He never hurt anybody. He liked soccer and Robert Louis Stevenson. When he grew up, he wanted to be a doctor. But not to get rich, he told me, time and again. He wasn't going to be a 'swimming-pool doctor.' He wanted to help people who really needed help, maybe go to a third-world country or something. And you know what? He would've done it. He would've made a difference. . . ." Her lips began to tremble. "He would've done some real good in this world. But all that potential is gone now. It's all been wiped away by an act of corporate callousness. Is that right? Is that acceptable?"

Before Ben could respond, Ralph opened his wallet and withdrew a photo. "This is my Roger." He laughed slightly. "He wanted to be an astronaut."

"My Donald," Margaret said, laying her photo atop the stack. "He talked about being an architect."

One after another, the tattered photographs fell into place. Jay Kinyon. Brian Bailey. Tracy Hamilton. Kevin Blum.

Colin Koelshe. Finally, Ben saw eleven sets of eyes looking up at him, eleven youthful faces that passed from the world well before their time.

And above those, all around him, Ben saw many more eyes staring at him. Waiting to hear what he would say next.

He found Harvey hidden in the clothes closet behind some fishing gear and a lifetime supply of shoes, just where his wife had said he would be. It was a walk-in closet, very spacious, with more clothes than a man could wear in a year. Harvey had always been obsessed with his appearance. He pushed the clothes to either side and found a hidden inner closet door. When he opened that, he found a private hidey-hole, just big enough for one. Harvey was cowering inside.

Harvey, a fiftyish balding man with a speckled turnip of a nose, was crouched in a near-fetal position, his hands covering his face. "Don't hurt me. Please don't hurt me."

He stared at Harvey with undisguised contempt. "Jesus Christ, Harvey. You ran off and left your wife to face the executioner?"

"She's crippled," he said, his voice quivering. "She had an accident last year. She couldn't move fast enough to get away."

He shook his head with disgust. "Pathetic." He grabbed Harvey by the scruff of his neck.

"Please don't hurt me!" Harvey screamed again. "I can't help you. I don't have what you want!"

"I wish I could believe you, Harvey. But of course, there's only one way to know for certain." He dragged Harvey forcibly back into the bedroom.

Upon arrival, Harvey saw his wife lying motionless in their bed. There was a red circle in the center of her forehead, and a pool of blood around her right leg. Her arms and legs were grotesquely splayed. "Oh, my God!" he screamed. "You didn't—you didn't—"

"Heck, no, Harvey. I didn't do anything bad. I just killed her." He threw Harvey onto the bed beside his wife's corpse. "What did you think, that I'd become some sort of rapist? Geez, Harvey. I haven't changed that much." He reached into his coat and pulled out a roll of duct tape. "Not that there was any need, anyway. Didn't you know, Harvey? I had your wife years ago."

Harvey's eyes widened, but just before he could shout, the man plastered a strip of duct tape right over his mouth.

"Oh, yeah, Harvey, it's true. It's been . . . what? Ten, eleven years now. We did it several times. Tried many different positions. Some pretty kinky stuff. One time you were in the house, sleeping. We did it right under your nose." He grabbed Harvey's arms and held them together, then wrapped tape around them and tied them to the bedpost above his head. "Not that it was any great thrill for me, if you want to know the truth. She was a bit pedestrian in the sack, wasn't she, Harvey? Too conservative for my taste." He smiled. "Although I did like that thing she did with her tongue. You know, during foreplay? Ooh-la-la."

He wrapped tape around Harvey's ankles, binding his legs together. Once Harvey was motionless, he clapped his hands together, as if celebrating a job well done.

"One last chance, Harvey." He ripped the duct tape off the man's face, taking bits of skin with it. "Where's the merchandise?"

"I don't know," Harvey said. Sweat poured down the sides of his face. "I don't have it. I never did."

"Wrong answer." Bending over, he grabbed a pair of dirty underwear lying on the floor and stuffed it into Harvey's mouth. Then he began systematically undressing himself.

"You're probably wondering what I'm doing, aren't you, Harvey? Wondering if maybe I really have changed, if maybe I have something perverse in mind. Well, you can relax." He removed the last bit of his clothing, folded them in a neat stack, and carried them to the edge of the room. "I'm not going to molest you or your wife's corpse. I just don't want to get any blood on my clothes."

He reached one more time into his coat, now folded in the pile, and withdrew a large hammer. A ball-peen hammer.

Harvey lurched forward, as much as he was able. His eyes bulged out of their sockets. He squirmed and twisted and made muffled cries for help.

"Oh sure, now you want to talk. But it's too late now, Harvey. Now you have to pay the consequences."

Harvey's muffled screams grew louder, but there was nothing he could do to help himself. The man drew back the hammer and smashed it into Harvey's left leg, shattering his kneecap.

"Wonderful. Now you and your wife are a matched set." He crouched down beside Harvey's spasming body, leaning forward against the side of the bed. "All right now, Harvey. Can we talk?"

Ben remained in his office after the parents departed. He had a lot to think about. He didn't emerge from his office until sometime after five.

Jones was sitting at his desk, waiting for him. "Well?"

A crease formed in the center of Ben's forehead. "Well, what?"

Jones fell back in his chair. "Damn everything! You took the case! I can see it in your eyes."

Ben cleared his throat. "I . . . uh . . . did agree to represent them, yes."

"*Damn!* I should've known. What am I saying? I did know! I just couldn't stop it!"

"Now, Jones, calm down. . . ."

"Do you have any idea what this kind of litigation costs?"

"I certainly do."

"Do you know what the odds are against you recovering anything?"

"Well . . . I think it's too early to say with certainty. . . ."

"Don't play coy with me. This is a trillion-to-one shot and you know it. We'll run up thousands in expenses and have no hope of recovering it."

"We've been through tough patches before."

"Do you know what our current financial situation is? I do. We're already on the edge. And this is just what we need to push us over!"

Ben nodded. "And since you've raised that issue, I'd like you to run downtown tomorrow and have a talk with The Brain."

"Aw, no, Boss. Not me!"

"You're the office manager. It's your job." The Brain was

the nickname they gave Conrad Eversole, the financial whiz at Nations Bank who handled the firm's accounts. He had loaned them money in the past. And he would have to loan them money again, if they were going to manage this case.

"What am I going to use as collateral?"

"Tell him about the lawsuit."

"Oh, right. Like he'll go for that pig in a poke."

"Well, use whatever you can. Take the title to my van."

Jones shook his head. "Ben . . . listen to me. This is a mistake. A big mistake."

"You're probably right. But it's already done. I've taken the case." He turned and started toward the door, then stopped. "Jones, I want you to know—" He paused. "I think we're doing the right thing here. Not the smart thing. Certainly not the safe thing. But the right thing. I think."

He continued to pummel Harvey's body with the hammer. After sixty or seventy strokes, Harvey at last expired, which must have been a great relief to Harvey, under the circumstances.

The man wiped the hammer clean in the sink, dried it, then returned it to its pocket in the inside lining of his coat. He put away his gun, then walked around the room, wiping his prints off everything he had touched. Finally, he washed off in the sink and put his clothes back on.

He had not learned what he wanted to know. Harvey had told him nothing. But he was now convinced that Harvey knew nothing. At first he thought it possible Harvey might be lying, but after the fifth or sixth swing of the hammer, to his other leg, his groin, his jaw, it just wasn't possible anymore. If he had known anything, he would have talked.

Harvey didn't know where the merchandise was. Which, sadly enough, was what Harvey had tried to tell him from the outset.

Well, if at first you don't succeed . . .

He walked downstairs, wondering which of the remaining three he would tackle first. It was tough, having to go about this business in such a random, hit-and-miss manner. But there was nothing for it. He would simply have to work his way down the list until he found what he wanted. Who he wanted.

He stepped outside, closing the door behind him. It was a glorious night. The moon was holding water, the stars were twinkling, and all was right in the universe.

All except for one thing, that was. One niggling detail.

He pushed his hands into his coat pockets and started across the street. He thought about the others, the three people who would be receiving visits from him in the near future. He smiled slightly as their faces came up in his mind's eye, one after the other.

Bang-bang, he thought. You're dead.

* 4 *

After he left work, Ben hopped into his van and headed homeward. He knew perfectly well there was nothing edible in his cupboard but cat food, so he made a stop at Ri Le's and grabbed some takeout—cashew chicken and lumpia dogs, his favorite. Ten minutes later he was outside his boarding house just north of the university. He parked on the street and headed inside. His mood was quiet, subdued. He had a lot on his mind.

Before he mounted the stairs to his apartment, he decided to stop in and visit Mrs. Marmelstein. She had been Ben's landlady when he first moved into this building. Technically, she still was, although since Alzheimer's set in, she had been a landlady in name only. Ben handled all the administrative duties attendant to keeping the house running—paying the bills, arguing with repairmen, and occasionally supplementing the always-wanting petty-cash drawer.

He rapped on the door. There was no answer. He cracked the door open slightly and poked his head in. "Mrs. Marmelstein?"

She was sitting in her favorite easy chair, watching television. The volume was turned up much too loud. She had obviously dressed herself: her socks didn't match; her blouse was reversed.

He walked to the television and turned it down. "Mrs. Marmelstein?"

Her eyes fluttered away from the TV set. "Paulie?"

Ben frowned. Her eyesight had been failing of late as well. But who was Paulie? "It's Ben, Mrs. Marmelstein."

"Oh, of course! Benjamin!" She pressed her hands together. Ben was pleased to see she still recognized him—and relieved. "Are you staying for dinner?"

"Nah. Tonight's Joni's night. I just stepped in to say hi." He winked. "Check on my favorite girl." Mrs. Marmelstein had been a bit dotty since the day he'd met her, but the Alzheimer's became progressively worse with time. Unfortunately, about six months ago, she had broken her hip. Since then, she'd been all but infirm. She had no living family of which they were aware, so Ben and Christina and Joni and Jami Singleton, two other residents of the boarding house, took turns looking after her. "Everything okay?"

Her eyes drifted back toward the television. "Well enough, I suppose. I do like that *Diagnosis Murder*. But I can't believe what Dick Van Dyke's done to his hair."

"What's that?"

"He dyed it! Dyed it blond. Can you believe it? At his age."

Ben glanced at the television. "Mrs. Marmelstein, I don't think his hair is dyed. It's just turned gray."

She blinked. "Gray?"

"Yeah. With age. Like—" He stopped himself. Mrs. Marmelstein's hair was currently a sort of bluish pink, courtesy of Hair Revue on Sixty-first.

Mrs. Marmelstein adjusted the lay of her blouse. "Well, it doesn't look good on him. Whatever it is. Have you been keeping an eye on my investments, Benjamin?"

"I certainly have." It was easy, since there was only one. This house.

"I'm glad to hear it. I depend on you. You know, that last oil well of mine was one of the biggest producers in the state of Oklahoma. Making money hand over fist."

Ben sighed. Mrs. Marmelstein hadn't owned any interests in oil wells since before her husband died, which was a good long time ago. They had made a bundle during the oil boom—but lost most of it in the crash.

"I'm keeping a careful eye on things, Mrs. Marmelstein. Nothing slips past me."

"Well, I'm glad to hear it. Don't think what you do goes unappreciated, Benjamin. You'll be well provided for when I'm . . . well, when the time comes."

Ben wondered what that meant. Probably she was planning to leave him her salt-and-pepper-shaker collection or something.

Her rather weary eyes drifted back toward the television. Ben could see he was coming between her and Dick Van Dyke. "Well, I'll be on my way. Joni should be here any minute."

She nodded. "Oh, Benjamin. Are you still seeing that redheaded girl?"

"You mean Christina? She's my friend, Mrs. Marmelstein. And coworker. That's all."

"Uh-huh." She didn't bat an eye. "You know, Benjamin, it's hard for an old gal like me to admit it, but . . . I think possibly my first impression of her was . . . mistaken. True, she doesn't act the way I was brought up believing girls should behave but . . . she's not as bad as I thought."

Ben marveled. Coming from her, this was the equivalent of blessing the marriage. " 'Night, Mrs. Marmelstein."

" 'Night, Benjamin. Oh, would you please turn the sound on the TV back up? I hate it when they start whispering."

When Ben popped open the door to his apartment, there was a surprise waiting for him.

" 'Bout time you got home. Man, you shysters keep long hours."

Draped across his sofa, staring at a football game on the television, was Ben's former brother-in-law, Mike Morelli. On the coffee table next to Mike was a large pepperoni pizza. Two beers were chilling in cozies.

"Took the liberty of ordering dinner," Mike said. "I knew you wouldn't have anything here."

Ben bent down and quietly slid his takeout bag out of sight behind a chair. "Great. I'm starved."

"Me too. It took some kind of restraint to wait till you got home, lemme tell you."

Ben snatched a slice. "You shouldn't've waited."

"Aw, well. I hate to eat alone."

"By the way, how did you get into my apartment without a key?"

"Hey, I'm a cop. I can get in anywhere." Mike picked up the remote and shut off the boob tube. "So tell me about your big day."

Ben spoke between bites. He really was famished. "Won a lawsuit. Well, settled it in a manner very favorable to my client. And . . . I got a new case."

"Anything interesting?"

"Oh, yeah. Very." Ben gave Mike a thumbnail sketch of the suit.

Mike peered at him intently. "You seem to have some reservations."

"Jones thinks it's going to bankrupt us. Christina thinks it's unwinnable."

"So you took it anyway."

"Yeah. Stupid, huh?"

"Extremely. And extremely predictable."

Ben grabbed his beer and leaned back against the sofa. "I kept telling the parents all the difficulties with their suit, explaining that courts aren't equipped to handle this kind of injury. But I also kept thinking, jeez Louise, if lawyers and courts can't help parents who have been through this kind of pain, what the hell good are we?"

"That's what the rest of us have been wondering for years."

"I kept telling myself there had to be something I could do. Unfortunately, now I have to figure out what that is."

"You've got your work cut out for you. As soon as you file the Complaint, you'll have the big boys from Raven, Tucker & Tubb crawling all over you."

"Don't I know it."

Mike took another man-size bite of pizza, then washed it

down with his Bud Light. "So," he said nonchalantly. "Heard anything from your sister?"

Ah, Ben thought to himself. So that's what this is about. "No. Not since she grabbed Joey and split for the East Coast."

"Some kind of big-time nursing program?"

"Yeah. Something like that." Ben bit down on his lower lip. What was it Mike wanted to know?

"I don't suppose she calls."

"Julia? No way."

"Not that I'm interested. I've put Julia totally behind me. I've moved on."

Sure, you have, Ben thought silently. That's why you still wear your wedding ring.

Mike changed the subject slightly. "Don't suppose you've heard from Joey, either?"

"She doesn't let him drop by for visits, if that's what you mean."

Mike propped his feet up on the coffee table. "That must be tough for you. I mean, you raised that kid on your own for what? About six months?"

"About that, yeah."

"And then she swoops in one day and takes him away. Man, I don't know what I'd'a done if she'd tried something like that on me. I wonder."

Ben wondered, too. Especially since he was almost positive Mike was Joey's father. He'd never mentioned it to Mike, since he'd never gotten any confirmation from Julia. But he felt certain just the same.

Mike slapped Ben on the back. "Well, it's just as well. You and I, bachelors, free as the breeze—we don't have any business raising kids."

"Probably true," Ben said halfheartedly.

"Personally, I wouldn't want to be tied down, locked into the ol' family straitjacket. It may look good from the outside, but it's really just a trap. Starts with a baby. Next thing you know, you've got a houseful of rugrats, in-laws, sky-high bills, and a mortgage to boot, all roping you in. Velvet handcuffs."

Ben raised an eyebrow. "Is this a new personal philosophy you're working on?"

"Nothin' new about it. I've always felt this way."

Always? Ben wondered. Always since he and Julia got divorced, anyway.

"Last thing a man in my position needs is a toddler running around the house. Hell, I wouldn't take that kid if he were my own flesh and blood."

Ben's lips parted. Did he know? Was this some kind of game he was playing? Or was he really as blind as he seemed?

The phone rang. Ben crossed the room and snatched it up. "Yeah?"

Ben listened to the man on the other end, then he covered the mouthpiece and spoke to Mike. "It's for you. Sergeant Tomlinson."

Mike waved a hand in the air. "Aww, tell 'em I'm dining out."

Ben dutifully repeated the message. "He still wants to talk to you."

"Please remind the good sergeant that I'm off-duty."

Ben did, but it didn't make any difference. "There's been a murder. Three of them, actually."

"Three?" Mike threw down the crust of his pizza. "Damn. Tell him I'm not home."

"Wait. There's more." Ben listened for another ten seconds or so. "He says, if you've just eaten, you might as well bring a barf bag to the crime scene."

"What?"

"He says you've never seen anything like this before in your life. Never."

Mike closed his eyes, inhaled, and pushed himself off the sofa. "I'm on my way."

* 5 *

Trying his best to maintain a stoic demeanor, Mike lifted the sheet off the corpse on the right-hand side of the bed.

"Sweet Mary, Mother of God," he whispered, without even realizing it.

He turned abruptly, fighting back the gorge rising in his throat. "I need to make a phone call," he said curtly, pushing his way out of the room.

"Sure," Sergeant Tomlinson said, pointing the way.

Mike walked into the hallway and didn't stop until he found a place where he could be alone for a moment. He passed though all the crime technicians working the scene—the hair and fiber men, the print dusters, the camerapersons, the body-fluid experts, the kids from the coroner's office. He avoided eye contact. He knew he wasn't fooling anyone, least of all Tomlinson, with that dodge about making a phone call. But he had a professional reputation as a "tough guy" to maintain, and he couldn't very well do that by vomiting all over the crime scene.

When he had fully recovered, Mike casually strolled back into the bedroom. For once, he removed his stained and tattered overcoat and slung it over a chair. It was incredibly hot in here. Or so it seemed to him, anyway. He was burning up.

"What the hell happened to this poor schmuck?" Mike asked.

Tomlinson shook his head. "The medical examiner can't tell us with certainty. Not till he gets the stiff back to his OR, anyway. But he appears to have been pummeled by some kind of blunt instrument. I'm thinking maybe a baseball bat."

Mike nodded grimly, trying to block out the chilling

mental image of this man, bound and gagged, being used for batting practice. Actually, he thought the baseball bat guess wasn't quite right, but it wasn't far wrong, either. "How many times was he hit?"

"Can't say yet. But I can see at least a dozen different points of impact."

Yes, Mike thought. But given the overall destruction to the body, the number was probably twice that. Maybe more. "How many times was the wife hit?"

"If you mean by the baseball bat, none." Tomlinson walked unexpressively to the other side of the bed, then lifted the sheet covering the other corpse. "She's been shot. Twice."

"But not hit?"

"Not that we can see. The medical examiner will be able to tell us for sure."

"What kind of gun?"

"We haven't extracted the bullets yet, so I can't say for sure. Looks like some kind of high-powered pistol, though."

Mike turned away. What the hell was this world coming to, anyway? It was enough to make a man vote Republican. "And the boy?"

"He was also shot. Once. In the center of the forehead."

"That's pretty damned efficient. Are we talking about a professional here?"

For the first time, Tomlinson hesitated just a beat. "I don't like to speculate in advance of the evidence, sir, but . . . that seems to me a distinct possibility."

"A hit man?"

"Or perhaps just a freelance serial killer. Or maybe just someone who's a damn good shot. But definitely someone . . . who's done this sort of thing before."

Mike nodded. The sour expression on his face seemed a permanent fixture, and was likely to remain so until he got the hell out of this house of horrors. "What have the forensic teams turned up?"

"Damn near nothing. Hair and fiber boys have turned up a few trace elements, but so far they all match clothing found in the victims' closets."

"What about prints?"

"None."

"None?" Mike was incredulous. "This killer must've been in here for a good long time."

"Just the same, the dusters found no prints, other than those belonging to the deceased. And not many of those."

"In their own bedroom?" Mike thought for a moment. "Our killer must've wiped the place. Before he left."

"That was certainly . . . professional of him."

"Yeah. So what have we got to go on?"

Tomlinson spread his hands. "Frankly, not a hell of a lot."

Mike took a step back and surveyed the gruesome scene. The sheets were off the corpses again; the videographers were making their record, preserving this nightmare for all time. The glare of the klieg lights did nothing to soften the grotesqueness of it all, particularly the inhuman mutilation on the right side of the bed.

There's something I'm missing here, Mike thought quietly. Something that doesn't add up. But what?

"Who was this guy, anyway?" Mike asked. "The victim, I mean." Tomlinson had been here barely an hour, but Mike knew he'd have the basics on all the victims. Since Mike had drafted him onto the homicide team a few years back, after a nasty serial killer case, he had proven himself to be a top-notch assistant. Best Mike had ever worked with, in fact. "What's his name?"

Tomlinson flipped his notebook open. "Name's Harvey Pendergast. He's fifty-three, white male, married, slightly over-weight and balding. Wears glasses for myopia."

"What's he do?"

"He works for the Blaylock Industrial Machinery Corpora-tion. Over in Blackwood. Some kind of middle-management executive. Makes about a hundred and twenty grand a year."

Mike whistled. "Not bad."

"I guess he needed it," Tomlinson commented. "He's got more clothes in that closet than JCPenney's."

Mike allowed himself a wry grin.

"So what do you think?" Tomlinson asked. "An enforcer?"

Mike slowly shook his head. "Doesn't seem quite right."

"You said yourself this was a very professional job."

"Well, it wasn't an accidental death, that's for damn sure. But a hit man wouldn't have taken the time to batter poor

Harvey around like that. He would've just put a bullet through the man's head and disappeared."

"Prescott thinks it was a robbery."

"Prescott?" Mike's teeth ground together. "Was he here?"

"Only for a while. He was in the neighborhood and heard about the killings on his scanner. He disappeared just before you arrived."

"Lucky for him." Prescott was the department's other homicide detective. To say that the two did not get along would be an understatement of monumental proportions. "I don't want that screwup anywhere near this case."

"Understood."

"You know these murders are going to get major play in the press. I don't want anyone mucking up our chances of making a collar."

"Got it."

"Why in God's name would he think it was a robbery?"

"Harvey's wallet was emptied. Some of his wife's jewelry appears to have been taken."

"But the mutilation—"

"Prescott says that was just a dodge. To throw the cops off."

Mike rolled his eyes. Was it any wonder he couldn't tolerate Prescott? In addition to being arrogant, in addition to getting his job through political connections instead of by merit, in addition to endangering prosecutions by flouting procedure—he was just stupid! "This was no robbery. No robber would stand around here banging at the victim when he had a gun in his pocket and there was so much more loot in the house."

"But the stolen jewelry—"

"That was the dodge. A bit of misdirection intended to confuse us."

"Then you agree with me."

"What's your theory?"

"Serial killer. I think this has to be the work of some kind of major crazy."

Mike thought a good long while before answering. "I don't know. Sure, the perp's got to be a little off-kilter to do what he did to that man on the bed. Tying him up. Beating him over and over again. Unless . . ." His eyes drifted back toward the bedroom. "Unless he had a reason."

"A reason? What sane reason could there possibly be for that kind of torture?"

Mike turned abruptly, grabbing his coat from the chair. "That's what I have to figure out."

Through the high-powered binoculars, his green eyes peered out toward the house that last night had been visited with so much carnage—at his hands. From his secure hiding place across the street, he could watch the furious come and go of the various crime technicians, all going about their separate and specialized tasks, rather like ants in an anthill. They would make all their tests and studies, use all their high-tech paraphernalia . . . and they would come up with nothing.

He smiled. There was a certain pride a man could take in this sort of work, he realized. To commit an act so horrible, at least by the standards of contemporary society, an act so vilified, and to get totally and utterly away with it—well, one couldn't help but get a little ego boost out of that. They couldn't catch him. It simply couldn't happen. Wasn't within the realm of possibility.

As he watched, he spotted a face he knew emerging from the house. A man wearing a stained and rather disgusting trenchcoat. He couldn't think of the man's name, but he knew he was a police detective. He'd seen the man's picture in the paper. The *World* seemed to think he was quite the Sherlock Holmes, that he could solve anything.

He laughed quietly. This time, Sherlock Holmes had met his Moriarty. There was no way that boob in the tacky coat could catch him. No way he could even get close. And even if he did get close—

He laid his hand gently upon the ball-peen hammer still in his coat pocket. He seemed to draw strength from its presence. A current of energy surged through it to him, reminding him that he was invincible, telling him he could destroy anyone who stood in his path.

No, there was no way he could be caught. Which was important. Because he still had work to do. If he was going to find the merchandise.

Still, he cautioned himself, it wouldn't do to get too cocky. Pride goeth before a fall. And advance preparation was the key to success. Perhaps he should take a few precautions. Vary his routine a bit. Just to keep the police swimming in circles.

His smile broadened. Yes, that was exactly what he would do. It would be smarter that way—and more fun, too. His eyes twinkled in anticipation. After all, variety was the spice of life, right?

And humans, being the resourceful creatures they were, had devised so many different ways to kill. So so many.

"Is something wrong?" Sergeant Tomlinson asked.

Mike rubbed the back of his neck, then scanned the surrounding neighborhood. They were standing in the driveway of the house where the murders had taken place, preparing to get into their respective cars. "I don't know. I just got a sudden chill for some reason."

"Probably the aftershock. That scene inside was pretty gruesome."

"Yeah. I suppose so. Look, when you get back to HQ, I want you to get all available personnel working on this case."

"Understood."

"Pick two men and have them start running the details of this crime through the FBI database. See if there are records of any recent murders resembling this one."

"Got it."

"And have someone run a background check on the victims. If there are any possible reasons why someone might want to wipe out this entire family—or any one of them—I want to know about it."

"Will do."

"I'm going to want someone to comb the area. Talk to all the neighbors. Ask if anyone saw anything suspicious."

"O-kay . . ." Tomlinson said, a bit slower than before.

Mike knew why he was hesitating. As any experienced cop would realize, this would be by far the most miserable of the assigned tasks. "Tomlinson, I'm sorry to do this to you . . . but I'd appreciate it if you'd handle that one yourself."

To his credit, Tomlinson didn't bat an eyelash. "Yes sir."

"I'm going to check out this guy Harvey. He seems to be the one the killer was most interested in. The one he wanted to hurt most. I'll go to his place of work, talk to his boss, his coworkers. Find out whatever I can. And when the background check is finished, maybe I'll have some more leads."

"Sounds good, sir." There was something about the inflection in Tomlinson's voice, the way he finished the sentence on an *up* tonality rather than a *down*, that told Mike there was more he wanted to say.

"Something else, Sergeant?"

Tomlinson licked his lips. "Sir . . . I expect you wanted me to get on this right away. . . ."

"You got that right."

"Sir . . . would it be all right if I made a quick dash home? Saw my family?"

A deep crease crossed Mike's forehead. He'd met Tomlinson's family a few times—a pretty wife named Karen. A daughter, probably about four or five years old now. He knew Tomlinson was very devoted to them. Which was probably why his marriage still worked, when so many other cops' marriages had failed. "May I ask why?"

"I don't know, sir. I just . . ." His eyes drifted back toward the house. The house of horror. The site of the most violent, grisly murder the two of them had ever witnessed. "I'd just like to check on everyone. That's all. Won't take a minute."

Mike laid his hand on his protégé's shoulder. "You do that, Sergeant. And give them a kiss for me."

"Yes sir."

He erased his smile. "And then get to work. Double time. Understand?"

"Yes sir!"

"Good." He turned and stared up at the house, at the bedroom window—the one splattered with blood. "I don't know what happened in there. But I intend to find out."

* 6 *

Ben passed copies of the three-page document to the rest of his staff: Christina, Jones, and Loving. He gave them ten minutes to scrutinize the document, although it could easily be read in half that time.

"This is what I've managed to come up with," Ben explained. "Think it'll get their attention?"

Jones flipped past the standard identification of the parties and their places of residence and cut to the gravamen of the Complaint. "Paragraph Eight. That Defendant H. P. Blaylock knowingly or with reckless disregard poisoned the plaintiffs' water supply with toxic chemicals. Paragraph Nine. That the chemicals discharged by Defendant H. P. Blaylock included TCE, a powerful neural poison, which causes symptoms ranging from dizziness and nausea to liver damage and cancer. Paragraph Ten. That the Defendant's aforementioned activities resulted in an epidemic of leukemia and the deaths of eleven children, as well as injuries to their families, including but not limited to emotional distress and the real and perceived danger of an increased risk of leukemia and other cancers and diseases in the surviving family members."

Jones looked up from the paper, his face deadpan. "Yeah, Boss. I think that might get their attention."

"So what're we askin' for?" Loving asked. Loving was Ben's investigator. He'd bumped heads with Ben years ago under adverse circumstances (Ben represented his wife in their divorce) but nonetheless became a fiercely loyal member of Ben's team. He was a huge bear of a man; his shoulders were broad enough to fit snugly between two goalposts. "What's the bottom line?"

Ben flipped to the last page of the Complaint. "Paragraph Fourteen. For the aforementioned injuries, plaintiffs seek actual damages for injuries incurred, damages for emotional distress, pain and suffering, and punitive damages for the willful and wanton acts of the Defendant in an amount not less than one million dollars."

Loving pursed his lips and whistled. "That's some Complaint, Skipper. You really think you could get a million bucks?"

"He'd better get more," Jones commented. "It'll probably cost that much just to try this sucker."

"The amount requested in the Complaint doesn't really mean anything," Ben explained. "I didn't want to stir up trouble by tossing out too huge a number. Between now and trial, we'll figure out what to ask the jury for. Frankly, a million dollars wouldn't even cover our clients' medical bills."

"When are you planning to file this, Ben?" Christina asked.

"Right now. Assuming you three don't have any changes or suggestions?"

"And when will the big boys down at Raven, Tucker & Tubb get it?"

"Just as soon as it's filed. I'm going to walk it over to the Bank of Oklahoma Tower and hand-deliver it myself."

"Uh, Skipper," Loving interjected, "have you considered, maybe, usin' a courier service?"

"Why?"

Loving tossed his copy down on a desk. "I don't think you wanna be around when the powers-that-be read this."

"You're exaggerating."

"I don't think so. A Complaint like this could do some real damage to an outfit like Blaylock. 'Specially once the press gets wind of it."

"Which they will," Jones interjected. "Blaylock will have to take this case very seriously."

Ben didn't respond. Deep down, he knew they were right. Blaylock would perceive this as a threat to their corporate integrity, not to mention their bottom line. Raven, Tucker & Tubb would perceive this as an opportunity to rack up some major billable hours. This suit would be big news throughout the legal community—in fact, probably throughout the state.

"All the more reason for us to get to work," Ben said. "I expect each of you to give this case your full attention. Whatever else you've got going, put it on the back burner. We have to move fast or we're going to get trampled." He handed each staff member a legal pad that outlined their assignments. "Christina, I know you're getting close to finals. Do you have time to do some intensive legal research?"

"Of course. I make it a practice never to study for final exams until the night before."

Ben rolled his eyes. "I think we can fairly anticipate Raven will try to bury us in a sea of motions. They'll take advantage of the fact that they have a hundred lawyers and we have one."

"One and a half," Christina corrected.

"As you say. You think you can anticipate what they'll file?"

She shrugged. "Sure. Discovery motions. Motion to dismiss for failure to state a claim."

"Exactly right," Ben said. "And the last is the one that scares me. Find some similar cases. Some legal precedent in our favor."

"I know I can find similar cases," Christina answered. "In fact, I've already found some. The Woburn, Massachusetts, case that was in that book *A Civil Action*. The Toms River case. The outbreaks in Montana and east New Jersey. The problem is—they all feature plaintiffs who get creamed."

"Find one that's different. It's critical that we be able to show the judge we have some potential for success at trial." He turned his attention to Loving. "We're going to need some witnesses to prop up all these claims in the Complaint."

"You mean experts?"

"No. We'll worry about that later. I mean fact witnesses. As I see it, our case has two basic premises, both of which we have to prove. First, that Blaylock poisoned the water. Second, that the poisoned water caused the leukemia outbreak. Of course, I'll conduct the traditional legal discovery, but I think we can fairly assume that everyone at Blaylock will deny all responsibility. I need you to ferret out someone who will tell the truth."

Loving tucked in his chin. "That's a pretty tall order, Skipper."

"I know. That's why I gave it to you." He smiled. "Blackwood has almost five thousand citizens. There must be someone somewhere who knows what happened and is willing to talk."

"If you say so."

"I do. And I'm not exaggerating the importance of this. We'll use experts to prove the contamination caused the cancers. But if we don't have evidence that Blaylock caused the contamination, we'll never get to trial. They'll take us out on a motion for summary judgment."

Finally, Ben adjusted his gaze to Jones.

"I suppose you'll want me to do some kind of high-risk heavy-duty investigating," Jones opined. "Perhaps some undercover work."

"Nooo," Ben replied. "I want you to figure out how we're going to pay for this."

"But Ben—"

"You're the CFO of this firm, Jones. It's your job."

"I know it's my job!" he shot back. "I spoke to The Brain this morning, just as you asked."

"And?"

"He's willing to advance fifty thousand bucks at twelve percent."

"Fifty thousand? That won't get us through the first month, even if we all agree to waive our salaries."

All three staffers shot out of their chairs. *"What?"*

"I was just speaking hypothetically," Ben said, although in truth, he doubted if he was. "We're going to need more money."

"What you don't seem to understand, Boss, is that The Brain works for a bank, not a charitable institution."

"Find the money, Jones."

"How?"

"I don't know how. But I'm confident you'll think of something."

"Oh, thank you very much."

"Look." Ben pressed his hands against the desk. "I know

this is going to be hard. This case—it isn't like just any case. It's—" He paused. "Frankly, most of what lawyers do these days doesn't amount to a hill of beans. It's paper pushing and moneygrubbing and no one's the better for it. But this case is different. This case matters." He paused again, making sure his words had a chance to sink in. "So I want to make sure we do the best job we possibly can."

Jones stared down at the floor. His voice was soft—but perfectly audible. "I still think we'll go down in flames."

Ben picked right up on it. "You know what, Jones? You may be right. Frankly, I don't know if this case can be won or not. But we're going to give it every possible chance, and when it's all over with—at least we can say we tried. Win or lose, we tried to do the right thing. We tried to find some justice for those parents who lost their children for no reason. And that's what matters in the end. That we tried."

Ben pushed away from his desk and sighed. "End of sappy speech. Now get to work."

Fred Henderson wadded the newspaper in his hands and tossed it across the room. Damn!

Well, he had wondered what everyone was whispering about at the Culligan cooler when he came to work this morning. Now he knew. After all, he wasn't the only person in the building who knew Harvey. Hell, half the people here probably did. And now everyone did; Harvey was famous. Not for anything he did during his life, but for the nightmarishly gruesome manner in which he died.

Fred could tell from the article that the police were doing their best to suppress the details, but how could you suppress a thing like that? In this tabloid world, sixty strokes with a blunt instrument was going to make the headlines. And that wasn't even mentioning what happened to Harvey's wife, his son. The whole family had been wiped out in a single hyperviolent stroke. The police were baffled.

Fred wasn't.

He pushed out his chair, suddenly moved by the desperate need to stretch his legs. He felt as if the walls of his cubicle were closing in on him, threatening to crush him like some elaborate comic book deathtrap. He walked to the edge of his space, catching a glimpse of himself in the glass in the dividers. He was fifty-eight, gray, liver-bespotted, slightly arthritic, and too damn old for this sort of thing. Way back then, when the whole mess began, it had been different. He was a different person, with a different body. Now he just wanted to be left alone. To forget. To fill out his final days in peace reading H. Rider Haggard novels and watching the History Channel. Hell, given the circumstances, there was no end to his retirement possibilities. If he lived long enough to enjoy them.

He knew what had happened to Harvey. He knew who did it and why he did it. And he knew that Harvey's killer had not found that for which he was looking. Fred knew that for certain. Because Fred had it.

Fred would be the last one the killer came after. He knew that as surely as he knew the sun would rise in the morning. No one had ever taken Fred seriously. He had never really been one of the gang—more like a mascot. Fred the Feeb, that's what they called him when he wasn't around. They thought he didn't know. But he did, of course. He always knew. He always knew everything. He was always one step ahead of them. Which is why he now had the merchandise. And the others didn't.

And Harvey was dead.

For some reason, Fred's mind began drifting backward, snatching back the calendar pages, remembering his boyhood back in Carter, a small town in western Oklahoma. He thought of his father, dead these past twenty years. His dad had been a poor hardscrabble farmer, barely eking out a living for his family of seven. He had rarely had time for play and too often had time to drink. And fight. And hit. They were too unalike, Fred and his father, and Fred's disdain for farming was too transparent. Instead of encouraging Fred's business ambitions, he actually seemed to resent them. They had never been very close.

And now that he was gone, Fred thought of him every day. And missed him, so badly that at times his chest ached.

What was it his father used to say? "You can't hang pumpkins on a morning glory."

What the hell had that meant? Fred asked himself time and again. If that was his father's idea of homespun wisdom, it was just as lame as everything else the man did. Or so it had always seemed. Now, today, his father's words came back to him, and they made perfect sense. He knew exactly what his father had been saying. He'd spent his whole life hanging those damn pumpkins. And the morning glory was the merchandise.

Fred had it, all right. But what good had it ever done him? He couldn't use it; he couldn't even tell anyone he had it. Not if he wanted to live. It was his little secret. He'd had to content himself with the knowledge that he'd fooled them all. That he'd succeeded where the others had failed.

Fred had never married. Who would want to marry Fred the Feeb? His family was all dead. His principal source of pride in his life had come from one dirty little secret. But how much longer would it remain a secret? He knew Harvey's killer wouldn't stop after one strike. He would keep on swinging that bat, or whatever the hell it was, until he found what he wanted.

Until he found Fred.

Fred pressed his hand against the glass pane, staring at the lines in his face, the deeply etched creases that reminded him how old he was, how long it had been. He was too old to track down his old friend. And too old to kill. Too old to do anything, really. But a countdown had begun. A countdown that could finish only one of two ways.

Either way you looked at it, someone was going to end up dead.

Like any good associate, Mark Austin came when he was summoned. He hoped he was dressed appropriately. It was such a tough decision, dressing to work in a large law firm. The blue suit, or the gray? The gray suit, or the blue? With the white shirt, of course.

The current summons had him scurrying out of the library with particular haste. For the entire two years he'd been at Raven, Tucker & Tubb, he'd been hoping for a chance to work with Charlton Colby. Colby was generally considered the top litigator in the city, if not the state. Certainly he was the richest. He had all the top blue-chip clients in his back pocket. He was the man holding the brass ring Mark hoped to grab.

He made a last-minute duck into the men's room to straighten his tie and adjust his hair, then sped toward Colby's office. He'd been waiting two years for this chance; he didn't want to screw it up now. This could be his ticket to the upper echelon of the litigation world. It all flashed past him in a heartbeat. Dining at the Tulsa Club, a vaguely bored expression on his face. Hobnobbing with CEOs and society debs. Weaving his spell in the courtroom, the eyes of the world upon him via the magic of television. Retiring to his majestic estate near Philbrook, neighbored by some of the oldest money in the city. That was what he aspired to. That was what he dreamed of. He knew it could all be his. He knew it.

He stopped just outside Colby's office and knocked on the open door. "You wanted to see me?"

Colby peered through his tortoise-tinted wire-rimmed glasses. "Yes. Come in, Mark."

Mark stepped into the office. He saw Colby was wearing his blue today, generally considered the warmer of the two acceptable lawyer fashion choices. He was glad he had done the same.

There were two high-backed plush chairs opposite Colby's desk—but one was occupied. "Mark, I'd like you to meet Myron Blaylock. Myron, Mark Austin."

Mark took the other man's hand, which was like ice. He had a weak, unenthusiastic grip.

"Mark, as you probably know, Mr. Blaylock is the CEO and president of the H. P. Blaylock Industrial Machinery Corporation. His grandfather founded the business."

Mark hadn't known, but now that he did, he would never forget it. "Of course."

"I've helped Myron with a number of cases over the years. Business litigation, mostly. Never anything like this." He lifted a stapled document off his desk and passed it to Mark. "Mr. Blaylock received an unwelcome bit of news this morning. A lawsuit."

Mark took the proffered paper. It looked like a standard civil-suit Complaint. He saw on the last page that the opposing attorney was someone named Benjamin Kincaid. Never heard of him.

"I'm going to need some help on this lawsuit," Colby continued. "A lot of it, in fact. I heard you had some time available."

"Of course," Mark said, straightening. "I'm ready to start immediately."

"Good. For starters, I'd like you to draft an Answer to this Complaint."

"Sure." The Answer was one of the simplest and most pro forma of all the pleadings in a suit. The defendant's approach was easy: Deny everything. "I assume we have the standard twenty days. Forty if we ask for the automatic extension."

Colby shook his head. "We want to file our Answer tomorrow."

Mark blinked. "Tomorrow?"

"Yes. Is that a problem?"

"No. Of course not." He concentrated on controlling his facial expressions. Had he already blown it? "I'm just . . . surprised. Normally, defendants—"

"Aren't in a big hurry?" Colby glanced at Blaylock, almost smiling. "I don't anticipate we'll stray from that standard strategic approach much throughout the course of this action. But we contemplate the press being interested in this. They'll run a story as soon as they learn of the Complaint. We want to be ready with our Answer. We can't let these charges go unrefuted. Not for a day. Not for ten seconds."

"I see." Mark scanned quickly through the Complaint. Leukemia, TCE, perc. Wrongful death, negligence, punitive damages. He didn't have time to soak in all the details. But it was apparent this was not your standard-issue business litigation. "May I ask what our . . . position is with respect to these charges?"

"We deny everything," Blaylock said. His voice had a raspy quality reminiscent of the creaking of a door in a haunted house. He was an old man, in his sixties at least, possibly older. His frame was long and gaunt, almost skeletal. "These charges are outrageous."

"No doubt," Mark murmured.

"I'm appalled that anyone would even suggest that H. P. Blaylock engaged in improper waste disposal. H. P. Blaylock has been an exemplary corporate citizen, from my grandfather's day to the present. We would no sooner poison the water wells than we'd poison our own watercooler. We employ over six thousand people in this state, and we take good care of them. To suggest that we are responsible for the deaths of children—it's unconscionable!" His indignation was so intense Mark worried that he might froth at the mouth. "It's outrageous. Libelous! Truly, Charlton, I feel the standard litigation responses are not enough. These people should be made to pay the consequences of these unjust and outrageous accusations. I think criminal charges should be considered."

"Rest assured that we will consider every realistic option, Myron," Colby said calmly. "And I can guarantee you that Mark's Answer will include a counterclaim for libel. Right, Mark?"

Mark hedged for a moment, torn between his desire to flaunt a morsel of knowledge and his hesitance to oppose anything Colby suggested. "Actually, sir, you can't bring a claim of libel against litigants based upon accusations made in a legal Complaint. They have qualified immunity."

Colby waved his hand absently. "If these plaintiffs are prepared to make these claims in court, I'm sure they've already made them somewhere else."

"But if we don't know—"

"We'll find out in discovery."

"Then perhaps we should wait and amend our Answer when we know—"

"Put the counterclaim in now." Colby still remained calm; only the slightest alteration in his intonation cued Mark that this discussion was over.

"Do you know anything about this pissant attorney who signed the Complaint?" Blaylock asked, keenly agitated. "This Kincaid?"

"In fact, I do," Colby said. His voice, his entire manner, was supremely dismissive. "Believe it or not, Kincaid actually worked here at Raven, for about ten minutes. Till we ran him out on a rail for gross incompetence. He's small potatoes.

Solo practitioner. Probably hoping for a quick and dirty nuisance settlement. We have greater resources, more talent, and more money." He shrugged dismissively. "We'll bury him."

"I expect nothing less. I want you to spare nothing, Charlton. I want this case prosecuted to the fullest extent. Do whatever it takes. Everything you can think of. Don't let these bastards come up for air. I want them to be sorry they ever heard of H. P. Blaylock."

"I understand."

Mark imagined that he could hear those old bones creaking as the scarecrow pushed himself out of his chair. "Keep me informed, Charlton. I want to know everything that happens in this suit, from now till the day we drive a stake through its heart. And everyone associated with it."

"Of course." Colby rose, removing his glasses. He walked to the door, exchanged a few more remarks with Blaylock sotto voce, shook his head, and bid him good-bye.

Colby returned to the office. Mark was still in the chair, waiting to hear what the man had to say next.

"Do I have your complete attention?" Colby asked. He walked to the window and gazed out at his view of Bartlett Square.

"Of course."

"From now until the day this case ends, your ass is mine."

"Completely, sir."

"Good." He turned, facing his new amanuensis, and inhaled deeply. "Do you smell what I smell?"

Mark was flummoxed. He didn't smell anything. Should he try to fake it? For some reason, he took the safer route and admitted his ignorance. "No, sir. What do you smell?"

A smile creased Colby's placid face. "Money."

* 7 *

Christina marched into Ben's office and let a flurry of pink message slips flutter down onto his desk. "Word is officially out."

Ben scanned the tops of the slips. Channel Two. Channel Six. Channel Eight. A couple of channels he didn't know existed. And the *Tulsa World*. "What do they want?"

"They want to talk to the man," she answered. "And you're the man. For the moment, anyway. They want to hear your plan for bringing one of the largest corporations in the state to its knees."

Ben frowned. "Pass."

Christina slid into the nearest chair. "Ben, I think you should consider talking to them. Just make a brief statement."

"No way. Only sleazebags try their cases on television."

"You don't have to deliver closing argument. Just tell them what it's all about."

"The Rules of Professional Conduct strongly disfavor lawyers talking to the media about pending cases. Judges don't like it. And neither do I."

"Ben, think for a moment." She reached out across the desk. "Once the public gets wind of this suit, the media will be all over Blaylock, trying to find out if they really poisoned the water supply in Blackwood. That's not going to be good for their public relations—or their stockholders. If you put the heat on them, they're much more likely to give you a favorable settlement."

Ben considered. "A generous early settlement would be nice. I'd give about anything not to have to try this sucker." He paused. "But I don't think it's going to happen. And I won't do it, in any case."

The interoffice phone buzzed. "Very insistent reporter from Channel Two on line one," Jones said via the intercom.

Reluctantly Ben picked up the receiver. "I'm not giving interviews."

There was a moment's hesitation before the male voice on the other end of the line spoke. "Oh, I don't want an interview. I just need a spot."

"A spot?"

"Yeah. You know, ten seconds. Twenty, tops. Just tell us succinctly why you think Blaylock contaminated the Blackwood water supply and what you intend to do about it."

Ben pursed his lips. "You're looking for a sound bite."

"Not a sound bite. A spot."

"What's the difference?"

"Sound bites are cheesy and uninformative. This'll be a first-class feature. It'll just be short, that's all."

"Sounds like a sound bite to me."

"Obviously, you're not in the industry. I only do spots."

"Well . . . out, out, damned spot." Ben started to hang up the phone.

"Wait!" the reporter shouted. "Don't you at least want to respond to Colby's accusations?"

"Colby?" Ben felt his blood quickening. When he had been at Raven, the other lawyers had referred to Colby as "the King." "Accusations?"

"Sure, haven't you heard? Don't you watch television?"

"Actually, no." Not entirely true, but there was no reason to confess his secret passion for *Buffy the Vampire Slayer* to this jackal.

"Well, turn it on. It'll run again on the noon news."

Ben hung up the phone and walked out to the reception area where Jones kept a small thirteen-inch TV. He switched to Channel Eight and waited.

He didn't have to wait long. Not five minutes later, the talking head announced the lawsuit filed against "corporate giant H. P. Blaylock by eleven Blackwood parents." Then they cut to counsel for the defendant, Charlton Colby, for comment.

Colby was sitting in a law library, back by shelves of impressive-looking legal tomes in matching colors. His face was calm and handsome, but his voice was one of moral indignation. "These charges are utterly baseless. An unscrupulous lawyer is taking advantage of the vulnerability of grieving parents and manipulating the media to blackmail one of Oklahoma's finest corporate citizens and line his own pockets. We will not let this happen. We will fight this to the fullest extent."

Ben checked his watch. Not bad. Colby pretty much covered all the bases—and he managed to do it in less than fifteen seconds.

Christina whistled softly. "He really is the King."

Ben nodded. "The King of sound bites, anyway."

"You see what he's trying to do, don't you? He knows that most people's natural sympathies will go to the parents who lost their children. He's trying to turn that around by casting them as innocent victims of a crooked lawyer who bullied them into bringing baseless claims."

"With me in the starring role."

"Yeah." She punched him on the shoulder. "Shame on you for being such a bully."

Jones called out from his desk. "You're very popular for a crooked bully, Boss. Another call on line one."

"Take a message."

"No. . . . I think you'll want to take this one yourself."

That sounded ominous. Ben crossed over to Jones's desk and grabbed the phone. "Yes?"

"Please wait for Charlton Colby."

Ben's teeth set on edge. In all the world, there were few things he hated quite so much as assholes who were so damned important they couldn't even dial the phone for themselves.

"Colby here."

Ben tried to suppress his irritation. "Kincaid here."

"Yes, Ben. Good to talk to you. How have you been?"

Ben couldn't believe it. Did the man actually think they were going to engage in amiable small talk just after he'd called Ben a crook on television? "I'm okay."

"Glad to hear it. Don't see much of you these days, since

you left the firm. We should get together sometime, play eighteen holes. Nothing I enjoy as much as spending an afternoon with fellow professionals. Perhaps out at the club."

"I'm not a member of any club. I don't play golf. And if you're going to spend any time with a lawyer, I'd recommend a libel lawyer."

There was a soft chuckling on the other end. "I guess you've been watching television."

"I guess so. And I didn't appreciate it."

"Now, Ben. You know it's all part of the game."

"I'm not playing a game. I'm representing eleven parents who lost their children because your client couldn't keep its waste in the trash can."

"Now, Ben, I must warn you, if you continue to make accusations of that nature—"

"Warn somebody who cares. Was there a point to this phone call?"

"Uh, yes. I'm afraid so." He released a soft exhalation of air, which Ben supposed was intended to indicate regret, although he didn't believe it for a moment. "I'm calling to inform you that I'm filing a Rule 12(b)(6) motion to dismiss, as a courtesy."

As a *courtesy*? "What kind of crappy tactic is that?"

"It's no tactic, Ben. Your Complaint is groundless."

"You're just trying to run up the bill and spin us around. Make things difficult."

"Litigation is never easy, Ben. That's why we get paid the big bucks."

"That's why you do, you mean. You get paid for pleasing your corporate masters by making life miserable for anyone who has the audacity to sue them."

"Ben, please. This is all too trite. I just wanted to give you the heads up. I expect a hearing will be set within a week's time." He mumbled a few more platitudes, then rang off.

Ben slammed the phone back into its cradle.

"What was that all about?" Christina asked.

"Colby's coming after us. Motion to dismiss."

"Son of a bitch." She fell soundlessly into a chair. "What kind of game is he playing?"

Ben could answer her with a single word. "Hardball."

* * *

Everyone had their own standards, Mike supposed, when it came to evaluating who they liked in this world and who they didn't. His father, for instance, God bless his soul, never trusted any man who had voted for Nixon—and would cop to it. His pal Ben Kincaid never trusted any man who liked to do a lot of hugging. His ex-wife, Julia, née Kincaid, had never trusted anyone who used a calculator to compute tips. And Mike himself? He never trusted anyone who was just too damn friendly.

Like the vice president in charge of operations for Blaylock Machinery, Ronald Harris. The man currently welcoming Mike into his office.

Harris had more teeth than a game show host, and they all seemed to be constantly on display. Frankly, most people weren't all that enthused when a homicide detective wanted to see them. Judging by the look on Harris's face, though, you'd think Mike was his long-lost billionaire uncle.

"Please come in," Harris said, escorting Mike to a comfortable sofa at the side of the office. His hair was slicked back in a sort of Reaganesque pompadour, and his handshake was of the manly bone-crusher variety. "I can't tell you how sorry we are about what happened to Harvey. And his family."

Mike made no comment. "I don't suppose you have any idea what happened to him."

Harris's reaction was a caricature of cluelessness. "Me? Jeez, no. I assumed it was a robbery. Weren't some of their possessions missing?"

"Some."

"You seem unconvinced."

Mike shrugged. "Burglars don't usually hang around for half an hour torturing the burgled."

Harris winced. "Tortured? Gosh—was it as bad as the paper seemed to suggest?"

"Much worse. Someone was really out to get him."

"Harvey? That astounds me. There's never been a sweeter guy."

Mike didn't know what to think. It was possible this was simply the usual deification that accompanied someone's passing, but somehow he didn't believe a damn word this unctuous clown said. "Can you give me some background on his work here? Tell me what he did?"

"Harvey was a headhunter."

"A headhunter." Mike scribbled nonsense into his notepad, just to keep his hands moving. "I gather that means he worked in personnel."

"Right. He was in charge of recruiting new executive talent."

"How long had he been here?"

"Let me check that." Harris thumbed through a file on his desk. "Yes, that's right. Twenty-three years."

Mike's eyebrows rose. "That long? Was he the head of his department?"

"No, no. Just a regular working stiff. I think he preferred it that way."

"He preferred being a grunt?"

Harris didn't lose his smile. "Of course, we don't use words like that here at Blaylock. Every one of our employees is an important part of the production chain. No, what I meant was, I don't think Harvey would've liked the pressure that comes with promotion. He was a quiet fellow. Simple, in his own way. Reserved. And he was earning a good salary. I think he preferred his relatively anonymous place as one of many hard workers in personnel."

Hard to believe anyone could be as contented as Harris made this poor stiff seem. "Did he have any problems?"

"None of which I'm aware. I see no notations in his evaluation file."

"Any conflicts with any of his coworkers?"

"No. Not here at Blaylock. We have finely honed our employee relations and dispute-resolution techniques. Frankly, that sort of thing just doesn't happen anymore. We don't allow it."

Mike frowned. The more he heard about this Stepford corporation, the less he liked it. "So you don't know of any motive anyone would've had to kill Harvey?"

"I'm afraid I don't. I can't even imagine."

Mike decided to try another approach. "Did he have any friends?"

"I would assume so."

"Do you know who they were?"

"Sorry. No."

"Would you object if I spoke to some of the other employees in his department?"

"N-nooo," Harris said, with decided hesitation. "But I don't think you'll learn much."

"And why is that?"

"Because for the most part, Harvey kept to himself. As I said before, he was an introverted man. Reserved."

No doubt, Mike thought. The question is whether he was reserved for a reason. "Anything else you can think of that might be of assistance?"

"I'm sorry, no." His plastic smile, however, did not admit a trace of sorrow. "This all comes as such a shock. Harvey was such a nice guy. Harmless, really."

"Harmless. Huh." Mike made another note. "Can you suggest anyone else I might talk to? Perhaps someone who knew Harvey better?"

"I'm sorry. I can't. Like I said—"

"He was reserved. Right. I got that." For all his smiles, Mike thought, Harris was being decidedly unhelpful. "You know, I really wanted to talk to your CEO. Blaylock. But I was told he was busy."

"Yes, very busy, I'm afraid. There's been a . . . legal development these past few days that I'm sure is occupying his time."

"Legal development?"

"Yes. I'm afraid I'm not at liberty to discuss it at this time. It has nothing to do with Harvey's murder, though."

So you say. "Well, I'd still like to talk to the top man."

"I'll let him know. Next time I see him. Which may well not be for some time."

"I see." Mike glanced up. Through the glass dividing wall behind Harris, he caught a fleeting glimpse of a face. Before he had a chance to focus, though, it was gone. "Who was that?"

"Who was who?" Harris twisted around, trying to look in the direction Mike was facing. "I don't see anyone."

"He's gone." Mike frowned. "I think it was a he, anyway."

"Someone you recognized?"

"No. Someone I did not recognize. But someone who was watching us."

"Watching us?" Harris drew up his shoulders. "Probably just idle curiosity. Someone wondering who's in my office. Wondering if perhaps you're going to be a new member of our family."

Or perhaps someone who knew Mike was a cop, wanted to talk to him, and was wondering how to do an end run around Harris. Mike leaned into the hallway and craned his neck, but he found no trace of the person he had seen before. Which was odd, because he had the distinct and creepy feeling that he was still being watched.

"I see. Well, I think that's about all I wanted to ask you." Mike pushed himself to his feet. "If you could show me where Harvey worked. I'd like to take a look at his desk."

"Sure." Harris rose and gestured toward the back door.

Mike followed, already planning how he was going to shake this walking, talking Ken doll. He knew he'd never learn anything as long as Harris was part of his entourage. He wanted to find out more about Harvey—who he knew and what he was doing. He wanted to know why the CEO was so busy he couldn't make time for the investigation of the murder of one of his long-term employees.

And most of all, he wanted to know who was watching him.

Damn everything, Fred thought, as he ducked into the kitchen. Did the cop spot him?

He thought he had been protected, hidden away by the combination of glare and fake foliage. And then all at once his eyes met the cop's, and he knew perfectly well he'd been made. He'd darted away as quickly as he could.

But was it quick enough? That was the critical question.

Fred had recognized the cop as soon as he'd walked onto the floor. He'd seen his picture in the paper a dozen times. He couldn't remember the man's name, but he knew he was some kind of detective, someone who was supposed to be pretty good at what he did. Someone who might actually be able to figure out what had happened to Harvey.

Which was the last thing Fred wanted right now. He had enough on his mind, worrying about the killer who would be inexorably making his way toward Fred. He didn't need some super sleuth dogging his heels, digging into the past, figuring out how this whole bizarre mess got started. What it's all about. Who's going to die next.

And most important of all, who had the merchandise.

Fred grabbed a paper cup and poured himself some water out of the cooler. This was the good stuff, the Culligan water that was supposedly purified of all foreign substances that sometimes made their way into the water supply. His hands were shaking as he held the cup under the spout. Damn!

He glanced casually over his shoulder, wondering whether anyone was watching. Happily, no one was. He had to get a grip on himself. He couldn't give himself away. He didn't want to go down in flames—another failure, courtesy of Fred the Feeb. He would not let that happen.

He brought the cup to his lips and let the cool, clean liquid trickle down his throat. It seemed to have a calming effect on his nerves; he was feeling better already.

Much better. But not better enough.

He polished off his drink, crushing the paper cup in his hands. It felt good, the satisfying folding of waxed paper between his fingers. It was an empowering act. Or so he told himself.

He walked briskly out of the kitchen, glancing over his shoulder, trying to look every which way at once. He was becoming paranoid; that wasn't good. Or perhaps it was—what did he know? Maybe he should be paranoid. He had a killer on one flank and a cop on the other. He had every right to be paranoid. Paranoia was a survival skill, right? And he was going to need every survival skill he could muster if he was going to get through this. Alive.

What he needed was a vacation. The idea came to him with such crystal clarity that he was stunned by its obviousness. He should get out of here, make himself scarce for a few days. Sure, the merchandise required him to wait until D-day, but he didn't have to wait here. He could disappear for a while. You can't kill a man you can't find, right? He might avoid the criminal investigation, too. Hell, they might be done poking around here by the time he returned. They might miss him altogether.

The problem was the absolute absence of cash in his bank account. The merchandise wasn't worth anything to him—not yet. And he had depleted his savings pulling that last fantabulous trickerooney on his former friends—and depleted his earned vacation time as well. Still, there were always possibilities. . . .

He ducked into Stacey Treadwell's office. She was the pert young twenty-something who was his personnel supervisor, meaning the one who decided whether a vacation was a possibility anytime in his near future. She was as pretty as they came, sexy as a Victoria's Secret catalog. She knew it, too, which was definitely a drawback. Although it hadn't prevented her from becoming personnel supervisor when she was barely old enough to vote, had it? He wondered if she was sleeping with Harris, or maybe had just given his zipper a workout in the storage room a few times. It was possible. Anything was possible, right now.

"Stacey," Fred said quietly, sliding into the empty chair. "What would you think about me slipping off to Beaver Creek for a few weeks? Just me and my fishing pole."

"I'd think you'd be out of a job when you got back." She was chewing gum, which Fred considered the most revolting of all vices. He'd rather come in and see her shooting up cocaine than watch her smacking that gum in his face. "You took your two weeks not four months ago. You haven't got any time."

"I could borrow against next year."

"Mr. Harris doesn't allow that anymore, Fred. You know that."

"Yeah. But I thought maybe, you know, you could maybe . . . pull some strings. Do me a tiny favor."

The utter absence of expression on her face made him sorry he'd even made the suggestion.

"Stacey, I really need to get out of here."

"Sorry, Fred." She pushed the gum out between her lips with her tongue. "Nothing I can do."

"There must be some way I can get off for a couple of weeks."

"Well, I can think of one way."

He leaned forward eagerly. "Yeah? How?"

"You could quit." The bubble popped. She licked her lips, collecting the splattered gum fragments and working them back into her mouth.

"I can't quit. I'm almost qualified for retirement."

"Then I suggest you get back to work." She turned her chair toward her computer, the ever-so-subtle signal that the conversation was over.

That was it then. The answer was no. He'd been summarily dismissed. By a twenty-something gum-cracking tramp.

He stumbled out of her office, entered the hallway—and saw the cop, standing not ten feet away down the corridor.

He bounced backward, flinging himself back into the cubicle.

Stacey looked up. "What is your problem?"

Fred stuttered for a few seconds before answering. "I—uh—don't—just—could—" He took a deep breath. Inhale, Fred. Inhale. "Did I mention how attractive that dress looks on you?"

Stacey glanced down at her bosom. "I'm not wearing a dress."

"Well, that—dresslike thing. Thingie. You're wearing."

"This blouse?"

"Yes, that." Looking out the corner of his eye, he saw the cop in the rumpled trenchcoat pass by without glancing his way. He hadn't spotted him. He thought. "That's it exactly."

"Fred, are you coming on to me? 'Cause I really hate that."

Fred raised his hands anxiously. "No, of course not."

"Do you know I could report you? You'd lose your job in a heartbeat." She shuddered. "Why do you people always choose me? Why would you think I'd want to get anywhere near some lifetime low-level clerk?"

"I got your message, Stacey."

"Do you creeps have some kind of club or something? Maybe a newsletter? You sit around and figure out who you're going to drool over next?"

"Stacey, I get the picture—"

"Yeah, well, this isn't the first time this has happened, so please put the word out to all the horny old geezers that I'm not available, okay?"

"Goodbye, Stacey." He ducked out of her cubicle, making

a beeline toward his own. Uppity tramp. She'd change her tune in a heartbeat if she knew what he had hidden away. He wondered if maybe Stacey would like some of the merchandise. No wondering necessary—she'd drop her blouse-thingie for him in a New York minute if she could get some of that action. Maybe he should give it all to her. It would be worth the loss, almost, just to put her on the hit list.

But no. He retreated into his cubicle and hid behind the relative security of his own desk. So he wasn't going on vacation. He'd have to deal with it. He'd have to figure out a way to keep clear of the police, and most important, to stay far away from his old friend. He had to keep his wits about him, keep one step ahead of everyone else. He could do that. He knew he could. He'd have to. Because the alternative was death. Death in a million pieces.

* 8 *

Given the events of the day, Ben didn't manage to get home until well after dark. He knew it was late, but he decided to stop in to see Mrs. Marmelstein anyway. Perhaps it was silly, but he just felt better when he'd checked on her with his own two eyes.

He knocked gently on the door. He heard soft footfalls on the carpet on the other side. Joni Singleton answered.

"Hi there, counselor," she said. "Heard about you on the evening news."

Ben groaned. "Don't you know better than to watch that crap? It'll rot your brain."

"Too late." When Ben had first moved into this boarding house, Joni, her twin sister, and their oversized family were already living in the room on the opposite side of the top floor. Back then, she was just a silly teenager with big hair and an equal-sized wild streak. Under Ben's tutelage, she had matured into one of the most nurturing caregivers he had ever known, first with Ben's nephew, Joey, and now with Mrs. Marmelstein. "Don't worry, Ben. Everyone who knows you knows those accusations are, like, total nontruths."

"That's swell. But what about the other half a million people in the greater metropolitan area?"

"I'm sure you'll prove it to them, too. Why is that skank saying all those nasty things?"

"To please his corporate bosses. It's a tactic. He's trying to get me to back off."

"Wow. Harsh."

"You could say that."

"But you're not going to back off, right?"

"Right. I've got a few tactics of my own."

She grinned. "Razor." She widened the door and motioned for him to come inside. "I'm glad you came by. I called earlier, but you weren't home yet."

A worry line creased Ben's brow. "Is something wrong with Mrs. Marmelstein?"

"To tell you the truth, I don't know. She got out an old photo album earlier this evening, and she's been acting strange ever since. She's sitting in her bedroom, practically in the dark. Every time I try to talk to her, I get no results."

That was disturbing. It was a shame, really, that Ben principally saw her at night, after work. Mrs. Marmelstein had a tendency to sundown; night was usually her least lucid period.

Gently, he pushed her bedroom door open and stepped inside.

"Paul?" She was sitting in an easy chair. The lamp beside her was the only source of illumination. "Paulie, is that you?"

He recognized her voice, although there was something odd, something different about it.

"It's Ben. Ben Kincaid."

"Paulie?" she repeated, her voice strange and breathless. "Paulie? I knew you'd come."

He took a step toward her. He turned on the overhead light, trying to brighten up the gloom.

"See? It's me. Ben. I'm sorry to be home so late. I've had . . . a busy day."

Her eyes lit upon his face and, after several seconds had passed, the light of recognition finally came on. Her shoulders sagged and her whole face seemed to droop. "I thought . . . I . . ."

Her voice drifted off into the darkness. Ben saw she was wearing a flannel nightgown, despite the fact that it was quite warm out. A slipper on one foot; nothing on the other. Her face was pale, almost ashen. Her hands trembled noticeably. He had never seen her look so feeble.

The photo album was in her lap. But in her hand, she held a gold-framed photograph he had never seen before.

"Can I look at this?" She didn't answer, but she didn't resist, either. He took the photo and held it up to the light.

It was very old; he judged it to date back to the Fifties at least. It had sculpted edges and was black and white, although the years had begun to give it a sepia tone. In the center of the picture a man and woman huddled close together. They were young—early thirties at best.

And between them, they cradled a tiny baby.

Ben had never seen any of the three in the photo as such, but even as old as the picture was, he could tell the woman was a much earlier version of Mrs. Marmelstein. The man, he assumed, was her late husband.

Ben pointed to the baby. "Is this Paulie?"

Her eyes darted away. "Paulie will come back. I'm certain of it. I always was. Paulie will come back."

"Who's Paulie?"

"He will come back. You'll see."

Ben frowned. "Where is Paulie?"

"Doesn't matter. Doesn't matter. He'll come back to me."

Ben ran his fingers through some of the other photos in her lap. He found another old one with three subjects, the Marmelsteins and a boy with jet-black hair, maybe twelve years of age.

"Is this Paulie?" he asked.

She seemed startled by the name, or perhaps by Ben's use of it. She glanced at the picture. "That was a long time ago."

"How long?"

She looked up abruptly. "Paulie's coming back to me, you know."

"He is?"

"Oh, yes. He's coming. I'm certain of it."

"When is he coming?"

"I don't know when exactly. But I know he's coming. I know it."

Ben gazed into her ashen face, then made a silent prayer that Paulie hurried.

He placed the photos on the end table and quietly left the room. Seeing her like this made his heart ache. For all her foibles, Mrs. Marmelstein had always been such a sweet, gentle person. He hated seeing time rob her of her personality, her sense of self, all the things that made her the special person she was.

And what was this business about Paulie? He'd never heard her mention a Paulie before. And she'd certainly never given the slightest indication that she had any children.

"How long has this been going on?" he asked Joni.

"Since we finished dinner. Normally, she eats and goes straight to sleep. But tonight, for some reason, she was determined to get out that photo album. And she's been in there muttering to no one ever since."

"Do you know anything about this Paulie?"

"Sorry. Clueless."

"Joni . . ." He was trying to think of a painless way to address this. "Mrs. Marmelstein . . . doesn't look so good."

Joni nodded her head somberly.

"Did you go with her to the doctor this week?"

Again she nodded.

"And?"

Joni gently placed her hand on his shoulder. "She's failing, Ben."

His eyes darted down toward the floor. "That's what I thought."

* 9 *

Christina met Ben at the door the moment he arrived at work.

"It's official," she said, waving a thin document in front of his face. "We're at war."

Ben snatched the paper from her hands. "As if I didn't know that already." He threw his briefcase down on his desk and gave the pleading a quick once-over. "They've filed their Answer? Already? Defendants usually let a month pass before they get around to that."

"It came accompanied by a Motion to Dismiss."

"That son of a bitch really did it."

"He did." She passed him the motion. "It's a tactic, Ben. That's all it is."

He did not appear appeased. "When's the hearing?"

She drew in her breath. She knew he wasn't going to like this part. "Three o'clock. This afternoon."

"This afternoon? What's the big damn hurry?"

"To read their motion, you'd think all of Western civilization was teetering on the brink."

"Who'd we draw?"

"Judge Perry."

"Perry! Jiminy Christmas!" Ben pounded his forehead. "You're full of good news today, aren't you?"

Christina held up her hands. "Hey, don't kill the messenger."

"I can't believe we drew Perry. The last thing on earth this case needs is a Reagan appointee. And not one renowned for his big heart, either." This was a critical blow. They needed a sympathetic ear, someone who would be moved by his clients' plight and perhaps even would cut them some slack occasionally as a result. But they didn't get it. And like it or not, this judge would be with them till the bitter end of the case. "I'm still surprised they went ahead and filed their Answer."

"I think they wanted to strike quickly while the story was still fresh and the press was still reporting each new development. Check out the section labeled General Overview."

Ben did as she instructed. It read:

> While the H. P. Blaylock Industrial Machinery Corporation regrets the loss of children's lives and sympathizes with the grief of their parents, Blaylock nonetheless states that it categorically and without exception is without fault or blame with regard to those deaths. H. P. Blaylock has always maintained and rigorously enforced a systematic policy for the disposal of its industrial waste, which has not at any time involved removal of such waste to any place where it could even conceivably contaminate the water supply of Blackwood or of any other community.

"Well, that just about covers it, doesn't it?"

"I have a question," Christina said, "as a struggling law student who can't possibly understand all the nuances of big-time litigation. What exactly is the purpose of a General Overview?"

"There isn't one," Ben said. "At least not in terms of the pleading. That section was clearly added for the press. They know the reporters will pick up copies of the Answer at the courthouse. This was designed to give the fifth estate a succinct, quotable quote for the front page."

He flipped to the second page, where the actual pleading began. The purpose of an Answer was supposed to be a paragraph-by-paragraph response to the allegations contained in the plaintiffs' Complaint. Here, the defendants managed to deny everything without actually saying anything:

"With regard to the allegations contained in Paragraph Four of Plaintiffs' Complaint, Defendant H. P. Blaylock either denies them or is without sufficient information to form a belief as to the truth of the allegations and therefore denies them."

A quick scan told Ben that most of the Answer repeated

this unenlightening language. Only the number of the paragraph referenced changed.

"Not very helpful, is it?" Christina said.

"Answers rarely are," Ben replied. "I wonder why courts require us to go through these hoops anymore, since they almost never convey any useful information."

"You mean this isn't unusual?"

"Unfortunately, no. Typical. This is time-tested language."

"Because defendants like to play it safe?"

"Actually, I think it's mostly laziness. You can draft this kind of response without doing the least bit of investigation. A lawyer can draft an Answer like this without even calling his client up on the phone. Heck, his secretary could probably draft this, without knowing a thing about the case. Just plug the names into the word processor and recopy it over and over." He rifled through the pages. "Is there anything useful in here?"

"Check out the last page."

Ben found one lone paragraph that broke the pattern. Christina had marked it with yellow highlighter:

H. P. Blaylock admits that the land behind its plant in the Blackwood area consists in part of forests and marshlands. Although this land has occasionally been used for the temporary storage of industrial equipment and drums, the contents of the drums have never been permitted to escape and no industrial waste materials have ever come into contact with the ground, ravine, or any groundwater stream.

Ben looked up. "Now that's interesting."

"I thought so. Why did they suddenly become so verbose?"

"Well, they had to say something. They could hardly claim that they 'lacked information sufficient' to know what was going on in their own backyard. Did we say anything in our Complaint about a ravine?"

Christina shook her head. "I didn't know there was one."

"And why single out drums? That's hardly the only way to transport waste."

"It must be the one they used."

"And they must think we know that. They're trying to suggest that the mere presence of drums on the land—to which there are probably witnesses—doesn't prove contamination. They're drawing the line at the point they think we can't prove—that the drums leaked."

"And what does that tell you?"

Ben placed a finger thoughtfully against his lips. "That they probably did."

Something about being in the presence of an ungodly attractive woman wearing a bikini put a man at an immediate disadvantage, Mike reflected, as Helen Grace stepped out of the pool, beads of water cascading down the sleek curves of her nearly naked body. Didn't matter how tough the man was. Didn't matter how attractive the man was. Didn't matter who he was or what he was doing. When a woman built like that stood there in as little as the law would allow, exuding sexuality from every exposed pore, she had the upper hand. And anything else she wanted.

Which made Mike more than a little uncomfortable. When he conducted witness examinations, he was accustomed to running the show. It wasn't ego; it was necessity. He almost never got to talk to anyone who actually wanted to talk to him. If he wasn't in a position to put on a little pressure, he would probably come up with a great big goose egg.

He handed the woman a towel, careful to keep his eyes up where they belonged. "Ms. Grace?"

"That's me. Are you the detective?"

"Guilty as charged."

She dabbed the towel against her body, drying herself. "It's such a nice day, I thought I'd take a little swim while I waited for you. I hope you don't mind."

"Of course not." And you wouldn't mind if I took a few pictures, would you? Just to show the boys back at the office?

"Did you have any trouble getting in?"

"Not to speak of." Which was a bit of an understatement. Southern Hills was one of the most exclusive country clubs in Tulsa. Visits from cops were neither frequent nor welcome. He'd had to bellow and bluster for ten minutes before he got in.

"I'm glad. Personally, I find all the elitism and exclusivity most annoying."

Really. Then why did you ask me to meet you here? "Is there someplace we could talk?"

"Sure." She led him to a small cabana near the north end of the pool. It was air-conditioned and, as he soon saw, equipped with a television, stereo system, and a stocked bar. Well, he supposed, it was important to have a nice place to change into your swim trunks.

She started to close the door, but he stopped her. "Leave it open a crack. If you don't mind."

"I . . . thought you'd want some privacy."

"This is private enough. We'll talk quietly." He didn't want to be paranoid, but with a woman like this, you couldn't be too careful. If the interview didn't go well, he didn't want any wild stories starting up about what went on while the two of them were alone in the cabana. "I wanted to ask you a few questions about Harvey Pendergast."

"Oh. Poor Harvey." A fraction of the strength and confidence washed out of her face. Her grief seemed genuine. "Sad enough to see him go before his time, but to go in such a hideous way . . ."

"It was pretty grim. So you can see why we're investigating every possible avenue. I don't want his killer to strike again."

"Oh, my God. Do you think there's a chance?" Her hand pressed against her very exposed cleavage. "That's terrifying."

"It is. I have a friend who tells me sales of security systems in Tulsa tripled the day after the *World* reported that murder." He paused, contemplating the best approach. "I'd like to ask you about your relationship with Harvey."

"What about it?"

"Well, for starters—what was it?"

"Lieutenant, let's not play games. I was Harvey's mistress, and apparently you know that or you wouldn't be here. So let's not beat around the bush."

Mike tried not to display his surprise visibly, but it took some doing. He was just interviewing all the people who worked in Harvey's department; she was the fifth one he'd talked to today. He hadn't known anything about any affair.

"That suits me fine. Since you know how much I already know, I hope you'll realize there's no point in lying to me." Jeez, did he have balls or what?

"The relationship had been going on for the better part of a year."

"How did it start?"

"I'm not sure I can explain it. No one was more surprised than me. Except maybe Harvey."

"Okay, I'll bite. Why was it such a surprise?"

She shrugged, sending provocative ripples up and down her torso. "Harvey was twenty-some years older than I. And not exactly Brad Pitt. But I'd just gone through a particularly nasty divorce. I'd had enough of hunks to last me a lifetime. Harvey wasn't like that. He wasn't like any man I'd ever been with before. There was something about him that seemed appealingly . . ."

"Safe?"

"That's not it exactly. More like . . . sweet. Comfortable." She took a deep breath. Mike tried to look elsewhere. "And I suppose I'd be lying if I didn't admit I felt a little sorry for him."

"Sorry? Why?"

"Don't you know? His wife was an invalid. Had been for some time. Their current sex life was nil. Zip. Not even a BJ under the covers."

This was a subject he definitely did not need to be discussing with an ungodly attractive woman in a bikini. "Do you know of anyone who had a grudge against Harvey? A reason to wish he . . . wasn't around anymore?"

"Enough to kill him? No way."

"Did he ever act . . . scared? Like maybe someone was out to get him?"

"No. Never. He could be secretive at times . . . but not in that way."

"In what way?"

She paused, reflecting. "There were times when Harvey tried to suggest . . . I don't know. That he knew something I didn't."

"Like what?"

"I don't know exactly. But he had big plans, and he liked to gas on about them. He'd talk about how we'd leave Blaylock behind. We'd go all around the world, and he'd show me the sights. He'd talk about how someday, when we had seen the world, he and I would buy a villa in France. Or a vineyard. Sit in a deck chair and drink wine all day."

"Expensive plans for a midlevel employee."

"Which I suggested to him, on more than one occasion. But he'd just get this coy little smile on his face. He wouldn't explain. He'd say something mysterious, like, 'You'll see, Helen. You'll see.' "

"Did he think he was coming into an inheritance?"

"Not that I knew about. And honestly, what kind of inheritance could pay for dreams like that? He'd have to be a Rockefeller. And I don't think he was."

Mike had investigated Harvey's background thoroughly. He wasn't.

"Was there ever any change in his demeanor? Anything out of the ordinary?"

"You know, now that I think of it, there was. It was subtle, but he started being . . . less carefree. More careful. That's when he had the dead bolts put on his doors. Iron bars on his windows. A big dog in the backyard. He told me it was because of his wife, because she was at home alone and helpless so often. But . . . I don't know. Something about that explanation just didn't ring true."

"As it turned out, he didn't spend nearly enough."

"Yeah. Sad, huh?"

"Very. Do you recall when this . . . change came over him?"

"Well, I think it was maybe six months ago. I remember it was about the time that loony broke into the law school and took hostages."

"Can you think of anything else that might be helpful?"

She thought for a while before answering. "I'm sorry. I can't."

"Mind if I ask you a question about yourself?"

Her eyes reflexively glanced down at her own goddesslike body. "I guess that depends on what the question is."

"You worked at the corporation with Harvey, so, if you'll

forgive me, I know more or less what you make. How can you afford to be a member in this joint?"

A wicked smile crept across her face. "Two words: divorce lawyer." She laughed. "I just work for the hell of it. If I didn't, my mind would turn to pudding and my body would bloat up like a balloon."

Unlikely, Mike thought. He handed her a card. "Thanks for talking to me. If you think of anything else, please give me a call."

"I will." She paused, and the expression on her face made a decided change. "You know, Lieutenant . . . I'm allowed to have guests at the club."

"Do tell."

"The air is cool, the cabana is private, and the bar is well stocked."

"And?"

"And"—she twisted around slightly—"there's a spot on my back I can't quite reach." She held out a towel. "Would you care to . . . be of service?"

His face widened with an unrestrained grin. "I can't tell you how tempting that is. But I gotta go with the advice my sainted mother gave me many moons ago."

Her lips pursed into a tiny pout. "And what would that be?"

"If something seems too good to be true—it probably is."

* 10 *

The lobby of the Adam's Mark Hotel was a little more public than he wanted when he was on a mission of this sort. In his everyday life, sure, he liked people, an audience. He thrived on it. But when he was on this kind of business, he thought of himself as a man of the shadows, a dark figure creeping through alleyways, a silhouette draped in a heavy overcoat, its pockets stuffed with gizmos and gadgets to aid him in his appointed rounds.

Like with Harvey. That had been a near-perfect operation. In and out, job done, mission accomplished. And no one the wiser.

Not that the hotel had a bad lobby. His cushioned seat was comfortable, and the bartender kept plying him with ginger ale. (No hard stuff; not while he was working.) The only immediate drawback was the restaurant just off the west end of the lobby, an Italian place called Bravo's, which unfortunately featured singing waiters. Every time he managed to find his quiet place, some fool in a tuxedo started belting out a tune from *Cats*. Really, there ought to be a law. If they could revoke a restaurant's license for health code violations, why not for mental health violations? Like this abomination called singing waiters.

She still hadn't shown. He'd been waiting for the best part of an hour. Not that he had any doubts. He'd been trailing her for days. He knew she was staying here, in her little room on the seventh floor, and he knew she would be back. But there was only so long he could sit here pretending to read *USA Today* over and over again. The damn rag only took ten minutes to read in the first place, and that only assuming you moved your lips and subvocalized every word as you read it. He hadn't spotted anyone who looked like a hotel detective, but eventually, even a civilian might become suspicious.

He wasn't sure why she was staying here, but he suspected she had read about Harvey's demise and thought she might be safer here than at home. He didn't know why people thought that way. The truth was just the opposite; compared to most homes, breaking into the rooms in this place was a cinch. Maybe she just thought he wouldn't be able to trace her here, that it would be a safe hideaway until she had her ducks in a row and could leave town.

Well, she'd been wrong about that, huh? It was always a mistake to underestimate him. Just ask Harvey.

He was having such a good time musing to himself that he almost didn't make her as she glided up the escalator. She was wearing a scarf around her face and had the collar of her coat turned up. Foolish girl. What did she take him for?

He waited calmly, dropping enough money on the table to cover the tab. He kept his distance as she punched the UP button on the elevator. He stayed put as the bell rang and the doors swung open, only moving when she slipped inside the elevator. She was alone, just as he had hoped. He waited until the last possible moment, then darted between the closing doors.

She looked up, just as the elevator doors closed behind him. One look, and she pressed herself into the corner, her eyes wide with fear.

"Relax, Maggie," he said, his voice calm and congenial. "I just want to talk."

"I'll scream." Her voice had an edge, but not enough to disguise the tremble. "I will."

"There's no need. This is just a social call. We have some business to work out, don't you think?"

"I think you're a sick maniac, and I wish I'd never met you."

"No doubt, but that's all water under the bridge now, isn't it? We did meet, long long ago. We were partners. And we have unfinished business."

"You're wasting your time."

"Please. It's never a waste to spend time chatting with a lovely woman like you, Margaret. You've always been my favorite. Did you know that?"

She moved herself as far away from him as possible. "The only person you've ever cared about is yourself." The bell rang; the elevator doors started to open. They were at the seventh floor.

She took a cautious step. "If you try to follow me, I'll scream."

He spread wide his hands. "Maggie, I assure you I have no intention of molesting you in any way."

She took another step forward. As soon as she was in front of him and couldn't see him, he whipped his arms around her throat. He was holding a roll of duct tape, surreptitiously removed from his ever-bountiful coat, and before she knew what had happened he had wrapped it tightly across her mouth. She tried to scream, but the sound was muffled most effectively by the sticky and impenetrable tape. Half a second later, her hands were taped together and her arms were taped to her sides. She tried to run, but he had an elbow lock around her neck she couldn't break. She tried to struggle, but he was a dozen, maybe a hundred times stronger. She was helpless.

The elevator doors began to close; he punched the 7 button, reopening them. He stuck a cautious neck out the doors. The coast was clear.

He dragged her, struggling, the short distance to her room. He dug through her purse: cosmetics, driver's license, fishing license, Kleenex—and room key.

Once he had her inside, there was no reason to maintain the remotest pretense of gentility. He grabbed her by the hair and slung her forward. Her knees crashed into the bed and she crumpled forward. He stretched her out flat on the bedspread, then taped her legs together, eliminating her last possible means of escape. He untaped her hands and arms, then retaped them above her head to the bedpost.

"Well, now, you're all trussed up like the Thanksgiving turkey, aren't you?"

Maggie squirmed from side to side, as much as she could, which wasn't much. Her eyes filled with tears. Try as she might, she could make no noise other than the insistent spasmodic whine that barely escaped from beneath the tape.

"You know, I hate to say it, Maggie, but Harvey was a hell of a lot braver than you are. And we're talking about a man so cowardly he let his invalid wife front for him while he hid in the clothes closet."

He paused for a moment, watching her desperate writhing, the veins popping out on her neck and the sides of her skull. He was enjoying this, to tell the truth. He didn't understand killers who just pulled the trigger, no muss, no fuss, and got it over with quick. What was the fun of it if you couldn't savor the moment? Wring it for every possible bit of pleasure. Moments of joy like this were few and far between.

"Of course," he continued, "one possible reason for your heightened reaction is the fact that you already know what happened to Harvey, and you're afraid it's about to happen to you. Well let me attempt to put all your fears to rest. First, I have no intention of molesting you. So put those rape fantasies right out of your mind."

He watched as her eyes fairly bulged out of her head. He hadn't had such fun in ages.

"Really, Maggie, if I never showed any interest in you before, why on earth do you think I would now? It's not as if I hadn't known it was available, if I'd wanted it. God, everyone knew you were available, Maggie. Everyone. You spread 'em for everyone, didn't you? Probably even Fred."

A fresh trickle of sweat dripped down the side of her face. He bent over and licked it off with his tongue.

"And let me also reassure you on another point. I didn't bring my hammer tonight. I am not going to do to you what I did to Harvey."

He watched as, gradually, her fevered thrashing subsided. Her eyes returned to normal. She was still breathing heavily but her body was more relaxed than at any time since they'd come into the room.

A brilliant, evil smile crossed his face. "I'm going to do something far worse."

Judge Perry's courtroom in the federal courthouse was an expansive room with high-vaulted ceilings, shimmering white wainscoting, and fluted columns lining the walls. There were no windows (they were in the middle of the fifth floor), which contributed to the claustrophobic, walled-in feeling Ben got whenever he came here. In this cavernous courtroom, every footfall echoed with an ominous resonance. Every sound was underscored by the faint hiss of the ancient air-conditioning system, working double time to keep the room reasonably cool in the midst of an Oklahoma summer. Above the judge's elevated perch, two bronze eagles were etched in bas-relief. A long, wooden railing separated the spectator's gallery from the counsel tables, the jury box, the witness stand, and the judge's bench.

Ben hated it here. Courtrooms were always nerve-wracking, even to the best of litigators, but there was something particularly intimidating about federal court. Ben hadn't opposed Colby's inevitable motion to remove the case here; a redneck state court judge might've dismissed this case without blinking twice. But in federal court there was always a sense that the stakes were raised, that everything you did was subject to greater scrutiny. And that wasn't entirely imaginary, either. Federal judges were notorious for holding those who practiced before them to high standards, and nowhere more so than in the Northern District of Oklahoma.

Ben and Christina sat patiently at the plaintiffs' table while Charlton Colby entered the courtroom—with his entourage.

"Is my math impaired," Christina whispered, "or does he have four other attorneys with him?"

Ben nodded. "One junior partner and three associates. And two legal assistants to boot."

"Is this supposed to intimidate us?"

"What do you think?" He craned his neck. "Is Loving ready?"

"Just like you told him."

"Good." Ben watched as Colby's group surrounded the defendants' table. With their intense expressions, they looked like Pentagon staffers huddled together in the war room. Almost as an afterthought, Colby broke from the pack and strolled casually toward Ben and Christina.

"Good to see you again, Ben."

"Wish I could say the same," Ben replied. "But I can't."

"Now, now, Ben. Let's not take this personally."

"I do take it personally. You've impugned my reputation."

He shrugged casually. "It's all part of the job."

"Maybe your job. Not mine." Ben rose to his feet. "I've managed to handle something like a hundred lawsuits over the past few years, and I've never once resorted to your kind of tactics."

"Which is why you're still a solo practitioner who has to represent whatever walks in the door."

"While you work in a penthouse representing blue-chip clients who don't care what you do as long as you win?"

Colby tilted his head. "Clients like results."

"And so you've developed your rep as the king of bare-knuckle litigation. You call out the attack dogs every time some big corporation has a plaintiff they want to screw."

"Jealous, Ben?" A smile crossed his face. "From what I hear, you could take a few tips from my playbook."

"I'd sooner starve."

"I suppose that is the alternative." His eyes narrowed. "Particularly if you continue to pursue this case."

Ben felt his neck stiffening. "Did you have some reason for coming over here?"

"Yes. Against my better judgment, my client has instructed me to make you an offer. Five thousand dollars per child. Take it or leave it. It won't be offered again."

"Five thousand dollars? These people have lost their children! What kind of settlement offer is that?"

"It isn't a settlement offer. It's go-away money. Your clients' loss is quite sad, but Blaylock bears no responsibility for it. We are, however, willing to pay a small sum to avoid the cost of litigation."

"Oh, I bet that's a big concern for you. What are you and your four helpers billing Blaylock? About a thousand bucks an hour?"

"That, of course, is none of your concern."

"It's certainly Blaylock's concern. Is that him?" Ben pointed toward an elderly gentleman sitting in the front row of the gallery. He was immaculately tailored in a blue pin-striped suit.

"It is."

Ben took a step forward. "I wouldn't mind meeting him."

Colby closed him off. "He doesn't want to meet you. Do you accept our offer or not?"

"Not. Big-time not."

Colby pivoted, his expression unchanged. "That is a decision you will live to regret."

About five minutes later, Judge Perry entered the courtroom. Ben had never known him to be particularly cheery, but today his expression was positively grim. He was middle-aged, around fifty, Ben guessed. Handsome for his age, with an ample shock of black hair and a strong face that had grown craggy without seeming wrinkled. Everything about him—his bearing, his voice, his appearance—gave an impression of strength. And, on this occasion, extreme intolerance.

"First of all," he said, "I want the parties to know I've read the pleadings and the Motion and Brief, so don't feel like you have to rehash anything therein. Second of all, I want the parties to know that although I am not in any way prejudging the present case or motion, my tolerance level for frivolous lawsuits is absolutely zero. The court's calendar is vastly overloaded. Legitimate litigants often have to wait years to get to trial, in no small part because unscrupulous lawyers accept clients' money to file lawsuits that are absolutely without merit. Whether they do it out of greed or mere stupidity I don't know, and it makes no difference. It's a drain on the taxpayer and this court and I will not tolerate it. If I find that this or any other suit is without merit, I will not hesitate to dismiss it, and furthermore, will take severe action against the lawyer who filed it with the harshest possible sanction."

Ben felt the color drain from his face. Well, this was certainly encouraging. . . .

"Mr. Colby, I believe this is your motion. Take the podium."

"Yes, sir." Colby launched into a long harangue that, despite the judge's instructions, mostly rehashed what he had already written in his brief. He talked about how the plaintiffs' suit was entirely frivolous, that even granted the most favorable interpretation of the facts, the plaintiffs did not state a claim upon which relief could be granted. He finished with a long-winded windup about the importance of stamping out frivolous suits, which managed to borrow key words and even entire phrases from the judge's earlier diatribe on the same subject. Ben could only marvel. Colby was nothing if not slick.

"Excuse me, counsel," the judge interrupted, "are you suggesting the plaintiffs failed to conduct a reasonable investigation prior to filing their claims?"

"Yes, sir, that's correct."

"Then I'd like you to address that issue. And please present any evidence you have."

"That puts me in a bit of a sticky situation, your honor. On the subject of what evidence the plaintiffs have to support their claims, the best witness is, of course, the plaintiffs' attorney. Therefore, as my first and only witness, I call Ben Kincaid to the stand."

Ben jumped to his feet. "What kind of sleazy tactic is this?"

Judge Perry rapped his gavel hard. "Mr. Kincaid, I will not have that kind of language in my courtroom. You will treat opposing counsel with respect or you will be excused."

"Your honor, I've had no notice that I would be called as a witness."

"I don't see why you need any time to prepare," the judge responded. "You're familiar with your own case, aren't you?"

"Of course, your honor. But I can't testify against my own clients. I'm the lawyer, not the witness."

"Your honor," Colby interjected, "who better knows what the basis for this suit might be?"

"Well, calling an opposing attorney to the stand is a bit irregular. Perhaps you could just describe your preliminary investigation to the court, Mr. Kincaid."

"Why should I have to preview my case in advance of trial? Colby hasn't previewed his for me."

Judge Perry's face was livid. "Counsel, you will comply with my request."

Ben was beginning to flush himself. He knew he was standing on the edge of a slippery slope. If he let Colby get away with this one, there would be no stopping him. "Your honor, the Rules of Professional Conduct say that an attorney's first and foremost duty is to zealously represent his clients. I intend to honor that duty. And I can't square that with taking the stand to testify against them or giving opposing counsel an advance look at our case."

Judge Perry rose to his full height. He jabbed his gavel in Ben's direction. "I'm going to assume you didn't understand me, counsel, so I'm going to explain it one more time. I'm a federal judge. I have the full authority of the federal law enforcement community, including the ability to lock you up, to bar you from practicing in the federal courts, or to initiate disbarment proceedings, until such time as you comply with my order. You will do as I direct."

Ben glanced over at Colby, who was standing calmly behind the podium, a smug expression on his face. This tactic was succeeding beyond his wildest dreams. Regardless of the result, Judge Perry was already alienated against Ben. "No, sir. I can't do that."

Perry was so enraged he was beginning to shake. "Last chance, Mr. Kincaid."

Ben squared himself. "I'm sorry, your honor. No."

With a flourish worthy of a master magician, he withdrew a small metal corkscrew from his overcoat.

"I give you the humble corkscrew," he said, holding it delicately between his fingers. "It doesn't look like much. You wouldn't run if you saw it coming. But in the right hands, it can be positively deadly. And best of all, painful."

Maggie screamed, so hard her temples throbbed, so hard it was just barely, almost, audible. But it was not nearly enough. He turned on the television and turned up the volume, just in case she managed to muster more power when the actual torture began.

"I've made quite a study of anatomy, you know. It comes in handy in this line of work." He grabbed the bottom of her blouse and literally ripped it off her body, tearing it at both ends till her bra and bare torso was exposed. He pressed his fingers against her bottom two ribs. "I know, for instance, that the doctors label these the T1 and T2 ribs. I also know that if I twist this corkscrew, slowly, between T1 and T2, it will not kill you. Not immediately. It will hurt like hell. It will likely puncture your lungs, which, if untreated, will of course kill you. But not right away. For the first several hours, all you'll have is pain. Pain like none you've ever experienced in your life. Pain so intense you'll wish you were dead. But you won't be."

He walked his fingers up her rib cage. "I'll go left, right, left, right, working my way up, until I finally reach right here." His fingers paused. "Here, I'll point the corkscrew upward and pierce your heart. Then you really will die, although even then not as quickly as you'd like. And we won't be there for hours. So let's get back to the beginning."

He pressed the tip of the corkscrew against the space between the first two ribs. She flinched, trying to pull away, but there was no escape.

"Here we go."

She clenched her eyes shut, bracing herself against the pain she knew was about to follow.

"Oh my goodness. I forgot something."

Her eyes popped open.

He punched her amiably on the shoulder. "I almost forgot. I'm supposed to give you a chance to tell me what I want to know. But can I tell you a secret?" He crouched down next to her ear and whispered. "I'm hoping you won't. At least not at first. That would spoil all the fun."

He grasped the edge of the tape covering her mouth. "Needless to say, if you even think about screaming, the tape will go down and I'll just start drilling. Without mercy."

He gave the tape a violent jerk. "So tell me, Maggie. Is the merchandise secure?"

Her lips trembled so she could barely speak. "I don't know." Her face was desperate and pleading. "It wasn't me! I never had it!"

"Wrong answer." He snapped the tape down. "Don't worry. I'll give you another chance. Sometime between T6 and T7."

He pressed the metal tip of the corkscrew against the soft flesh covering her two bottommost ribs. Her gut-wrenching cries for help were almost completely muffled. The only person who heard them was the one who not only didn't care, but rather enjoyed it.

"That was an order, Mr. Kincaid!" the judge bellowed. His voice boomed all the way up to the high-vaulted ceiling and reverberated back down again. "You will take the witness stand."

"With regret, your honor, I must refuse."

"Bailiff!" Judge Perry's lips quivered. "Take Mr. Kincaid to a jail cell, where he will remain unless and until he decides to comply with my order."

The bailiff was a burly, balding man who was obviously startled, since most days his only job was to keep himself from falling asleep. He strode hastily toward Ben.

Ben held up one hand. "Your honor, may I make a suggestion?"

"No!"

"The issue here is whether we have sufficient basis for filing a Complaint, right? And whether the Complaint is legally sufficient to state a claim? I can't take the stand against my clients, but I can offer affirmative proof to support our position."

"This is nonsense," Colby interjected. "A ploy to delay the inevitable."

"How can he know that?" Ben shot back. "He has no idea what we have or what we know."

"I know he has no evidence against Blaylock. Because none exists."

"What about the EPA report?" Ben replied.

Judge Perry appeared surprised. "There's an EPA report?"

"Yes, your honor," Ben continued. "A report on the contamination of the Blackwood water well. And it mentions H. P. Blaylock by name."

Perry slowly lowered himself back into his seat. "That wasn't mentioned in Mr. Colby's brief."

"It's inconsequential," Colby said, maintaining his calm demeanor. "Bureaucratic guesswork. All it says is that Blaylock is a possible contributor. It's not even admissible."

"The issue isn't whether it's admissible, your honor. It's whether the plaintiffs have any reasonable basis for their claims."

"There's nothing reasonable about relying—"

"And what about the toxicology reports from the contaminated well? What about the geologists' report on the ravine running from Blaylock's property? What about the information from the Centers for Disease Control on possible toxicological causes of leukemia? None of which Mr. Colby mentioned in his brief."

Colby hesitated for a moment, and Ben thought he knew why. Colby hadn't mentioned all this other evidence because he didn't know about it. But he didn't want to admit that to the judge.

"This is all bluff," Colby said, eventually. "Bluff and bluster. If Mr. Kincaid really has all this evidence, let's see it."

"I was hoping you'd say that." Ben motioned to Christina, who was standing at the back of the courtroom. She pushed open the back door. A moment later, Loving entered pushing a dolly loaded with four large bankers boxes.

He flashed Ben a next-round's-on-me grin. "Where should I put it, Skipper?"

"Next to the table will be fine." Ben turned back toward the judge. "This is the evidence we obtained from the EPA under the Freedom of Information Act," Ben explained. "Before filing suit." As soon as Loving deposited his load, he scurried back out of the courtroom for more.

"This is the information we obtained from the Centers for Disease Control," Ben said, as Loving returned with another equally ample load. All eyes in the courtroom watched as Loving returned not once, not twice, but six more times, each time bringing in another load of bankers boxes. "This is the information we obtained from the Blackwood city engineer," Ben explained. "This is what we got from the state health department." By the time Loving was done, a mountain of evidence had piled up so high, Ben had to step in front of it just to be seen.

"That's the evidence we've collected to date, your honor." Ben leaned gently against the Everest of evidence. "And we haven't even entered the discovery phase yet."

Judge Perry swiveled. "Do you have a response, Mr. Colby?"

Colby cleared his throat. "I, uh, was not . . . aware of this additional evidence."

Judge Perry nodded. "Which suggests to me that this Motion may have been premature. Now don't misunderstand me." He turned back to Ben, a stern expression on his face. "I am not in any way saying I believe the plaintiffs will prevail. It appears to me, based upon my review of the pleadings, that the plaintiffs have a very difficult causation problem, and if that is not addressed to the court's satisfaction, I will not hesitate to dismiss this case. Before it goes to a jury. But to dismiss now, before formal discovery has taken place, would not be appropriate. Defendant's motion is denied." Judge Perry rapped his gavel, then left the courtroom.

Ben glanced over at Colby. He was not smiling. Colby had not only lost the motion—he'd been embarrassed in front of his megabucks client. Hard to explain why you're billing someone a thousand bucks an hour to get creamed in court.

He felt Christina's hand on his shoulder. "Congratulations, champ. You must be ecstatic. You won the motion."

"I'm ecstatic not to be spending the night in jail."

She grinned. "That was a pretty good gimmick, having Loving haul in all those boxes. Did you learn that in law school?"

Ben shook his head. *Miracle on 34th Street.*

Christina laughed, then moved to the back of the courtroom and sidled up beside Loving. "Nice work, Loving."

The big man shrugged. "Just followin' orders."

"Uh-huh. Thing is—I was back at the office when we were packing up all this stuff, and I don't remember there being quite so many boxes."

"Well . . . don't tell the Skipper, but . . ." Loving glanced over his shoulder, making certain no one else was listening, then winked. "Half of them are empty."

Strike two! *Damn!*

Calm soul though he was, this was getting irritating.

Maggie wasn't the one. He had held out high hopes; she had always been a little too clever for her own good.

But it wasn't her. She didn't have the merchandise. He was certain. Frankly, he thought she would've spilled all before he even started, but certainly by the time he pressed the corkscrew between T3 and T4, she would've sold her mother into white slavery if it would've stopped the torture. She wasn't capable of lying at that point. No one would be.

She didn't have it.

Well, two down, two to go. But good as he was, he had to assume the police were looking for him, and the search would intensify as soon as Maggie turned up looking like a slice of Swiss cheese. He had tried to make this murder distinctive, to create a different M.O., but he feared two torture-murders in the same area in so short a time—no matter how different— would attract attention. He needed to do something to prevent that cop in the grungy raincoat from putting two and two together as long as possible.

Suggestions, anyone?

He rifled through Maggie's purse. He found an extraordinary quantity of cosmetics. Could he smear them all over her face, try to pass this off as some kind of perverted sex crime? Maybe make it look like she was a prostitute done in by her john? Or perhaps a slumming rich bitch done in by her male hustler?

Nah. She just didn't look the part. Even cops wouldn't be stupid enough to fall for that.

He went through her wallet, checking all her membership cards, all the photos of kids he knew weren't hers, not coming up with anything. Inspiration didn't strike until he found a thin document on white paper folded into fourths.

It was some kind of legal thing, he realized immediately. He recognized the name of the case: *Elkins et al. v. H. P. Blaylock Industrial Machinery Corp.* It was a case with which he was, of course, familiar, as was probably everyone in Tulsa.

Now that had some potential. If he could get her well-ventilated corpse out of the hotel without being seen . . .

And he knew he could. He could do anything, couldn't he? And he would keep on doing anything, anything at all. Anything necessary. Until at last he found what he wanted.

* 11 *

Ben brushed away the bits of eraser nub and tried again.

Drafting written interrogatories for the other side was not his favorite activity. Although it was a time-honored discovery procedure for civil lawsuits, it was a difficult process and rarely a productive one. He would spend several hours trying to come up with specific airtight questions that could lead to useful information. But even though the interrogatories were technically addressed to the opposing party, Ben knew perfectly well that they would in fact be answered by the opposing party's attorneys. Whether through laziness or a deliberate effort at obfuscation, the lawyers would go to extreme lengths to avoid providing any concrete information. Lawyers had vast banks of excuses for not answering: "The question is too vague, too narrow, too unclear, not relevant, yada, yada, yada." Or that time-honored chestnut: "The documents to be provided by Defendant will be the most reliable source of information on this subject." In other words—look it up yourself. Of course, Ben could object to any incomplete or evasive answer, but by the time they got a hearing, they would be taking depositions, so it seemed simpler just to ask the witnesses. Interrogatories could be a simple, inexpensive discovery tool, but lawyers had made them worthless.

So why was he bothering to draft them? Ben asked himself. Hope springs eternal, he supposed. And he would feel negligent if he didn't, even if he knew it to be a futile process.

Document production might be more helpful. There was a time when drafting requests for documents was just as complicated as the interrogatories, but today, in the Northern District of Oklahoma, anyway, document production was automatic and mandatory. Parties had an obligation to produce all relevant documents as soon as the suit was active. Anyone who failed to do so could be severely sanctioned, either monetarily or by having judgment entered against them. Written requests were only necessary to request specific documents that, for one reason or another, had not already been produced. Which was good. Ben would be very anxious to read any documents relating to Blaylock's waste-disposal procedures.

Just to make sure he didn't miss anything, Ben drafted a few requests for physical examination. He wanted to tour the Blaylock plant, and particularly to examine that ravine behind the property. And he wanted to send in his experts to test the soil and water. It was possible that Blaylock might cooperate voluntarily, since refusal would only lead to a court order, but Ben thought it best to have his formal request on file, just the same.

And finally, there was the matter of taking depositions. Of all discovery procedures, depositions were the most time-consuming, the least pleasant—but by far the most productive. Ben could require any witness to appear and answer his questions under oath in the presence of a court reporter who would take down every word the witness said. Pretrial depositions were usually the best opportunity to learn what the other side had up its sleeve. Although opposing counsel could be present, they were not allowed to prevent the witness from answering, with a few very rare exceptions, such as when the questions impinged upon the attorney-client privilege.

No one liked giving depositions. With attorneys sitting all around the table, unfriendly questions, and a reporter taking it all down, it became a high-pressure affair. Almost as bad as testifying in court. But it was essential. Deposition answers could lead to new evidence, new theories, other witnesses. And the transcript could be used to impeach a witness should the person attempt to change his or her story at trial.

Ben was unsure where to begin. He knew he wanted to talk to the president of the company, and anyone responsible for waste disposal, but after that, he was unsure. He couldn't talk to everyone who worked at Blaylock; they had thousands of employees. But at this early stage of the game, it was hard to know who was important and who wasn't.

Ben felt a shadow pass over him, as if a mountain was approaching. Which, as it turned out, was correct.

Loving was on the other side of his desk. "Christina said you wanted to see me?"

"Yes. Thanks." Ben set down his pencil. "How's the research coming?"

"Slow, Skipper. No one at Blaylock wants to talk to me. They all seem to think they might lose their jobs if they talk."

"A distinct possibility." He thought for a moment. "How about former employees?"

"S'possible. How would I know who's a former employee?"

"I'll request a list in these interrogatories. They surely have some computer files they can print out without too much trouble." He made a note on the draft. "That isn't why I wanted to see you, though."

"It ain't?" Loving pulled up a chair.

"No. Loving, you've met my landlady, haven't you?"

"Sure. That's Mrs. Marble . . . Marmalade . . ."

"Marmelstein."

"Yeah. That's it. How's the old girl doin'?"

"Not well, I'm afraid. I'm worried that . . ." His voice drifted. He didn't like to think about it, much less say it. "Anyway, all these years I've lived in her house, I've thought she had no living family. But now, crazy as it seems, I think she may have a son. And I'd like you to find him."

"A son? Didn't she ever mention him?"

"No. Not when she was lucid, anyway. Which suggests to me there may be some bad blood, on one side or the other. Maybe both."

"That's too bad. You know his name?"

"I think it's Paul. Paulie, she called him."

Loving tore a scrap of paper off Ben's legal pad and made a note. "Okay. Got anything else for me?"

"I'm afraid not. I've tried to get more information out of her, but . . ." He sighed. "Her Alzheimer's is pretty bad. I've got a picture." He passed the brown-tinted photo he'd taken from Mrs. Marmelstein's photo album. "It's dated, of course. But it's better than nothing."

Loving appeared skeptical. "I'll see what I can do. If there is a son, there should be a birth certificate around somewhere."

"Thanks, Loving. I appreciate it. I know it's a long shot, but I think it's important." He paused. "It's think it's important that we find him as soon as possible."

About thirty minutes away from Ben's office, in the tiny town of Blackwood, a meeting took place on the top floor of the H. P. Blaylock headquarters building. Myron Blaylock, looking particularly crochety this morning, sat at the head of a long conference table. Charlton Colby, lead counsel for the defense, sat at the other. Several vice presidents and other functionaries sat in between, including Ronald Harris.

Mark Austin sat behind Colby, legal pad at the ready, anxious to perform whatever task his master wanted, whether it be handing him exhibits or making him a sandwich. The faithful associate didn't ask questions; he did what he was told. And Mark wanted very much to make a success of this assignment. This was his ticket to the big time.

"Thank you for coming," Colby said. He leaned forward, making it clear that, despite his placement at the table, he was running this meeting. "Since it appears that the lawsuit will be proceeding, I wanted to gather everyone together and discuss our strategy."

"I hate this, damn it all," Blaylock barked. "I hate wasting our time and money on this lawyering. I've got a business to run."

Colby took it all in stride. "And the purpose of this strategy session is to insure that you continue to have a business to run."

Blaylock folded his arms in a huff. "The whole idea is ludicrous. Blaming us because the well water is poisoned. Can't we get rid of this thing?"

"We have attempted to do so," Colby patiently explained, "and will do so again. But for the time being, the case will continue. We're entering the discovery period now, and I want everyone to be prepared for it."

"Goddamn it, I'm not going to have to give another deposition, am I?"

"I fear that is inevitable, Myron."

"Blast! Don't these idiots know I have better things to do than waste an entire day answering their fool questions?"

"Nonetheless, they will insist upon it. Unless I miss my guess, the plaintiffs will want to depose everyone in this room. They don't really know what they're looking for or who knows what, so they're likely to use a shotgun approach. Aim their guns at everything in sight."

"Excuse me," a balding man named Gregory Steinhart said, "but would that include me? I don't see how Personnel relates—"

"They will. Probably they'll subpoena your records. Try to find out everyone who worked in waste disposal, or might've come into contact with hazardous materials."

"Oh." Steinhart appeared to find this a sobering prospect.

"Of course, they'll want everyone and everything to do with waste disposal. They'll want everyone who ever ordered, used, or handled the chemicals listed in their Complaint— TCE and perc. Maybe some others as well. I know Kincaid's been talking to chemists and geologists. I need to know what Blaylock's official policy is with regard to disposing hazardous materials."

A short, slight man on the other end of the table cleared his throat. "Ronald Harris here. Our official policy has always been to store potentially dangerous chemical waste in steel drums, then to have the drums transported to authorized waste-disposal sites."

"And your actual practice?"

Harris glanced quickly at Blaylock, then back at Colby. "Our practice has always been to conform with our official policy."

"Good," Colby managed to say, without the slightest trace of irony. "I'm glad to hear that. So there's nothing dangerous or contaminated on the grounds behind the plant."

"Absolutely not."

"No trace of TCE or perc in the ravine or groundwater."

"Of course not."

"Then you won't object to letting the plaintiffs' attorney examine the grounds."

"What's this?" Blaylock rolled forward in his chair. "I don't want attorneys running all over my plant. We've got work to do, damn it! Has he asked for an inspection?"

"Not yet. But he will. You can count on it. He'll bring experts with him. Geologists, toxicologists—"

"That's going to cost them a pretty penny."

"The plaintiffs are playing for big stakes. They'll be willing to spend a few dollars."

"Who's going to pay for all this? Those plaintiffs can't afford to play ball in our court."

"I don't know the answer to that question, Myron. But I'm working on it."

"Maybe we should see if we can run up the bill. These jerkwater clowns might lose their fervor for litigation."

"That defense strategy is not exactly unknown, Myron. Of course, we wouldn't want to do anything unethical."

Blaylock snorted. "No, of course not. Is the tape recorder on?"

Colby smiled thinly. "I'll delay whenever possible. But the inspection will happen. So be ready for it." He scanned the rows of eyes on both sides of the table. "Prepare."

"What exactly are we allowed to do?" another vice president asked.

"Well, of course, you can't hide any evidence. But you can continue with your normal practices. And since your normal practice is to dispose of chemicals in drums and have the drums transported elsewhere, I suggest you do that. In a big way."

The vice president nodded. "I think I got you. I'll take care of it."

"Damn right you will," Blaylock added. "Every last drop."

Colby continued. "Now I've already sent each of you a memo regarding the production of relevant documents. I assume that work is already in progress."

"The photocopiers are working double time," Steinhart answered.

"I should also warn you," Colby continued, "that it's possible the plaintiffs' attorney or his representative might attempt to talk with you or your employees at any time. Under no circumstances should you talk with them. No matter what they say. No matter how simple it seems. If Kincaid wants to talk to us, make him go through me. Make him go through official channels. Trust me—it will be better for us all. Okay?"

Everyone in the room nodded their consent.

"Good. That about covers it, then. Of course, I'll see you again and prepare each of you before your deposition is taken. We'll review documents, discuss potential answers. Refresh your memory, if necessary."

"I have a question," Blaylock said. "About the production of documents."

"Yes?"

"Does that include our own . . . internal documents?"

"I'm afraid it does."

"Even things we just wrote . . . just for our own use?"

"Even that."

Blaylock shifted what little weight he had. "Charlton, you may remember a report I once sent you. In a dark-blue folder."

"I distinctly recall it."

"We don't have to produce that, do we? 'Cause if we do—"

Colby cut him off. "As I recall, I instructed you to include me on the report's circulation list."

"Correct." Blaylock removed a slim blue folder from his

briefcase. He checked the first page. "There you are. CC to Charlton Colby."

"Good. Since I was included in the distribution list, the report was, at least in part, prepared for my benefit. Therefore, I believe we have a tenable claim that it is covered by the attorney-client privilege and therefore should not be produced."

"And what if your esteemed colleague disputes your claim and wants the document?"

Colby answered the question with a question. "How can he request a document he doesn't know exists?"

"Mmm. Good point."

Mark leaned close to Colby. "I'll prepare a claim of privilege form, sir."

"That won't be necessary, Mark."

"It's traditional—"

"But not required." Colby's expression barely changed, but he nonetheless managed to give Mark a look that told him to back off in no uncertain terms. "There is no rule that expressly requires me to identify documents that have been withheld under a claim of privilege. I'm a member of the bar. I can determine in good faith whether a document should be produced."

Mark buttoned his lip.

"I think that covers everything," Colby said, gracefully rising to his feet. "Please don't hesitate to call if I can be of service."

"Don't call him too often," Blaylock grumbled. "He bills by the second."

"Please remember what I said, though. Loose lips sink ships."

"And lose overpaid executives their jobs," Blaylock added.

The men in the room rose to their feet. Not a one of them was laughing at Blaylock's little joke. Not so much as a smile.

* 12 *

The Outsider was a creature of unspeakable horror. He had no body in the traditional sense, only a fluid gelatinous ooze that slithered out at the monster's whim. He had no features as such; only careful examination revealed two large eyeballs, veined and protruding, unlidded, and a hideous mouth—a gaping, slavering maw with two fanglike tusks jutting out, each of them sharpened to a deadly point.

Scout did not know exactly where the Outsider was, but he knew the beast was somewhere in this dense thicket, and he knew the beast was looking for him. Hunting him.

The Outsider was not an intelligent creature, not in the sense that he could think, reason, plan ahead. But he was a creature of unrelenting instinct, a natural born predator. He hunted humans. He fed on them, devouring them, starting with the eyeballs, which the monster considered a great delicacy. His hunger was intense and unyielding. Once he caught the spoor of prey, he became a killing machine. He did not tire. He did not reconsider. He did not quit. So long as his prey lived, the hunt would continue.

Scout swerved his bicycle between two tall trees on the side of the dirt road. Good thing he'd talked his dad into buying this mountain bike for Christmas; that old green Schwinn he'd had before could never have handled this kind of punishment. His only chance of escaping the Outsider would be to cut across the thicket, then make a northwest shortcut across the Reinholtz farm property. He could duck into the ravine at the far side; its higher wall might protect him from view long enough to allow him to make his escape.

Pedaling with all his might, Scout crossed the farmland

and tumbled down into the ravine. He didn't think he'd been spotted, but he was certain the Outsider was nearby, his instinctual telepathy primed for any signs of his prey. It was like a sixth sense, an indelible intuition, intangible, but no less certain for it.

Scout had to keep moving. That was his only hope.

He had moved north less than ten feet when he heard the sound. He whirled around, his eyes wide with anticipation. Where was it? Why was the creature toying with him like this?

Pedaling as fast as he could, Scout raced down the ravine. Barely a second later, he heard the unmistakable growl of the Outsider. It was above him, nestled in the branches of a nearby tree. Before Scout had a chance to move, the monster plunged down on top of him, knocking him off his bike. Scout and the Outsider rolled onto the muddy ground.

Scout fought with all his might, but the monster was stronger than he was. Before long, the creature was on top of him, pinning him down. Scout was unable to resist. He knew now that the hunt was over. The prey had been caught. He was finished.

"Gotcha!"

Scout's friend Jim rolled backward, laughing with glee.

Scout sat up. "I think you broke my neck."

Jim did not seem particularly repentant. "Man, you should've seen your face when I came flying out of that tree. I've never seen anyone look so scared. I bet you peed your pants!"

"I did not," Scout said angrily. At any rate, he hoped he hadn't. That would make it even more embarrassing.

Scout liked Jim—sort of. Since Scout and his family had moved to Blackwood, he'd been Scout's best friend. You needed a friend, when you were a nine-year-old kid who'd just moved to some podunk town you'd never heard of before. Jim was kind of rough-and-tumble, but he had a good imagination. He played the Outsider game better than anyone, even if he did tend to bend the rules around.

"Who said you could climb up into trees, anyway?"

"All's fair when you're the Outsider," Jim replied. "I nailed your butt but good. Gimme five."

They went through the whole routine—high five, low five, on the side five. . . .

"All right," Jim said, still ebullient. "Your turn to be the Outsider."

"Great." Scout examined his clothes, which were torn in two places and covered with mud. "I look like a monster."

"Agreed." Jim laughed. "Ready to go again?"

"Yeah, I'm ready." Scout was always ready. He loved this game—even if Jim did always manage to beat him. Scout's father wouldn't play it with him; he said Scout was too old for this nonsense, too old to be pretending about monsters. But it was Scout's favorite thing—good scary fun. Even better than the movies.

"Okay," Jim said, "here I go. You gotta count to a hundred before you come lookin'."

"Right." Scout turned away. Just before he closed his eyes, though, he noticed something unusual. It was about a hundred feet away, across the field, behind that great big plant where half the town worked, including Scout's father. "What is that, a bulldozer?"

Jim stood beside him. "Nah. It's a Brush Hog. Looks like they're digging something up."

Scout peered more intently. The giant mechanical claw was hauling something out of the dirt. But what was it? Buried treasure, maybe? An Indian graveyard? "Let's take a closer look."

Scout started forward, but Jim grabbed his arm, holding him back. "Don't go over there!"

Something about the look in Jim's eyes frightened Scout. "Why not?"

"Don't you know what that is? That's the Blaylock plant."

"Yeah. So?"

Jim leaned forward. His voice dropped to a hush. "My daddy says it's poison!"

"What, the whole plant?"

"Nah. The water. But if you go onto their property, you might get some of it on you."

"Poison water? That's silly."

"If my daddy says it, then it ain't silly!"

"Yeah, well, I don't believe it." It was crazy; it couldn't be true. Especially since his father went to work there every day.

"Do you remember Billy Elkins?"

"Never heard of him."

"Oh, that's right. It was before you came." Jim glanced over his shoulder. "Billy was a kid at our school. He was pretty cool. But he got real sick. And then he *died*."

Scout's eyes widened. That didn't happen to kids their age, did it? "He died?"

"Yup. And so did a bunch of other kids in Blackwood. And it's all because of the poison water. There's some big lawsuit going on about it in the City. My daddy says they oughta burn the plant to the ground and execute all the men in charge."

Scout was no Einstein, but he knew enough to realize that was unlikely. "I still don't believe the water is poison." Something in the field behind the plant caught his eye. "Hey, look at that."

The Brush Hog had hauled something large and cylindrical out of the ground. It was encrusted with dirt; Scout couldn't quite make it out. But he could see enough to know that it hadn't grown underground naturally. Something had been buried down there. And for some reason, the men operating the Brush Hog were digging it up.

"What is that?" Jim whispered. "Looks like a big trash can."

"Storage drum," Scout replied, his voice hushed. "I've seen pictures in my dad's office. But why would they be underground?"

"I don't know. What do you think's inside them?"

"Trash, maybe."

"Oh, don't be so boring. Maybe it's pirate gold!"

Scout grinned. "Or maybe it's the lost treasure of a wandering Mayan tribe."

"Or maybe it's the eyeless remains of the Outsider's victims!" With that, Jim jumped on top of Scout, scaring him out of his skin and knocking him to the ground. They wrestled about in the mud, one on top, then the other, until they were both even more filthy.

They tumbled out of the ravine. Scout scrambled to his

feet and started to run—when he was startled by an abrupt cracking noise.

It came from the field behind the plant, where the Brush Hog was doing its digging. One of the drums had slipped out of the claw and fallen to the hard earth below. The drum split. The contents tumbled out.

Scout gasped.

From his distance, it was impossible to tell whether it had its eyeballs or not. But it was definitely a human body that had spilled out of the drum. And the body was unmistakably dead.

* 13 *

Mike Morelli was not happy about the discovery of yet another corpse. He was still buried in his investigation of the brutal murder of Harvey Pendergast and his family. He felt he was making progress, even if he didn't exactly know toward what he was progressing. When a new murder hit, though, the pressure was always on from the Chief to give it the full-court press, on the theory that most murders are solved shortly after they occur, if they are solved at all. Therefore, Mike was faced with the prospect of either adding a new unsolved murder to his workload, or relegating this one to Lieutenant Prescott. Neither possibility pleased him.

As he trudged through the muddy grounds behind the Blaylock plant, he was glad he was wearing his trademark trenchcoat. The sky was gray and overcast; for once, the coat seemed appropriate. He just wished he'd worn some old shoes as well. The ground was wet and muddy and he was getting it all over himself.

He saw Tomlinson standing just outside the huddle of

activity that inevitably surrounded the corpus delicti. "Over there?" he asked, pointing.

"Yes, sir. But if you've had breakfast . . . you may want to go slow."

"Isn't that what you said the last time?"

Tomlinson nodded grimly. "More or less."

"Well, this can't be worse than the last one."

Tomlinson did not reply.

"Great. Just great." Mike trudged past him, brushed the other crime scene personnel aside, and pulled the white sheet off the naked corpse.

He couldn't tell what exactly had happened to this woman, but whatever it was, he knew it was bizarre. And sadistic. And painful. Her torso was riddled with punctures, sizable blood-ringed holes running up and down her rib cage on both sides. There was one over her heart as well. That was no doubt what had killed her, if she wasn't dead already. Dried blood was everywhere.

Mike threw down the sheet. "Goddamn it, I hate my job."

Tomlinson was at his side. "You don't hate your job. You hate the person who was capable of doing this."

"I hate my job because it forces me to think about sadistic bastards who are capable of doing this." He walked away from the crime scene, putting a good distance between it and him, trying unsuccessfully to soak in some fresh air. Trying, because the air wasn't that fresh; it seemed sooty and polluted. Probably the plant had a smokestack or incinerator somewhere on the premises. Not that it mattered. Right now, a sudden jolt of pure oxygen probably wouldn't make him feel any better.

When at last he returned to the center of activity, he was all business. "How did they come across the body?"

"According to the foreman, they were readying waste-disposal drums for transport to a waste-disposal site. He says it's a regular procedure—something they do every week or so."

"That's all there is to it? They put the waste in the drums, then haul it off?"

Tomlinson nodded. "So they said. On a frequent and regular schedule."

Mike crouched down, grabbed a handful of dirt, and let it trickle through his fingers. "This soil has been disturbed."

"I noticed that," Tomlinson said. "But the foreman explained that it was just the result of many feet trampling over the ground after the body was discovered, combined with the wet weather."

Mike scanned the area surrounding him. The soil had been disturbed for a wide radius in all directions. It was almost as if the dirt had been turned, like something a farmer might do to freshen the topsoil.

Mike pushed back up to his feet. "Do we know who she is?"

"No clue. She was stripped naked when we found her."

"Any idea how she was killed?"

Tomlinson shrugged. "Just the obvious. Something sharp and thin. Ice pick, maybe."

"Maybe. Lot of tearing of the surrounding skin, though. What does the coroner say?"

"He says not to bother him until he's finished his report."

"Pompous ass. He'll talk when I want him to talk." Mike pressed a hand against his forehead. Calm down, he told himself. Don't let it get to you. "Doesn't look like the same M.O. as the last murder. Harvey."

"Agreed. They don't seem to have anything in common. Except above-average cruelty."

"Christ. What a wonderful world we live in." He turned, trying to think clearly. "Still, it's a hell of a coincidence. Last victim was a Blaylock employee. This one turns up in Blaylock's backyard."

"True. But coincidences do happen."

"Not on my turf." Mike surveyed the scene, watching the technicians go about their specialized tasks. "Still, we have to go by the book. Until we have reason to think different, we'll treat this as a separate murder inquiry." He paused. "Even if my gut tells me otherwise."

Mike fumbled pointlessly in the pocket of his coat. Days like this he really wished he hadn't stopped smoking. "Find out who she is, okay? Start by taking her picture inside the plant. Show it around. I'm betting someone will recognize her."

"Consider it done, sir."

"I want all the reports from the crime scene teams on my desk as soon as possible."

"Understood."

"There's not much I can do until we know who she is. But the longer that takes, the less likely we are to find the killer."

"Right."

"Until we have a tangible reason to think otherwise, we have to assume these killings are unrelated. Which means there are two killers on the loose." Now that was a chilling thought. Two killers. Two men in one county capable of committing hideous and sadistic atrocities. And both still at large.

He cast his eyes toward the steely sky. "We have to catch them before they strike again." He paused, then looked directly into Tomlinson's eyes. "We have to."

It was the cop again.

His piercing green eyes, pressed up against the high-powered binoculars, recognized the detective as soon as he arrived. Sherlock Holmes at the scene of the crime.

He would be lying to himself if he didn't admit he was a trifle concerned. He had thought this investigation would be handled by some local yokel Blackwood cop. The fact that Tulsa's top homicide investigator had been called in suggested that someone somewhere at least dimly perceived the possibility of a connection. True, the great detective was still light-years behind him. He had no clue what was happening, much less why. But at the same time, certain facts could not be denied. All had not proceeded according to plan. When he had planted the body in the barrel, then put the barrel in line with the others for the usual Saturday burial, he had expected the body to disappear, not to be seen for decades, if ever. How was he to know that, contrary to all prior procedure, the corporation had decided to start digging up the drums?

What were they thinking, anyway? He didn't know what the deal was, but he had a strong hunch it related to the lawsuit, the one described in the document he'd found in Maggie's purse. Someone was trying to bury the evidence. Or unbury it, in this case.

Could the great detective put two and two together? True, he now had the corpse, and he would undoubtedly discover who she was. He would discover the connection to Blaylock—but that wasn't all that unusual, especially in this one-horse town. Would he realize that the killings were linked? Even if he suspected as much, would he ever be able to uncover the secret?

There was one way, he was forced to admit. If the cop discovered the connection between the victims—and found the others.

Now more than ever, the green-eyed observer realized he had a double reason for eliminating his former colleagues. To recover the merchandise—and to wash away the only trail that could lead the authorities to him.

He laughed, safe and secure in his distant hiding place. That detective had no idea what was going on, any more than he realized he was being watched at this very instant. He could never catch him. He was Moriarty, wasn't he? Even the original Holmes was never able to outthink Moriarty; he could only defeat him by brute strength, by tossing him off a waterfall. This detective would never have that opportunity. He would never come close.

And if he tried—punitive measures would be taken. Immediately.

It was time for a celebration, he declared silently. He reached into his always-loaded overcoat and withdrew a bottle of white wine, a still-chilled bottle of chardonnay. From another pocket he withdrew a corkscrew—its spiral blade caked with blood.

He plunged the corkscrew into the bottle and slowly withdrew the cork. The wine fizzed over the top, the effervescent yellow liquid mixing with the blood—creating a faintly crimson overflow.

He poured it into a glass and drank with great enthusiasm. Even if he had not yet recovered that which he sought, he could take time for a bit of revelry.

And then, when he was finished, it would be time to kill again.

* 14 *

Ben tried to remain calm as he scanned the front lobby of his office.

"You know, Christina, when I told you I thought we needed to redecorate our office space, this wasn't exactly what I had in mind."

Christina smiled thinly. The decor of the front lobby had indeed changed—it was buried in paper.

"Couriers from Raven, Tucker & Tubb dropped by this morning. Twelve of them. They had to cart the stuff over in a truck."

Ben reeled as he looked at the vast quantity of documents. Stacks upon stacks of photocopied documents filled the waiting room. Thousands upon hundreds of thousands of pieces of paper—he couldn't even begin to make an accurate estimate. The cost—not to mention the manpower involved— must have been enormous.

"You think they've produced everything they have?" Christina asked, although in truth she already knew the answer.

"Of course not," Ben replied. "They've given us a little bit of what they have, and buried it in a huge mass of crap that has nothing to do with the case. The problem is, we can't complain to the court about what they've failed to produce—"

"Until we know exactly what they have produced. Which, judging from the magnitude of the production, would take roughly—"

"Forever. Which is exactly the point." Ben pressed his lips together. "Colby is well aware of the fact that he's up against a firm with one lawyer—"

"One and a half," Christina corrected.

"—while he has dozens of associates at his disposal. He's going to press that advantage to the max. He's going to try to bury us."

"He also sent this," Christina said.

It was a bill for the photocopying—a huge bill, which the plaintiffs were obligated to pay. "And now he tries to exercise his other great advantage. The fact that he has tons of money at his disposal. And we don't."

"That's so . . . unethical. Trying to win a lawsuit with these bullyboy tactics."

"Unethical, maybe. But hardly uncommon. More like standard practice, for big defense firms."

"So what are we going to do about it?"

"Well, we can't begin to afford to hire help. So there's really only one thing we can do." He grabbed a pile of paper from the nearest stack. "We roll up our sleeves and get to work."

One glance at the front page of the *Tulsa World* was sufficient to give Fred a piercing headache. Damn, damn, *damn*!

The membership roll of their little club was once again diminished.

He walked out of the kitchen, strode through his living room, and turned the dead bolt on his front door. What was he going to do? He had to do something. He couldn't just sit here, waiting for his former friend to come sashaying through the door, swinging his sledgehammer or whatever gruesome instrument of torture he was using this week.

But what could he do? He'd tried to get vacation time; no go. The merchandise was worthless to him now, although it would be riches beyond measure in such a short time. . . .

Which would not do him a damn bit of good if he was dead. He had to face reality—he was not safe. Anywhere. He had tried to pretend he would be safe if he stayed at home at night and kept the doors locked. Yeah—that's probably what Harvey thought, too. And Fred's house wasn't nearly as secure as Harvey's. Plus, he lived alone.

There were things he could do to make his place more secure. But would that be enough? He could run, flee the city, hide out somewhere. Of course, that's probably what Maggie did. And she still ended up stuffed in a steel drum.

Bottom line—if his former friend wanted him—and he did, or would, at any rate, when he realized the truth—

There was no stopping him.

A chill rippled down Fred's spine. His mouth went dry. There had to be something he could do. He had to prove once and for all that he was not Fred the Feeb. That he was better than all of them. Even—

He heard a clattering sound in the kitchen. Fear paralyzed him. He felt his knees grow weak and wobbly. He stumbled across the room, struggling to escape. His heart was pounding, beating so hard he felt he might have a stroke at any moment. Sweat dripped from his temples. It was all over now. All done. *He was here!* Here, now! Coming—

Actually, it was his cat—a mousy-looking calico he called Charlotte. God, he hated that cat. Now more than ever.

He collapsed into an easy chair. He couldn't go on like this, living in terror, having his heart stop every time he heard a noise. He had to do something. But what?

There were only three of them left now. One killer. And two future victims.

And for all he knew, he could be next.

Ben's discovery motion had been sloughed off to a federal magistrate, a sort of assistant judge who dealt with matters federal judges were either too busy or too important to handle. Discovery disputes almost always went to the magistrates; judges would do anything to avoid that inevitable and interminable mudslinging. This referral to a judicial officer of lower rank hadn't bothered Ben at first; after all, it wasn't as if he had exactly charmed his way into Judge Perry's heart. Who would have guessed the magistrate could be worse?

His first clue was when Charlton Colby walked into the small conference room and Magistrate Grant all but hugged him. He grabbed Colby's hand and shook it vigorously. "Good to see you again, Charlton."

"And you," Colby replied. "How's Dorothy? And the boys?"

"They're fine." The magistrate was an older man, about

Colby's age, with gray hair, prominent cheekbones, sunken temples, and a long face. Whether it was true or not, the combined features gave the impression of a weary, impatient man. "You need to come over again. See what Dorothy's done to the garden."

"I'd like that. It's been too long. Perhaps you should drop by for dinner when—"

"No, no. I owe you." His voice dropped a notch. "I haven't forgotten what you did for me. Before the committee. When the magistrate's post was being filled."

"It was an honor. My pleasure."

Ben sat quietly. Somehow, this conversation did not awaken great hopes for the success of his motion.

Colby took a seat at the conference table and, almost as a afterthought, waved vaguely in Ben's direction. "Magistrate, I assume you know my opponent, Mr. Kincaid."

A sour expression passed over Magistrate Grant's face. "Only by reputation." He riffled through the papers he'd brought into the room. "I gather this is your motion, Mr. Kincaid?"

"Yes, your honor. We're having some problems with discovery." Technically, a magistrate wasn't "your honor," but Ben thought it best to overlook that detail for the time being.

"Has the defendant failed to produce documents?"

"No. Much to the contrary. They've produced hundreds of thousands of documents."

"Then what is your problem?"

"Your honor, I've made a preliminary review of these documents, and I can tell you that most of them are not even arguably relevant to this case."

The magistrate's eyes narrowed. "Let me see if I've got this straight. You're complaining because the defense has been too generous."

"Your honor, the defense is clearly engaging in a deceptive scheme to hide the ball in a morass of useless information."

"You stop right there, Mr. Kincaid." The magistrate's eyebrows formed a solid ridge above angry eyes. "In my conference room, members of the bar will treat one another with respect."

"But your honor—"

"I've known Mr. Colby for years. We went to school together. I know from experience that he is a man of honor and a distinguished member of the bar, and I will not have you refer to him in that abusive and derogatory manner."

Oh, great, Ben thought silently. He would get nowhere as long as this suckup was calling the shots. "Pardon me, sir. I know your honor has always upheld the highest standards of decorum—"

"Flattery won't win your motion, counsel."

Ben drew in his breath. This guy had it in for him, big time. "Your honor, it's my sincere belief that this document production violates the spirit, if not the letter, of the discovery code and this court's new mandatory production guidelines. No effort has been made to sift out the documents that actually pertain to the case."

"The defendant didn't ask to be sued, Mr. Kincaid."

"Yes, your honor. I realize that."

"You can't expect an ongoing corporate concern to stop everything and start reading every document in sight. They have a business to run."

"But the discovery code still applies to them."

"Let me be blunt with you, counsel. I'm not remotely interested in your whining about getting too many documents. As far as I'm concerned, that just means you should stop complaining and get to work."

"But, sir—"

"Do you have any evidence that there are relevant documents that have *not* been produced?"

"Yes, your honor." At last, they were getting to his motion. "I discussed that in my brief. They have produced no internal studies relating to Blaylock's waste-disposal practices."

"Do you know that there are in fact any such studies?"

"No, not for certain. But if there are—"

"So basically this is a big fishing expedition. I might have known." He adjusted himself to face Colby. "What about it, Charlton? Do you know if your client has conducted any internal studies that are relevant to this case?"

Colby didn't hesitate a moment. "I assume your honor is only interested in documents subject to production."

"Of course."

Ben felt an alarm sound inside his head. What did that mean?

"I have no knowledge of any such studies. I see no reason to believe there are any."

"You would agree that, if the studies exist, they should be produced."

Again he did not hesitate. "Certainly, your honor. Assuming there is not some other factor that renders them not subject to production."

"Wait a minute," Ben said. "What is all this wishy-washy talk about documents subject to production? Every relevant document is subject to production."

Colby glanced at Ben benignly, as if he were trying to deal kindly with the village idiot. "What opposing counsel has just said, your honor, is of course not accurate. Sometimes otherwise relevant documents must be withheld. For instance, when they are subject to a claim of privilege."

"Are you saying you're holding back documents under some claim of privilege?"

"I did not say that."

"Don't mince words with me, Colby. Are you holding back documents?"

When Colby spoke, it was to the magistrate, not Ben. "A very few documents have been withheld, of course, as always occurs in cases of this nature. Communications between client and counsel are naturally protected by the attorney-client privilege."

The magistrate nodded. "Of course. Nothing unusual about that."

"Wait a minute!" Ben said. "If he's holding back documents, I want to know what they are."

Colby used the same patronizing tone. "The provision of such information would, of course, violate the privilege."

"Naturally." The magistrate stacked his papers before him. "I think we should move on—"

"I don't!" Ben shouted. He knew he wasn't going to win any points with the magistrate with this outburst, but that was just too bad. "If he's holding back documents, I want to know about it."

The magistrate's dander was rising. "If documents are privileged, you are not entitled to know anything about them."

"Fine. Make him submit them to the court in camera. You can decide whether they're privileged or not."

The magistrate's reply was succinct. "No."

"Your honor! He could be suppressing anything under some fishy claim of—"

The magistrate rose, his face red with anger. "Mr. Kincaid, I have already warned you about these disparaging remarks. I will not have them in my conference room, particularly not regarding a lawyer of the caliber of Mr. Colby. His professional reputation is unparalleled and unblemished. Quite the opposite of yours, I might add. If Charlton Colby tells me a document is privileged, then no further inquiry is required."

Ben bit down on his lower lip. The magistrate's good ol' boy favoritism was enraging, but making a scene wouldn't help. The best thing he could do now was control his temper and try to salvage what little he could from this disaster.

"May I ask for a ruling on my motion, your honor?" he said quietly.

"Your motion is denied."

"As to what?"

"As to anything. I will not punish a busy defendant for producing too many documents. That's the stupidest thing I've ever heard."

"And about the internal studies?"

The magistrate pursed his lips. Clearly his patience was being pushed to its outer limits. "To the extent that any such studies exist, they must be produced. Assuming they are not subject to privilege or any other infirmity."

"Understood, your honor," Colby said quietly. "I'll institute a thorough search immediately. Just to be sure."

"I know you will. Thank you for your cooperation. It is much appreciated and"—he glanced quickly at Ben—"most refreshing." With that, the magistrate rose to his feet and strode out of the conference room.

"I'll expect those documents by the end of the week," Ben said to Colby, once they were alone.

"Or what?" Colby replied, arching an eyebrow. "You'll complain to the magistrate?" He allowed himself a small chuckle, then quietly slid through the door.

*   *   *

Late that night, Charlton Colby arrived at the private office of Myron Blaylock, on the top floor of the Blackwood headquarters building. They were alone. The room was mostly dark. A green shaded banker's lamp on Blaylock's desk provided the only illumination.

"What happened?" Blaylock snapped. Colby wasn't surprised. A man Blaylock's age had no patience for small talk.

"It went precisely as I anticipated."

"So . . . we don't have any problems?" Although his eyes did not avert, his hand touched the blue-covered report on the corner of his desk.

"None at all."

"We have a reason for not producing it?"

"We not only have a reason"—a tiny smile crept across Colby's face—"we have the magistrate's blessing."

"Excellent. Excellent." Blaylock rubbed his spindly fingers together. "Maybe you are worth that outrageous fee you charge, after all."

"I try."

His hand returned to the report. "This must never get out."

"Then it won't."

"And we must win this lawsuit. Whatever the cost."

"Understood."

"Any more settlement talk from the plaintiffs' lawyer?"

"No. He still thinks he can win."

"You don't seem too worried."

"I'm not." Colby turned slightly, gazing out the window at the night sky. "What Kincaid doesn't understand is that I've got an ace in the hole. No matter what. Even if he makes it to trial. And whatever the result. He cannot prevail. It's not possible. No matter what happens." He turned back toward Blaylock, his eyes unblinking. "No matter what."

Friday night, Ben was still in his office working late, as he had been every night since he'd accepted the Elkins class action. His staff was all present as well. Jones was on the phone, trying to line up the corps of experts they would need to prove this case and, even more challenging, trying to figure out how to pay them. Ben was talking to Loving about his two ongoing investigations—one of Blaylock employees, the other of Mrs. Marmelstein's "Paulie."

"I didn't find a birth certificate anywhere in Oklahoma," Loving told him. "If there is a son, he must've been born in another state."

"Keep looking," Ben said. "There must be record somewhere."

They were interrupted by a knock on the office door. A moment later, Christina stepped inside. "Courier from Raven, Tucker & Tubb."

Ben glanced at his watch. "What do you know? Colby made the deadline. Just barely."

He took a large manila envelope from Christina. A note on the outside said it contained "all additional documents to be produced pursuant to the magistrate's order." Ben opened the envelope.

It was empty.

Ben tossed it over his shoulder and let it slowly flutter down to the trash can.

"They're not going to give us a damn thing," Ben said quietly. "And there's nothing we can do about it."

"So where does that leave us, Skipper?" Loving asked.

"In your ball park. I don't want to put the pressure on you, Loving, but the fact is, they're not going to tell us anything. I could probably depose every employee in the whole damn corporation. As long as Colby's hovering over their shoulders, it won't make any difference."

"What can I do?"

"What you are doing. Only more so. You've got to find someone who will talk. Someone in that corporation must have a shred of decency. Someone's conscience must be bothering them."

"I've been tryin'—"

"Try harder. As soon as the depositions are done, I can guarantee you Colby will file a motion for summary judgment. If I can't prove Blaylock is responsible for tainting the Blackwood water supply, we'll never get to trial."

"I'll do everything I can, Skipper. And then some."

"Good. Good." Ben nodded slowly. "And I'll take all the

depositions we can afford. Maybe someone will slip, tell us something we don't know. But I doubt it." He leaned forward. "You're our last best hope, Loving. The last one we've got."

* 15 *

Christina offered Cecily Elkins a glass of apple juice. She was taking her off coffee; the woman was jittery enough without another shot of caffeine coursing through her veins.

"I don't understand why this is necessary," Cecily said. "Why would they want to take my deposition?"

"Because you're the principal plaintiff." They were sitting at a round table in one of the smaller conference rooms in Ben's office. Christina had tried patiently to explain the ins and outs of depositions, as she had done before for other clients on dozens of occasions. It was always the same. Nobody liked it. The thought of being face-to-face with an opposing attorney who had the right to ask you virtually anything was enough to intimidate the hardiest of souls. "You're suing them."

"My little boy died! We all know what happened. It's not as if there's any doubt about it."

"There is doubt about why it happened. At least in the defendant's camp."

Cecily was dressed in what Christina suspected was her Sunday best—a pretty print dress with a blue bow. Her black hair was brushed back and pinned on top of her head. She was wearing makeup—probably more than was her norm. Witnesses always dressed for depositions, Christina had noticed, even though the court reporter would only record what they said. She supposed that there was a subliminal hope that if she made a good appearance the attorneys would go easier on her. Fat chance.

"There's no point in asking me questions about causation," Cecily said. "I don't know anything about chemicals or leukemia."

"Which I'm certain they will point out repeatedly." Christina placed her hand over Cecily's. She could feel it trembling slightly. "Anyway, Ben wanted me to go over a few points with you. To prepare you for the deposition."

"Where is he, anyway? Why isn't he doing this?"

"He's taking the depositions of some of the defendant's employees. You're not scheduled until later in the week."

"I hope he makes them suffer as much as I am."

"Fear not," Christina reassured her. "He will." Actually, Ben was rather courteous, as deposers went, but why tell her that? "Let's go over the ground rules. When the deposition begins, you'll be sworn in by the court reporter. You have to tell the truth; if you don't, you're subject to prosecution for perjury."

"Does that actually happen?"

"Next to never. But it'll be pretty embarrassing if someone proves at trial that you lied at your deposition. That's the main reason they take these things. To get a preview of your testimony, and to keep you from changing your story. If you do, they can read the contradictory passage from your deposition at trial to impeach you."

"What can they ask?"

"Virtually anything. See, there won't be a judge present to rule on objections. Attorneys can make objections, but they're reserved till trial. That means you have to answer the question, pending a future ruling. Only in very rare instances can Ben instruct you not to answer—like if the question impinges on the attorney-client privilege."

"It seems like, if a question is objectionable, I shouldn't have to answer at all."

"Yeah, but think about it. There's no judge present. If the deposition stopped for a ruling every time an attorney made an objection, the deposition would never be finished. It would go on forever. Which, of course, would be fine with most defendants." Christina could see that her explanations were not calming Cecily in the least.

"What if they ask me something I don't know?"

"Then that's what you say—I don't know. Don't guess. Don't speculate. These are the three most important words to remember when you're being deposed; you'll use them often. I—don't—know."

"Got it."

"Second only to the three other most important words. I—don't—remember."

Cecily frowned. "Doesn't that sound a little feeble?"

"Who cares? They'll be asking you about things that happened years ago. They'll ask you about where you grew up, what you studied in school, every job you've ever had. No one can remember everything. So when you don't remember—say so. Don't guess. Don't speculate."

Cecily pressed her hand against her forehead. "Fine. Anything else?"

"Yeah. Don't make jokes. They may sound funny at the time, but typed up and set down on paper the humor won't play. Sarcasm could end up sounding incriminating. So don't do it."

"Okay."

"Don't bother trying to cozy up to the opposing attorney. Some deponents insist on believing they can charm the guy, win him over to their side. It's a fool's dream. It won't happen. So just answer the questions succinctly and get it over with." She paused. "Any questions?"

"Yes." Cecily's eyes widened. "Is there any way I can get out of this?"

"Not unless you want to dismiss your lawsuit."

Her hesitation suggested she was actually considering it. "No," she said finally. "I owe this to Billy."

"I agree." Christina squeezed her hand once more. "Don't worry. You'll be fine. Remember—Ben will be with you at all times. He won't let them beat up on you. It won't be pleasant, but you'll survive."

"I hope so."

"You're in the right here, Cecily. Your cause is just. There's nothing they can do to you."

Cecily didn't reply, but her eyes expressed her disbelief in Christina's statement more plainly than words could ever have done.

Mike was in the office of the Tulsa County medical examiner, Bob Barkley. Bob, an amiable man even younger than Mike, was new to the job. He had replaced Dr. Koregai, who'd served in this office since the dawn of time, or at least as long as Mike had been a cop, until he died recently of a heart attack. Koregai had been as irascible as Bob was amiable. Talking to Koregai was always a game. Koregai never wanted to tell him anything; Mike had to bend over and scrape just to pry out the most rudimentary information. He was pompous, arrogant, and difficult in the extreme.

Mike missed Koregai, damn it.

"How did this woman die?" Mike asked, referring to the corpse that had been dragged back from Blaylock's backyard.

"Extensive punctures to the lungs. Also to the heart." Bob was fair-haired and clean-shaven; indeed, Mike wondered if he had to shave at all. "The puncture wound to the heart would've been almost immediately fatal. But I think she may have been dead before that happened."

"Then what was the point?"

"That question falls outside my area of expertise." He removed the blue sheet, exposing the corpse. Under the harsh fluorescent lights of the examining room, it almost seemed to glow, a milky gray color.

"D.R.T.?"

"No way. She's been moved. A fair distance, I think. Then stuffed into that drum."

"Why?"

"Can't say. Perhaps the killer thought she'd be taken out with the rest of the trash."

"Hell of a way to get rid of a corpse. But I suppose it might've worked. No one's too anxious to open a can of industrial waste. Especially if it starts smelling bad." He glanced down at the woman's body, then quickly looked away. "Can you speculate as to the weapon?"

Bob nodded. "Corkscrew."

Mike's eyes widened. *"Corkscrew?"*

"You heard me. And not a very nice one. Probably cheap plastic, like the kind you see in hotel rooms. Put the handle beneath your fingers and twist."

Mike wiped his brow. "A corkscrew? Jesus Christ."

"At first I thought maybe it was a drill. You know, like a power drill. A little electricity would've simplified this nasty piece of work. But there would've been more tearing, more striation. No, I think it was a corkscrew."

Mike's face was ashen. "For God's sake—why?"

"I can only tell you what I know. It would've hurt like hell, like nothing you can imagine. Worse than a gunshot. And death would not have been instantaneous."

"You think she was being tortured?" The thought of it made Mike's gorge rise.

"Clearly the killer wanted this woman to feel some major pain. Just like that last one you brought in."

"Harvey? The guy with all the smashed bones?"

"That's the one. Clearly his killer also wanted him in serious agony before he actually expired. Probably got his rocks off by inflicting pain."

"Maybe," Mike said quietly. "Or maybe there was another reason."

"What other reason could there possibly be?"

"I don't know."

"If the killer isn't a psycho—what the hell is he?"

"Something far worse, I fear." Mike shook his head. "I don't know enough to say. But this isn't like a pure serial killer, someone who kills just for the pleasure of it. There's a pattern here. A method."

"So you're saying the killer is someone who isn't insane—but is still capable of inflicting pain of this magnitude?"

"Scary thought, isn't it?"

"Damn straight."

"Give me your opinion, Bob. Were both of these victims killed by the same person?"

Bob shook his head. "I can't say with certainty. The M.O.s are different. Still, how many people can there be who are capable of inflicting this kind of pain?"

"Too damn many," Mike spat back. "But there's a difference between capability and actuality. Most people are capable of extreme behavior in extreme circumstances. But that doesn't mean they're out on the street wielding corkscrews." He pulled a notepad out of his back pocket. "We've learned that the woman's name was Margaret Caldwell. She worked at Blaylock. She was in the legal department." He put away the notepad. "Which means both victims had a connection to Blaylock. Which is pretty damn coincidental. And I don't believe in coincidences."

"There is one similarity between the two killings." Bob crouched over the corpse and elevated her right hand. "See these marks on her wrist? Those were left by some kind of heavy-duty tape. Electrical tape. Duct tape. And I found similar marks on Harvey's wrists. What was left of them."

"Unfortunately, that's not an altogether uncommon way of restraining a victim these days. Everyone's seen it in the movies."

"Still, it doesn't happen every day."

"No. It doesn't." He drew in a deep breath of mentholated air. "So, give me the bottom line, doctor. Am I looking for one killer, or two?"

"Impossible to say, based on the medical evidence. There's not nearly enough here for me to assume a common killer." He gently pulled the blue sheet back over the corpse's head. "But however many of them it is—I hope to God you catch them. Soon."

Mike thrust his hands deep into his coat pockets. "So do I."

Ben sat at a conference table at the Raven, Tucker & Tubb law firm opposite Myron Blaylock, easily one of the most unpleasant men he had ever met in his entire life. It was a beautiful room; it spoke volumes about the kind of money this firm had at its disposal. Lush Oriental carpet, porcelain vases, rich mahogany table. A large bay window with an expansive view of downtown Tulsa. Unfortunately, Ben was not in a position to appreciate any of it.

The deposition had gotten off to a rocky start. Blaylock had barged into the conference room twenty minutes late, refused to shake Ben's hand, and immediately launched into a hot-blooded tirade.

"How dare you question the integrity of H. P. Blaylock?" he

shouted indignantly. "This corporation has served this state for more than sixty years, since it was founded by my granddaddy, and we have never done anything to harm anyone. Never!"

Once the man was finally seated and sworn in, Ben tried to begin the deposition, but Blaylock stopped him before he could ask the first question. "I want to state for the record that I am grossly offended by these entire proceedings. These claims have no basis in fact and are utterly without merit. I am only here today because my attorneys inform me that I have no choice, but I am indignant about being forced to participate in these sham proceedings."

"Indignation noted," Ben replied, and he began the deposition.

The hostility only escalated. Ben's initial questions dealt with Blaylock's employment background, as was traditional with corporate deponents. "What business is it of yours?" Blaylock exclaimed on repeated occasions. "What the hell has this got to do with this lawsuit?"

Ben refused to be baited into justifying his own questions. He maintained a placid face (regardless of how much he secretly wanted to wring the man's scrawny neck) and reasked the question until it was answered.

An hour into the deposition, Blaylock was treating Ben with open contempt. Ben's tongue grew sharper in response; it had to. If he hadn't toughened up, he'd never have gotten an answer to anything. War was being waged amongst burnished curtains and mahogany furniture.

Colby interrupted repeatedly. "There's no reason to make this unpleasant."

Ben ignored him. There was a reason. It was sitting across the table from him.

Finally, about two hours from the start, Ben got to the heart of the matter. "Have you or any of your employees ever used TCE or perc at your plant?"

"No," Blaylock answered, his voice dripping with hate. His eyes were small and narrow, almost porcine. "I have not."

"What industrial solvent do you use?"

"Do I look like the janitor? I have no idea."

"If you don't know what you use, how can you know that you don't use TCE?"

"I know I didn't cause those kids' cancer, that's for damn sure!"

"That wasn't the question, sir. How can you know that you don't use TCE?"

Blaylock sneered. His message was clear. I'm not giving you anything. And you can't make me. "I assumed you were asking whether I had knowledge of any such use."

"No, sir. That was not the question. Let me ask it again. Have you or your employees ever used TCE or perc?"

Colby leaned forward. "If you know."

"Don't coach the witness!" Ben said.

"I'm not coaching," Colby said calmly. "I'm counseling."

"If there's a question pending, you should keep your mouth closed. Period."

Colby rose slightly out of his chair. "Don't presume to instruct me on how to perform my job, Mr. Kincaid."

"Don't you coach the witness!" Ben shot back.

"If you can't control yourself, Mr. Kincaid, I will remove the witness and cancel this deposition."

"I issued a subpoena for this deposition. You try to leave and I'll have the sheriff drag his cranky butt back to the conference room!"

Colby glanced at the court reporter. "Are you getting all this?"

The court reporter nodded. She glanced up at the screen of her laptop. " 'You try to leave and I'll have the sheriff drag his cranky butt—' "

"That'll be enough," Ben said, cutting her off. None of this colloquy of counsel was getting him answers to his questions. "Mr. Blaylock, have you or your employees ever used TCE or perc?"

"If you know," Colby interjected.

Ben gnashed his teeth.

Blaylock glanced at his lawyer and took the cue. "I . . . don't know."

"Then it's possible?"

"Objection," Colby said.

"Anything's possible," Ben insisted. "The witness will answer the question."

Colby gave Blaylock the nod. "I don't know what solvent every single person has used since the dawn of time. But it doesn't matter. Because whatever it is, it was properly disposed of, as we do all our waste."

"Please describe your waste-disposal procedures."

Blaylock waved a hand in the air. "I have people who take care of that."

"Does that mean you don't know?"

"We store it in steel drums."

"What do you do with the drums?"

"We have them hauled off to an authorized and regulated disposal site. Exactly as we're supposed to do."

Ben didn't let up. "How is the waste transferred to the drums?"

"I don't know what you mean."

"I mean, how does the waste get put in the drums?"

"How do you think?"

"I don't know, sir. That's why I'm asking."

"Like this." Blaylock leaned across the table, grabbed the end of Ben's tie, and dunked it in his coffee. "Understand, now?"

Ben jumped to his feet. "Let the record reflect that the witness has just soaked my necktie."

"Not true," Colby interjected. "Only the tip of the tie."

They took a short break, but relations between witness and examiner did not improve. Ben asked a question; Blaylock dodged it. Ben pressed harder; Colby made an objection. Blaylock made a rude remark; Ben made a ruder one. And in this manner they proceeded to argue a dispute potentially involving millions of dollars and the lives of eleven innocent children.

* 16 *

Mark Austin sat quietly, his hands folded in his lap, and watched his mentor, Charlton Colby, prep yet another Blaylock employee for deposition. This was the seventh one they had drilled tonight—and there were still several more waiting in the wings.

Mark's early expectations regarding this case had been fulfilled—and then some. He had hoped this case would boost his billable hours, and that wish had come true beyond his wildest dreams. He'd billed eighty hours a week since the case began, and he wasn't the only one, either. At least a dozen other associates had worked on the case in one capacity or another—doing legal research, drafting briefs, reviewing and cataloging documents. Colby himself had also billed high numbers, which at his hourly rate added up to some significant dollars. Colby had reportedly been billing time seven days a week, fifteen and sixteen hours a day. *Elkins v. Blaylock* had become the biggest cash cow Raven, Tucker & Tubb had seen in some time.

Mark had also hoped this case would give him an opportunity to work with Colby closely, to study under the man commonly considered to be Tulsa's master of corporate litigation. That wish had also come true. Mark had been involved in every aspect of Colby's work—the motions, the discovery, the tactics. The experience had been extremely illuminating if, at times, surprising. And a bit disturbing.

The current witness was a man named Archie Turnbull. Although Colby had allowed Mark to prep some of the witnesses on his own, he had insisted on personally preparing all of the top executives and anyone who was personally involved in waste disposal. Turnbull fell into the latter category.

Turnbull was a tall, thin man with an elongated countenance; he looked rather as if he had been grabbed at both ends and stretched. He was beyond balding; there were two patches of graying hair over each ear, with a few pathetic wispy strands stretched across his head, masking nothing from no one. He was nervous, but then, so was everyone when they came in here. And even more so when Colby started in on them.

"I want to impress upon you the importance of what you are about to do," Colby said in solemn tones. It was late at night, and Colby had been working all day, but he still cut an impressive figure. He was athletic and handsome for his age; his gray pinstriped suit was well tailored and immaculate. "Sometimes corporate employees think, 'Oh well, I don't really know anything, so my deposition won't be important.' But they're wrong. Every statement is important. The tiniest slip could change the course of an entire lawsuit."

Turnbull nibbled at the corners of his fingernails. He had been nervous before, and this lecture from Colby evidently wasn't helping.

"Make no mistake about what is happening here. These plaintiffs are after the heart and soul of H. P. Blaylock. They want to suck out its profits and drain it dry. They are greedy and undeserving, but they wouldn't be the first undeserving plaintiffs who succeeded in the courtroom. If they prevail, there may well be nothing left of this company. You'll be out of work—you and all your friends. And if that happens, what will you do? Where will you go?" He paused, allowing Turnbull to contemplate this unpleasant prospect. "Do you hear what I'm saying?"

"Of course I do," Turnbull said. He had to remove his fingers from his mouth to speak. "I'll do whatever I can to help."

"Good. That's what I like to hear." Colby briefed him on basic deposition procedure. "Here's the most important thing for you to remember—don't volunteer anything. Answer the question succinctly and then be quiet. If it's a yes-no question, then say yes or no and clam up. Don't explain. Don't try to please the questioner. Don't try to make everything clear to him. You're not there to help, and you wouldn't succeed, even if you tried."

Turnbull's voice squeaked a bit as he spoke. "Surely we don't want to leave them confused."

"And why not? Confusion is good. They can't prove a case if they don't understand what's going on. Listen to me, my friend. I've been in the litigation game for a long time now. You start trying to be Mr. Helpful and you'll end up putting a noose around your neck. So you just answer the question succinctly and clam up."

"All right," Turnbull said meekly.

"This assumes you know the answer. If you don't, by God you just say so. You don't guess. You don't say what probably happened or what usually happens. Got it?"

Mark noticed that Turnbull's left eye was beginning to twitch. "Got it."

"Now let's talk a moment about your testimony." Colby eased back in his chair, relaxing his intimidating posture a hair. "Of course, I wouldn't presume to tell you what to say. That would be improper and unethical. I would never encourage a witness to do anything but tell the truth."

Mark wondered why Colby paused. It was almost as if there was a *but* coming.

"Given the work you did at the plant, it is inevitable that you will be asked about the waste-disposal process. The plaintiffs' lawyer is desperate to prove that somehow Blaylock poisoned the Blackwood water aquifer—which of course was more than half a mile away from the plant. It's ridiculous, but that's what they want to do. So it's important that we be firm and consistent in our description of the waste-disposal plan H. P. Blaylock maintained at all times and without exception."

"Of course," Turnbull said quietly.

"As I understand it, the runoff from all equipment tables—anyplace these chemical solvents would have been used—was collected in plastic bins. When they were approximately two-thirds full, the bins would be poured into steel drums; a drum was conveniently placed in every workroom. When the drums were nearly full, they were sealed—airtight—and carried to the back of the plant, where every two weeks they would be hauled to a federally approved waste-disposal site.

There is absolutely no way any of that waste could have contaminated the groundwater. None whatsoever."

Colby paused again, as if waiting for Turnbull to make some kind of response.

"Is that your understanding of the situation, too?"

Turnbull's neck stretched. "Well . . . yes. More or less."

Colby pounced forward. "More or less? What the hell does that mean? A wishy-washy answer like that could cost your employer millions."

"But—you know"—Turnbull was struggling for words—"there were times—"

"Excuse me? Are you saying that wasn't the policy? Because I have it from Myron Blaylock himself."

"But . . . there's a difference between policy and . . . implementation."

"Are you saying there was someone who didn't follow the official corporate policy?" He grabbed a legal pad. "Because if there are such persons, I want their names now. They will be subject to summary termination."

Turnbull licked his lips, parted them, acted as if there was something he might say. But nothing came out.

"I'm waiting, sir. Was this waste-disposal policy followed or not?"

Turnbull finally managed to speak. "It . . . was."

"Good. I'm glad to hear it. You should have said so in the first place." He peered directly into Turnbull's eyes. "Please remember what I said. Answer yes-no questions with a yes or a no. Period."

"Sorry," Turnbull said, tucking his chin. "Yes. That's how it was."

"Fine," Colby replied calmly, a small smile playing on his lips. "That's how I thought it was." He stretched out in his chair, his hands placed casually behind his neck. "Mark, bring in the next one."

* 17 *

After Myron Blaylock, Ben decided he needed a break from overtly hostile witnesses, so the next day he scheduled a few who didn't work at Blaylock but whose testimony could nonetheless be critical.

He started with Blackwood's city engineer, a quiet man named Nathan Tate. He had principal responsibility for the water wells in Blackwood—in theory, anyway—and he was the one who had finally shut down Well B, after chemical poisons were identified by the EPA. Unfortunately, he had conducted no studies of his own; he took action solely on the basis of the EPA report. He also had no idea how the contamination occurred.

"Have you made any effort to determine how the well became poisoned?"

Tate cleared his throat. "The EPA report suggests some possibilities."

"I'm aware of that," Ben replied. "But have you or anyone in your office tried to learn how the contamination occurred?"

"Er, no. I'm afraid we don't have a budget for that sort of thing."

"You're saying you can't afford to keep the wells safe?"

"As soon as we learned the water was tainted, I closed them."

"But you haven't determined the cause. Doesn't that fall within your responsibility?"

Tate straightened a bit. "Sir, chemical testing is expensive. If the city chooses not to fund me adequately, there is precious little I can do."

"So for all you know, the other water wells in Blackwood may be contaminated as well."

"After the EPA discovered the contamination of Well B, they systematically tested the other water wells. None of them had any problems."

"So there must be some specific distinctive event which caused the Well B water to go bad."

"I . . . suppose that's true."

"But you have no idea what that event was."

Tate glanced across the table at the Blaylock team, then returned his eyes to Ben. "I have no concrete evidence on that subject, no."

Ben nodded. "Thanks a million."

The government official who had direct authority over Tate was the state inspector, a man named Paul Schoelen. He was no more help than Tate—possibly less. He had received all kinds of complaints about the water in Blackwood, but nothing that concerned him until the EPA report was released. After that report, he would've closed down Well B— except that Tate had already done it.

"What kind of reports did you receive about the water in Blackwood?" Ben asked.

"Oh, the usual sort of thing." The inspector was an average-looking middle-aged man, with a haircut that dated back to the Seventies and wire-frame glasses. He'd held his position for over twenty years and, as far as Ben could tell, had survived that long by doing as little as possible. "Mothers complaining that their water smelled funny. That it had a bad aftertaste. A few letters suggesting that children developed rashes after baths or showers."

"Did you investigate these complaints?"

"Not at that time."

"Why not?"

He flipped his hand in the air. "You have to understand— there are literally thousands of water wells in the state of Oklahoma. I have a very small staff. Our budget is minuscule. We can't go running around every time some mommy thinks the water smells funny."

"So you did nothing."

"Nothing at that time."

"At any time?"

Schoelen squirmed slightly. "Well . . . after the EPA report . . ."

"You're saying you didn't become involved until after the well was closed?"

"That would be correct."

"When did you first receive complaints about the water in Blackwood?"

"Oh, I couldn't say for sure without checking my files. About five or six years ago, I'd guess."

"Five or six years ago?" Ben was aghast. "Every one of the parents in this lawsuit lost their child in the last five years. If you had acted on those complaints, they might have been saved."

"Now don't you try to blame those deaths on me. I didn't poison the well."

"I didn't say you caused the deaths. I said you might've prevented them."

"Do you have any idea how many complaints I receive every week?"

"No," Ben said, "but I know this. I know when people give their tax dollars to a state inspector, they have the crazy idea that he's out there inspecting, not sitting behind a desk ignoring complaints."

"I resent that remark."

"And I resent the fact that if you'd done your job, some of these tragedies might've been avoided." Ben pushed away from the table. "Taxpayers finance people like you to protect them from dangers they can't possibly detect on their own." He shook his head sadly. "But all that money really doesn't buy them much, does it?"

After the lunch break, Ben started in on the Blaylock employees. There were dozens of potential witnesses, any one of whom might know something about the waste-disposal procedures followed at Blaylock. Ben had no way of knowing which witness might be more important than others, and of course Colby's interrogatory answers had intentionally given him no clue. So he would have to depose them all. And taking depositions was very expensive—usually a couple of thousand dollars per day.

In order to save time—and money—Ben tried to move as quickly as possible. But he knew that if he hurried too much he might miss something important, thereby defeating the whole point of the deposition in the first place. For the most part, he had to plod methodically through the long list of witnesses, doing his best to learn what he could, trying not to think about the huge bill he was running up but would eventually have to pay.

The first two Blaylock witnesses were executive types, vice presidents of this or that. Although Ben couldn't avoid deposing them, he knew his chances of getting anything out of them were slim. They had far too much invested in their careers. They had fancy cars, stock options, and a medical plan. They weren't going to risk angering Blaylock by giving Ben anything useful.

After the executive parade was over, Ben began deposing some of the men and women who worked in the plant—chemical employees, machinery cleaners, janitorial squads. The timbre of these depositions was different; Ben didn't sense so much evasion, so much artifice, so much concerted effort to mislead. Some of them had no idea how the chemical runoff was disposed of. Those who had an opinion on the subject toed the party line: it was carefully transferred to steel drums, which were then transported off the premises. Nothing ever spilled on the ground. They could not have contaminated the water supply.

On the fourth day of these depositions, Ben questioned a man named Archie Turnbull. He seemed a simple, prepossessing fellow; Ben initially liked him, which had not been the case with most of the witnesses he'd had to tackle. Turnbull had been supervisor of the machine room in the rear of the plant that transferred waste to cans and packaged them. Part of his duties included supervising the removal of the waste product.

"What kind of waste are we talking about here?" Ben asked.

"Principally spilled machine oil and grease." Turnbull had a habit of biting his nails that reasserted itself anytime Ben asked a sufficiently long question.

"Any solvents?"

"We . . . do use solvents in the plant. To keep the machinery in top condition."

"What solvents do you use?"

"I'm not in charge of ordering that stuff."

"But you are the area supervisor. You must know."

The nibbling intensified. "All those chemical names sound alike to me."

Ben removed a document from his notebook. "Mr. Turnbull, during document discovery we received a copy of a receipt for the purchase by Blaylock of twelve gallons of perc."

"Oh?" he said, raising his eyebrows.

"Yes. And unless I'm mistaken, those are your initials at the bottom." He pointed to the spot. "Right?"

Turnbull swallowed. "Yes. I suppose they are."

"So your plant does in fact use perc."

"I . . . guess so."

"And you also use or have used TCE, right?"

"Well . . . I . . ."

Ben reached into his notebook and retrieved another piece of paper.

"Yes, that's correct," Turnbull conceded. "We have used TCE. Though I don't believe we do anymore."

"Have you used it in the last five years?"

"Uh . . . yes."

"I see." Ben was glad to hear it—especially since the last piece of paper he'd retrieved from his notebook was an interoffice memo discouraging employees from spending too long in the bathroom. "So it's possible that some of these solvents could have been included in your waste product."

Turnbull glanced unhappily at Colby. "I . . . suppose it's possible."

"Tell me how you dispose of the waste."

"Well, of course, I didn't do it myself."

"The workers under your supervision, then."

"Basically, we collect it in plastic bins placed beside every worktable in the area. When they start to get full, we carefully dump the contents into steel drums. The drums are placed out back, until they're taken away."

"Do the drums ever leak?"

"Oh, no. They're made of steel."

"But perhaps if the lids are not placed securely?"

"That never happens." His eyes darted one way, then the other. "We're very careful."

"Where are the drums taken?"

"I forget the name of the place, but it's an approved disposal site somewhere in the southern part of the state. Near Texas."

"How often is this done?"

"Every two weeks."

"Without fail?"

"That's correct."

"Was there ever a time when this procedure was not followed?"

Turnbull's hands were shaking so much that he lowered them out of sight and sat on them. "No."

"Not to your knowledge?"

Turnbull glanced over at Colby. "Never. I would've known. The procedure was always followed."

"You're sure about this?"

His voice squeaked slightly. "Absolutely positive."

Ben leaned thoughtfully back in his chair. He hated to leave the matter like this, but his current approach was getting him nowhere. He needed to try something different.

"Mr. Turnbull," he said eventually, "do you have any children?"

"Yes. Six."

"Six?" Ben blinked. "That's quite a family these days."

He looked down shyly. "My Carrie Sue and I love kids."

"Good thing." Ben pushed out a map of the city of Blackwood. "Sir, do you and your family live in the Well B region?"

"Objection," Colby barked. "What's that got to do with anything?"

"Objection noted," Ben said. "The witness will answer."

"No," Turnbull said. "We're over here." He pointed on the map. "In the newer part of town. The Well D area."

"Lucky for you. Do you know anyone who lives in the Well B area?"

"Again I must object!" Colby said. "This is absolutely of no relevance."

"But the witness must still answer the question. Please answer, sir."

Turnbull cast a nervous sideways glance toward Colby. "Sure. I know lots of people in that part of town."

"Did you know any of the children who died?"

"This is outrageous!" Colby said, slapping his hand down on the mahogany table. "Irrelevant—and abusive!"

Ben didn't blink. "But the witness still must answer the question, regardless of how hard you slap the table. Mr. Turnbull?"

Turnbull cleared his throat. "I—did, yes. That boy—Billy Elkins. My Becky knew him. They both sang in the church choir together. Before he died."

"Why do you think Billy died?"

"I'm warning you, Kincaid." Colby was on his feet now. "If you continue in this abusive manner, I will take the witness and leave."

"The witness will answer the question," Ben said calmly.

Turnbull began to stutter. "I-I guess he died of leukemia."

"And what do you think caused the leukemia?"

Colby objected again, but Ben ignored him. He kept his eyes trained on the witness. "Please answer."

"N-no one knows what causes cancer."

"Do you really believe that?"

"That's it, Kincaid," Colby shouted. "This deposition is terminated."

Ben kept going. "I wonder how you would feel, Mr. Turnbull, if you had lived in the Well B region. If your Becky had started developing strange rashes. A cough that wouldn't go away. Bruises that appeared for no reason."

"It's over, Kincaid!" Colby shouted. He pointed at the court reporter. "Pack up your stuff. Stop taking this down."

"I wonder if your testimony would change if Becky had been the one who died. Died for no good reason, simply because someone somewhere was careless or negligent and didn't care who got hurt as a result. I wonder what you would say then."

Colby jerked Turnbull up by the arm. "Come along, Mr. Turnbull. We're leaving."

Colby dragged Turnbull out of the conference room, but

Ben never broke eye contact with him, not the entire time he remained in the room.

And to his surprise, Turnbull never stopped looking at him, either.

A few minutes later, Christina entered the conference room and slid into a chair beside Ben. He seemed lost in thought.

"Well, I don't know what you did in here, but whatever it was, you sure worked Colby up into a froth."

"Thanks, Christina. That makes me happy."

"He's screaming about calling the magistrate, getting a restraining order to prevent you from taking more depositions."

"Bluster from a blowhard. He can't do any of those things. He's just trying to impress his client with what a hardball player he is." He turned slightly. "Christina, call Loving. Tell him to start concentrating his efforts on a man named Archie Turnbull."

"You think Turnbull is lying?"

Ben shrugged. "I don't know exactly. But something is bothering him."

"Is that a surprise? No one likes being deposed."

"Yeah, maybe. But I had the sense . . . there was something else. What's more—I got the impression that Turnbull is basically a good person. That he actually has a conscience."

"What—in this day and age?"

"Yeah. And if we have any hope of success, it will be thanks to people like that. So have Loving contact him. See if he can get anywhere."

"Will do."

"And quickly. Colby will be filing his summary judgment motion soon, now that he's decided to show how tough he is. And if we can't prove Blaylock caused the well contamination—we're going to be blown right out of the courtroom."

Turnbull was surprised when Colby asked him to remain in his fancy skyscraper office after the conclusion of the deposition, but he was even more surprised when he saw his ultimate boss, Myron Blaylock, enter the room. He jumped to his feet, as if he were being received by royalty. In all his years at the plant, Turnbull had never actually met Blaylock, only passed him a few times in the corridor or the cafeteria.

"Archie," Blaylock said, extending his hand. Turnbull was stunned that Blaylock even knew his name.

"Mr. Blaylock," Turnbull said. He grabbed the elderly man's hand and pumped it like a madman.

"Call me Myron."

Turnbull was speechless.

Colby took a seat casually behind his desk and propped his shoes up on the edge. "Archie, I asked Myron to step in so I could tell him what a fine job you did during your deposition today."

Turnbull blinked. "I did?"

"Yes." He adjusted his gaze toward Blaylock. "He held the line, Myron. And let me tell you—some of the questions that bastard Kincaid asked were downright dirty pool. That man will stop at nothing. But Archie didn't let it get to him. He did H. P. Blaylock proud."

"Indeed. I'm glad to hear it." He faced Turnbull. "You know I need someone like you in the executive suite, someone I can trust."

Turnbull's tongue felt like cotton. "The executive suite?"

"And why not? Who have I got now? A bunch of college graduates, more interested in their stock portfolios than in serving my company. I need men like you—men who know what hard work is." He leaned closer. "Who know the meaning of loyalty."

"That's what I like to see," Colby said. "A man rewarded for his loyalty."

"I thought I'd create a new position for you. Vice president of floor management. We've needed someone who has hands-on knowledge about the way the plant works. I think you will be an invaluable asset."

"I-I'd like that," Turnbull managed.

"Of course you'll have the usual perks. Company car—I see you as a BMW man. Am I right?"

"T-That would be fine."

"Increased vacation time. Increased medical. Could be quite a help with a brood like yours, Archie. And of course, increased salary." He scribbled a number on a scrap of paper. "How would that be, just for starters?"

Turnbull couldn't believe this was happening. "That would be . . . twice what I make now."

"And long overdue." Blaylock slapped him on the back. "I don't want to see a man like you slip away."

"There is one thing," Colby said. His voice had the laconic tone of one who has suddenly recalled a trifling detail after his third mint julep. "I know you think that since your deposition is completed this is all over for you . . . but it isn't necessarily so."

"It isn't?"

"It's entirely possible the plaintiffs—or their representatives—will attempt to contact you. Try to get you to change your testimony. Say things that aren't true. Persuade you to spill confidential secrets. It's important that you not be suckered into any of that."

"Loyalty," Blaylock said. "That's what's important to me."

Colby nodded. "You wouldn't let the plaintiffs lure you into anything like that, would you, Archie?"

"I—I certainly wouldn't lie to them."

"Archie . . . I don't want you to talk to them at all."

"Loyalty," Blaylock repeated to no one in particular. "Careers are made or lost on that factor alone."

"It is important," Colby continued, "that we maintain a strong defense. A firm resolve." He peered across the desk. "We can count on you, can't we, Archie?"

Turnbull swallowed. "Of course you can."

"Good. I'm glad to hear it." He rose and shook Turnbull's hand. "Thanks for staying late."

"I'll have my assistant meet you at the front gate tomorrow morning," Blaylock explained. "To show you to your new office."

Turnbull glanced again at the scrap of paper with the unbelievable six-digit figure on it. It was too good to be believed. It almost made him forget—

"Will that be acceptable?" Blaylock asked.

"Of course," Turnbull said quickly. "I'll see you tomorrow morning."

* * *

After Turnbull was gone, Blaylock rose to his feet and began pacing back and forth across Colby's office.

"I hope that satisfied you. Personally, it made me sick to my stomach."

"Stay calm, Myron." Colby smiled. "It was necessary."

"I don't see why. We didn't do it for any of the others."

"This man is different." Colby's eyes narrowed slightly. "I sense . . . a stirring inside him. The potential for trouble."

"Damned high price to pay to avoid trouble."

"The cost will be far higher if you don't." He slid his feet off the desk and sat up. "And it's only temporary. Kincaid hasn't discovered anything. I'm filing my summary judgment motion immediately. Once this case is dismissed, you can do anything with Turnbull you want."

"That will be a happy day," Blaylock spat out, as he grabbed his briefcase and headed for the door. "For more reasons than one!"

* 18 *

"Ready to go?" Ben asked.

Cecily glanced at Christina, then nodded. Not an enthusiastic nod, but the best she could muster under the circumstances. "If I must."

"Christina gave you the lowdown on what's going to happen?"

"About a hundred times," Cecily said sourly.

"That's my Christina," he replied. "Nothing if not efficient."

He took Cecily's elbow and led her to the corner conference room where the deposition would take place. As was traditional, when Ben wanted to depose Blaylock's witnesses, he had to go to Colby's skyscraper office, but when Colby wanted a shot at his witnesses, he had to come onto Ben's turf. Ben tried to whisper comforting words as they approached the conference room, but he suspected his words accomplished little.

Colby was full of easy gentility when they arrived. "Mrs. Elkins," he said, taking her hand. "It's a pleasure to meet you."

Cecily wasn't sure what to do—shake hands with the Big Bad Wolf or run out of the room screaming. She took his hand.

"And before we begin, let me express my deepest sympathy for your loss. I have children of my own; I can't imagine what you must've gone through."

"Well . . . thank you."

"I'll try to make this as easy as possible for you. It shouldn't take more than an hour or two."

Cecily's eyes widened slightly. Could that be true? Done before lunch? Ben could see her hopes elevating—a potentially dangerous development, since the higher they rose, the further they had to fall.

Colby began with the softball stuff—name and address, former occupations, college education. He spoke slowly and was more than accommodating. None of which put Ben's mind at ease. It only reminded him of something his friend Mike Morelli once said. When the devil is stalking you, beware. But when the devil is making nice—run.

"You went to college at Rogers University, is that right?"

"Yes." Ben could tell Cecily was amazed this was still so painless. Ben, on the other hand, was more concerned about how well-informed Colby seemed to be.

"You studied biology, I believe?"

"That's correct."

"Took you five years to get your undergraduate degree?"

"Well, you know how it is. I changed my major about eighteen times."

Colby chuckled. "Yes, I know what you mean." His smile gradually faded. "But that wasn't the only problem, was it?"

"Uh—excuse me?"

"That wasn't the only reason it took you longer than usual to get your degree, was it?"

"I'm . . . not sure what you're getting at."

"You had a problem with drugs, didn't you, Cecily?"

The other shoe had dropped. The room was filled by a silence that seemed deafening.

It took a good while for Cecily to frame her response. "I . . . did a normal amount of experimenting. When I was young."

"I feel I must remind you," Colby said, "that you are under oath, and that you are subject to the penalties of perjury if you answer falsely."

"That's unnecessary," Ben cut in.

Colby plowed right ahead. "In fact, Mrs. Elkins, you were suspended for an entire semester after you were arrested by campus security officers on a drug-related charge, weren't you? I have a copy of your transcript right here."

"I was at a party," Cecily tried to explain. "A couple of the kids had joints on them. It was really nothing."

"The campus administrators didn't feel it was nothing."

Cecily shrugged. "Rogers is a small college in a small town."

Colby looked indignant. "Mrs. Elkins, I consider drug abuse a serious matter, as do most right-thinking people I know."

Ben thought it was time to jump in, even if he didn't really have an objection. "Colby, does this abusive line of questioning have any relevance to the lawsuit, or are you just being cruel for the fun of it?"

Colby was unfazed. "This is of the utmost relevance, counsel. Mrs. Elkins, when was your son Billy born?"

"About a year after I got out of school."

"Which was about a year and a half after you were picked up on drug charges. You have heard, no doubt, that illegal narcotics can have a negative effect on pregnancy, haven't you?"

Cecily's nostrils flared. "I never used drugs when I was pregnant. Not even aspirin."

"You mean, after you knew you were pregnant, don't you? But you were probably with child for at least a month or two before you realized it."

"I did not hurt my baby!"

"I'm sure you want to believe that," Colby said calmly. "I'm sure you would much rather blame his illness on some mysterious unseen corporate evil—than accept responsibility for your own actions."

"I did not hurt my baby!"

Colby turned away, shuffling his papers. "That, of course, will be for the jury to decide."

"I did not hurt my baby!"

"Let's take a break," Ben said, jumping up.

"This is my deposition," Colby said calmly, "and I did not call for a break."

"I don't give a damn whether you did or you didn't."

Ben took Cecily outside the conference room. He tried to calm her, but had little success. He put her in Christina's hands, hoping she somehow might be able to settle her nerves.

A few minutes later, Ben returned to the conference room. "Congratulations, Colby," he said. "You've managed to achieve an all-time high on the depravity meter."

Colby barely blinked. "We have angles like this on all your clients, Ben."

"What's that supposed to mean?"

"It means this is a scruffy bunch you've taken under your wing. They all have secrets—except they won't be secrets anymore, if you continue to pursue this lawsuit."

"You're a disgusting person, Colby. Disgusting and unethical."

"Excuse me, O High and Mighty One, but the Rules of Professional Conduct require me to zealously represent my client to the best of my ability. That's exactly what I'm doing."

"What you're doing is using blackmail to suppress a legitimate claim. That isn't honorable. Profitable, maybe. But hardly anything to brag about."

"I'm not going to waste time bantering with you. Bring your witness back into the conference room so we can continue."

"Forget it. She's done for the day."

"Fine. Then bring in the next one. Mrs. Hardesty." His eyes narrowed. "You're going to love what I do to her."

Loving parked his pickup and strolled toward the Blackwood Bowl-O-Rama. As far as he could tell, this was the local grown-up hot spot. The parking lot was almost full; the only other place in town that came close was the Sonic Drive-In, and that was mostly teenagers cruising in and out. The crowd he sought was inside here, amidst the clang and clatter of heavy balls and falling pins.

Loving liked Blackwood; it reminded him of the tiny town in western Oklahoma where he grew up. He had no problem relating to the folks in this burg. They were cordial, direct, simple. Not stupid, mind you. Simple. Uncomplicated. There was a difference. He'd put these folks up against some of the would-be highbrows he came across in Tulsa any day of the week.

Before he pushed through the front door, Loving drew in his breath and mentally put himself in his "tough guy" mode. Contrary to popular opinion, this was not something he particularly enjoyed. But it was necessary. In his line of work, the courteous just didn't get results. Whether he enjoyed this routine or not, he owed the Skipper a lot, and what's more, he thought this case was important, more so than most. So he didn't want to disappoint.

He stopped at the front desk and rented a pair of ugly red-and-beige bowling shoes, size twelve, but did not rent a lane. He wasn't here to play. He was here to persuade.

He spotted his quarry on lane ten. There were six of them, all wearing matching green jerseys. This was an H. P. Blaylock bowling-league team. The league had many teams, but this one was made up of men who worked in the waste-disposal department—including Archie Turnbull. The logo on the back of their matching shirts read TONY'S TIGERS. Loving had learned that this was a tribute to Tony Montague, a Blaylock employee who had died six years before in a horrible bus accident.

"Excuse me." Loving walked up behind where five of them were sitting, while the sixth took his shot. "Could I speak to you gentlemen for a moment?"

Heads turned. "Who are you?" one of them asked. The smell of beer was thick on his breath.

"My name's Loving. I'm a private investigator. I'm workin' for Ben Kincaid."

Mostly frowns. "Kincaid? Don't know him."

Except from Archie Turnbull. "I do. He's the lawyer representing the parents. The ones suing Blaylock."

The bowlers could not have moved away from Loving more quickly had Turnbull told them he had an advanced case of leprosy. "Get outta here!" one of them shouted.

"We don't want nothin' to do with you!" said another.

"I've just got a few simple questions," Loving said. "It won't take long."

Beer Breath was the first who decided to get tough. "Maybe you didn't hear," he said, leaning into Loving's face. "We told you to get out!"

"Look, I don't want any trouble—"

"Well, you're gonna get it! If you don't clear out!"

Loving drew himself up to his full height, which was somewhere between six foot two and the sky. He didn't have to make threats; his body made the threats for him. Beer Breath retreated to the safety of the ball carousel.

"All I want to do is ask a few questions about how you boys disposed of waste at the plant."

"I've already told your boss everything I know," Turnbull said.

"Have you?" Loving replied, cocking an eyebrow.

"Yes." Turnbull turned away.

"Don't talk to him," Beer Breath said, tugging on Turnbull's shoulder. "They're just ambulance chasers."

"The only thing I'm chasin' is the truth," Loving said. "We haven't got that yet. But I'm bettin' one of you boys could remedy that."

"We're not tellin' you nothin'," Beer Breath barked. He hoisted his bowling ball up with one hand. "And if you don't clear out, I'm calling security."

"That go for you, too, Archie?"

Turnbull didn't answer.

"You know, Mrs. Elkins's boy Billy—he loved to bowl, too. He was kind of a little guy; it was prob'ly his best sport. I wonder if maybe your Becky didn't come bowlin' with him on occasion."

Turnbull's head jerked up, riveted by the sound of his daughter's name.

"Billy's mother loved to bring him out here. They did it

two, three times a week. 'Course, that all came to an end. She won't be able to enjoy the simple pleasure of takin' her son bowling anymore. Never again."

Three of the green-jerseyed men walked on either side of Loving, surrounding him. "We want you out of here," Beer Breath growled. "Now."

Loving made a show of being unimpressed. "Let me give you my card. If one of you wants to get in touch, just call me. Or call Ben Kincaid's office."

Beer Breath took the card, tore it up, and let the pieces flutter to the ground. "Last chance, asshole. Leave."

Loving nodded. "Be seein' you, Archie." Loving burned a path to the man's eyes and didn't blink until Turnbull finally turned away.

As Loving casually walked away, in no great hurry, he realized that he'd learned one thing: the Skipper's instincts were better than he'd expected. Turnbull did know something—Loving was certain of it. Unfortunately, he had every reason in the world not to tell what he knew. But there had to be some way to get past that, to get the man talking.

If only Loving could figure out what it was.

Presumably, Colby thought the element of surprise was gone by the time he got to Mrs. Hardesty, another of the parents in the class action against Blaylock. He made no attempt to charm or seduce her. There could be no accusation of subterfuge in a deposition that began with: "Your husband beats you, doesn't he, Mrs. Hardesty?"

Martha Hardesty's jaw dropped an inch. Nothing Ben or Christina had told her prepared her for this.

"I'm sorry, ma'am," Colby said, "but you have to answer verbally. So the court reporter can take it down."

"But . . . my . . . Jack—"

"He beats you, right? You are under oath, ma'am."

Martha was in her mid-forties, average weight, flaxen hair. She had once been quite thin, but three pregnancies had a way of changing that. "He . . . doesn't. Not really."

"Not really? Please." He shuffled the papers before him. "I have a hospital report. You came in with two black eyes. You told the attendant your husband did it."

"W-well . . . but—"

"So which is it, Mrs. Hardesty? Were you lying then, or are you lying now?"

"Objection!" Ben shouted. "Colby, if you don't shape up, I'll terminate this depo just like the last one!"

"Which will only continue it to another day. Frankly, Ben, I don't care if you stretch this case out for a year. I'm in no hurry." He turned back toward the witness. "Mrs. Hardesty, there's no point in hiding. We all already know the answer. Your husband beats you, doesn't he?"

Martha's eyes turned downward. "He . . . has before."

"How often?"

"N-not often. . . ."

"Two times a week?"

"No!"

"You went to the emergency room three times last year alone."

"But—it wasn't because of Jack."

"Yes, that's what you said before. I'm afraid we can't trust anything you say now."

Ben clenched his teeth. "Colby!"

Colby proceeded. "On one of these occasions, your arm was broken. Surely you realize that violence of that magnitude could potentially damage an unborn baby."

"But—Tommy was born long before that—"

"True. But while you were pregnant, the hospital records show you" —he cleared his throat—" 'tripped and fell down the stairs.' Right?"

"That had nothing to do with Jack! I just got dizzy—"

"Mrs. Hardesty, you're aware that an injury like that could potentially damage an unborn fetus, aren't you?"

"The doctors said there was no damage."

"None that they detected at the time. But it's always possible. For that matter, almost anything is possible in a home with a man as violent as your husband."

"Jack did not cause Tommy's illness!"

"How can you be sure? Are you a doctor?"

"No, but—"

"Do you know what causes leukemia?"

"I'm not a doctor, but—"

"But when your son died prematurely, you didn't blame your violent husband, who had shown a repeated tendency for violence—which, I might add, you could have curtailed by pressing charges, something you never bothered to do. Instead, you trumped up some preposterous unprovable claim against a corporation."

"That's not true!"

"We'll let the jury decide, ma'am. We'll let them decide what they think is more probable—death due to some fantastic pseudoscientific water problem, or death due to habitual unchecked physical abuse."

"That's not what happened!"

"This deposition is concluded," Colby said, folding up his notes. "If you wish to dismiss your suit now, Mr. Kincaid, this would be a good time. Otherwise—bring on the next one."

Loving was leaving the bowling alley when he heard a whisper from the alleyway separating the Bowl-O-Rama from a closed pawn shop.

"Psst! Mister!"

Loving had to grin. Was this really happening? It was like something out of a spy movie.

"Over here!"

Well, he never passed up a lead. Loving ambled into the alley and found . . . not James Bond . . . not Humphrey Bogart . . . but two kids on bicycles. They couldn't be more than ten, if that.

"You talkin' to me?" Loving asked.

"Are you the one asking all the questions about the plant?" the towheaded boy asked.

Loving saw his reputation had preceded him. Well, spend a day asking questions in a small Oklahoma town, that sort of thing was bound to happen. "Yup. I'm the one. Why?" He crouched down to the kids' level. "You know somethin'?"

The two boys looked at each other. "Yeah," the blond said finally. "We were there when they found the body."

Loving's chin rose. This was turning out to be more interesting than he had imagined. "You were at the plant?"

"No. Just outside. Hiding in the ravine."

"Hiding?"

The other boy jabbed his friend in the stomach. "He was hiding from the Outsider."

"The Outsider?"

The blond boy looked mortified. "It's just a game we were playing. It isn't real. But what happened at the plant sure was."

"You were there when the workers found the drum behind the plant with the corpse?"

"Yeah. Except it wasn't behind the plant. It was buried."

"Buried?"

"Yeah. Under the ground. Lots of them were."

Loving's eyes bulged. "Let me see if I've got this straight. Waste storage drums were buried in the ground?"

"Yeah. They had a big Brush Hog diggin' 'em up. 'Cept it dropped one of them and it burst open. And a body tumbled out."

Loving couldn't believe what he was hearing. This was not the official Blaylock account of how the body was discovered—not by a long shot. "Are you sure you boys aren't maybe . . . confusing what really happened with your game? Imaginin' stuff that didn't strictly speaking occur?"

The blond boy seemed offended. "What d'ya think I am, some kind of jerk?"

"No, no. And you say barrels were buried?"

"Yeah. Lots of them. Fifty or more."

"Fifty?" It was more than he could believe. "Why didn't you say anything about this before?"

"I wanted to, but my dad told me to keep my mouth shut. See, he works out at the plant. He's a floor manager. You understand?"

Loving nodded. He was beginning to, anyway. "Look, kid, would you be willing to testify about what you saw? So we can make a record?"

"Sure, I would. But my dad says I can't."

Loving placed his hand firmly on the boy's shoulder. "Let me see if I can't persuade him otherwise."

* 19 *

Finally, after more than three weeks of excruciating depositions, they had reached the last of the plaintiff parents, Ralph Foley. It had been three weeks of hell, not just for Ben, but more important, for the parents themselves. Every fear they had ever held, every cliché they had ever heard about the nastiness of litigation and lawyers, had been paraded before them. Colby had proven he was willing to stop at nothing, to inflict any measure of pain or humiliation to badger the plaintiffs into dropping their case or accepting a trivial settlement. And there was nothing Ben could do to stop it.

To their credit, so far, neither Cecily nor any of the others had talked about dropping the lawsuit. But Ben could see some of their fervor was ebbing. The fire was draining out of their eyes. "These people killed our children!" he heard on more than one occasion. "Why should we have to bear this abuse just to see justice done?"

Ben had no answers for them. No answers to those questions existed.

Colby was taking the slow route this time, dancing around Ralph's college days for no apparent reason—*apparent* being the operative word. Ben could see Ralph's stomach was tight as a drum. It must be horrible, he thought, sitting there like a clay pigeon waiting for the shot, wondering what dark secret this demon had dredged up about you. At least his nervousness wasn't showing too badly—not like some of the others. Ralph drove an ambulance; he was probably more accustomed to working under pressure.

"How long have you been driving the Blackwood ambulance?" Colby asked.

"Over eleven years now," Ralph replied.

"Looks like you have a spotless record. No accidents since the day you took the job."

Ralph looked at Colby warily. "That's true."

"But appearances can be deceiving, can't they?" Colby reached into a manila folder previously clamped under his elbow. "Can you tell me what this sheet of paper is?"

Ralph gave it a quick once-over. "It looks like . . . a job application." He looked a little closer. "This must be the application I filled out to get the job with EMSA."

"That would be correct. Of course, you filled it out truthfully."

Ralph didn't answer immediately. He was smart enough to see the red flags flying.

"You wouldn't lie on your job application, would you? Take a job under false pretenses?"

"No," Ralph said. "Not intentionally."

"Just the same, I couldn't help but notice your answers in the box at the bottom left. Where it asks about your driving record."

Ralph remained silent.

"Do you see that section?"

"Yes."

"You say you have a clear driving record, correct?"

"That's what it says."

"But that wasn't true, was it?" Colby reached once more into his magic folder. "You had a traffic accident. Sideswiped a car at the intersection of Park and Lincoln."

Ralph's jaw clenched. "I was just a kid."

"You were nineteen. Which does not in any way justify lying on your job application." He reached into his folder again. "It was a pretty bad accident. A little girl in the other car was almost killed."

"Do you think I don't know that?" Ralph said quietly. "It was horrible. She was screaming, crying. Took twenty minutes to get her to the hospital. She was in such pain."

Colby looked at him squarely. "You're lucky her parents didn't decide to bring some big lawsuit against you."

"My insurance covered her medical costs. She recovered."

"But you lied about it on your application."

"I wanted the job!" Ralph said. "She shouldn't have had to wait so long to get to the hospital. I wanted to make sure that didn't happen again, to anyone else. So I took a special course to sharpen my emergency driving skills and applied for the job."

"And lied in the process."

"If I had told them about the accident, there's no way I would've gotten the job."

"So you lied. *Didn't you?*"

Ralph was trapped, and he knew it. "Yes."

"You lied in order to get something you wanted. And now, eleven years later, there's something else you want. A lot of money. And to get it, you're making all kinds of outrageous claims—"

"They're not outrageous."

"The question I have to ask myself—and will ask the jury at trial—is, if you were so willing to lie before, how can we believe what you say now?"

After the questions were done and Ralph had left the room, Ben asked the court reporter to remain. "I have an objection," he explained.

Colby cocked an eyebrow. "The deposition is over."

"I can still make an objection. For the record."

"On what grounds?"

"On grounds that you're an embarrassment to every man or woman who ever practiced law."

Colby was nonplused. "I'm only doing my job."

"Yeah. That's what the boys at Nuremberg said, too."

Colby pushed away from the table. "If you'll excuse me—"

"Not so fast, Colby. It's only three in the afternoon."

"But—he was the last of the plaintiffs."

"Good. Then we can depose someone on my list. Someone I just added."

"And who, pray tell, would that be?"

"You don't know him," Ben answered. "But after today, I bet you never forget him."

"What have you got, Kincaid? Some crackpot witness?"

Ben smiled. "Close. A nine-year-old boy."

* * *

Loving only had to ask a few questions to find out where the Blaylock group was hanging today. Apparently they were regulars; everybody knew them.

They were congregated over by the bar. Four of them—Archie Turnbull, Loving's old pal Beer Breath, and two other guys he hadn't seen before. They were well into their cups—or Beer Breath was, anyway. His displays of hilarity far exceeded the amusement quotient of his jokes, and he was having a bit of trouble staying on his bar stool.

He would prefer to catch Turnbull alone, but it hadn't been possible. Turnbull seemed to surround himself with these goons whenever he was out of the house. Like it or not, he'd have to go after the man here. Loving knew this wasn't going to be pleasant, so he figured it was best to just get it over with. He positioned himself directly behind them, hoping the element of surprise would buy him some extra time.

"Good evenin', gentlemen," he said in an unnecessarily loud voice. "Can I buy you all a drink?"

"You?" Beer Breath gasped, then collected himself. "Again? I can't believe it. What are you, some kind of tar baby?"

"Private investigator, actually."

"I told you to get lost back at the bowling alley. But some of the boys tell me you've been following them around all over town. Hounding them in restaurants and chasing after them at the grocery store."

Loving threw back his enormous shoulders. "My ex-wife always said I was a persistent cuss."

Beer Breath slid off his stool. "What the hell is it you want, anyway?"

"I told you already. I want to ask you a few questions about how Blaylock got rid of its waste product."

Beer Breath leaned into his face. "Yeah? Well, we don't wanna talk to you!"

Enough spit flew to make Loving feel good and drenched. He snatched a cocktail napkin off the bar and dried his face. "That go for all of you?" He scanned the unfamiliar faces in the group. They were looking away from him, practically hiding. "That go for you, Archie?"

For a moment, it looked as if Archie might actually speak, but before he could, Beer Breath interposed himself between them. "Is there somethin' goin' on here I should know about? Why the hell are you always pickin' on Archie?"

"No reason," Loving said hastily. He didn't want to alienate Turnbull from his friends—or cause any problems that would make his coming forward even less likely. "He just looks like an honest man. And I understand those are in short supply up at Blaylock these days."

Without warning, Beer Breath drew back his fist and clipped Loving hard on the jaw. It knocked him a few steps back. He'd had a lot worse in his time, but it stung, just the same.

"There's more where that came from," Beer Breath said, sneering.

"No, actually, there ain't."

"Oh yeah? How come?"

Loving hovered over the much shorter blowhard. "Because if you try anything like that ever again, I'll bend your arm back and snap it in two like a toothpick."

Beer Breath laughed, trying to save some face, even though he was obviously terrified. "Oh, yeah?" he finally managed.

"Snappy comeback," Loving replied. "You'll probably get on Letterman with that one." He walked over to a bulletin board covered with business cards at the end of the bar. "I'm pinning my phone number up right here. I'm thinkin' that since this is public property, no asshole'll come along and tear it up. If any of you boys wants to come clean and talk about what really happened, call me."

He heard a voice from the bar. Archie's. "No one's gonna talk to you, mister."

"Really?" Loving said. "I'll bet your Becky would. Course, she knew what a swell, special kid Billy Elkins was. And she still knows the difference between right and wrong."

Normally, Ben wouldn't depose his own witness; depositions were for obtaining information from the other side. In this case, though, it was critical that he get Scout on the record. It would eliminate the danger of Scout getting scared at trial or forgetting what he'd seen, and would also give Ben some ammunition when Colby filed his inevitable summary judgment motion.

When Scout took his seat at the huge mahogany conference table, he was so short his head was barely visible. Christina found the blond-headed boy a thick cushion to sit on, and Ben started the deposition. Scout—whose real name, as it turned out, was Harold—spoke clearly and answered to the best of his ability, even though he was obviously intimidated by his surroundings.

"Scout," Ben asked, "do you know the difference between right and wrong?"

"Sure I do. I go to Sunday school. Most times, anyway."

"And you know the difference between the truth and a lie, don't you?"

"Sure. When I tell the truth, my momma says I'm a little angel. And when I tell a lie, my daddy turns me over his knee and beats the tar out of me."

Ben tried to keep a straight face. "I'm going to ask a favor of you, Scout. I'm going to ask you to answer my questions, but only tell the truth. Okay? Nothing but the truth."

"Sure. That's what I promised."

Ben took Scout back to the day several weeks ago when he and his friend Jim had been playing in the ravine near the Blaylock plant. They heard all about the elaborate game of "Flee the Outsider," how they had been wrestling in the mud, and how they'd spotted the Brush Hog at work behind the plant.

"Could you tell what the Brush Hog was doing?" Ben asked. It was important not to lead the witness. He wanted this testimony to be pristine, so he could read the transcript at trial if necessary.

"Sure. It was diggin' up the ground behind the plant."

"Digging up the ground? Could you tell why?"

"They were haulin' big containers out. Those big drums."

"Storage containers? Like this?" Ben showed him a picture of some of Blaylock's waste-disposal drums.

"Yeah. That's it exactly."

"And they were buried in the ground?"

"That's what I said. That big Brush Hog would haul them out of the earth. Saw them pull up twenty or thirty of them. Till one popped open and that body dropped out."

"Are you sure they weren't just stored behind the plant? Waiting to be carried away?"

Scout didn't blink. "That's not what I saw. They were in the ground. Deep down there, judging by the size of the hole they dug."

Ben nodded. "Waste-filled drums, buried deep in the earth." He glanced at Colby. "Not exactly your federally approved waste-disposal procedure."

For once, Colby looked just a tad ruffled. In two months of depositions, this was the first time Ben had made the slightest dent in his case. "Mind if I ask a few questions?"

"Be my guest." Ben figured he might as well be magnanimous—since he had no choice about it. Cross-examination was an absolute right, even in depositions.

Colby smiled, apparently trying to put the boy at ease, to make him think he had nothing to fear. And Scout was just innocent enough to believe it.

"Scout," he said pleasantly, "at the time you say you saw the drums being dug up, you were playing a game, weren't you?"

"Sure."

"You and your friend were both pretending, is that right?"

"Uh-huh."

"Have you played that game often?"

"Yup. Lots of times."

"I expect you're pretty good at it by now."

Scout shrugged. "S'pose so."

"A game like that—it probably takes a lot of imagination, doesn't it?"

"I guess."

"You have to do a lot of pretending—pretending things are there that really aren't there."

Ben could see where this was going, but there was nothing he could do about it.

"Like for instance, you pretend there's a monster chasing you—even though it's really just a little boy. Right?"

"Yeah."

"You make everything more exciting and mysterious than it really is, don't you?"

"I guess so."

"I'm glad you're willing to admit it, Scout. Because I'm wondering if that's not what's happened here. With your testimony in this case."

Scout frowned. "Whaddaya mean?"

"It's probably fun being a witness, isn't it? Feeling important. Having grown-ups cater to you. Having Mr. Kincaid wine and dine you."

Scout glanced at Ben. "I didn't get no wine."

Colby grinned. "You know what I mean. I'm wondering if your testimony is what you really saw—or if maybe you used your imagination a bit. Made things more interesting than they really were."

"I told you what I saw."

"Yes, Scout, you did. But I know for a fact that isn't what happened."

Scout glanced at Ben. His breathing grew rapid. "I told the truth, mister. Just like it happened."

"Scout," Colby said calmly, "we've had something like two dozen men testify in this case. Important men. Grown-ups. Executives. And every one of them has said something different than what you did. They say the drums were carried away. No one said the drums were buried."

"Well, they were."

"You're saying all those men were liars, and only you are telling the truth?"

"Well . . ."

"Why would all those men lie, Scout?"

The boy looked distinctly uncomfortable. "I dunno . . ."

"They wouldn't. And I'm sure you didn't mean to lie. You just let your imagination get away from you."

"That's not so."

"I'm sure it makes the story more interesting. It's sort of like finding buried treasure your way, isn't it?"

"I'm telling the truth!"

"Let me show you some photographs of the area behind the plant." Colby pulled the relevant photos out of the shared document file. "Now, you were down here in the ravine, weren't you?"

Ben could see that Scout was treating Colby much more warily than before. "Yeah."

"So you were downhill from the plant at the time you watched the Brush Hog working."

"Yeah."

"But the crane of the Brush Hog was dipping down on the other side. Past the crest of the hill."

"Okay."

"You couldn't see the crane once it dipped out of sight."

" 'Course not."

"So you never actually saw the drums come out of the ground."

"Well, not the instant it happened. But it was obvious—"

Colby's voice became hard and cold. "You didn't actually see it, did you?"

Scout scrunched down in his chair. "No, sir."

"Don't let him intimidate you, Scout," Ben interjected. "You tell what you saw."

"But what did you see?" Colby jumped in, not missing a beat. "You only saw the drums after the crane hauled them into the air. You thought they were coming out of the ground, but in fact the crane was simply picking them up off the surface and moving them to a different location so they could be picked up by the delivery truck."

"I don't think so. I saw the dirt dug up—"

"Scout, you said you didn't actually see the drums come out of the ground!"

"Right."

"Is it possible that what I said was what really happened?"

"I don't think—"

"Listen to the question, boy." His voice was loud and harsh; his eyes accusing. "Is it *possible* that what I said is what really happened?"

Scout's reply was tiny, but audible. "I guess it's possible, but—"

"So what you actually saw happen might have been exactly what every single other witness said happened. Right?"

Scout squirmed. "I guess it's possible, but—"

"Thank you, Scout. I appreciate your honesty. And I don't blame you for this . . . error in your testimony." He glanced up at Ben. "I blame the grown-ups who were exploiting your innocence for their own personal gain."

Colby rose to his feet, smiling. "Any more surprise witnesses, Kincaid?"

Ben's lips were pressed firmly together. "No."

"Pity. I do love surprises. You'll get my summary judgment motion tomorrow morning. Then we can finally put this travesty of a lawsuit to rest."

* 20 *

"Stop!" Mike shouted breathlessly. He was running as fast as he could, which in street shoes and a heavy overcoat was not all that fast. The man he was chasing was staying ahead without even trying hard.

"I said, *stop!*" He raced down the trail, no time to admire the scenery, panting, sweating like a pig. His right hand pressed against the stitch in his side. "Stop! Police!"

The man stopped. He cocked his head to one side, then slowly turned around. "Were you talking to me?"

"Of . . . course . . . I . . . was . . ." Mike said, gasping for breath between each word. He limped forward till he caught up with the man. "I'm . . . Lieutenant Morelli . . . Tulsa PD. Now . . . don't run off again or . . . I'll"—he bent forward, gasping, hands on his knees—"have to get . . . rough. . . ."

"Now, now, take it easy. Relax. Breathe naturally. You'll only make it worse if you start hyperventilating."

"I don't need your help. I'm in top shape."

"Uh-huh." The man, who was wearing a color-coordinated

gray running suit with a neon pink headband, did not appear convinced. "Do you by any chance smoke?"

"Used to. Gave it up."

"Good for you. When you smoked, you were flirting with death."

"Yeah. But I was a lot happier." He pulled himself up and wiped the sweat from his brow. "Why didn't you stop sooner? I started chasing you half a mile back there."

"Sorry. Didn't hear you." He pointed to the Discman strapped to his belt. Headphones dangled around his neck. "Smashing Pumpkins."

"Wonderful. Are you George Philby?"

"Guilty as charged."

"Good. Can I talk to you for a moment?"

"I suppose. But I'm on my lunch break. I have to be back by one."

Mike nodded. They were standing on a jogging trail that wove through a forest not far from the Blaylock headquarters office building. "It's about Margaret Caldwell."

"I figured you weren't here to root out financial irregularities. You've been talking to a lot of people in the office, haven't you?"

"Yeah. And they tell me you were one of Margaret's best friends. Probably her best friend at work."

"That may be so." Philby was in his late forties or early fifties, but he still had a full head of thick brown hair and the waistline of a nineteen-year-old. The result of spending lunch running instead of snarfing cheeseburgers, Mike supposed. "God, I still can't believe she's gone."

"Any idea why someone might want to get rid of her?"

"No. Margaret was a precious person. Sweet. Kind. Good-natured. Generous. Those qualities aren't that common anymore. Especially in the legal department."

"But Margaret wasn't a lawyer, right?"

"Right, right. She was what we call an executive assistant. Fancy term for a glorified secretary, really. But Margaret was great at what she did. One of the best ever."

"Now, you *are* a lawyer, am I right about that?"

"Guilty again."

"But you hung out with a secretary?"

"I hung out with Margaret, and Margaret was as smart and witty as any lawyer. More so than most. She could've practiced law, if she'd wanted. I wasn't going to hold a grudge against her just because she didn't spend three miserable years in law school."

Mike nodded. Couldn't fault the man for that. "Was there anyone who didn't like her?"

Philby took a moment, but he didn't come up with anything. "I can't think of anyone. And if there was someone, I think I'd know about it."

"What did the two of you do together? When you weren't working, I mean."

"Well, our friendship was largely work-based. But we did meet occasionally outside the hallowed halls of H. P. Blaylock. You know. Friday night happy hour. Birthday parties. And we went on fishing trips together. That woman loved to fish."

"Did she? That seems unusual. For a woman, I mean."

"Not really, Lieutenant. You've got to chuck those sexist attitudes. I know lots of women who like to fish. It's peaceful. Calming. Meditative."

"So, was it just the two of you on these meditative excursions?"

"Oh, no no no no." He held up his hands. "I hope people haven't given you the wrong idea. There was never anything . . . intimate between us. We were just good friends. There would usually be other work friends along on these occasions."

"Uh-huh." Mike scribbled something into his notebook. "What was she working on? At the office, I mean."

"Oh, everything, really. Whatever came through the door."

"Was she working on that toxic waste case?"

Philby arched an eyebrow. "I see you stay informed on the latest and greatest in the legal world."

Mike shrugged. "I have a buddy who keeps me up to date."

"Like most big corporations, Blaylock farms big litigation matters to outside counsel. We in-house lawyers monitor, but we don't do much of the work."

"That must rankle a bit."

"How do you mean?"

"You guys are permitted to handle the grunt work, but if something important comes along, they take it elsewhere."

Philby shrugged. "It's the way of the corporate world. Whenever any significant dollars are at stake, they send the case out. It's the greener grass syndrome—corporate bigwigs always assume the best lawyers are the most expensive ones."

"And that's not you?"

"If I was into glory and prestige, I'd be working in a big skyscraper in downtown Tulsa." He smiled. "Look, I know what mountains I have and haven't climbed. I decided a long time ago how I was going to live my life. I intentionally chose a job that would pay less—but would leave me more time for a real life. A family. So, no—my ego isn't bruised by this sort of thing."

Darn mature of him, Mike thought. But he wondered if anyone could possibly be that mature. "So you don't know of anyone who would have a reason to kill Margaret?"

"I'm afraid not."

"Was she acting . . . unusually? Before she was killed, I mean. Was she . . . doing anything odd?"

"No. Everything seemed absolutely normal. Until she disappeared, of course. She was gone for some time before her body was discovered in that waste drum."

"Yeah, I know. What about that, anyway? Why would anyone want to stick her body in a steel drum?"

"I can't imagine. Just convenient, I suppose. They're always lined up outside, behind the plant. Anyone could've gotten to them."

"Great. I'll narrow my list of suspects to 'anyone.' " Mike shoved his hands into his coat pockets. "Can you think of anything else that might be helpful?"

"I'm sorry. I can't." He paused. "The article in the paper seemed to suggest that her death was very . . . unorthodox. Grisly, even."

"I'm afraid that's true. I'm not at liberty to discuss the details."

Philby's voice slowed, as if he was suddenly choosing his words more carefully. "Do you think her death . . . is connected to . . . that other employee who was murdered not long before?"

"I don't know. The M.O.s are significantly different, but still . . ." He cut himself off. No reason to explain his hunches to this fellow.

"Some of the guys at the office say Blaylock is cursed. That's why all these people are dying."

"And why would Blaylock be cursed?"

"Beats me." Philby winked. "Revenge of the Blackwood water wells?"

Mike didn't smile. "Here's my card," he said, pulling it out of his pocket. "If you do think of anything—"

"I'll call you immediately."

"I'd appreciate it. I'd really like to catch this killer. As soon as possible. Thanks for your time." Mike turned away, then stopped. "Oh—one other thing I wanted to ask. Do you know whether Margaret knew Harvey Pendergast?"

"Harvey . . . Pendergast?" Creases formed across his forehead. "He was the first victim, wasn't he?"

"Right."

"I think I read . . . Did he work in Personnel?"

"That's right. Did she know him?"

Philby shrugged. "I don't know. Why would she?"

"What about you? Did you know him?"

"Me?" He pressed his hand against his sweat suit. "Why would I know him?"

Mike noticed that Philby had suddenly started failing to give yes or no answers. "Does that mean you did or you didn't?"

"Didn't. I didn't know him at all." He cleared his throat. "Don't think I ever met the man. It's a big plant, you know. Thousands of employees."

Mike peered deeply into the man's eyes. There was no objective reason to doubt what he was saying. And yet . . .

"Well, I'll stay in touch," Mike informed him. "I may have more questions later. If I do—I'll try to catch you when you're not running. My heart can't take much more of that."

"Now that you're off the smokes, you should take up jogging. It'd be good for you. You'll live longer."

"Says you. I have a theory. I think we're all born with so many heartbeats. So why waste any of them?"

"Well, who knows? You might be right."

"Exactly." Mike tucked his notepad into his back pocket. "And in this world of uncertainty, I prefer to take the options that don't involve getting sweaty."

The green-eyed man peered through his binoculars from behind the trees and brush about a hundred feet from the jogging trail. He was well hidden; they couldn't have seen him if they'd been looking, which they weren't. He was totally safe, as long as he didn't step out. Which, unfortunately, he had almost done.

He was planning to put the snatch on Party Member Number Three today—his old pal George Philby. A lunchtime snatch seemed not only audacious but unexpected enough to escape detection and distinctive enough to confuse the cops. He had transportation all arranged, as well as a big surprise for George when they got back to his apartment. Something new and exciting.

He smiled. And shocking.

But then the damn cop had put in his appearance. Of course, he'd grown accustomed to seeing his plodding figure circling around the plant. That was all right, he supposed. The man was only doing his job, and not doing it particularly well.

But this was different. Instead of cleaning up the mess after he was gone, this time, the cop was talking to his next intended. Why? Was it just dumb luck? It could be coincidence; he knew the cop had been talking to damn near everyone in the company. Or was there something more? Had he actually uncovered the connection?

Of course not, the man reassured himself. How could he? There was no way it could happen. Unless one of them talked. And he was in the process of systematically ensuring that never occurred.

Still, he had to admit it was a bit unsettling. What if the cop had arrived a few moments later, after he'd started the snatch? That could have led to some seriously unpleasant consequences. Sure, he could've handled it, he thought, as he reached deep into his coat pocket and fingered the handle of his trusty ball-peen hammer. But unexpected events like that were not his specialty. Careful planning had been the hallmark of his success. Advance planning. Research. When plans began to unravel . . . anything could happen.

He would have to keep a close eye on Lieutenant Morelli. And he might have to step up his timetable. But he would stick to the master plan. Get the job done. Recover the merchandise.

And if Morelli tried to get in his way . . .

Well, he'd keep his hammer polished. Just in case.

Fred the Feeb raced down the jogging trail back toward the plant. This had been a stupid idea from the get-go. Stupid, stupid, stupid. And now it threatened to turn into a full-fledged disaster.

He had known it was risky, trying to talk to George. But, Jesus Christ, what were they supposed to do? Sit here like cattle and get slaughtered one after the other? Maybe if they conferred, banded together, they could figure out what to do. Of course, he would've had to lie to George. Pretend he wasn't the one who had the merchandise. But that was okay. George would never suspect, even if there was no one else in their little group left alive. Who would ever suspect Fred the Feeb?

Just as he was about to approach George, he saw the cop. Christ, wouldn't that have been great? He'd been ducking that lug since Harvey was killed, and now he almost blundered right into the man's lap.

He stood on the sidelines for a moment, acting like he was admiring the scenery, not paying any attention to them. He was there long enough to hear George tell the cop he hadn't known Harvey, that he couldn't imagine what connection there might be between the victims. What bullshit. And he did it all with a straight face.

Before he attracted too much attention, Fred had turned and headed back in the opposite direction. But not so fast he didn't see . . . something else. Just a glimpse, a blurry image as he swerved around on the trail. But it was definitely something. He hadn't imagined it.

Someone was hiding in the brush just beyond the trail. Watching.

He didn't stop to see who it was, of course. He was already

running, and that only made him run all the faster. Could have been anyone. . . .

Who was he kidding? he asked himself as he raced back toward the plant, his heart pounding in his chest. Who else would be hiding in the bushes? Who else would be stalking George? It could only be one person.

The killer. Harvey's killer. Maggie's killer.

George would be next.

Which at the least meant Fred himself wasn't next. But it also meant he couldn't be far behind.

Forget about talking to George, he counseled himself. George was a dead man. The best thing Fred could do now was stay as far away from him as possible. And figure out how to get himself to safety. Without giving up the merchandise.

That was the trick. A smarter man would've probably just given it up. You can't spend it when you're dead, right? But he had worked so hard for this. Had invested so much time. It was his ultimate triumph over those clods who had always treated him like a second stringer. His final in-your-face.

He couldn't give that up now. No matter how stupid it was. Or lethal. He just couldn't do it.

He slowed as he approached the office building. He was safe now, for the moment at least, and he didn't want to arouse suspicion.

He strolled calmly through the back door. He ducked into the men's room, ripped off a paper towel, and mopped his brow.

He couldn't go on forever like this. He had to do something. But what?

What could he possibly do?

* 21 *

It was a beautiful Oklahoma day—the sun was shining, the ozone count was down, the azaleas were blooming—and how was Loving spending this magnificent day? Trapped in a suit and tie, standing in a reception line outside the First Baptist Church of Blackwood, Oklahoma.

Such a job he had.

Loving grabbed the man's hand and pumped it enthusiastically. "Great sermon, Reverend."

The Baptist minister smiled modestly. "Oh, it was nothing."

"Nothin'? I thought it was dynamite. The best I've heard in years." Which was absolutely true—because Loving hadn't been inside a church in years. Not since he married Laverne, and that was one hell of a long time ago now.

"Well," the reverend beamed, "sometimes the Holy Spirit does move me. I'm only a vessel, you know. Only a vessel."

"I 'specially liked that part about not bearin' false witness. And not holdin' back when you have a chance to help someone in need." Loving whipped around to face the man behind him. "Didn't you, Archie?"

Archie Turnbull was stunned. His lips parted speechlessly.

Turnbull was wearing what was obviously his Sunday best, which was still not very good. He was standing next to his wife, a middle-aged woman with a pleasant expression, and six children of various ages, including a young preteenaged girl.

Turnbull's wife smiled, a bit uneasily. "I don't believe we've met."

"My name's Loving," he said, extending his hand. "I'm your husband's conscience. So it's only natural that I would come to church with him."

Her brow furrowed. "I don't quite understand—"

"Archie can explain it to you."

"You . . . know Archie?"

"Archie and I have met," Loving said, not taking his eyes off the man. "Several times."

"What are you doing here?" Archie said urgently. He glanced around, trying to see if anyone was watching. "This is our *church*, for God's sake!"

"What better place?" Loving replied. "The truth shall set you free, Archie." He glanced over at the girl. "I guess this must be Becky." He smiled. "I can see why Billy Elkins liked her."

"Leave my family alone!" Turnbull pushed his wife and children toward the parking lot as quickly as possible.

Loving watched as they scurried away from him. Coming to the man's church had been a pretty extreme tactic, but time was running out. Soon the summary judgment motion would make the truth a moot point. He had wanted to take one more shot at cracking Turnbull before it was too late.

One last, desperate shot. And he had failed.

Mike was surprised to find out how many people worked at the Blaylock plant on a Sunday. He was also surprised to see that there could be so many employees he hadn't talked to yet. It seemed like he had grilled everyone here, some of them twice. But of course, even using every available man in his department, that wasn't possible. The best he could do was quiz those who seemed most closely related to the victims. But if there was one thing of which Mike was now certain, it was that whatever the link between them might have been, if there was one, it wasn't immediately apparent. So for all he knew, he could be interviewing exactly the wrong people.

And on that happy note, he decided to go to the bathroom. Some daily chores were inescapable, even for a master detective. He pushed into one of the stalls, locked the door, pulled down his pants, and took a seat on the porcelain throne.

Maybe a minute later, he heard the rush of air that told him someone else had entered the bathroom. He didn't think much about it—not until he heard the footsteps stop just outside his stall.

"Psst."

Mike stared at the closed stall door. Was this for real?

"Psst. Are you the cop?"

Mike considered lying about it, but what the hell. "Yeah. Who wants to know?"

"I gotta talk to you."

Mike wondered to whom he was speaking. He didn't recognize the voice. All he could see was that he was wearing badly tattered brown Hush Puppies. "Give me a minute. I'll be right out."

"I don't have a minute."

Mike rolled his eyes. Everyone was in such a goddamn hurry these days. "Just one minute and I'll—"

"Here's all I wanted to tell you. Follow the money."

Follow the money? What the hell did that mean? It sounded like something out of *All the President's Men.* Or was that "*Show* me the money?" He could never keep his movies straight. "Look, who are you, anyway?"

"Gotta go." Mike saw the Hush Puppies disappear from the opening below the stall door.

As quickly as possible, Mike pulled up his pants and opened the door.

His informant was gone.

He raced out the door, well aware that he had not yet taken time to attend to such amenities as zipping up his fly.

No sight of his mysterious informant. The people working in the offices outside looked as if they hadn't moved in a year.

After he'd pulled himself together, Mike walked the floor, checking for the Hush Puppies. He didn't find any. Could be the guy had another pair of shoes. Could be he didn't work on this floor. For that matter, could be he didn't work in the whole damn building.

Mike interrogated several people on the floor, but no one had noticed anyone going into or out of the men's room.

Which left Mike back at square one. Exactly where he had been before. With one minor difference.

Follow the money?

Archie Turnbull sat in a darkened room. All the lights were off, although the television was on, casting an unearthly flickering blue glow over his skin. There was a bottle of Jack Daniel's on the table beside him, half empty. He was cradling a glass in his hands, half full.

The booze had hit his stomach like a Molotov cocktail. He hadn't eaten all day, several days maybe. He hadn't slept well for weeks, not since this whole business began. Tonight, he had snapped at Becky for no reason. Well, that wasn't true. There was a reason. But the fault was his, not hers.

He heard the soft shuffle of his wife's slippers in the room behind him. "I'm going to bed now," she announced.

"Good," he answered. "It's late."

"Are you coming?"

"No. Not now." He turned slightly. "I'll be up later."

There was a long pause. "Is there anything I can get you?"

He didn't answer her directly. "Gloria, have you ever been over to see Cecily Elkins? I mean, since . . . Billy."

"No," she replied. "I've thought about it often enough. I wanted to . . . I don't know. To take her a pot roast or something. Anything that might help. But every time I started, I . . . I just never made it."

She didn't need to explain. He knew exactly what she was talking about. He had been through the same thing himself. He'd also thought of going over, trying to comfort Cecily. God knows he'd been over often enough when Billy was alive; he'd always liked and admired Cecily. And the boy. But since Billy died, somehow, that house had become off-limits. It had become a house of death. And whether due to superstition or just plain fear, he didn't want to go there. No parent would. He knew that, after the initial burst of sympathy, most of the other families in Blackwood had stopped visiting, too.

His wife spoke again. "I guess in part I thought she wouldn't want to see me. I mean, since you work at Blaylock and all."

Turnbull nodded his understanding. When he'd first heard that Cecily was blaming the plant for her son's death, he thought she'd gone off the deep end. A pathetic lonely mother desperately grasping at straws. But now . . .

"You know, Archie . . . it wouldn't matter to me"—he could sense she was struggling with words, struggling to express something she only barely understood—"whatever you want to do. I've always trusted you. You've always taken good care of me."

"That's what I'm trying to do now."

"But I don't need money or . . . promotions or cars or any of that to be taken care of, Archie. And that goes for the children, too. All we need is you. All we want is for you to be happy."

Thank you, he thought silently, into the void surrounding him. Thank you for releasing me.

"I love you," he said, after a long while.

"I know you do," she replied. "It's one of your best qualities."

He listened to the soft swishing sounds of her slippers as she padded up the stairs. After she was long gone, he pushed the Jack Daniel's bottle away, picked up the phone, and dialed 4–1–1.

"Yeah. I need the number for an attorney. No, I don't know exactly where he is. Somewhere in Tulsa. The last name's Kincaid."

Ben knew if he formally announced that he wanted to redepose Turnbull, Colby would fight tooth and nail to prevent it, and Blaylock would bring every ounce of pressure he could on the poor man. So he decided to surprise them. Why not? Colby had said he liked surprises.

Colby was expecting a middle-level functionary from the EPA when he instead saw Archie Turnbull enter the deposition room. "What's going on here?" he said, rising.

"I've got a few more questions for Mr. Turnbull," Ben said nonchalantly.

"You can't do that. You've already deposed him."

"I kept the depo open in the event further information was uncovered, remember? And boy, has it ever been uncovered."

Colby turned his attention to Turnbull. "What's happening here? I told you if you had any questions about the suit or your testimony, you were to call me."

Turnbull averted his eyes nervously.

Colby blazed ahead. "I don't know what you think you're up to, Kincaid, but it won't wash. This man works for H. P.

Blaylock. That makes him de facto my client. I will not permit him to be deposed or redeposed unless and until I've had an adequate opportunity to prepare him."

"I think you've already prepared him quite enough," Ben answered. "Are you ready to proceed, Mr. Turnbull?"

"I am."

"Then I see no reason to delay. Please take a seat."

Colby was enraged. "Have you been talking to Turnbull behind my back? In case you've forgotten, Kincaid, the Rules of Professional Conduct preclude you from speaking to my clients outside my presence, and in the case of a corporation, that includes all the employees."

"I haven't said a word to the man," Ben replied. "All I've done is listen. And I got an earful. Now stop whining and sit down."

The witness was resworn. Ben saw no point in repeating the preliminaries. He cut straight to the quick. "We're on the record. Mr. Turnbull, this deposition is a continuation of your previous deposition taken in this suit two weeks ago today—"

"To which I object," Colby cut in. "For the record, I have not had proper notice. Mr. Kincaid is deposing my witness without giving me an opportunity to prepare. I move to strike the entire proceeding."

"Objection noted, but this is just a continuation of the previous deposition, for which Mr. Colby had notice and ample time to prepare." He knew he had to keep moving. If he gave Colby a toehold, he'd never get through this. "Mr. Turnbull, have you had a chance to reflect on the testimony you gave two weeks ago?"

"I have."

"Is there any aspect of your prior testimony you wish to . . . change? Or amend?"

"Objection!" Colby fumed. "Leading the witness!"

"I can lead. He's your witness."

"Not today, he isn't. Again, I object. This is outrageous."

"The witness may answer the question," Ben intoned, ignoring Colby.

"Yes," Turnbull replied. "There are some things I . . . didn't get quite right last time."

"With regard to what?"

"Blaylock's waste-disposal procedures."

"Please describe to me what really happened."

"Objection!" Colby shouted. "What is this, deposition by ambush?"

Ben kept his eyes focused straight ahead. "The witness will answer the question."

Turnbull started, but Colby cut him off.

"No, he will not!" Colby rose to his feet. "This is the most grossly inappropriate procedure I've encountered in twenty-three years of practicing law. As the representative of the defendant and the witness's employer, I instruct the witness not to answer."

Ben drew in his breath. He had suspected Colby would try something like this. And planned accordingly. "Are you claiming this question intrudes upon the attorney-client privilege?"

"No, I'm claiming this whole procedure is grossly inappropriate!"

"Because the witness is trying to tell the truth? Yeah, I can see how that might put your nose out of joint."

Colby looked as if the top of his head might fly off at any moment. "This deposition is over." He walked behind the court reporter and yanked the power cord to her laptop out of the wall socket.

"You don't have the right to terminate my deposition, Colby," Ben said.

"This is my conference room," he growled. "I'll do whatever the hell I please."

Ben walked around the large mahogany table. He opened the door a crack. "Christina?"

She appeared in an instant. "He's on line one. We've been talking about cocker spaniels."

Good old Christina. She knew everyone, or at least knew someone who knew someone who knew someone. He reentered the conference room and strolled to the phone.

"That's my phone," Colby spat out, "and I'm not taking any calls."

"Oh, I think you'll want to take this one." He punched the button to activate the speakerphone. "Are you there?"

"This is Magistrate Grant. What seems to be the problem?"

As red as Colby's face had been before, it became absolutely ashen when he heard the voice on the phone.

"Magistrate Grant," Ben said, "we're having a bit of a discovery dispute here. I remember when we were in your office you said you were available to resolve any problems that might arise. I appreciate you being good to your word."

The magistrate's voice crackled over the speaker box. "What's the problem, Mr. Kincaid?"

After the initial shock faded, Colby recovered himself. "The problem is," he shouted across the room, "Kincaid's trying to depose my witness without giving me advance notice!"

"That's not precisely so," Ben said calmly. "This is a continuation of a deposition taken two weeks before, of which Mr. Colby had notice and ample prep time. Last night, the witness called me on his own initiative and told me he wanted to amend his testimony. Naturally, I want to give him a chance to do so."

"It's grossly improper!" Colby shouted. "Kincaid can't contact my clients!"

"He contacted me," Ben emphasized. "The only thing I told him was where and when to show up."

"Well, that doesn't seem improper to me," the magistrate remarked. "A bit irregular, perhaps, but not improper."

"But I haven't even had a chance to talk to the man!" Colby insisted.

"Is the witness there?" the magistrate asked.

Turnbull cleared his throat. "Uh, yes, sir. I am."

"Do you wish to speak to your attorney?"

"No, sir. I don't. We've spoken before and . . . I'm ready to proceed now."

"Well," the magistrate said, "I'm not going to force a man to consult with counsel against his will."

"He's my witness!" Colby spat back.

"Yes," the magistrate said. His voice had acquired a bit of an edge. "He's your witness. He's not your property. If he wants to testify, he can. So get on with it. I'll remain on the line, just in case there are any additional problems."

Colby lowered himself into his chair, so angry he could

barely contain himself. The court reporter plugged herself back in. Ben retook his seat.

"Mr. Turnbull, please describe Blaylock's waste-disposal procedures. As they really were practiced."

"Objection," Colby said. "Asked and answered."

"Overruled." The magistrate's voice came in clear over the speaker box.

"Then I object for lack of personal knowledge."

"Overruled," the magistrate repeated, without missing a beat. "The witness will answer."

"The liquid waste was collected in drums, and sometimes the drums were hauled off to designated disposal sites," Turnbull said. "But that was expensive, and Mr. Blaylock was always trying to cut costs. So sometimes he wouldn't do it. Especially during busy periods when a great amount of waste collected."

"What did you do instead?"

"Objection," Colby said. "Assumes facts not in evidence."

"Overruled," the magistrate said. "Mr. Colby, please don't interrupt unless you have an objection that is at least arguably applicable."

Colby burrowed down in his chair, his lips pressed tightly together.

"I'll ask again," Ben said. "What did you do when you didn't have the drums hauled away?"

"We buried them."

Ben nodded. Scout had been right. He *had* seen drums coming out of the ground.

"We had a big Brush Hog behind the plant. So someone would dig a hole and bury the drums. Saved Blaylock a significant amount of money."

"How many drums were buried? Five? Ten?"

"Try fifty or sixty."

Ben's eyes widened. "How sturdy were the steel drums?"

"We didn't use steel drums. At least not most of the time. We did keep a few out back, but they were mostly for show. The ones we actually used were made of corrugated cardboard. They were less expensive than the steel variety, obviously. They might look the same from a distance, but they weren't the same. They broke much more easily."

"And did they break?"

"All the time. Frequently. Particularly when we were trying to bury them. And when they broke, the waste would spill all over the ground."

Ben nodded. And from the ground to the groundwater to the ravine to the aquifer to the water well. Just like that.

"Are the drums still buried behind the plant?"

"No. Mr. Blaylock ordered that they be removed about two months ago."

Exactly when Scout and Jim were playing the "Outsider" game. Scout had seen exactly what he thought he'd seen. "Do you know why they were moved?"

Turnbull's head turned slightly. "I believe it was done on the advice of counsel."

Ben's chin rose. "Mr. Colby, I believe you are guilty of tampering with evidence and obstructing justice."

"Mr. Kincaid." The magistrate's voice crackled. "Don't make accusations you can't substantiate. I've told you before I won't tolerate that."

Ben kept his silence. He would never be able to prove that Colby deliberately hid evidence by advising Blaylock to get rid of the drums. But he had. Ben knew it, and the court reporter knew it, and the magistrate knew it. Soon, everyone in town would know it. Colby's reputation would never be the same.

"Anything further to tell us, Mr. Turnbull?" Ben asked.

"No," he said, head down. "That's all. Except—I'm sorry."

"Sir, you have nothing to be sorry about. You're a brave man." He glanced up at Colby. "Care to withdraw your motion for summary judgment?"

Colby coughed into his hand. "I . . . may have to amend my brief. Refile on other grounds."

"You do that." Ben thanked the magistrate for his assistance, then disconnected him. "Mr. Turnbull, would you like to walk back to my office with me? Cecily Elkins is back there. I think she'd like to talk to you."

Turnbull's eyes brightened. "Yes. I'd like that very much." He pushed out of his chair. "I have a few things to say to her, too. And I've waited far too long to do it."

* 22 *

Ben drove his van back toward Tulsa after spending the morning in Blackwood. It was the most pleasant morning he'd had in weeks—possibly since this lawsuit began. He'd assembled Cecily and all the other plaintiff-parents to give them an update on the status of the case.

Ben started the meeting with the good news: they had a witness who would testify—had testified—that Blaylock's waste product had seeped into the soil, just as the EPA suspected. The bad news? Their work was just beginning. They would need expert witnesses to prove Blaylock's TCE and perc did in fact seep into the water supply. That would be expensive, but Ben believed it could and would be proven. But even after they met that burden, they would need experts to prove that the contaminated water had caused the children's leukemia. That would be far more difficult—but essential to their case.

Ben left them on an upbeat note, but made it clear they still had a long way to go before judgment. It was hard, staring out into that sea of faces, confronting those hopeful, wide-eyed expressions. He had the sense that, strange as it might seem, he had taken the place of their children, that they had bundled up all their remaining sorrow and guilt and lost hopes and deposited them on one Ben Kincaid. They were counting on him to give some meaning to all those days they had spent raising a child who never reached adulthood, all those messy diapers and sleepless nights, all those dreams.

He only hoped he wouldn't let them down.

*   *   *

Back at the office, Jones was fuming. "Guess what we got in the mail this morning?"

Ben wasn't in the mood for guessing games. "Judging by your expression, I'd say it must be a bill."

"Darn tootin'. Do you have any idea how much you blew taking all those depositions?"

Ben peered at the bottom line on the invoice Jones was waving. He did a double take. It was twice what he had expected.

"Sorry, Jones. It was necessary."

"Necessary? Thirty-two depositions? Couldn't you have skipped the losers?"

"Unfortunately, you can't separate the winners from the losers until after you take their depositions."

"Well, then couldn't you have asked fewer questions? Or asked them faster?"

"There's no point doing it if you're not going to do it right. You have to be thorough if you hope to drag anything out of unwilling witnesses."

"Fine." Jones folded his arms. "Tell me, Mr. Thorough, how exactly are we going to pay this bill?"

"I thought the last loan—"

"Long gone."

"Gone? That was supposed to last us through the trial."

"Well, surprise, surprise. It didn't even come close."

"Where did it go?"

Jones threw his hands up in the air. "Where do you want me to begin? This case has been a money pit since day one— as I predicted. You totally wiped us out with that battery of experts you hired. Geologists and hydrologists and all that rot."

"We can't make this case without expert testimony."

"Did you need so many?"

"I didn't get nearly as many as I would've liked." Ben felt himself getting hot under the collar. This was ridiculous. He was being put on the defensive—by his employee. "I needed a geologist to analyze the soil behind the plant, in the ravine, and at the water well to prove it was contaminated. I needed a hydrologist to prove the groundwater from Blaylock made it to Well B. They all have to conduct tests, which must be run twice for confirmation, once by themselves, once by independent analysts. They've got to consult with specialists, prepare exhibits."

"It's too expensive."

"It's only just begun. I still need doctors to provide medical testimony about each of the children's illnesses. I've got to have a cancer specialist talk about the causes of leukemia, to tie it to the tainted well—"

"Which you don't have yet."

"The point is, I've already cut expenses to the bone. If I do any more, we'll be throwing the case away. And if we do that, we have no chance of recovering anything."

Jones sat in his chair and stewed. A long period passed during which neither of them spoke.

"I'm not going back to The Brain," Jones said finally.

"Jones, you have to."

"I've done it the last three times. I'm not doing it again."

"It's your job."

"I don't care. I'm tired of groveling for change. I feel like a little boy asking for an advance on his allowance. I refuse."

Ben could see they were at a stalemate. "Fine. I'll go."

"Wonderful. I'll make you an appointment." He pointed across his desk. "By the way, you got a big package from Colby. I think he's taking his revenge for the Turnbull depo."

Ben picked up the hefty stack of paper and rifled through it.

"Eight motions? *Eight?*"

"Guess he thought you had too much free time on your hands."

"*Eight?* How can he do this?"

"When you have forty or so associates at your disposal, you can do about anything." He smiled thinly. "The one that matters is on top."

Ben glanced at the titles of the motions and their attached briefs (few of which were, in fact, brief). Three motions in limine, trying to keep out various pieces of evidence, including Turnbull's testimony. Two discovery motions, one requesting not only medical records, but requesting that each of the plaintiffs undergo an extensive (and no doubt humiliating) battery of medical and psychological tests. A motion for physical inspection of the plaintiffs' homes. A motion for censure against that notorious embarrassment to the local bar, Benjamin Kincaid. But as Jones had said, the best was the one on top.

A motion for summary judgment.

"Son of a bitch," Ben murmured. "He did it anyway."

"He came up with different grounds," Jones explained. "Some legal mumbo jumbo I didn't begin to understand."

Ben thumbed rapidly through the brief. It seemed the legal scholars at Raven, Tucker & Tubb had been working double time. The motion hinged on a Supreme Court case called *Daubert v. Merrill Dow Pharmaceuticals* which, according to the Raven brief, established standards for scientific testimony. According to the brief, this case precluded Ben from putting on evidence at trial about the causes of leukemia—which of course would make the parents' case unwinnable. Therefore, Raven argued, summary judgment should be entered against the parents now.

After all this work. All this time and money. Summary judgment. Ben's chest felt as if his heart had stopped beating.

"Can this be right?" Ben said softly, under his breath.

"Don't ask me," Jones replied. "But it looks good on paper. And they've got a lot of cases supporting their position."

Which was true. The brief's table of cases went on for three pages. Most were cases Ben had never heard of.

"What are you going to do?" Jones asked.

Ben dropped the briefs on the desk, feeling forlorn and useless. "I don't know. When she comes in, ask Christina to go to the library and start working on all this."

"Boss, she can't possibly—"

"She's a law student. She knows her way around the library."

"But Boss—*eight motions*?"

"I'll help."

"You've got your own work to take care of. You've got stacks of documents you still haven't waded through. Depo transcripts you haven't read. Experts to locate and prepare."

"We have no choice."

"Boss—you need help."

Ben arched an eyebrow. "What did you have in mind?"

"I don't know. Can't you . . . hire an associate?"

"Hire an associate with what? No money, remember?"

"You're going to have to do something."

Ben blew air through his lips, suddenly feeling enormously tired. "Thanks for telling me something I didn't already know." He started toward his office. "Did I mention that I hate civil litigation?"

"No," Jones said, with a wry smile. "Why?"

"Because there's nothing civil about it."

Mike stared glassy-eyed at the mound of paper covering his desk. He hated paperwork. Hated it with a passion. Avoidance of paperwork could well be the secret reason he'd decided to become a cop in the first place. He wanted to be Starsky and Hutch, not Bob Cratchit.

So why was he—top homicide detective in the Tulsa police department—going over these blinking accounting records?

It had taken him more than a week to pry these financial statements out of H. P. Blaylock. He'd had to bully, swagger, threaten, cajole, wave subpoenae in the air. Finally, experiencing a rare moment of triumph, he got what he wanted.

Except, now that he had it, he didn't know what to do with it.

He couldn't read this spreadsheet crap. He couldn't even balance his checkbook. He'd been an English major, for God's sake. And although there were many reasons for that choice, one of the highest ranking was definitely—no math.

He couldn't begin to decode all this accountant gobbledygook. Much as he hated to admit it, he needed assistance.

He punched the intercom button on his phone. "Nita?"

The floor secretary was there. "Yes, Mike?"

"I need a consultant. Who's the top accountant in our white-collar crimes division?"

"That would be Pfieffer."

"Not Pfieffer!"

" 'Fraid so."

Mike groaned. "Okay, who's the bottom accountant?"

"That would also be Pfieffer."

"Are you saying he's the only accountant we have on staff?"

"Where do you think you are, New York City? Of course he's the only accountant we have."

Great. Just great. "Would you please tell Mr. Pfieffer that I would like to request an audience with him at the earliest possible opportunity?"

"I will." She giggled. "Can I come and watch?"

"No." He slammed the phone receiver down. He hated to be harsh with a sweetie like Nita. But some things just weren't funny.

Ben checked his watch again. Thirty minutes. He'd been waiting thirty minutes. If he were in a doctor's office, of course, that would be nothing. But in a bank, it seemed like an eternity.

Finally, a bleached blond secretary escorted him into The Brain's interior office. He was actually named Cecil Conrad Eversole II. He was twice as old as Ben and about half the size, a tiny man who seemed almost entirely enveloped by his white starched shirt and pinstripes.

The Brain was sitting at his desk, bifocals poised at the end of his nose, staring at some documents. When he spotted Ben, he offered a slight smile. "Always a pleasure to see you, Ben."

Ben scrunched down in a chair, already feeling cranky. "If it's such a pleasure, why did I have to wait so long?"

"Sorry about that. Busy day. Hope you weren't too miserable."

"I was. I hate banks."

The Brain did a double take. "You hate banks? Why?"

"Because I don't have any money in them."

The banker smiled. "Anyway, how much will it be?"

Ben blinked. "How . . . much?"

"Of course. I assume since you're here in person this time, you're planning to pay back some—"

He froze. The expression on Ben's face told him how mistaken he was.

"Oh, no," he whispered under his breath. "No, no. Please no. Don't tell me—"

"I need more money."

"I made it clear to Mr. Jones last time that it was absolutely your last trip to the well."

Ben squirmed. "We've got this big lawsuit going—"

"I know all about the class action suit. Mr. Jones has briefed me extensively."

Ben fingered his collar. "Well, then, you must realize that the potential for recovery is . . . unlimited."

"I think it's speculative in the extreme. I think you were foolish to take the case."

Well, that was going to make this more complicated. "We've had some unforeseen expenses. But I've no doubt that in the end—"

The Brain cut him off with a wave of his hand. "Let me make this easier for you, Ben. No."

"Excuse me?"

"No. Absolutely not. Not a penny more."

"But—we're in the middle of a lawsuit!"

"All the more reason. This is a responsible financial institution. We can't throw good money after bad."

"But—"

"Ben, I'm trying to make this easy for you because I like you. I'm trying to spare you the mortification of making a lot of desperate pleas. They won't work. I cannot loan you any more money."

"But I've got to hire experts—"

"My colleagues think I was crazy to humor you as long as I did. Making loans with a lawsuit as collateral is preposterous."

"Then—take something else as collateral. Take the title to my van."

"Already got it."

"Take a lien on our office equipment."

"Did that months ago."

"Then—take a lien on my personal possessions."

"I can't, Ben. You don't have anything anyone else would ever want to have." He fidgeted with a pencil. "This is making me most uncomfortable, Ben. Please desist."

Ben threw himself back in his chair. "There must be some way. I can't just abandon the case."

"I don't think you have any choice. I can't loan you any more money for a lawsuit. And no one else in town will, either."

Ben felt his weight sinking into the cushioned pads of the chair. There had to be some way to continue.

"Hear what I'm saying, Ben. I cannot loan you any more money for a lawsuit."

Ben tilted his head slightly. The way The Brain was overemphasizing some of the words—it was almost as if he was trying to tell him something. Tell him something without saying it.

The light dawned. "What if the money . . . wasn't for a lawsuit?"

The Brain arched an eyebrow. "Go on."

"What if it were something more . . . ordinary?"

"An ordinary business expense?" He shuffled his papers around. "That, of course, would be an entirely different matter."

"What if I simply wanted to . . . expand my business?"

The Brain shrugged. "A loan of that nature would be a far simpler matter. Principally the decision would be based upon an analysis of your most recent financial statements and your potential gains after the implemented expansion. I believe I have a copy of your last year's profits."

"I had a pretty good year last year. Well, for me."

"What kind of expansion did you have in mind?"

"Well . . . I've been thinking of bringing in another lawyer. So I could handle more business."

"A sound business move. Assuming you have more business."

"Oh, I do. More than I can handle. And I've been thinking about hiring some . . . outside consultants. To enable my firm to handle a . . . wider variety of legal matters."

"That, too, is a sound business practice." For all his stoicism, The Brain seemed to be suppressing a smile. "Of course, you're carrying a lot of debt already."

"But that's all secured. Valuable collateral."

The Brain made a sort of humming noise. "Well, let's not dwell on that point too much. I think I can agree to a reasonable business loan for expansion purposes."

Ben jumped out of his chair and grabbed the tiny man by the shoulders. "Thanks. I really appreciate this."

He held up a finger. "But listen to me, Ben. Listen carefully. You've been to the well once too often already. There is no more water."

"I understand."

"I mean it. Nothing more. Not for any reason. And you must begin repaying your outstanding debt. Soon."

"No more loans will be necessary." He grabbed his coat and smiled. "I'll invite you to the victory celebration."

The Brain smiled wearily. "Just send me a check."

Mike found Pfeiffer at the New York Deli on Seventy-first near Yale. He was sitting upright and precisely consuming his Brooklyn Bomber pastrami sandwich in measured, equal-sized bites. He had removed his suit coat; all that was visible above the booth was his white shirt and his trademark suspenders and bow tie.

Pfeiffer spotted Mike as he approached. "Ah, Lieutenant Morelli. I was told you'd be visiting me." He gestured toward the empty seat on the other side of the booth. "If I'd known you were coming here, I'd have ordered you a sandwich. Still, it's not too late. I particularly recommend the pastrami. It's hard to get genuine deli meat here in Tulsa, you know. Shall I order one up?"

Mike crawled into the booth and faced him. "No thanks. I'm not hungry."

"Are you sure? Man does not live by murder alone."

"Cut the crap, Pfeiffer. This is unpleasant enough without having to put up with your baloney."

Pfeiffer's eyes widened. "Beg pardon? Have I done something to offend?"

"You know damn well you have. Let's not talk about it." Mike pushed the snaps on his briefcase and drew out some papers. "I need your help."

Pfeiffer nodded. "So I gathered. Something of a financial nature, I assume."

"You assume correctly." Mike pushed the documents across the table. "This is just the tip of the iceberg. I've got mounds more of this stuff in my office."

Pfieffer gave it a quick once-over. "Look like the monthly financials for some large business entity."

"Correct. H. P. Blaylock Industrial Machinery."

"Ah." He fingered through some of the documents. "This must relate to your current murder investigation."

"You know about that?"

"Of course. I've reviewed all your expense reports. Lots of trips out to Blackwood. Too many, really."

Mike felt his blood pressure rising. Control yourself, he said silently. Keep it under wraps.

"I hope everything was in order," Mike replied. The edge in his voice was nonetheless unmistakable.

"So far." Pfieffer didn't look up. His eyes were trained on the documents Mike had provided. What bored Mike to tears seemed to fascinate Pfieffer. "So tell me, Lieutenant. What exactly is it you're looking for?"

"I don't know."

"Excuse me?"

"You heard me," Mike barked. "I don't know."

"Are we on the trail of an embezzler? Tax fraud? Illegal campaign contributions?"

"I don't know."

Pfieffer seemed incredulous. "But this pertains to a murder investigation?"

"I got an anonymous tip, okay? Someone told me to . . . follow the money."

"Follow the money? You're joking."

"No, I'm not."

"And what exactly does that mean?"

Mike had reached his own personal boiling point. "I don't know, you pompous twit. That's why I have to resort to getting help from you!"

Several heads turned their way. Mike made a show of not looking like he was about to throttle the man, even though that was exactly what he wanted to do.

Pfieffer, of course, maintained the same even-tempered demeanor. "You don't . . . like me very much, do you, Lieutenant?"

Mike was never one to mince words. "No. I don't."

"May I ask why?"

"Why? You have to ask why? After what you did?"

Pfieffer seemed utterly flabbergasted. "What I did? What did I do?"

"You got me hauled in front of Internal Affairs!"

"Oh. That."

"Yes, that! What the hell did you think you were doing?"

"My job."

"I've been on this force since I got out of college. I've worked on some of the toughest murder investigations this town has ever seen. And I never got hauled before IA. I never had a blemish on my record." His eyes narrowed. "Until you changed all that."

"It is my duty to scrutinize all expense reports and to report any instances of fraud."

"Fraud! Fraud!"

"You attempted to receive more money than that to which you were entitled. That comes out of the taxpayer's pocket, you know."

"I made a math error!"

"If we allowed that excuse to prevail, everyone on the force would be overcharging."

"Four dollars and twenty-three cents! I overcharged the department four dollars and twenty-three cents!"

"Of course," Pfieffer said diffidently, "it's the offense that matters, not the amount. That would be like saying, well, it was only a little murder."

"Murder! This has nothing to do with murder! My calculator was broken!"

"My, you do have a plethora of excuses, don't you? No wonder you were hauled before Internal Affairs."

Mike leaned across the table. "I was completely exonerated."

"Then what are you getting so hot under the collar about?"

"It's the principle of the thing. You damaged my reputation."

"You damaged your reputation when you filled out the expense report incorrectly. Did you pay the money back?"

"Of course."

Pfieffer spread wide his hands. "Then why don't we let bygones be bygones?"

I'm simply going to have to kill him, Mike thought. Perhaps I could stuff the body into one of those steel drums.

"Good," Pfieffer said, clapping his hands together. "I'm glad we got past all that unpleasantness. Now let's see if I can't help you with your investigation."

I've got a ball peen-hammer in my toolshed, Mike thought, continuing in the same vein. Although that murder method might be too humane for this man.

"I'll take all these," Pfieffer said, stacking the documents neatly. "And I'll send a clerk around to pick up the others."

Or there was the corkscrew option. Corkscrews were everywhere. Could probably get one at that QuikTrip across the street.

"It won't be easy," Pfieffer said. "Since I have no idea what I'm looking for. But if there's an irregularity in here, I'll find it." He stood, beaming. "I'm glad we've been able to come to this understanding, Lieutenant." He extended his hand. "Let's shake."

Mike took his hand and shook. Defenestration, he thought. Exsanguination. Castration. Mutilation. Decapitation. A stake through the heart.

* 23 *

Ben was cheered by seeing the TU law school again. Since the class action suit had shifted into high gear, he'd asked a colleague to teach his classes, and he missed it. He had accepted the adjunct position because he wanted the opportunity to do something other than try lawsuits; he wanted the occasional chance to interact with people in a more positive, less adversarial manner. He liked the kids; he tried to extend their enthusiasm and idealism just a bit beyond its natural life span. He hoped to get back to teaching as soon as possible.

But he felt a shiver run down his spine when he approached the large forum classroom. He hadn't been in there since that horrible day several months ago when a madman had broken in with a shotgun and taken him and all the students hostage. He'd been filling in for another professor that day, Professor Canino, a.k.a. The Tiger, who disappeared soon after and, as far as Ben knew, had never been found. It had been the most frightening experience of his life. He would never forget it.

Especially not the way it ended. That was still a constant source of nightmares. And guilt. It haunted him day and night.

Professor Jack Matthews held court in the forum classroom today. He was one of Ben's better friends among the faculty; he was also the last professor Ben had seen before he entered the classroom on the fateful day his whole class became hostages. He was renowned as the leading expert on torts, the area of the law relating to personal injuries, in the state. He was also well known (perhaps notorious) among the students for his slightly cockeyed but always engaging slant on tort law.

Today was no exception. As Ben peered through the window glass in the door, he spotted Professor Matthews—riding on a tricycle.

Ben slipped quietly inside so he could see what was happening. All eyes in the classroom were fixed on the professor, whose tall, gangly frame was scrunched down into a child's three-wheeler. He had a thick, bushy salt-and-pepper beard, very academic-looking, accented by his tweed jacket and bright red bow tie. He was pedaling from one end of the apron to the other. The students were entranced, smiling merrily but completely attentive.

"So," the professor said, pedaling furiously, "Little Johnny Prosser is pedaling down the street on his tricycle when another kid in the neighborhood, that bully Little Learned Hand, lights a firecracker. We don't know what he planned to do with it, but just as he lights the thing, his bratty big sister, Little Sandra O'Connor, who thinks they're still playing tackle football, broadsides him, knocking his feet out from under him. The lit firecracker flies forward, landing just inches from Little Johnny Prosser and his tricycle. It explodes. Although the noise is not such as would normally startle a child, Johnny is preternaturally afraid of loud noises because of a traumatic accident he had as a tot involving a Hoover vacuum cleaner. So Little Johnny is scared out of his wits and falls off the tricycle, injuring himself."

At that, Professor Matthews threw himself sideways, capsizing the tricycle. The classroom burst into laughter. Matthews lay on his side, wheels spinning in the air.

"So the question, students," he said, still lying sideways on the floor, "is this. Who was the proximate cause of Little Johnny's accident? Who's liable? The bully with the firecracker? The bratty big sister? Johnny himself? Or no one?"

Hands shot up into the air. An engaging discussion of proximate cause, one of the most difficult issues in all of torts, ensued. Ben marveled at the professor's quick wit, his cleverness, his ability to get students engaged in a topic that was dense, difficult, and often esoteric. Ben knew his own lectures, which involved no tricycles or other such theatrics, must seem dull in the extreme by comparison.

After class ended, Ben cornered the professor.

"Ben," Matthews said warmly. "Good to see you. I heard you were taking a brief sabbatical."

"That's true. Someone else is covering my classes. Can I talk with you for a moment?"

"Sure. Just let me park my tricycle." He pushed the three-wheeler behind the podium. "Care for some coffee?"

Ben didn't, but he followed the man to the pit outside the library where the vending machines were located. Matthews treated for both of them, then led the way to a nearby table. He started drinking almost immediately. Ben held his in his hands, blew on it, and tried to look as if he might actually drink it at some point in the future.

"What can I do for you, Ben?"

"It relates to a case I'm working on," he began.

"The class action? I've heard about that. And read about it in the paper, of course. How's that coming?"

"Well, I've survived discovery, but the real litigating is just getting started. My worthy opponent is trying to heat things up. Put the pressure on to settle for peanuts."

"That's Charlton Colby, right?"

Ben nodded.

"I hear he's one tough son of a bitch."

"I would have to concur with that academic evaluation." Ben grinned. "He's trying to bury me in motions practice. I got eight in one day."

"Eight? You should complain to the magistrate."

"Trust me, I've already gotten everything I'm ever going to get out of the magistrate. Besides, they're not frivolous motions. In fact, much as I hate to admit it, some of them look downright scary."

"You're afraid he'll shut your case down before you get to trial."

"In a nutshell."

"Sounds grim. What can I do for you?"

Ben cleared his throat. He'd practiced this a hundred times driving over, but he never got it where it sounded halfway persuasive. "I was hoping you might be willing to join the plaintiffs' team. To be our legal scholar."

Matthews was obviously surprised. "Me? Why me? I'm just a law professor. I haven't practiced in years."

"A law professor is exactly what I need. You're the expert in torts—best in the state, most say. I can handle the courtroom. But I know I'm not the best at these esoteric legal arguments. You are."

Matthews tugged at his bow tie. "That's very flattering, Ben. But I'm sure there's nothing in those motions you couldn't handle yourself—"

"Given enough time, you're probably right. But I don't have enough time. I've got a hearing date that's fast approaching and a million other things to do to get ready for trial. I can't afford to spend a couple of weeks in the library. Which the opposition knows. Which is exactly why they filed the motions."

"Kind of dirty pool litigation, isn't it?"

"It usually is."

"Still, Ben, I must be honest with you. I think you overvalue me. I'm an academic, basically. There's no reason to think that anyone out in the real world is going to listen to a word I say. Or write."

"I have a reason," Ben said. He had planned to keep this detail to himself, but he could see now it would be necessary if he was going to win Matthews over. "You wrote an article for the law review. On the nature of causation. Which has been and will be the big bugaboo in this case."

"So what? No one reads the law review."

"I know someone who does," Ben replied. "I saw it on Judge Perry's desk, last time I was in chambers. And it was open to your article. I have to assume he was consulting your piece to aid him in resolving the issues this case raises. In other words, he already considers you the expert."

"On the printed page, perhaps—"

"So just imagine what will happen when I walk into the courtroom with you in tow. My credibility will shoot up a thousandfold."

"Ah." Matthews fingered his beard. "Now we're getting to the real reason you want me on the team."

"They're all real reasons," Ben insisted. "These are serious motions. I need someone who can make a serious reply."

"Sounds like a hell of a lot of work. And on short notice, too."

There was no point in lying about it. "It will be a major headache." But he was relieved to see Matthews was at least considering it.

"Probably have to cancel some classes. Forgive me for being so venal, Ben, but—are you planning to compensate me for my time?"

"Of course. I just secured an advance for that express purpose." More or less. . . .

"Remind me who the defendant is?"

"H. P. Blaylock. Industrial machinery company out in Blackwood."

"Oh, right, right. I did some work for them, actually. Years ago. Back when I still practiced."

Ben's heart clutched. If Matthews had done legal work for Blaylock in the past, he might be barred from taking representation in opposition to them now by the conflict of interest provisions in the Rules of Professional Conduct. "What kind of work?"

"Oh, nothing much. I drafted some documents. It was a million years ago."

Ben slowly exhaled. "Then it didn't have anything to do with this lawsuit?"

"It didn't have anything to do with any lawsuit. It was purely pro forma stuff. Don't worry; there's no conflict."

Thank goodness. "Then what do you say?"

"I should say no. I'm carrying a full class load, plus I'm working on a textbook that I'm way behind on."

"Tell me we're coming to a 'but.' "

Matthews smiled. "But it is tempting. I've done all right in the academic world, but I have to admit, I've always been a bit jealous of the legal eggheads who have really made a name for themselves. Dershowitz. Miller. Those guys became famous—by getting involved in some high-profile lawsuit."

"This one's very high profile, Jack. And then some."

Matthews nodded. "Damn. I'm probably crazy—but I'll do it."

"Great!"

Matthews rose to his feet. "So, I'll want to get copies of those motions as soon as possible."

"As it happens, I have copies in my car."

Matthews arched an eyebrow. "Very confident, weren't you?"

Ben shook his head. "Hopeful."

Matthews laughed. "Well, I want to get those motions. Let me get my briefcase."

"Forget the briefcase," Ben replied. "You'll need a dolly."

Fred the Feeb was running scared. He had tried to pretend otherwise, tried to act like he had everything under control. But he did not have everything under control. Things were spiraling totally out of his control. People were dying. And he might be next.

Since he had spotted his murderous friend out in the woods near the jogging trail behind the office, he had been in a state of abject panic. He had tried to keep his mind on other things—without success.

He had to do something. He didn't need to see a doctor to know his blood pressure was rising. His hands shook. He sweated spontaneously, for no apparent reason. His heart was doing a tap dance inside his chest. And why shouldn't it, for God's sake? That maniac was killing them! All of them! One by one.

Fred pushed away from his workstation. He had to get a grip on himself. He had to stay calm and think rationally and—

"Fred?"

He damn near hit the ceiling. A tiny shrieking sound emerged from his lips and his body bounced into the air.

"I'm sorry. Did I startle you?"

It was Stacey, his personnel supervisor. He hadn't seen her since she'd turned down his vacation request. And threatened him with sexual harassment charges.

"Oh—no," Fred mumbled. "I was just thinking about something."

"No doubt." She dropped a pink sheet of paper on his desk. "Your request has been denied. Sorry," she added, although there was not much regret in her voice. She sashayed out of his office.

Fred scooped up the paper and read. He had requested an early withdrawal from his pension fund. He didn't care if he had to pay a penalty; he needed money and he needed it now. He wanted to get far, far away from this place, even if it did cost him his job. Money wouldn't matter, not once the merchandise came into play. He just needed to get the merchandise to safety. Most important, he needed to get himself to safety.

But his request was denied. DENIED—that's what it said, stamped in big red letters. There was only one signature at the bottom of the form—Stacey's. Goddamn that big-assed bitch, anyway. What was her problem? She was probably still carrying a grudge about their last meeting, still deluding herself into thinking he had propositioned her. She was striking a blow for herself and women everywhere. At his expense.

What could he do now? He twitched onto his feet, ideas

rushing through his head like quicksilver. He could just leave, hit the road, travel, go places his former friend wouldn't think to look. Except how long could he afford to keep that up? Not long enough.

He could at least move, get an apartment somewhere. Yes, he could definitely do that. But how long would it remain secret? Urban reality—if someone really wanted to find you, eventually they would. He could buy alarms and dogs and guards and the whole nine yards. But he would never be safe. He knew that, deep in his heart. Never. Not as long as his friend lived. And Fred had the merchandise.

He stepped outside his cubicle, then froze. George Philby was in the hallway, talking to some executive. He hadn't seen George since that day out on the jogging trail. He whirled around—and saw someone else. Someone who sent a cold chill racing down his spine.

Fred ducked back into his cubicle, hyperventilating. Was it *him*? He thought it was; he was almost sure of it. But why was he here? What was he doing?

He continued hyperventilating, gasping for air in short, ineffectual bursts. There were, of course, only two possible answers to that question. He was either looking for George—

Or he was looking for Fred.

One or the other of them was next on that bloodthirsty killer's hit list.

God—let it be George. It was George, wasn't it? He'd been sure of it, when he'd seen the hidden figure skulking out in the brush while George was jogging. But now—

He had to do something. He had to do something quick. But what? *What?*

On his way up to his apartment, Ben made a preliminary visit at Mrs. Marmelstein's. Joni answered the door.

"Ben-a-rino. How go the lawyer wars?"

"Poorly. But improving. Thanks again for taking double shifts with Mrs. Marmelstein. This case has been running me ragged." He nodded toward the living room. "How's she doing today?"

"Actually, Mrs. Marmelstein's having a good one. She's

relatively lucid, especially for this late in the day. She's been in good spirits. Can't pry her away from those pictures, though."

"Any improvement . . . healthwise?"

The gleam faded from Joni's eyes. "No. We saw the doctor this morning, but . . . the prognosis has not improved. And her eyes are still failing. Doc says soon she won't be able to see at all."

Ben stepped into the living room of the apartment. The television was on. Vanna White was spinning letters, but Mrs. Marmelstein did not appear to be paying much attention. Her eyes were on the photo in her hand—the one of the two parents at the beach. With their son.

"Paulie?" she said as Ben entered the room.

"No." He walked around in front so she could see him. "It's just Ben."

"Oh." Not that she was unhappy to see him, exactly. But it clearly wasn't what she'd been hoping for. "Good to see you, Benjamin."

"Good to see you." He stepped closer and crouched down beside her chair. "How are you feeling?"

"Oh . . . about the same, I suppose." The lines in her creased face seemed to sag. "I saw that doctor again today. I don't much like the man, though. So many tests. Always something new. So tiring. And he wants to take me away from my home."

Ben was surprised—but delighted—to see how cogent she was. He was always thrown by the irrationality of Alzheimer's—addlepated one day, lucid the next. "He does?"

She made a sniffing sound, then drew her afghan closer. "Wants to put me in some kind of house."

"House? You're already in a house."

Joni was standing behind them in the doorway. "In a home."

"Ah." Ben laid his hand gently on her arm. "I don't see any need for that."

"That's what I keep telling the man. I like it here. This is my home. It's all I—I—" Her eyes drifted down again to the photo.

Ben seized his chance. "Mrs. Marmelstein, a friend of mine has been looking for your Paulie, but so far, he hasn't had any luck. Is there anything else you could tell me about him?"

Her eyes wandered from side to side. "He was always a good boy. Not like some of those little monsters. Always tried to do the right thing."

No doubt, Ben thought, but that wasn't going to help them track him down. "What's his full name?"

"His name?" She tilted her head to one side, as if she hadn't heard properly. "His name is Paulie."

"Is that a nickname? Is his real name Paul? Does he have a middle name?"

"We called him Paulie. Always did. Even as an adult. I don't think he minded."

Ben sighed. "When was he born?"

"Oh, my, that was a happy day. We had worried that . . . well, that the Good Lord wasn't going to bless us with any children. And just about the time we had resigned ourselves to that—here comes Paulie. He was a miracle, that's all. A miracle boy."

Ben glanced again at the photo. Judging by the clothing styles and haircuts, Paulie was a little boy in the Fifties. Was he born, then, in the late Forties? "Do you have any idea where he is now?"

Her head trembled a bit. "Hasn't . . . really . . . kept up with us the way he used to. He was a great letter writer. But not anymore."

Ben became concerned. "Mrs. Marmelstein . . . did something happen to Paulie?"

"Happen? No. Not like that. It happened to . . . all of us."

Ben pushed himself to his feet. He was getting nowhere fast.

He leaned close to Joni. "Do you have any idea what she's talking about?"

Joni shook her head. "Clueless. Except that she seems certain this boy—former boy—is alive. And she's desperate to see him."

"Why now? When she hasn't seen him for years?"

"I think you know the answer to that, Ben."

He did, of course. She was desperate to see him now because, even in her troubled mind, she realized that her time was growing short.

"Mrs. Marmelstein," he said quietly, "did something happen? Between you and Paulie?"

"It all seems so foolish now. So much fuss about so little. But you know how men are. Always butting antlers. Paulie never got along with his father. Never, never. They were both good men. Just very different."

Now they were getting somewhere. "Paulie had disagreements with your late husband?"

"All the time. You can't imagine what it's like when a father and son are so . . . angry with one another."

"I can imagine," Ben said quietly. "What did they argue about?"

"They didn't see eye to eye on anything. Clothes, hair, lifestyle. Nothing. Albert wanted Paulie to follow him into business. Paulie had his own plans. That was bad. But the worst came when he brought home that woman. That shiksa."

Ben blinked. "She . . . she wasn't Jewish?"

"She wasn't anything. Except pretty. Very, very pretty. Had what they called 'It,' in my day. Lots of It. Totally turned his head."

"You didn't approve of the relationship?"

"Oh, I didn't care so much. Let the boy make his own mistakes. He'll learn, that's what I said. But Albert didn't see it that way. He was a very . . . controlling person. He threatened . . ."

Ben was beginning to get the drift, even if he did have to piece the story together like letters in a cryptogram. "Did you try to intervene?"

Her head fell. "No. I supported my husband. That's the way I was raised. What I thought I was supposed to do. It all seemed very important at the time. But now . . ."

Ben could see her eyes filling. He took her hand and squeezed it.

"Now . . ." she continued, "I just want to see my Paulie."

"I'll find him," Ben said. "I promise. I'll find him and bring him back here."

Wordlessly, Mrs. Marmelstein threw her arms around Ben and hugged him tighter than he thought he had ever been hugged before.

* 24 *

The last time Ben had been out on a golf course, he'd managed to run up a score somewhere in the high three digits. And that was just on the first hole. This time, he decided to leave the playing to others.

He was invading the third cubicle in a South Tulsa driving range, watching in respectable silence as the man in the matching Polo shirt and shorts knocked another one well past the two-hundred marker.

"How did you find me, anyway?" the man asked. He was Dr. Abbott K. Rimland, Ph.D., specialist in hematology—the expert witness he and Jones had been trying for weeks to persuade to testify for the plaintiffs in their class action suit.

"My office manager called your office," Ben answered. He was being circumspect, careful not to talk when the man was swinging. He knew from prior experience how much golfers hated that.

"Who? Karen?" The man shook his head. He was in his late fifties, but still quite handsome, graying at the temples. "I can't imagine. She's under strict instructions. I don't get that much time off, and I don't like to be bothered when I finally manage to escape."

Ben cleared his throat. "I believe your secretary was under the impression that she was speaking to your wife."

"What? Karen knows what my wife's voice sounds like."

Ben's eyes darted toward the ground. "So does my office manager. He's a very talented mimic."

Dr. Rimland shook his head, then set another ball on the tee. "I suppose I have to give you points for determination. But the answer is still no."

Ben grabbed an available driver, just to have something in his hands. "Doctor, if you'd just let me explain—"

"I explained my position in detail to your man on the phone. And I told him the matter was closed."

"Which is why I came to see you in person. Your participation is absolutely vital to this case."

Rimland glanced up, adjusting his sun visor. "Then you're in big trouble, my friend." He brought his club around and knocked another one high into the sky.

"With respect, sir, this is not just any lawsuit. This is important. We're talking about parents who have lost their children for no good reason—"

"Spare me the soft-soap routine. I know all about the case. I read the papers."

"Then you must know how important it is that—"

Rimland cut him off. "I already gave you my answer. No." For the first time, a trace of annoyance crossed his face. "Look, you don't need me. There are any number of doctors around who will take the witness stand and say whatever the hell you want, if you pay them what they ask."

"I don't want just any doctor," Ben said firmly. "I want someone who is knowledgeable, someone who's worked and researched in this field for years. I want you."

Rimland lined up another shot. "I'm not the only scientist doing research on leukemogenesis." He paused, smiling slightly. "Close, though."

"I'm familiar with your work."

"Then you must know how inconclusive it is."

"I didn't think so. I read the chapter you wrote in Coswell's *Case Studies in Hematology*. You said that the existence of leukemia clusters was too prevalent to be coincidental. You wrote that the existence of such clusters was an undeniable medical fact."

Rimland's eyes stayed on the golf ball. "I was young. I may have been wrong." The club whipped around faster than the eye could see. "But even if it's so, what does it get you? So you've got a leukemia cluster. So what?"

"If clusters do occur, and it isn't just coincidence, then something must be causing them."

"Ay, but there's the rub. Something must be causing them—but what?"

"That's what I need you to explain to the jury. You've done the research."

Rimland took the last golf ball out of his bucket and placed it on the tee. "Really? And suppose I tell them that TCE and perc have nothing to do with it. That they can't possibly cause cancer."

Ben's lips parted. "You are up to date on my case."

Rimland shrugged. "It's my field."

"I've read the results of the studies you did on the East Coast. You proved that both TCE and perc instigated leukemic diseases."

"In laboratory animals. White mice developed cancers of the lymph system. But mice have decidedly different chromosomal structures, as defense counsel will undoubtedly point out. Different metabolisms. Those results don't necessarily mean it happens that way in homo sapiens."

"Common sense tells me—"

"But common sense won't get you far in the courtroom, will it? You need proof."

"I need an expert opinion. So what's yours? Do you believe that TCE and perc are harmless to human beings?"

"No—"

"Then you have to testify—"

Rimland raised a hand. "Stop right there. Sure, I think chemically tainted water can cause leukemia. In fact, there's not the slightest doubt in my mind. It may not be the only cause of cancer. But I find the reticence of my colleagues on this issue embarrassing. Why do we go on pretending we don't know what causes cancer when, in some cases at least, the causes are evident? Why do we deny as scientists what is obvious to common sense?"

Ben was barely able to contain himself. "If you'll just take the stand and say that, sir. That's all we need. That's all I would want you to—"

"But it wouldn't be all you'd ask, would it?" He paused. "You'd ask me if these chemicals could cause cancer, and I'd say they could. But eventually, either you or the man on the other side would ask if the chemicals did in fact cause the leukemias suffered by the children of the plaintiffs. That is the ultimate question after all, isn't it? And I would hem and haw. I'd say, it could've. Might've. Perhaps even, probably did. But I can't say with absolute certainty that it in fact did."

"All of the children were exposed to the tainted water—"

"A compelling fact, I agree. But it is still possible that their leukemia was caused by some other instigating factor. We just don't know enough about it to trace the disease back to a single cause with certainty. After all, there were presumably dozens of other children who drank the water and did not die of leukemia."

"My parents' kids may have had a genetic predisposition to the disease. I can live with that. It's the eggshell skull principle. The law permits recovery, so long as I can show the defendants caused the inception of the disease."

"Which you'll never get from me. All I can do is affirm the possibility."

Ben bit down on his lower lip. "Fine. I can live with that."

The bucket of balls was exhausted. Rimland set down his club. "Mr. Kincaid, I don't think you've been listening to me. I do not wish to be your witness. I've testified in lawsuits before, and I found it unpleasant in the extreme. It's a dirty process. And cross-examination—"

"I'll be in the courtroom," Ben said. "I'll protect you during cross."

"That's what they all say. But when the opposition attorney starts in, there'll be little or nothing you can do. He'll use everything in his power to paint me as a lunatic, a fringe scientist, a paid mouthpiece. He'll drag out every little secret he can find. And frankly, I have a few stones I don't want turned over."

"Lots of major scientists have served as expert witnesses."

"Yes, and lots have regretted it, too. I have an academic reputation to protect. I won't endanger it. My work is too important."

Ben realized it was time to play his trump card. "Really? I thought your work was coming to an end."

Rimland's eyes dimmed. "What have you heard?"

"That your project is being discontinued."

"That's nonsense. Just . . . delayed, that's all. A momentary funding snag."

"Then let me unsnag it. Take this job, and use the fee to revive your project."

Rimland shook his head. "It wouldn't be enough. Even at my hourly rate."

"Are you sure? Think about it. You'll have to meet with all the parents. Do medical workups on them. Review the victims' medical records. Perhaps run some tests of your own."

"Time consuming, yes. Which is another drawback. But it still wouldn't be nearly enough—"

"I'll pay you fifty thousand dollars." Ben felt his heart stop even as he said it. But he was desperate. He needed this man in the witness chair.

"You mean—as a flat fee?"

"That's right." It would take every penny Ben had managed to wheedle out of The Brain. But he had no choice.

"Regardless of what conclusions I reach?"

"Correct."

"Regardless of what happens when I take the stand?"

"I'm not looking for a mynah bird, Doctor. I just want someone with unimpeachable credentials and experience in the field to take the stand and tell the jury what happened."

Rimland touched a finger to his lips. For the first time, Ben had the impression he was considering it. "Give me twenty-four hours. I'll get back to you."

Ben felt his heart slowly restarting. "I'll be waiting for your call."

∗ 25 ∗

Ben decided to forgo the usual shaking of hands and pretending to be collegial as he entered the judge's courtroom for the hearing on Colby's many defense motions. What was the point? Everyone involved knew he had absolutely no feelings of collegiality toward Colby. And by not going through the usual greeting process, he left Colby wondering: Who was that distinguished-looking gentleman with the salt-and-pepper beard Ben brought to court with him? It was pleasant to think he might be introducing a tiny bit of uncertainty into Colby's master plan. It might not be much, but even the tiniest chink in the defense armor could only work to Ben's benefit.

Colby sat at the defense table with his team, trying not to stare at the newcomer. He had brought his client, Myron Blaylock, along for the ride, too. Ben couldn't imagine why. Perhaps the old man just wanted to be here to watch Ben's case go down in flames. Colby also had brought no fewer than five other Raven lawyers—practically one per motion. Once again, it seemed Colby's firm was sparing no expense in their effort to bury the plaintiffs' case—or to run up as big a bill as possible trying.

They didn't have to wait long this morning. Almost the instant the big hand touched twelve, Judge Perry emerged from chambers. He appeared as serious as ever. He smiled briefly at Colby—and did not smile at all at Ben. He took his seat, plopping a large stack of books and papers beside him. He was ready to go. Presumably the vast number of defense motions had inspired him to get the show rolling as soon as possible.

"I have read the parties' briefs," Judge Perry said, "so don't feel obligated to regurgitate every word. I should say at the outset, however"—he cast an evil eye in Ben's direction—"that I take these issues very seriously. Despite the enormous pretrial publicity, of which I do not approve"—another evil look Ben's way—"I will not hesitate to dismiss this case if that course seems appropriate after the court has heard these motions. Why don't we begin with—"

"Your honor," Ben said, rising to his feet, "before we begin, may I introduce the newest member of the plaintiffs' team?"

Perry did not appear annoyed at having been interrupted. Apparently he was curious about who was sitting beside Ben, too. "Of course, counsel. Proceed."

Ben's companion rose. "This is Professor Jack Matthews, author of several books and professor of tort law."

The judge cleared his throat. "Did you say Jack Matthews?"

"Yes, your honor." Ben had to resist smiling. He knew the name rang a bell with the judge. He had seen the judge's eyes dart downward to the stack of books he had brought in with him—including a gray-colored paperback Ben knew was the issue of the TU law review that contained Matthews's most recent article on causation issues in complex tort litigation.

"And . . . Professor Matthews is assisting the plaintiffs?" the judge said, apparently trying to mask his incredulity.

"That's correct, your honor. He's already filed his entry of appearance." Ben proceeded to recite a brief but nonetheless impressive litany of Matthews's credentials and academic achievements.

The judge drank it all in, still amazed and surprised. He could be imagining it, but Ben had the distinct impression his credibility rating with the judge was rising like the mercury in a thermometer on an Oklahoma summer day. "Will you be . . . splitting witnesses with Professor Matthews at trial?"

"No, your honor," Ben answered. "I'll still be handling the trial. Professor Matthews will be consulting with me on legal issues. Particularly those causation difficulties the court earlier expressed concerns about."

"I see." Judge Perry fingered the rim of his glasses, obviously still not quite sure what to think of all this. "Well then, let's proceed."

"Your honor. If I may," Colby said, with his usual calm, direct, supremely confident manner. Ben had seen out the corner of his eye that he'd been whispering with Myron Blaylock. "I believe we may have a bit of a problem here."

Ben didn't need any problems, not just when it appeared there was some chance of surviving this hearing. What did they have up their sleeves now?

"It appears we may have a client conflict issue," Colby continued. "I am reliably informed that Professor Matthews has worked for the defendant H. P. Blaylock in the past. That being the case, it would be inappropriate for him to now act against their interests. Although we mean no disrespect to the distinguished professor, I'm afraid he must be disqualified."

The judge peered intently through his black-rimmed half-glasses. "Is this true, Mr. Kincaid?"

"If I may address that issue," Professor Matthews said, rising. "I'm probably the best equipped to respond to this charge. It is true that I worked for the Blaylock company in the past. It was several years ago. I worked in-house, and was responsible principally for the drafting of corporate documents. I never did any work on the present case and I have not worked for them since."

The judge coughed. "Still, if there's any question—"

"With respect, I believe there is no question of disqualification in this instance. The Rules of Professional Conduct, at Rule 4.2, combined with comments one through ten, make clear that disqualification only occurs when there is ongoing representation or a substantial connection between the former matter and the present one."

"Your honor," Colby interjected, "I must insist that the present case touches or may touch upon literally every aspect of the Blaylock company's business. It seems to me that any corporate work may have exposed the professor to trade secrets or insider knowledge that he could use, even unwittingly, to his former client's disadvantage in the present litigation."

Professor Matthews didn't miss a beat. "That may be Mr. Colby's viewpoint, your honor, but it is not the viewpoint of the Rules of Professional Conduct or the considerable case law that has developed pursuant to these rules. I could cite numerous cases, copies of which I have with me today, in which former connections far more prominent than mine were found to not preclude representation. Furthermore, I have prepared an affidavit, filed with the court this morning, in which I state that I learned nothing during my brief prior relationship with the company that could possibly be of use in this suit. That is the only evidence on this subject on record at this time. Since it is unrebutted, I believe the rules of this court require that it be accepted as fact."

Ben drew in his breath. Wowzah! Hiring this dude was the best move he'd ever made.

Colby didn't even bother responding. There was nothing he could say. He'd lost, and he was smart enough to know it.

Judge Perry leaned back in his chair. "Mr. Colby, if you

come up with additional evidence at some time in the future, I'll allow you to introduce it. But for now, I see no problem with Professor Matthews proceeding in this case. His insight on these complex tort issues may be of benefit to us all."

Ben had to restrain himself from jumping up out of his chair. He knew he could never overcome the fact that Perry had history with Colby and considered him a friend. But if he could establish Matthews as the brains of the case, Colby's motions and tactical maneuvering would be futile.

"Well then," the judge said, "now that that's out of the way, shall we get started on the motions? I suggest we begin with the defendant's motion for summary judgment. After all, if that one is granted, the rest of the motions will become moot." He nodded toward the defense table. "Mr. Colby, it's your motion. Why don't you begin?"

"Thank you, your honor." Colby took his position behind the podium. "It's really a very simple motion, based upon the express language of *Daubert versus Merrill Dow Pharmaceuticals*. In that case, the distinguished nine justices of the Supreme Court, the highest court in the land, held that scientific testimony cannot be accepted unless—"

"Excuse me. Your honor?"

It was Professor Matthews again. Rising to his feet. "If I could make a clarification."

Colby's cheeks puffed up. "Sir, here in court, unlike the classroom, it is traditional to allow the first speaker to finish what he has to say before beginning the rebuttal by the opposition."

"Oh, I know, I know," Matthews said, the picture of harmless gentility. "But I hate to allow a misstatement to stand uncorrected."

Colby arched an eyebrow. "A misstatement?"

The judge leaned forward. "What would that be, Professor?"

Matthews didn't hesitate. "The *Daubert* case was not decided by the full Supreme Court. Two of the justices recused themselves. Therefore, only seven members actually voted, and the final decision was a four-three split—a slim plurality."

Even from where he was sitting, Ben could feel the heat rising off Colby's collar. "I don't see that the exact count is of much importance, your honor. Whatever the count, the case is now law."

"But there are many matters the case does not address," Matthews replied. "And given the slimness of the plurality, it suggests that on some issues even that slight consensus could not be reached."

Colby drew himself up. "Be that as it may, the *Daubert* case, which is now the supreme law of the land, held that courts may not accept expert scientific testimony unless it first determines that it will aid the trier of fact—the jury. That means the court must rule on its relevance and the scientific validity of the reasoning, methodology, and principles underlying the testimony."

"Agreed," Matthews said quietly.

"In the present case, the plaintiffs intend to admit scientific testimony that is speculative in the extreme, and that has not been generally accepted by the majority of the medical community."

"Mr. Colby is now, of course, referencing the language of the *Frey* test," Matthews interjected. "Totally rejected by Rule 702 of the Federal Rules of Evidence and the *Daubert* decision."

"Be that as it may," Colby continued. His voice was acquiring a bit of a tremor. "The plaintiffs' proposed testimony is not supported by any credible scientific evidence. It is quackery of the worst sort—the sort that is bought and sold by unscrupulous persons willing to do or say anything to make a buck."

Ben started out of his chair, but Matthews waved him back. "Your honor, I must protest. While I recognize that Mr. Colby has an ethical duty to provide zealous representation, the statements he has just made are simply incorrect."

The judge appeared interested. "How so?"

"The medical expert we propose to put on the stand, Dr. Abbott Rimland, is perhaps the world's leading expert on the subject of leukemogenesis."

"He's practically the only man on earth who believes these chemicals can cause cancer!" Colby bellowed.

"An open mind is often the doorway to great discoveries," Matthews replied. "Galileo said that, your honor. And he was right. In this case, Dr. Rimland's pioneering work has allowed him to reach trailblazing conclusions relating to the causes of urban cancer."

"He has a theory," Colby responded. "No credible proof."

"Again, that is not true. He has performed extensive controlled studies involving laboratory animals—"

"Which is not the same thing as performing tests on human beings," Colby said firmly. His expression suggested that he felt they had finally arrived at a point he could win. "This very issue has already been visited by the federal courts, in the case of "—he paused momentarily as an associate handed him a photocopied case—"*Vernon versus Maplewood Medical Arts*. This court concluded that tests on lab animals were insufficient to justify testimony as to probable effects on human beings." He paused, smiling, and held the case out. "If the learned professor would care to peruse the case . . ."

Matthews didn't even glance at it. "The *Vernon* case was decided by unconvincing reasoning based upon a state statute which does not exist here in Oklahoma. Most commentators have agreed that the dissents are the best reasoned portions of the entire case. And, as Mr. Colby failed to mention, the case comes from the Third Circuit, so it is not mandatory authority over this court. Since the *Vernon* decision, three other cases have visited the same issue"—Matthews rattled three more case names off the top of his head—"and every one of them permitted the scientific testimony, holding that while testing on lab animals might not be conclusive as to effects on humans, it was certainly sufficient to support a reasoned expert opinion." He paused, allowing himself—and everyone else— to catch their breath. "The latter of these cases, your honor, the *Buchner* case, is from the Tenth Circuit, and therefore *is* mandatory authority as to this court."

Judge Perry leaned back in his chair. "Well then," he said with a slight chuckle, obviously impressed, "that would seem to decide the matter. Anything further to say, Mr. Colby?"

Colby's eyes were as dark as night. "No, your honor."

"Very well, then. The defendant's motion for summary judgment is denied. Furthermore, based upon the argument I have heard, I will allow the plaintiffs' medical experts to testify at trial. I will warn counsel, however, that I will be listening to that testimony very carefully. Although the professor has convinced me that the jury should be permitted to hear the evidence, if the court determines that the evidence is not sufficient to support a finding in the plaintiffs' favor, I will not hesitate to intervene."

Matthews bowed his head slightly. "Understood, your honor."

"Very good. Let's move on to the rest of these motions." He glanced up at Matthews. "They shouldn't take too long."

They didn't. The court whipped through Colby's remaining seven motions in less than half an hour. Matthews handled all the arguments, and it was clear that, from the judge's viewpoint, Matthews could do no wrong. Colby might be his friend, but Matthews was the legal expert, and when he spoke, Judge Perry listened. Matthews was prepared for everything, anticipating Colby's arguments and deflecting them with seeming ease. The results were never in doubt.

With Matthews at the helm, the plaintiffs defeated six of the remaining seven motions, and took a partial victory on the seventh. All the motions in limine were defeated. The motion to censure Ben was defeated, almost without discussion. The judge ruled that the plaintiffs would have to produce medical records and submit to medical tests, although at Matthews's suggestion, the tests were significantly scaled down from what the defendant had requested.

All in all, it was a smashing victory for the plaintiffs, and a crushing defeat for the defendant. Ben could see Myron Blaylock's dander rising with each ruling. Best of all, Ben felt that, for perhaps the first time since this case began, the court was treating him with deference and respect. Apparently, the feeling was that if the distinguished Professor Matthews was willing to work with Ben, he couldn't be all bad.

Ben caught Colby's eye on the way out. "Looks like there's going to be a trial, Colby. You must be crushed."

"Crushed?" Colby walked close to Ben, so no one else could hear. "Sure, I tried to stop the case from going to trial. I had an ethical obligation to do so. But now this case is going to be tried, and the trial will last, probably, what? A month? Two? Maybe longer. I'll have to staff appropriately. My client has no choice but to defend to its utmost ability. So I figure my firm will make something like half a million dollars." He paused. "Crushed? Yeah—I'm devastated."

Colby stepped even closer, close enough that a whisper was more than enough. "No, Kincaid, I'm not crushed. But by the end of this trial, you will be."

* 26 *

For once, Ben came home from work in a relatively jubilant mood. True, he was staring down the throat of the worst, most complex, most expensive trial he had ever attempted in his entire career. But he had scored a major victory—two, actually. He'd gotten Arthur Turnbull's new and improved testimony on the record, and he'd won the hearing on Colby's motions, won with flying colors. There was still much to be done, but at least he was coming into the trial on a winning streak. So he was naturally in high spirits—

Until he saw the note from Joni pinned to his door. It was only four words long, but those four words spoke with magnificent clarity:

WE'RE AT THE HOSPITAL.

He found Joni in the fifth-floor corridor, hovering outside Mrs. Marmelstein's room.

"They won't let me go in," she explained. Her usually perfectly coiffed hair was a mess; her face was streaked and blotchy. "They've been in there for more than an hour."

"What happened?" Ben asked.

"I don't know. I just . . ." She ran her fingers through her hair. "I was only gone a minute. Somehow—she must've fallen trying to get out of bed."

Ben winced. "How bad?"

Joni's eyes started to swell. "It's bad, Ben. Real bad. I don't know how—I didn't know—I was only gone a minute. . . ."

Ben put his arm around her and lowered her to a chair. Joni was so dependable and so good at caretaking that he almost forgot how young she was—barely more than a teenager. She was shouldering enough responsibility to break people much older and more experienced than she. "It isn't your fault," he said.

"I thought she was sleeping. I needed to call my friend to see if I could borrow his notes—"

"It isn't your fault," Ben said firmly. "There's nothing you could have done."

"But if I'd just been there. I was supposed to have been there."

"Don't blame yourself. Accidents are inevitable with the elderly. You can only do so much. What do the doctors say?"

"She's hurt her hip. Again."

Ben shook his head. It was—what? Barely more than a year ago that she'd had hip-replacement surgery. It had taken her forever to recover from that.

"The accident seems to have worsened her glaucoma. She can barely see."

She can't walk. She can't see. This was hopeless. Joni could no longer provide the kind of care Mrs. Marmelstein would need. No one could, not on their own. "She's going to have to be institutionalized."

"I don't think we're going to have the chance, Ben." Joni's lips quivered. "She's dying."

Mike was in his office working late, as he had been since the first of these grotesque murders had been discovered. The night was dark and starless, and through the window behind his desk he could see the lights of downtown Tulsa, the fluid ooze of headlights, the orange fires of the refineries just across the Arkansas. He was trying to concentrate on his work, trying to block the most horrific details out of his mind, trying to pretend he didn't still hanker for a quick jolt of nicotine. The aching was worst late at night, when he was alone, perhaps even a little bored, and craved something to elevate his spirits, something to do with his hands, something to make him feel less alone. Since he'd quit smoking, he'd gained almost twenty pounds—and he still felt a pang of desire every time he walked past the smokes machine in the lobby.

The telephone rang, jolting him back to business. He put on his nononsense voice and answered. "Morelli."

The voice on the other end affected an equally sonorous tone. "Pfieffer."

Mike's expression soured. "What's up?"

"I've got something for you."

"Let me guess. You've discovered that I took a cup of coffee from the kitchen twelve years ago without putting a dime in the kitty. You'll probably bring me up on charges."

Pfieffer must've been in a good mood. He opted to ignore the sarcasm. "Not this time. I've got something on Blaylock."

Mike sat up. "So soon?"

"Hey, can I cook or what?"

"You couldn't possibly have had time to—"

"Well, I've only managed to go back in their financial records twelve years."

"Twelve years? You've been through twelve years of that gobbledygook?"

"Hey, it may be gobbledygook to you, but it's my first language. Did you know that a few years back Blaylock got ripped off for sixty million clams?"

"Sixty million? No way. I would've heard something about that."

"Not unless they reported it to the police."

"You're saying someone could lose sixty mil and not call the cops?"

"That's how it looks to me. At any rate, the money departed, and the ledger entry attributes it to theft."

"Must be some kind of cover-up. A bad investment or something."

"Maybe. But there's no record of any such expenditure, and the money is gone, just the same. A hit that size could dent even Myron Blaylock's deep pockets."

"No doubt."

"Mind you, finding this wasn't easy. Those Blaylock

accountants use so many different interlocking documents, reading the financials is like solving a crossword. Even for me. I suspect different pieces of the financial puzzle are shipped out to different accountants, so no one person really knows what the hell is going on. Except ol' Myron himself."

That was interesting, Mike ruminated. Why would the distinguished president be so determined to keep his financials private?

"Anyway, that's the biggest single-entry suspicious item I've identified. Found that sometime last night. But I just uncovered the second largest, which is why I called."

"Yeah? What is it?"

"A lump sum payment to a corporate employee—in the amount of slightly more than two million dollars."

"Two million? What the hell did he do to deserve that?"

"Beats me. The ledger entries just call it a 'capital contribution.' "

"Must be a top vice president. Or maybe an inventor who came up with a new kind of machinery."

"Wrong on both counts." Pfieffer seemed to be deriving a good deal of pleasure from being light-years ahead of Mike. "He's a lawyer."

"A lawyer? Since when do lawyers make two-million-dollar bonuses?"

"Since never, unless they're representing former Heisman trophy winners. But this guy is a salaried employee. Supposedly makes eighty thousand a year. Works in-house at Blaylock."

That triggered a memory in Mike's mental notepad. "What's this guy's name, anyway?"

"Ronald Harris. Ring any bells?"

"Yeah, it does. I interviewed him not too long ago. When was this payment made?" Pfieffer gave him the date. "That was long before the murders."

"Any idea why he'd get that kind of money?"

"I can't imagine," Mike said, rising. "I think I'll drop by and ask."

"Cool. Hey—does this mean I've been helpful to you?"

Mike felt his teeth grinding. "Possibly."

"Excellent. So am I back in your good graces?"

"Never," Mike said, and hung up the phone.

Ben gathered his staff together in his office for the traditional pretrial cram session. Christina was putting everything in order, using her supreme organizational skills to make sure there were no unpleasant surprises at the trial. Loving hovered over Ben's desk, assembling all his witness profiles and investigative reports. At the same time, Professor Matthews ran hypothetical objections past Ben, anticipating potential snags and developing potential responses. They tried to run through every contingency, making sure they were prepared for anything. Ben had learned some time ago that, contrary to what spectators sometimes thought, the secret to being good at trial was not being quick on your feet. It was being prepared. And with the stakes as high as they were in this case, Ben planned to make damn sure they were prepared.

They had walked through the trial notebooks, making sure everything was in place, everything Ben might need—witness outlines, exhibits, notes. They had combed through the enormous quantum of documents, pulling those few that might conceivably be of importance at trial. They had researched the legal issues that they could expect Colby to raise whenever he had a chance.

"Enough," Ben said, well past midnight. Preparation was a good thing, but at some point, it had to yield to other considerations. Like the need for sleep.

He had tried to focus on the tasks at hand, although his mind tended to wander back to Mrs. Marmelstein's hospital room. He had told Joni to call him if there were any developments. So far, no calls.

"Loving—any news on the search for Paulie?"

The mountainous man shook his head. "Sorry, Skipper. I've hit a wall. And what with this big trial comin' up . . ."

"Keep looking," Ben urged. "It's important. Now more than ever. We . . ." He hesitated. "We probably don't have much time."

Ben craned his neck around. "Where's Jones, anyway? We need to review his stuff, too. Some of those motions will have to be filed—"

"Here," Jones said, as he rushed through the doorway. "Sorry. Got trapped on the phone."

Ben didn't bother hiding his annoyance. "Why didn't you tell whoever it was that you had work to do?"

"Because whoever it was was The Brain."

"Oh." Thank God he hadn't picked up the phone. "What did he have to say?"

"He found out somehow about the good professor here. He's angry. Says that's not what he loaned the money for."

Geez, Ben thought. If The Brain was upset about Matthews, it was a damn good thing he didn't know about Dr. Rimland.

"He says he was protecting his investment by making sure we could complete the trial, not so we could take on additional unnecessary expenses."

Professor Matthews cut in. "If I'm going to be a problem, I can drop out."

"No, actually, you can't," Ben said. "Colby will have a fleet of associates running research for him at every turn. I need you in my corner."

"Still, if your money man objects—"

"Let him object. There's nothing he can do about it now."

"Except refuse to loan us any more money," Jones said.

"He said he was going to do that, anyway," Ben rejoined. "If we need more cash—"

"Which we will."

"—then we'll have to try something else."

"Such as what?"

The entire staff stared blankly at one another.

"We could hold a bake sale," Christina offered, perky as ever.

Jones's expression suggested he didn't feel that was worthy of response.

"We'll cross that bridge when we get there," Ben said. "For now, I want everyone thinking about the trial. The trial, the trial, and nothing but the trial. We're the plaintiffs in this suit. We have to take control."

Christina's brow creased. "How do you mean?"

"I mean, since this lawsuit began, we've been reactive, not proactive. Plaintiffs are the ones who normally take the ball and run with it, but in this case, from the day it was filed, we've let Colby take charge. We've been his hostage." And, Ben thought silently, our lives have been hostages to this case. "He's taken the lead on pretrial publicity, on motions practice, even on discovery. All we've done is deflect his blows and try to keep our heads above water. But that won't be good enough at trial. We have the burden of proof. If we don't meet our burden, we'll go down in flames."

He paused. "We know they outdollar us. We know they outman us. We know they have more resources than we ever dreamed of having. But we have to take the offensive. Because we have a room full of parents who are depending on us to make their children's lives mean something. And to make sure this doesn't happen again." He gazed at each of them in turn. "They've put their trust in us. I don't want to let them down."

Mike sat at his desk in the dead of night, frustrated.

Ronald Harris was not at home, or if he was, he wasn't answering the phone. Which was understandable, given the hour. But Mike couldn't wait. He wanted to ask Harris about the two-million-dollar payoff, not to mention the disappearing sixty million from the corporate coffers. He didn't know why, but he felt certain it was important.

But Harris wasn't at home. So he would just have to wait until tomorrow. Unless . . .

A few synapses inside his weary brain fired back to life.

What was it George Philby had said when they'd met? "I figured you weren't here investigating financial improprieties."

Mike pondered. Could be just a coincidence. A smart aleck trying to make wise. But as he had mentioned before—he didn't believe in coincidences. Why would Philby's mind take that turn?

It was probably nothing. But then, his last fifty or so interrogations had been nothing, too. What did he have to lose?

He picked up the phone, hoping George Philby was a light sleeper.

Just as Ben was almost out of the office, the phone rang. Jones scurried out to take the call, then returned. "Ben?"

"Take a message. We're busy."

"It's Colby."

Ben's head cleared with amazing alacrity. The weariness that had been seeping into his bones evaporated.

Colby? At this hour? What the hell did he want?

Ben punched the blinking red light on his phone and picked it up. "Yes?"

"I want to say up front, this was not my idea." Colby's voice was flat and unemotional, even on the phone. "I personally am against this. But I am required to act at the instruction of my client. And my client has instructed me to make a settlement offer."

Ben felt a clutching at his heart. A settlement offer! Could it be true? He had discussed this possibility with his clients earlier in the afternoon, had considered what they would and would not accept, even though he thought an offer was unlikely. But here it was! And if they accepted—the whole hideous spectacle of a trial would become unnecessary!

"What is it, Colby?"

"Here's the terms. We want a confidentiality agreement. No one talks to the press. The numbers are not revealed. The settlement will be structured, with a payout over ten years."

"Yeah, yeah, yeah," Ben said. "Cut to the part that matters."

"We admit no liability. We're doing this strictly to avoid the inevitable expense of going to trial."

"Spare me the sermon. I wasn't born yesterday. How much?"

Colby drew in his breath. "I'm in a position to offer you a cash settlement of two hundred and twenty thousand dollars."

Two hundred and twenty? In other words, twenty thousand per dead kid. Barely more than what Colby had offered at that first hearing. Not nearly enough to compensate the parents for their medical expenses. It wasn't an offer—it was an insult.

"Your offer is rejected," Ben said.

"Excuse me, counsel. Don't you have an ethical obligation to take the offer to your clients? Or have you decided to disregard the ethics code entirely now?"

"I've already discussed settlement with them, and they've given me parameters for what they will and won't accept, to avoid the trouble of tracking them all down every time we need to make a decision. Your offer isn't even close."

"It's a mistake to get greedy, Kincaid. Twenty thousand is a lot of money. And a lot better than nothing."

"The answer is no, Colby."

"At least this way they take something and save some face. If they go to trial, they're going to be humiliated—and take home nothing."

"I gave you my answer. If there's nothing else—"

"You plaintiff's attorneys are all alike," Colby snarled. "You claim there are great principles involved. You say it isn't about money. But it always is. You and your pack are just looking for a quick financial fix. Someone else's money."

"It isn't about money, Colby," Ben shot back, "and I can prove it to you. Here's a counteroffer which my clients have authorized me to make when I think the time is right. They're willing to settle for this amount: one dollar."

The silence on the other end of the phone was satisfyingly long. "What?"

"You heard me."

"What's the catch?"

"No catch. Blaylock pays us one dollar—and admits that what it did was wrong. Admits they poisoned the well and caused those unnecessary deaths. And pays to clean up the Blackwood water supply. That's the whole deal, Colby. No greed involved. So what do you say?"

Colby's voice was low and subdued. "You know we can't accept that."

"One measly dollar, Colby. Not a very greedy offer."

"Your offer is rejected," Colby said.

He hung up without another word.

"What was that all about?" Christina asked.

Ben shook his head. "Nothing important. You people go home and get some sleep." He pushed himself up and snapped his trial notebook shut. "Tomorrow morning, we're going to trial."

* 27 *

George Philby sat at home, waiting.

Why the hell was the cop chasing him tonight, when there was a killer on the loose? Morelli had called a few minutes ago, said he wanted to come over and ask a few more questions. Fine, jerk-off—whatever amuses you. The cop was clueless; he still hadn't tumbled onto what this was all about. As long as he was in the dark, he was helpless.

George wasn't excited at the prospect of talking to Morelli, but what could the man do? He had no grounds to arrest him. George would bluff, lie—whatever it took. The far greater danger lurked in the killing hands of his former friend.

The doorbell rang. That would be the cop. George wondered if he knew about the money. Probably not, but even if he did, so what? It wasn't illegal to give an employee a big paycheck. The police might frown on the motivation for the payout, but they had no way of learning about that. No one could tell them—except George, or Blaylock himself. Maybe Ronald Harris. And none of them was likely to start talking.

He peered through the peephole in the door. He saw the back of the cop's trenchcoat. He was gazing at the stars. Probably fancied himself the romantic type, George mused. What a fool. He'd blow wind up this guy's ass, get him out of the house, then go upstairs and catch some sleep.

He opened the door. "Okay, Lieutenant, let's get this over with. I've got a big day—"

George froze. His expression disintegrated, from impatient tolerance to unmasked horror.

"Hello, George," his old friend said, as he peered out with his piercing green eyes. "Miss me?"

*   *   *

While he steered his Trans Am with his left hand, Mike punched the number into his cell phone again with his right. No answer. That was odd. He had spoken to George Philby just ten minutes ago, telling him that he wanted to talk to him tonight. Sure, come on over, the man had said. I'll be here all evening. So why was it that when Mike called now, just to tell him he was going to be a little delayed, there was no answer?

Something strange was going on here. Mike felt a tingling somewhere at the base of his brain. There were, of course, a thousand possible explanations. Maybe the man was in the bathtub and didn't care to get out. But would he do that when he was expecting a police detective to drop by? Maybe he had call waiting and he didn't want to ditch his first caller. But Mike had tried three times; surely he would've eventually taken the call. It was possible the man was taking out the trash, or doing some moonlight weeding, or had fallen asleep. . . .

But Mike didn't buy any of that. Something was wrong. Either Philby had something to hide, and he'd decided to hit the road before Mike got there . . .

Or Mike wasn't the only visitor dropping by the Philby residence tonight.

With his free hand, Mike yanked the portable siren out of his backseat. He rolled down the window, snapped the thing on tight, and let it rip. The siren wailed, and Mike's face was bathed in a fuzzy, red glow. There weren't that many cars on the road this time of night, but Mike didn't want to take any chances.

The killer had gotten past him twice already, had already killed four people in hideously grotesque ways. He didn't want to see what the maniac might have cooked up next.

"Comfortable?" he asked, as he smeared lubricating jelly under each of the handcuffs. "I hope so. This isn't supposed to hurt you, George. Well, not yet, anyway."

George's eyelids began to flicker open. Good. It would be more fun with him awake. And they were supposed to be friends, right? So they should be facing one another, eyes open in eager anticipation. He hadn't meant to knock George out cold. He just wanted to apply enough force to make the man compliant. To get him on the bed and handcuffed to the bedposts without resistance.

"Rise and shine, Georgie-Porgie." He slapped the man's face a few times, harder than was necessary. "It's showtime."

George's eyelids fluttered open. "What . . . is it? What do you want?"

"I think you know the answer to that question, George."

As he regained awareness, George first realized he'd been stripped naked. Then he realized he was lying flat on the bed. A horrible moment later, he realized he couldn't move. He jerked his arms down, jangling the cuffs. "Wha-what is this?"

"This is the way the world ends, George. For you, anyway."

"What are you going to do? Where are my clothes?"

"You won't need them." He crawled off the bed, bent over, and picked up a breadbox-sized metal device. "See this? It's a portable battery charger. I had it in my car."

George's eyes widened. He tugged again at his chains, unable to get free. He tried to squirm, but found his feet were tied to the end of the bed. He could barely move at all. Sweat poured down the sides of his face.

"You're not getting away, George. Not possible. So don't waste your energy. You're going to need it."

"What are you planning to do, you sick bastard?"

He made a tsking noise. "Language, George. Language." He patted the top of the charger. "You were always mechanically minded, George. I'll bet you've already got the whole thing figured out."

"Don't get any ideas, you asshole. A cop'll be here any minute!"

"Oh, I'm sure. I suppose you called him telepathically." He giggled, then withdrew the two charging cables, one positive, one negative, and attached them to the metal frame of the bed. "Forget it, George. I cut the phone line before I came in. You couldn't call the cops even if you could get free. Which you can't." He ran his hand along the smooth metal frame of the bed. "So convenient of you to have this old-fashioned brass bed. Very attractive. And conductive."

"What are you going to do to me?" George screamed.

"Here's the game plan." He withdrew a small timer from his overcoat pocket and plugged it into one of the AC jacks on the back of the charger. "I plugged the charger into the handy-dandy wall socket. Had to unplug your VCR, though. Sorry about that—you're going to miss tonight's episode of *Frasier*. Anyway, when activated, this charger is capable of transmitting something like a thousand volts of electricity per second. That'll really supercharge your brain cells." He laughed, loud and horribly.

When his hysteria finally subsided, he wiped his eyes dry. "I was being facetious, of course. It'll fry your brain like a poached egg. A minute or so of this and you won't be able to do more than sit in a chair and drool on yourself. But it won't really matter, because after two minutes, you'll be dead."

"Don't do this," George said. "Please."

"The electricity will travel through the cables, into the bed, into your handcuffs and, greased by that jelly I rubbed over each wrist, right into your body. Oh, you'll feel it, all right. You'll feel it in every neuron and synapse of your being. I'm sure you've felt pain once or twice, George, even in your pampered existence. But you've never felt anything like this before. You'll be begging me to stop it. Crying like a baby. But it won't stop. It won't stop until you're dead."

"Please," George said. His quiet voice was nonetheless urgent. "Please. I'll do anything."

The man smiled. "Here it comes."

"*No!* Please, no!"

He reached behind the battery charger and flicked the power switch. George braced himself. His body arched up into the air, stiff—and a moment later, he realized there was no charge.

The man practically fell over himself laughing. He pressed a hand against his side, reeling. "You're such a sucker, George! Such a fool!" He laughed some more, until finally, almost a minute later, he had settled down enough to explain. "The power is on, George. But you didn't get shocked. Know why?"

George shook his trembling head.

"There's only one thing saving you from the big shock-eroony, George. And that's this timer. You've probably seen them before. People use them to turn the lights on and off while they're out of town. I got this one set for five minutes." He walked over to the side of the bed and pressed close to George's face. "For the moment, the timer is blocking the flow of electricity. But unless I do something to prevent it, in five minutes, the juice will flow." He poked a finger into George's rib cage. *"Zzzht!"*

Why were all the lights out in the house? Mike wondered as he steered his Trans Am toward George Philby's house. Did he have the wrong address? He checked his notes. No, this was the place. But if Philby was expecting him, why wasn't the porch light on? Or at least the living room light. Why didn't he see the same blue television glow he saw in most of the other houses he'd passed?

As before, there were a thousand possible explanations. Philby might be in a room that only had a window on the back of the house. There could've been a power outage. But coupled with Philby's failure to answer the phone for the last fifteen minutes, it gave Mike the inescapable feeling that something was wrong. Call it the influence of years of cop work, or just call it gut instinct. Whatever it was, it told Mike he was heading toward trouble.

He parked on the street, then slipped out the side door quietly, his Sig Sauer at the ready.

"Please," George said. Tears were welling up in his eyes. "I don't want to die. I'll do anything. Tell you anything."

The man leaned all the closer. "Will you? I'd really appreciate that. And you know what I want to know."

"How do I know you won't kill me? Even if I talk. Like you did the others."

The man leaned all too close to George's face. "You don't. But that timer is still ticking."

"I don't have the merchandise. I was as surprised as you when I found out."

This was the third time he'd heard this same song and dance, and he was getting tired of it. "Then who does have it?"

"I don't know. Maybe Fred has it."

The man was incredulous. "Fred? Fred the Feeb?"

"I don't know. If I knew, I'd tell you. Hell, if I knew, I'd go and get it myself."

"George, I want to know where it is."

"I don't know!"

The man pushed away from the bed. *"Am I going to have to kill every damn one of you?"* He turned away, pressing his fingers against his forehead. Control, he told himself. Control. That's the secret. That's why you've come so far so well. Preparation and control.

He walked into the bathroom and splashed cold water on his face. He took several deep breaths, focusing on recapturing his inner tranquility. Then he grabbed a towel, dried himself off, and returned to the bedroom.

He glanced at the timer. "One minute, George."

"Please!" George pressed his chest forward, straining, pulling the cuffs to the full length of their chains. "I do not have it. I don't know where it is."

The man shrugged. "Then you'll die."

"Okay, then—I do know where it is. I admit it. I can show it to you. But you'll have to let me go."

"I don't think so." The man glanced again at the timer. "Thirty seconds. Where is it?"

"It—it—" George's eyes raced. "It's in my office."

"I've already searched your office. Thoroughly."

"I didn't mean my office. I meant—the den. Here at home. I sometimes call that my office."

The man shook his head from side to side. "You're pathetic, George." He sighed. "And you don't know where it is any more than I do."

"Then let me go!"

"Why should I?" A second later, they both heard the click. A tiny sound, but one that sent shock waves of terror through George like nothing he had ever known in his life.

The timer had reached zero.

More than a thousand volts of electricity coursed through George's body. He flew up into the air, his back arched, his handcuffs holding him to the bed.

The man shook his head in disgust. "I never liked you

anyway, George." He turned away and returned to the bathroom. He had never cared for the smell of cooked flesh, and he felt an urgent need to relieve himself.

There was no sign of forced entry, Mike noted as he approached the porch. And the front door wasn't locked. Curiouser and curiouser.

He pushed the door open quietly, then stepped inside, gun at the ready. The downstairs was just as dark as it had appeared from the outside, but up the central staircase he saw a trace of light. A moment later, he heard talking, a voice, and—something else. A low humming sound, like powered machinery in operation.

What the hell was going on here?

He considered calling for backup, but decided against it. What would he tell them? He didn't really know what he had here. Maybe it was nothing at all. And if he left, it was just possible the man he'd been chasing might escape. And he couldn't live with himself if that happened.

Slowly, he crept up the stairs, gun poised, ready for anything. Catlike, he told himself. That's what the manuals always told officers to do when they didn't want to be heard. Walk catlike. What the hell did that mean? He weighed almost two hundred pounds and he was wearing street shoes. There was no catlike.

He heard the carpet creak—could a carpet creak? Something did. The floorboards, whatever. Fortunately, the humming noise upstairs was far louder than he was. He didn't think he'd been heard.

At the top of the stairs, he saw the lights were on in a single room. The humming was coming from that room—and something else. What was it? It sounded like running water.

He walked cautiously to the doorway, then jumped inside. He whirled around, scanning in all directions with his gun at the ready, covering the room in the usual police-manual manner. Till his eyes were riveted by the spectacle at center stage.

There was a naked man handcuffed to the bed. He recognized him—it was George Philby. His body was arched up in the air. His eyes were clenched shut, as were his fists. His whole body was tight as a drum. He appeared to be in immense agony.

And Mike quickly saw why. He knew the gizmo at the side of the bed was a battery charger. The cables were attached to the bed and the man was handcuffed. . . .

Mike's jaw literally dropped. My God, what kind of sick mind—

It came to him like a bolt out of the blue. He was here. The killer was *here*, he realized.

But too late. The blow struck Mike on the back of his neck, hard. He reeled forward, neck feeling like it was broken. Hold onto the gun, he told himself, as he tumbled across a chair and fell onto an end table. Hold onto the gun.

He felt a kick to his ribs. He clenched his teeth together. That hurt. He rolled around, trying to get his bearings. He saw a dark figure moving toward him. In an overcoat. He didn't have time to think or focus. He brought his gun around and aimed.

The steel grippers on the battery cable touched Mike's gun, and an instant later, he felt a thousand volts of electricity rocket through his body. He reflexively fired, but the bullet went wild and lodged in the ceiling. He dropped the gun, then fell back spasming onto the carpet.

"Son of a bitch," he whispered, as he fought for consciousness. The room was darkening, or so it seemed to him. A dark blur was surrounding him, blanketing him. . . .

It was the killer. He still held one of the battery cables. And he was reaching for something.

Mike's wedding ring. He still wore it, even after all these years. And now someone was going to use it to kill him.

He tried to roll around, escape, but he was too groggy. His body felt uncoordinated; it didn't respond properly to command. The steel grippers came closer, and he couldn't move fast enough, couldn't get away. . . .

A moment later Mike felt as if someone had stuck a knife inside him and started peeling away his skin. From the inside. He felt his body trembling, rocking back and forth with the surge of electricity rippling down his spine. He felt his whole

body tense like a brick. He thought his heart was doing
flip-flops in his chest, thought his flesh was on fire, and a few
moments after that, was beyond thinking anything at all.

TWO

* *

Here He Lies Where He Long'd to Be

* 28 *

Christina stood at the front of Judge Perry's courtroom trying to explain things as best she could. "I'm sure it will only be a moment, your honor."

"A moment is too long." Judge Perry's usual impassive expression today seemed positively grim. "When I say a trial will begin at nine o'clock, I mean it."

"I understand that."

"If this is part of a plaintiff strategy to delay, let me tell you right now that I will not tolerate it."

"No, sir." Christina felt the prickly heat rising up her neck. "It's nothing like that. He's just . . . late."

"Then we'll proceed with co-counsel at the helm. Approach the bench, Ms. McCall."

"Your honor . . . I can't." Christina was twisting her fingers into knots. "I'm only an intern. I haven't finished law school."

Judge Perry's shoulders began to heave. "Fine. Then we'll proceed with Professor Matthews."

Matthews awkwardly pushed himself to his feet, making minute adjustments in the lie of his tweed jacket. He did not approach.

"Is there a problem?" the judge asked, with an edge that could cut through butter. "Haven't you finished law school?"

"Your honor," Matthews began. "I do have a law degree. But I've never tried a lawsuit. I'm here strictly to advise on legal issues."

Judge Perry's face was so tight he had difficulty speaking. "I will not tolerate this in my courtroom! Where is Mr. Kincaid?"

"I-I don't know, your honor," Christina stuttered. "I can't

imagine what happened. But I'm sure, whatever it is, it was unavoidable. . . ."

"Mr. Kincaid is in contempt of this court. If he does not appear in five minutes, I'll dismiss the plaintiffs' suit."

Cecily leaned across the plaintiffs' table to Christina. "Can he do that?" she whispered.

"Oh, yeah," she whispered back. "He's the judge. He can do whatever he wants."

"I'm setting my stopwatch," the judge informed them. "Five minutes. And counting."

"That won't be necessary."

The last voice came from the back of the courtroom. Everyone present swiveled around to see Ben Kincaid rush up the center aisle. He had a document box under each arm, with his briefcase precariously balanced between. His tie was unknotted, dangling over his neck. He looked a mess.

"I apologize to the court for my tardiness," Ben said as he raced to the front. "It was unavoidable. I . . . uh . . . had car trouble."

"That's not good enough!" Judge Perry barked. He seemed even more enraged now that Ben was here. "When I say a trial begins at nine sharp, I mean nine sharp. Not a second later."

"Yes, sir. I understand that, sir. And I'm very sorry."

"In your absence, you were found in contempt of court. You are directed to pay a five-hundred-dollar fine to the court clerk on your way out of the courtroom today."

Ben closed his eyes. "Yes, sir." Five hundred dollars!

"Now please take a minute to . . . pull yourself together. And then let's get on with this trial!"

"Yes, sir. Thank you, sir." May I have another, sir?

The judge stepped into chambers. Ben avoided Colby's smarmy smile; obviously he thought the trial was already drifting his way. He'd had nothing to do with Ben's absence, but he was more than happy to exploit it to the fullest.

Christina began knotting his tie. "What happened to you? Sleep late?"

"No. Couldn't get to the courthouse. Ended up calling for a taxi. And you know how long that takes. Since there are only two taxis in all of Tulsa."

"What happened? Van wouldn't start?"

"No." He craned his neck as she slid the knotted tie up against his Adam's apple. "When I walked out to the curb this morning, it was gone."

"Stolen?"

"Repossessed."

Christina's jaw dropped. "No."

"Yes." He popped open his briefcase and started organizing his materials. "It seems we've reached the end of our financial tether. The Brain is calling in the markers."

Once he was finally dressed and groomed properly, Ben scanned the courtroom gallery. It was jam-packed. Spectators were wedged together on the long-tiered pews like travelers on an overbooked bus. People stood at the back of the room and filtered along the walls. Ben suspected Judge Perry wouldn't tolerate that for long; surely it violated the fire code.

All in all, he counted more than two hundred people crammed in the relatively tiny gallery. Members of the press and sketch artists occupied most of the first row. Members of the plaintiffs' families took the second, except for Cecily who, as the designated plaintiffs' representative, sat at the table up front with Ben. And directly behind the relatives sat a phalanx of gray-suited Blaylock executives and employees. Most of the people who had been deposed were present, including Turnbull—although Ben noticed that he sat a good distance away from everyone else in the Blaylock camp. Ben knew Turnbull hadn't been fired, but he was probably receiving a chilly reception from his old pals, just the same.

And some of the people crammed into the courtroom were simply spectators, folks with no connection to the case at all. Some were VIPs or lucky ducks with well-placed friends who'd managed to get them in without waiting in line. It was supposed to be first come first served, but Ben knew that, as a practical matter, connections counted. He also knew Colby had sent in a squadron of young associates at the crack of dawn to hold seats until the Blaylockians arrived. He wanted as many friendly faces in the courtroom as possible.

The Brain was out there, too, the son of a bitch. Keeping an eye on his collateral, Ben supposed. He wondered if he'd driven to the courthouse in Ben's van. Ben's former van.

Ben marveled at the high-tech appearance of this far-from-new courtroom. Although federal courts still did not permit trials to be televised, monitors for internal use were everywhere. A huge television screen, six feet by six feet, faced the jury box. It was on wheels so it could be moved as necessary. In this way, exhibits could be shown to the jury as they were discussed. Two smaller television screens appeared at each end of the jury box. All of these monitors, of course, had wires and cables and feeder mechanisms cluttering the courtroom. There were also computer monitors at the judge's bench, and it looked like Colby's team had no fewer than three laptops.

Not exactly Clarence Darrow's courtroom.

Ben stifled a yawn. He had not gotten much sleep last night and, despite the excitement swirling around the courtroom, it was beginning to catch up with him. Even after he left the office, he had a hard time sleeping. Sometime around four he finally drifted off. Good thing he hadn't gone outside—he might've seen the repo man swiping his van.

The old-style steam radiators in the federal courtroom emitted a discernible hum; once you focused on it, it seemed deafening. The spectators had a hum of their own, an expectant buzz, an anticipatory excitement about what would soon begin. Why did people come to watch trials to which they had no connection? Ben wondered, for about the millionth time. Don't they get enough of this on television? Don't they have lives of their own? It never made sense to him. But after all the pretrial publicity this case had received, he supposed it was inevitable.

Around nine fifteen, Judge Perry returned to the courtroom. He appeared to have suppressed some of his anger, although Ben knew he had a long way to go before he'd be back in this man's good graces.

"Good morning, ladies and gentlemen," the judge said. "The court case set for trial is *Elkins et al. versus H. P. Blaylock Industrial Machinery Corporation*, case number JP00-065. This case is set as a jury trial. Counsel, is there any reason we should not proceed at this time with jury selection?"

Ben and Colby both rose to their feet, shaking their heads. Ready or not, the trial had begun.

Compared to most of the criminal cases Ben had handled, voir dire in federal civil court was a piece of cake. Voir dire in criminal cases could go on for days in some jurisdictions; voir dire in this case took less than an hour. In the Northern District of Oklahoma, the judges still handled all the questioning of prospective jurors. Lawyers could submit questions in advance, which the judge might or might not read. But at any rate, when the judge was in charge, there would be none of the mostly irrelevant questioning designed to help the lawyers "get to know" the jurors, and none of the questions designed to preview trial theories. If the question didn't pertain to rooting out potential bias, the judge didn't read it. As a result, federal voir dire was always more direct—and shorter. Even though it limited his ability to select a favorable jury, Ben had to admit that, objectively speaking, the federal court approach was a lot quicker and probably better.

Judge Perry methodically quizzed the twenty potential jurors he had called to the witness-box. Although he was probably less persistent than a private attorney might've been, he didn't hesitate to follow up when a juror statement revealed any possible bias.

Probably the most interesting moment occurred when the judge asked if any of the jurors had any ties, past or present, with the defendant, H. P. Blaylock. A black woman in the back row, Etta Thompson, raised her hand.

Ben almost salivated. What would it be? he wondered. A disgruntled employee? An angry mother? Even if Colby removed her from the jury, all the others would get to hear her complaint.

"My husband Manfred worked at that company for twenty-four years. Till two years ago."

"But he doesn't work there now?" Judge Perry followed up.

"No, sir."

"May I ask why not?"

Ben rubbed his hands together in anticipation. Fired. Laid off. Industrial accident.

"He's dead, your honor."

The judge was taken aback. "Oh—I'm sorry. I didn't know—"

"Don't worry, sir. We had twenty-six good years together."

"Oh." He paused a few respectful moments. "Well, was there anything about your husband's work experience that might make it difficult for you to treat the Blaylock corporation just as you would any other defendant?"

"Yes, sir."

Ben sat up.

"You think you might have some bias?"

"Yes, sir. I do."

Now we're back on track, Ben thought. Let 'er rip, lady. Give us the dirt.

"Did the corporation treat your husband poorly, ma'am?"

"Oh, no, sir. Far from it. They were a godsend."

Ben felt his heart thump down to the pit of his stomach.

"They've been so fine. So generous. They continued paying us six months after Manny's heart attack. They paid out his pension immediately, in cash. They even paid all the medical expenses. And they've kept his health insurance coverage in place for my children."

The judge seemed confused. "Well then . . . why . . . you said you were biased."

"I am, sir. I'm biased in Blaylock's favor. It think it must be the best little company that God ever put on this earth. I just . . ." She turned her head slightly toward plaintiffs' table. "I just can't understand why anyone would ever want to hurt those good people."

Ben felt a throbbing in his temples that didn't desist. First his car was repo'd, then one of the jurors nominates the defendant for sainthood. This case was already off to a rotten start—and they hadn't even had opening statements yet.

Judge Perry didn't see fit to remove any of the jurors for cause—not even Mrs. Thompson, who ultimately swore she could treat all parties fairly despite her undying love for H. P. Blaylock. So Ben had to use his first preemptory to remove her. Colby removed a woman from the front who had a son with cerebral palsy; no doubt he thought she would be too sympathetic to the plaintiffs. Ben then removed a school janitor who had opined that jury awards were "getting out of hand"; Colby removed a woman who felt that "big corporations have too much power."

Ben hated to remove the janitor; he had two boys of his own about the age of Cecily's Billy. But he couldn't afford to leave anyone who might, even if he managed to win the suit, argue against awarding major damages. Ben didn't have any illusions; this case wasn't going to break the record set by *Pennzoil v. Texaco*, in which the jury awarded plaintiff Pennzoil eleven billion dollars in damages. But he had hoped to keep open the possibility of a significant damages award. He'd better—if he ever hoped to see his van again.

Ben wasn't sure what to do with his last peremptory. Christina steered him toward a plumpish woman in the center row.

"Why her?" Ben whispered.

Christina shrugged. "I think she's stingy. And we definitely don't want stingy."

"Stingy? How can you tell?"

"I just have a feeling. Look at the way she sits, all bottled up tight. Look at the way she clutches her purse in her lap; she hasn't let go of it since she came into the courtroom. And look at that dress. Most people dress up for court. If that's her idea of dressing up, it's been a good long time since she went shopping."

Ben wasn't entirely convinced, but he didn't have any better ideas. The woman was dismissed. Colby removed another mother, which left them with fourteen people—twelve jurors and two alternates. Ten women and four men, ages ranging from twenty-one to sixty-eight. Twelve white, one black, one Hispanic. One with a college degree, thirteen not. A secretary, a sales clerk, two fast-food restaurant employees, a bookkeeper, a retiree, a hospital nurse, a stay-home mom, a student, a man who owned a body shop, an architect, and two waitresses. A randomly chosen group of average citizens who would be charged with finding the facts in one of the most complex cases Ben had ever encountered, a case where millions of dollars were at stake, a case that would determine culpability for the deaths of eleven innocent children.

The preliminaries were over.

The trial had begun.

* 29 *

"Ladies and gentlemen of the jury," Ben said. He addressed them squarely, standing directly behind the rail that separated the jurors from the rest of the courtroom. "There's a little town not twenty miles away from Tulsa called Blackwood. It's a nice place; I bet most of you have been there at one time or another, or at least have driven through. It has lovely green rolling hills, tall trees, abundant parks. The Arkansas River runs right through the center of town. Main Street is filled with what I'm told are some of the best antique stores in the area. It has homes, families, and schools—one of the best school systems in the state. But it also has something else. It has more than its share . . . of death."

Ben spoke quietly, almost intimately, as if he were speaking to them one-on-one on a living room sofa rather than delivering a speech in a crowded courtroom. He didn't use notes. He didn't need them. "I represent eleven sets of parents, moms and dads, who live in the Blackwood area. These parents are different in many ways. They are teachers, physical therapists, ambulance drivers, accountants, office clerks, secretaries, post office employees. Some of them went to the same church; some of them had never met before. But they all share one element, one tragic common denominator. They all lost a child between the ages of eight and twelve."

Ben proceeded to describe some of the leukemia cases, some of the heartaches his clients had endured. If anything, he soft-pedaled the drama; it was still early in the case and he didn't want to seem as if he was trying to win a verdict on sympathy alone.

"Those of us who have not experienced it are simply incapable of understanding what these good people have been through. There can be nothing worse than losing your own child. Nothing in the world. But the aching is only intensified when it turns out the death was caused by factors that could've been prevented, factors that never should have arisen in the first place."

Ben's voice acquired a harder edge. He began describing the waste-disposal practices at H. P. Blaylock, how they used TCE and perc, both "identified by the EPA as dangerous carcinogens." He was careful not to argue—this was opening statement, after all, not closing argument. The attorney was only supposed to preview the evidence that would follow, so he was careful to preface his points with the catchphrase: "The evidence will show . . ."

"The evidence will show that H. P. Blaylock engaged in practices that systematically contaminated the Blackwood water supply. They lied about it when initially asked, pretending they were having the waste carried off to a federally approved disposal site, but in fact much of the waste was buried underground, in permeable containers, making contamination of the groundwater inevitable. The groundwater seeped into a nearby ravine which traveled directly to one of Blackwood's water wells—Well B. The well that serviced the homes of every one of the children who died."

Ben took a step closer, leaning against the dividing rail. "The defendant will undoubtedly deny all responsibility for their actions, just as they formerly denied they contaminated the water supply by burying waste underground. They will deny they did anything wrong, and furthermore will say that even if they did, it didn't cause those poor children's cancer. We will put on evidence demonstrating just the contrary— that a cancer cluster of this magnitude cannot be an accident, that contaminated water will in fact cause leukemia, particularly in vulnerable young growing bodies. But I will suggest, ladies and gentlemen, that this medical testimony will just be rubber stamping what each of you already knows. You don't need medical evidence to tell you what happened here. Common sense tells you what happened here. Common sense tells you that when an entire neighborhood's children start dying, the fact that the water supply is loaded with carcinogens is not simply a coincidence. It's the cause."

He paused, drawing himself up. He wanted to end on a calm, unemotional note. He knew Colby would accuse him of playing on the jurors' emotions. He didn't want it to be any truer than necessary.

"You might be wondering, 'Do I think the Blaylock company hurt those children on purpose?' No, of course not. They weren't trying to hurt anyone. They did it because they didn't care. They did it because it was cheaper than spending money to have the waste hauled away. It wasn't malice that killed those children. It was corporate indifference. Well-compensated executives putting profits above lives. That's what killed my clients' children."

Ben paused, carefully looking each juror in the eye. "This didn't have to happen. They knew this was wrong. But they did it anyway."

After Ben was finished, the gallery, packed as it was, remained silent for a very long time.

Judge Perry broke the silence by calling for a recess, to everyone's relief. It was almost as if everyone in the gallery released their breath at once, a collective sigh. Gradually people found their way to their feet and shuffled out to the hallway.

Ben noticed the judge was frowning at him; he wondered if His Honor had frowned all the way through his opening. He probably hadn't liked the part about "common sense." Perry had already lectured Ben about the necessity of proving causation, and threatened him about the consequences if he didn't. They both knew it was the weakest part of the plaintiffs' case—which was exactly why Ben had addressed the issue right off the bat.

When the recess ended, it was Colby's turn to talk to the jury. Although he had the option of reserving his opening until it was time for him to put on the defense case, he of course chose to speak now. He'd have to be crazy to let Ben's impassioned speech go unrebutted.

Colby didn't mince words, didn't beat around the bush. "Counsel for the plaintiff would have you believe that H. P. Blaylock is in the business of murdering children. Well, we're not. We did not do this. This is not our fault. This is not simply the plea of a defendant being defensive; this is a fact. We did not do this. And more to the point—the plaintiffs are unable to prove that we did."

Despite his strong words, Colby appeared to be playing it cool. Ben supposed he had been practicing long enough to know that an impassioned plea from an injured party simply has more rhetoric force than an impassioned denial from the accused. Natural sympathies would be with the parents who lost their kids, no matter what he did. So he took the Spock approach, played the cool, logical friend bringing reason to those who have been temporarily led astray.

He was also smart enough not to deny the undeniable. "A little bit of what counsel for the plaintiffs has told you is actually true. Blaylock employees—contrary to the procedures established by upper management—did in fact bury some waste underground, in a vacant lot behind the plant. That, however, does not prove that any of the waste spilled onto the ground. If in fact there ever was any spillage—which has yet to be proved—the amounts were so small they couldn't have contaminated anything. Moreover, there is no proof that anything from the Blaylock lot ever made it to Well B—which is almost half a mile away."

Colby had a strong, forthright voice, one that made it seem inconceivable that he could speak other than the truth. Ben knew it was that voice that had won Colby so many trials; when he was speaking, even Ben found it hard not to believe him.

"But that isn't the biggest whopper in the plaintiffs' case. The largest hole in their scheme is where they suggest that these tiny chemicals caused those kids to develop leukemia. That statement is simply absurd. And unprovable. The fact is—no one knows what causes leukemia. Don't take my word for it. Ask anyone. Every one of you could call up your family doctors tonight and ask them what causes cancer, and every one of them would say the same thing: 'No one knows what causes leukemia.' That's the truth of the matter. Regardless of what Mr. Kincaid's paid professional experts say."

Colby paused, patting his vest pockets, then removing a pocket watch. He didn't look at it, but simply fiddled with it, twisted the watch and chain in his hands. It may have seemed strange to the jurors, but Ben knew exactly what he was up to. He was making them wait—drawing out the suspense, making them hang on his every word. It was a great gimmick, although Ben had liked it better when he first saw Gregory Peck do it in *To Kill a Mockingbird*.

"These parents who have brought this lawsuit have been through a terrible tragedy. We can all agree about that. No parent should have to endure what they've endured. No one should have to bear so much pain. But they did. And when it was all over, it was only natural for them to want . . . something more. They start thinking, 'Is that all there is?' 'Did I spend all those years raising that boy . . . for nothing?' That's when they start looking for someone to blame. It's easier to think such a tragic loss is the fault of some evildoer, rather than to simply accept the truth—that fate is sometimes cruel and the Good Lord works in unfathomable and mysterious ways. They want to turn this tragic loss into a crusade."

He tossed back his shoulders. "Those parents have my utmost sympathy. But ladies and gentlemen of the jury, H. P. Blaylock is not an evildoer. Blaylock is a fine, family-run business, the kind that made America great, one that has employed and supported thousands of families throughout this century. Our hearts go out to all parents who have lost a child—but we did not cause this tragedy. It is not our fault. And the plaintiffs—who bear the burden of proof—cannot prove otherwise. It's that simple, really."

* 30 *

Ben rushed into Room 452 at St. John's Hospital, ignoring the nurse shouting after him.

"Mike?" He pushed the swinging door open and ran inside.

Mike was sitting upright in bed, wearing the traditional ill-fitting gown. He set aside the Anne Tyler novel he was reading. "Ben. Nice of you to drop by."

Ben was so flustered he could barely order his thoughts enough to speak. "What are you doing here? Why didn't you tell me?"

"Apparently you found out anyway."

"I came to see Mrs. Marmelstein. I saw Tomlinson in the hall and he told me you were hurt."

"Tomlinson never could keep his mouth shut."

The floor nurse peeled through the door, glaring at Ben. "Sir! I'm afraid visiting hours are over, and in any case, you can't simply barge into a patient's—"

Mike waved his hands. "It's all right, Emily. He's a friend."

The nurse made a sniffing noise. "Even so. This is not how a visit should be conducted. There are procedures—"

"He's a lawyer," Mike explained. "He can't help himself."

Nurse Emily's lips pursed. She pivoted on one white plat-form heel and left the room.

"So how is Mrs. Marmelstein, anyway?" Mike asked amiably.

"Bad, getting worse. Her strength is fading. She seems to be losing the will to live. In fact, she seems to be losing the will to do anything except see her long-lost son, who we have been totally unable to locate. But that's beside the point. What the hell are you doing in the hospital?"

Mike tugged at the skirt of his hospital gown. "I found my killer."

"The one who killed the two Blaylock employees?"

"Three." Mike's lips pressed together tightly. "We haven't found the third body yet. But I'm sure he's dead."

"What happened to you?"

"I got fried." Mike lifted his bandaged hand. "I went in ready for almost anything—corkscrews, ball-peen hammers, whatever. But I sure as hell never expected a portable battery charger."

"A battery charger? What was he doing with that?"

"Electrocuting his victim. And me." He lifted the bandage slightly, just enough that Ben could see the charred, blackened flesh underneath. "Got me on the wedding ring. Gave me a shock that just about fried my brains."

"But you're all right now?"

"They say I'll be back on my feet tomorrow. Next day at the latest."

"Thank God." Despite this ostensibly good news, Ben noticed that his friend still wasn't smiling. "I guess you must be upset because he escaped."

"That's not what bothers me most. I never should've let that creep get the drop on me."

"How could you know he'd be administering electroshock therapy on the cheap? At least you weren't killed. I'm sure you gave a description to the cops. Let them catch him."

Mike shook his head. "No description. I never really got a look at him."

"So that's what bothers you most."

"No. I know this creep will kill again. I can feel it."

"Another Blaylock employee?"

"How should I know? Why—do you have a Blaylock victim you'd like to suggest?"

"Several. So that's what you're most upset about—you think this crazy will kill again?"

"No. And just for the record—I don't think he's crazy. He doesn't fit the profile for any serial killer we've ever encountered. Even the FBI agrees with me on this one. There's a reason this man is killing these people. Torturing these people. He wants something. I just don't know what it is."

"So that's what bothers you most."

"No." He inhaled deeply. "This guy is eliminating people because he thinks they pose some kind of threat to him. I don't know why exactly. But I'm certain self-protection is at the heart of it. He's covering himself."

"Yeah. So?"

"So—he let me live. Could've killed me. Easily. But he didn't. So what does that tell us?"

"I give. What?"

"That he doesn't consider me a threat. He knew who I was. But he was so damn sure of himself he didn't think I could touch him. So he didn't kill me. Not because he couldn't. He just didn't bother."

Ben slowly began to understand. "And that's what bothers you most."

"Damn straight." Mike pulled himself up by the metal braces on either side of his bed. "I wanted this bastard before. But it's gone beyond that, now. I have to get him. I *have* to. You know what I'm saying?" Mike pounded his fists together. "I have to get him. And I will."

Fred meticulously typed the ten-digit number into the green-glowing keypad next to his front door. Let's see . . . the year of the Battle of Waterloo, followed by my mother's age when she died, followed by the last four digits in my social security number. . . .

He punched in the last number, then hit the pound key. The keypad responded with a satisfying beep.

His spiffy new high-tech alarm system was officially armed.

He stepped back and beamed at the keypad, like a father admiring his daughter as she waltzed down the walkway in Atlantic City. It had cost him every spare penny he could scrape up, but it was worth it. Worth the money to know he was safe. Worth almost any amount to know that he wouldn't end up like George. . . .

He had of course read the article on page two of the *Tulsa World*. Sure, they hadn't found a body yet, but they knew what had happened, as did he. In the words of the immortal Queen . . . another one bites the dust.

Somehow he found this one harder to believe—harder than Harvey, harder than Maggie. After all, George had considerable advance warning. He must've known about the first two murders, and he must've realized who was behind it. He'd talked to the cop; he knew the score. What the hell was he thinking? What was he waiting around for?

Not what he got, that's for damn sure. The paper was skimpy on the details, but it supplied enough about "death by electrocution" for Fred to recognize the Master's hand. This was not a coincidental killing. This was the same old self-centered bastard, blowing away anyone and everyone he thought stood between him and his precious merchandise.

Including the cop. Lieutenant Michaelangelo Morelli, whom the *World* clearly considered God's gift to law enforcement, all but obliterated by a few kazillion volts of electricity. Paper said he was recovering nicely, which surprised Fred no end. Why would his former friend leave any witnesses, potential or otherwise? He wouldn't. He must've been in a hurry, must've simply not had time to mess around with him. Must've been determined to take care of George while he had the chance.

Which was lucky for the cop. Less so for George.

Fred stared glassy-eyed at the green-glowing keypad. Somehow it wasn't making him feel quite as secure as it had a moment ago.

He was the only one left. Assuming Professor Canino was dead, which he thought a fair assumption since he hadn't been seen in months, Fred was the only obstacle between the killer and the certain acquisition of the merchandise. Even as low as the killer's opinion of Fred was, at this point, he would have to realize that Fred was the one who had the goods.

He would come after Fred.

What was he worried about? he asked himself. He had one of the best security systems known to man. He was totally safe and secure.

An errant thought wandered unbidden into his cranium.

Didn't Harvey have an alarm system?

Fred turned, his face abruptly ashen, shuffled into the kitchen, and opened up the yellow pages. Maybe a guard dog. Yeah, that would be the thing. A great big scary Doberman.

Maybe even a Rottweiler. Nothing could get past a Rottweiler. Then he'd be safe. Then he'd be absolutely, totally, without question, safe. . . .

* 31 *

Ben wasn't used to going first. In the criminal trials that had been his mainstay over the past several years, he was never first. The prosecutor always started. Which had its pluses and minuses. It meant the opposition got the initial opportunity to influence the jury. But it also meant Ben had time to think and plan, time to absorb what the prosecution was trying to accomplish and to figure out a way to circumvent it.

Today, he didn't have the luxury of time. He had the burden of convincing the jury of the rightness of his cause, holding their attention, and persuading them—by a preponderance of the evidence. If he failed to do that, the defendants would never even have to stand up. The case would be dismissed before it got to them.

Ben had spent days agonizing over whom to call as his first witness. Conventional wisdom would say he should lead with his clients, so the jury can understand who and what this case is really about. The obvious sympathy factor involved in putting bereaved parents on the stand was also a consideration. Ben didn't want to exploit their grief; at the same time, he'd been hired to win this lawsuit, not to show how sensitive he was. And if he led with some of the more technical experts, the jury's mind might be permanently dulled before he got to the heart-gripping stuff.

He finally decided to start with two witnesses from the Blackwood hospital. From a legal standpoint, these witnesses would establish the fact of an injury—an essential component in any case for damages. As a practical matter, Ben hoped they would do much more.

The first witness was a man named Adam Nimsy. He worked as a photographer at the hospital, and at Dr. Freidrich's request, had photographed most of the children at various stages of their leukemia.

Nimsy was a middle-aged man, heavyset, with a seemingly permanent tired expression on his face. Ben introduced him to the jury, then started on the real questioning.

"What's your current position?"

"I'm a freelance photographer," Nimsy answered. "But most of my work comes on assignment from the hospital."

"And how long have you been doing this kind of work?"

"Interminably," he said dryly.

"What exactly do you do?"

"Whatever the doctors tell me to do," he explained. "If they say shoot, I shoot. If they say print, I print. If they say bark, I bark."

Ben tried to ignore the alleged wit. This was not supposed to be a "funny" witness. "Why do the doctors have you take pictures?"

"For legal reasons, usually. If they're getting ready to do something risky or controversial, they want an accurate record, either via photos or videotape. Sometimes they want pictures for comparative purposes, to analyze the progress of a disease—or a cure. Sometimes they want pics they can send to outside specialists for consultations."

Ben turned slightly toward the section of the gallery where his clients sat. "Do you know the parents who are the plaintiffs in this lawsuit?"

"Some of them. And I knew most of their children. I photographed most of them."

"How did that come about?"

"It was at Dr. Freidrich's request. He didn't ask me to photo the first two boys. But after that, I guess he started to suspect that something strange was going on. So many leukemia deaths of young children at the same time in the same neighborhood couldn't possibly be—"

"Objection," Colby said, rising to his feet. "Is this witness a medical expert? I don't recall hearing his credentials."

"The objection is sustained," Judge Perry replied. "The witness will restrict his testimony to what he has seen and heard and not offer the jury opinions on matters outside his field."

"Of course, your honor," Ben said, not remotely repentant. "Mr. Nimsy, did you photograph the subsequent nine leukemia victims?"

"Yes. All of them."

"How often?"

"Whenever the doctor asked. About every two months."

"Do you have those photographs with you today?" Like any good trial attorney, Ben was only asking questions to which he already knew the answer.

"I do." He looked up at the judge. "May I?"

With Judge Perry's consent, Nimsy retrieved the photos from the gallery. They had been enlarged (at Ben's expense) and mounted so that the jury could see them easily on their monitors—and take hard copies back to the deliberation room when the trial was over.

The photos told a story more eloquent, more gut-wrenching, more devastatingly sad than anything the finest poet could have conceived. Nimsy, of course, was not allowed to comment on what the photos contained—and there was no need for him to. All he did was authenticate the evidence—that is, talk about how and when and where the photos were taken. None of which anyone cared about. What was important remained unsaid. But the pictures spoke volumes.

Through these photos, the jurors were able to chart the course of the disease for each of the nine photographed children. Billy was up first. In his first shot, he still looked essentially normal. He had been diagnosed with leukemia, but the bruises didn't show and he hadn't started to lose weight yet. The next photo, taken two months later, revealed a startling change. He'd begun chemotherapy; his hair was gone. By the third photo, his face was drawn and his cheekbones protruded from a gaunt, emaciated face. By the fourth photo, he appeared discolored; bruises covered his body. Ben saw the jurors' shock as they viewed the hollow concavity surrounding his eyes, his gaping, seeping, open wounds. In the fifth photo,

Billy seemed skeletal, weak, and brittle; his eyelids were barely open. And in the sixth . . .

Well, as Nimsy explained, there was no sixth. Ever.

Like a slide show from hell, the flurry of photographs showed nine youngsters progressing from healthy poster children to a tragic mutated travesty of humanity. The witness shed no tears and had no tremble in his voice—but the impact was profound, just the same.

Colby did not cross-examine, and Ben thought he knew why. What was there to be gained? There was no question about the authenticity of the photos, and Nimsy had not officially offered any opinion as to the cause of their illness. But as Ben peered into the jurors' collective eyes, he knew there would be no further discussion about whether an injury had occurred. Colby would have to win his case on other grounds.

After the break, Ben put on Dr. Freidrich, the Blackwood pediatrician who'd treated seven of the boys and girls. Words met pictures, as Freidrich systematically took the jurors through the stages of the disease. In a way, it was almost overkill; the pictures had already said it all. Still, Ben needed medical testimony on the record, so there could be no question but that he'd made a prima facie case as to injury.

It was hard on the parents—Cecily in particular. They had been through this nightmare once already; they didn't need to relive it in the courtroom. Still, they managed to get through it without losing control or pretending as if it didn't hurt. Only one of the mothers had to leave the room. Two cried, but under the circumstances, Ben didn't think they could be accused of improperly trying to influence the jurors—two of whom were crying themselves.

As before, Colby did not cross-examine. He knew better than to dispute the fact of the tragedy. The fight for control of this case would be fought on another battleground.

In the afternoon, Ben started the technical testimony. This he knew would be less than heart-stopping, but it had to be done. He started with his geologist, Edward Drury. Drury essentially repeated what he had said at his deposition, updated with the information he had gathered since that time (at Ben's expense). He described the extent of the contamination of the soil and groundwater behind the Blaylock plant and the adjoining ravine.

Colby did cross-examine, although it was brief:

"You say the ground behind the plant is contaminated with TCE?"

"That's correct."

"When did this contamination occur?"

"Well . . . I couldn't say exactly when it happened. But it's definitely there now."

"Was it there six months ago?"

"It seems like—"

"Don't guess, sir. Do your studies indicate whether the soil was contaminated six months ago?"

Drury frowned. "No, they do not."

"For all you know, it could have happened last week."

"I suppose technically that's so. But as a practical matter—"

"In fact, the soil could have been recently contaminated, intentionally, by some unscrupulous person trying to assign blame to Blaylock—and your test results would be just the same, wouldn't they?"

"I suppose. But—"

"And since you don't know when the soil was tainted, you have no idea if it began before"—he paused meaningfully—"or after the tragic deaths of the plaintiffs' children."

"Common sense tells me—"

"We don't want to hear about common sense," the judge said. Ben hoped that would be the sound bite for the evening news. "We want to know what your study shows."

"My study didn't address the question of when the contamination occurred. I don't think any study could. But it can't be a coincidence that the plaintiffs—"

"I admire your loyalty to the plaintiffs," Colby said, cutting him off. "It's touching. Now—remind me again—how much have the plaintiffs paid you to be a witness in this case?"

When he gave Colby the number, the jury gasped.

Next, Ben called his groundwater specialist to the stand—Harry Campbell. Campbell was even dryer and duller than Drury had been (and, as Colby revealed on cross, more expensive). But he did manage to demonstrate how, at least theoretically, water could travel from the Blaylock plant into the ravine, percolate for a while in the aquifer, then get sucked into Well B. Colby did not cross; apparently he didn't think it necessary. Proving the water could travel from the Blaylock plant to the well was one thing. Proving that the poison did in fact come from the Blaylock plant was something else altogether.

In the late afternoon, Ben called his EPA expert to the stand. Ben considered him a relatively safe witness. Although he wasn't in Ben's back pocket in the sense that he was being paid to cooperate or had a vested interest in the outcome, he was definitely on the side of the angels. He knew the EPA was as concerned about the Blackwood water as his clients were—and was equally anxious to do something about it.

Kenneth Thorndyke was as large as any man Ben had seen in his entire life, and yet he entirely defied the stereotype of overweight. According to him, at least, he was a man of action. He was the first to suspect that there was something wrong with the water in Blackwood, and he led the research team that went out to run tests.

"What caused you to suspect the water was tainted?" Ben asked.

"Actually, I didn't," Thorndyke replied. "I was just investigating a complaint. Common everyday procedure. Several Blackwood residents reported that they thought the water tasted funny, or smelled funny, or felt funny in the shower. Frankly, these complaints are not uncommon, and we can't investigate them all. But when the number of them rises above a certain threshold, we try to check it out."

Ben took the witness through a detailed chronology of just exactly what tests were performed and how and why. He wanted to make sure the EPA study couldn't be attacked on scientific grounds.

"What did you learn from these tests?" Ben asked.

"We learned the water was poisoned. We—"

"Objection." Colby was on his feet again. "Your honor, I object to the use of that inflammatory and misleading word."

Ben assumed he wasn't referring to the word "water."

"Your honor, I'm not aware that counsel has the right to restrict my witnesses' vocabularies. Surely they are permitted to choose their own words."

Judge Perry frowned. "Well, I don't plan to stifle anyone's testimony. But I would appreciate it, Mr. Thorndyke, if you kept your language factual and unemotional."

"Very well, your honor," Thorndyke said, nodding. Ben appreciated the fact that Thorndyke was being so compliant. He also appreciated that he hadn't mentioned that Ben had asked him beforehand to use the word "poison" as many times as possible. "Anyway, we ran chemical analyses on the Blackwood water wells and found severe contamination in Well B."

"What were the contaminants?"

"We found traces of TCE and perc, both industrial solvents."

"Were you familiar with these substances?"

"Of course. They're both on the EPA's list of suspected carcinogens."

"Which means what?"

"It means they give you—"

"Objection!" Thorndyke had tried gamely to get it in, but Colby was too quick for him. "Once again, counsel tries to slip in medical evidence from a nonmedical witness."

"Sustained," Judge Perry said wearily. "Mr. Kincaid, please keep your witness on the subject upon which he has actual knowledge."

If I must. "Without getting into a discussion of the possible medical side effects, could you please explain why the discovery of these chemicals concerned you?"

Thorndyke twisted his immense girth around awkwardly. He could only barely move in the witness box. "People expect their water to be pure, but most times it isn't. Some things that filter into water aren't harmful— although people would be pretty grossed out if they knew what they were. Some pollutants, like fluoride or certain minerals, are actually helpful. But we try to single out the ones that, uh"—he glanced up at the judge—"that . . . are not helpful."

"Such as TCE and perc?"

Thorndyke nodded. "Exactly."

"Did your study attempt to determine the source of the pollution?"

"Objection," Colby said, predictably enough. "Once again, Mr. Kincaid tries to lure his witness outside the proper scope of his testimony."

"How does he know that?" Ben replied. As always, he addressed the judge, not the opposing attorney. "I just asked if the EPA study considered the source. Why don't we hear the answer?"

Judge Perry nodded. "I suppose I'll allow it. But I caution you, counsel—I don't want any improper testimony."

"Of course not, your honor." Perish the thought. "Mr. Thorndyke, you may answer the question."

"We did try to determine the source. We found trace elements of TCE in a ravine that feeds into the well. We followed the ravine less than half a mile to—"

"Again I must object," Colby said. "This is not testimony relating to a scientific study. The mere fact that some TCE is found in a ravine does not prove—"

Judge Perry waved him down. "Quite right, counsel. I agree entirely. Mr. Kincaid, I want you to discontinue this line of questioning. And I instruct the jury to disregard what little has been said."

Ben could live with that. He'd gotten further than he'd expected. And he felt certain even the densest juror realized what was half a mile up the ravine.

This time, Colby did not waive cross-examination. He strode to the podium, fidgeting with his pocket watch, peering at the witness through a squinted right eye.

"You're not a medical doctor, are you, Mr. Thorndyke?"

"No."

"And you're not a scientist, are you?"

"No. Although I made a B in high school biology."

Thorndyke grinned, but no one grinned back. Ben had warned him about the dangers of cracking jokes on the stand. Ben had been right.

Colby's squint intensified. "And you don't want people to be misled into thinking you are, do you?"

"No-oo. . . ."

"You're not qualified to say what is or is not a carcinogen, are you?"

"No. But I'm qualified enough to say I don't want any in my drinking water. Or my son's."

Yes! Ben thought. He restrained himself from giving the witness a high five.

"Mr. Thorndyke," Colby said, his voice dark as the grave, "this is a very serious matter, and I would appreciate it if you treated these jurors with the dignity they deserve."

Ouch. Ben winced. Slung that one back in our faces, didn't you?

Colby continued. "You are not the man who made the decision to put these chemicals on any list, are you?"

"Well . . . no."

"And you do not know what tests—if any—were conducted to determine whether they should be placed on said list, do you?"

"I didn't do it, but I know how it was done. Concentrated injections were given to laboratory rats—"

"Lab rats?" Colby allowed himself a small grin. "All this fuss is over lab rats?"

"The rats died."

"I'm sure rats die all the time. This will probably sound like a crazy question, but—did any of these studies involve—say—human beings?"

"You can't test poi—" He stopped himself. "—Suspected carcinogens on people!"

"People are probably a little hardier than lab rats, wouldn't you imagine?"

"We're all mammals. We've learned that lab rats can be good indicators—"

"Sir, you keep saying 'we.' But you are not a scientist and you were not involved in this testing in any way, were you?"

"No, but—"

"Excuse me," Judge Perry said, interrupting. "Just answer the question posed to you."

"Thank you, your honor," Colby said, bowing his head slightly. If these two old pals became any more deferential to one another, Ben was going to barf. "Mr. Thorndyke, you said you found traces of TCE in the ravine. But you don't know how it got there, do you?"

"It's obvious to me that—"

Again, Judge Perry cut in, doing Colby's work for him. "Sir, this court is not interested in your speculations. You are here to tell us what you know. If you don't know, say so."

Thorndyke drew in his breath. "I cannot say with utter certainty how the TCE got into the ravine."

"Thank you." The judge settled back in his chair. "This court appreciates honesty." He cast a wayward glance toward Ben. "Even if you may have been encouraged to avoid it."

"Exactly how much TCE did you find in the ravine?" Colby asked.

"How much?"

"Yes. What quantity?"

Thorndyke shrugged. "It would have been a tiny amount. Less than one part per thousand."

Colby appeared stricken. "Less than one part per thousand? All this fuss is for less than one part? Barely a decimal?"

"In the ravine," Thorndyke added. "In the well—"

"In the well," Colby interrupted, "you also found what you yourself referred to as 'trace amounts.' "

"Yes, but it doesn't take—"

"In fact, the quantities you found were less than one gram per gallon of water, correct?"

"That's true. But you have to realize—"

"Those traces would be diluted by immersion in water, correct? If you know. I realize you're not a scientist."

Thorndyke did a slow burn. "They would be diluted. But they would still be TCE. And TCE would still be—"

"Just answer the question," Judge Perry said, cutting him off. "I won't warn you again."

Colby proceeded apace. "And that water would be distributed throughout the hundreds of homes serviced by Well B, thus diluting it even further."

"This stuff is deadly!" Thorndyke burst out. "You don't have to have—"

Judge Perry leaned forward. "This is absolutely your last warning, mister. Another outburst like that and I'll have you evicted from the courtroom and have your entire testimony stricken."

"You will admit," Colby said, "that the TCE is greatly diluted when it enters the well."

"It doesn't take much!"

"Really? And just how much does it take?"

Thorndyke twisted around in his seat. "Well . . . I couldn't say exactly. No one knows—"

"Mr. Thorndyke, that's the first thing you've said today that I agree with totally. No one knows. No one knows if TCE is harmful, especially in such tiny amounts. No one knows how it got into the well. And no one knows what causes leukemia. Including you."

* 32 *

It had taken Mike weeks to get an appointment to see Myron Blaylock. He had been desperate to get in, desperate to see the man before there was a fourth victim. And now that he was finally in, Mike was certain there was going to be a fourth victim—Blaylock himself. Because Mike was going to kill him with his bare hands.

"I can give you ten minutes," Blaylock said, snapping his pocket watch closed. "So let's not shilly-shally about."

A pocket watch? Mike wondered. What kind of affectation was that? Although, as old as Blaylock was, he might own the original model. "Mr. Blaylock, I've been waiting for weeks to talk to you—"

"My apologies." The elderly man's spindly legs quivered a bit when he stood in one place too long. Mike was relieved when he lowered himself into a chair. "I've been quite busy of late."

"The lawsuit?" Mike asked.

Blaylock tilted his head. "I see you stay abreast of current events, Lieutenant."

"I do my best."

"You've heard about this frivolous suit?"

"A little bit." Mike decided not to mention that his best friend was the plaintiffs' attorney. Somehow, he didn't think that would endear him to the old codger. "Are you sure it's frivolous?"

"Of course it's frivolous. No one knows what causes cancer. To blame it on chemicals used half a mile away . . . it's just preposterous." It could be his imagination, but Mike thought Blaylock's face did not quite bear the conviction of his words. Was it possible the geezer was having doubts? "Your time is running, Lieutenant. I assume this is not what you wanted to talk about."

"No. It isn't. I'm trying to figure out who's been bumping off your employees."

"Well, I wish you'd get on with it." Blaylock's voice caught fire. "I don't like this kind of turmoil in the workplace. Absences have risen to an all-time high. Apparently some people are afraid to come to work, afraid they might be the next to go."

Mike noted that Blaylock's consternation was all related to business; he hadn't said a word about the minor inconvenience to the people being murdered. "I've talked to most of your top executives," Mike said. "And a lot of your employees. Everyone who worked with the deceased. I've been trying to learn why anyone might want to kill these people."

"And what have you learned?"

"I haven't learned scratch. That's why I've come to you."

"Me?" Blaylock pressed a gnarled hand against his chest. "You think I could help you? I didn't even know those people."

"You must've known something about them."

"Lieutenant, I have thousands of employees—"

"And three of them—who are now dead—had been with the company more than fifteen years. Two of them for more than twenty."

"Nonetheless, I am not the personnel manager. I'm afraid I can't help you."

Blaylock pressed his hands against the desk, as if signaling that the interview was over.

Mike quickly jumped in; he hadn't nearly gotten his ten minutes' worth yet. "Was there anything these three victims had in common? Other than working here?"

"Not that I'm aware. I believe I was told they worked in different departments."

"That's true."

"Perhaps there is no connection. Perhaps there are multiple murderers."

"Perhaps."

"The murders themselves were each quite different, were they not?"

"They were different," Mike agreed. "But I think that was an intentional ploy to mislead me. Different as they were, they were all hallmarked by extreme violence. Cruelty in the first degree. How many people can have the capacity to inflict that magnitude of pain?"

"In my experience," Blaylock said, "quite a few."

"I just can't believe it. I think there's one killer—the man who slipped away from me at George Philby's house. And I think there's a rational—or at least explicable—reason for these murders. These three people must've had something in common. Do you have any idea—"

"I told you, I didn't know them."

"Perhaps they all worked together at some time—"

"They didn't."

"Or were members of the same club. Ate lunch together. Worked on a joint project."

"No, no, no," Blaylock said. "If anything like that were true, I'm sure one of my executives would've reported it to me. And to you."

"There must be some connection," Mike repeated.

"Must be? Or you want there to be? That would make your job easier, of course. If the man is simply a crazed lunatic, picking off victims at random, you'll probably never catch him."

"There is a connection," Mike said. "I just have to figure out what it is."

"Well, I'm afraid I can be of no use to you," Blaylock said. He pulled his watch out of his vest pocket and checked the time. "And I see that your ten minutes have expired."

"I'm not done," Mike protested.

"But I am." Blaylock pushed the button on his intercom. "Janice, would you please escort Lieutenant—"

"Where did the money go?" Mike asked abruptly.

Blaylock blinked. "Excuse me?"

"The money," Mike said calmly. Now it was his time to relax and let the old gasbag squirm. "The sixty million. That disappeared. Six years ago."

"Cancel that, Janice." Blaylock took his finger off the intercom. "It seems we're not done talking."

Ben had spent an hour the night before preparing Scout to take the witness stand. By normal standards, an hour would be a very short prep period, especially for such a vulnerable witness, but Ben was concerned about overwhelming the boy. Hard as he tried not to show it, Scout was obviously nervous about sitting in that chair next to the judge and talking to a lot of strangers. Who wouldn't be? So Ben simply reviewed what he would say, tried to give him some glimmer of what to expect on cross-examination, and let his father take him away for an ice cream.

The next morning, after Judge Perry called the case back into session, Ben called the boy to the stand. He bravely soldiered his way to the front of the courtroom, brushing a ridiculously long shock of blond hair out of his eyes. He was dressed in a suit with a clip-on tie—and looked miserably uncomfortable in it. The suit must've been his father's idea. Ben had the impression Scout wouldn't have chosen it in a million years, not even if he was on the way to a funeral.

After he was sworn, Judge Perry asked the boy the usual series of questions to determine whether he was competent to testify despite his tender age. Scout asserted proudly that his daddy had taught him the difference between the truth and a lie, and apparently the judge was satisfied.

After Scout settled in, Ben began the questioning. "Would you state your name please?"

"Scout," he said. "Er—I mean, that's what they call me. I guess my actual name is Harold Marvin Michaelson."

"Thanks. We'll just call you Scout, if that's all right with the court." Judge Perry nodded graciously. "How old are you, Scout?"

"Nine," he said quietly.

"Speak into the microphone," Judge Perry instructed him. "Doesn't do anyone any good if the jury can't hear you."

"Yes, sir." Scout cleared his throat and leaned closer to the mike. "I'm nine. 'Bout to be ten, though."

Calmly, with frequent stops to deflect Scout's inadvertent diversions, Ben led Scout through a recitation of what he saw that day, now months past, when he was playing in the forest and ravine near the Blaylock plant. Scout described how he and Jim hid in the ravine, how he saw the Brush Hog unearth the waste drums, some of them cracked or broken, and how he saw the Brush Hog drop one, which split apart on impact. Following the court's prior instruction, Scout did not mention the dead body found in the drum. Judge Perry didn't want the jury distracted by details that weren't pertinent to the present case.

"Scout," Ben said, winding up, "do you have any idea how many drums you saw hauled out of the Blaylock property that day?"

"Well . . . I didn't have a chance to count. But there musta been at least forty. Probably more like fifty."

"Forty or fifty waste drums buried in the ground. And how many of those were leaking?"

"Gosh. I couldn't say for sure. Prob'ly—"

"Objection," Colby said calmly. "If he doesn't know, he doesn't know."

"Sustained," the judge said quickly. "Son, we don't want to hear any guessing up there. We just want to know what you know."

"Okay. Well, I don't know exactly how many drums were broke." His voice dropped a notch. "But it was a lot."

Ben smiled. "I have no more questions for this witness, your honor."

Unfortunately, Colby did. Ben watched as the master trial

lawyer approached the podium, his eyes fixed on Scout like a predator eyeing its prey. He wondered what approach Colby would take. He would, of course, try to poke holes in Scout's testimony; it was the first evidence that tangibly linked Blaylock to the contaminated water. But he couldn't come on too strong. Scout was only a boy, after all, and the jury wouldn't like it if he started in with bully tactics.

"First of all," Colby said, "let's cover everything you don't know. You don't have any idea what was in those drums, do you?"

Scout glanced at Ben, then back at Colby. "N-no. . . ."

"Could've been water, for all you know."

Scout swallowed. "I don't know what was in the drums."

"And you don't know when those drums were placed on the property. Could've been the day before."

Scout tilted his head to one side. "They looked pretty dirty. And they were buried deep."

Colby looked at him sternly. "You don't know when they arrived, do you?"

"No, sir."

"And if they were placed recently, it would be impossible for those waste drums to have caused the well contamination. If there was any. Right?"

"Right."

"Good. I'm glad we got that settled. Now let's talk about something else." Colby leaned forward, resting against the podium, tilting it slightly. "You were . . . playing a game that day, weren't you, Scout?"

Scout hesitated. He undoubtedly remembered what Colby had done during his deposition. "Y-yes."

"You were . . . pretending. Right? About the Outsider and all the monstrous things he did. Make-believe."

"Yes. . . ."

"Pretending. Making it up."

"Yes. . . ."

Colby fingered his chin thoughtfully. "I wonder how much of the rest of your story is . . . made up."

Scout straightened. He wasn't going to let Colby do this to him twice. "I'm telling the truth. About the drums and all."

"So you say. So you say." Colby opened a manila folder

he'd brought to the podium with him. "But you have been known to tell lies on occasion, haven't you? When it was convenient. When it got you a lot of attention."

"I'm not a liar."

"Are you sure about that, Scout? Didn't you tell some of the other boys at school the other day that your father was the president of a big company?"

"Well . . ."

"But he isn't, is he? He's a janitor. Scrubs floors nights at the Blaylock plant."

"Your honor," Ben said, rising to protect his witness. "This is not relevant. He's just trying to embarrass the boy."

"That's not so," Colby said quickly. "It goes toward the witness's propensity for truthfulness. That's permissible cross."

Judge Perry shrugged. "That's what the rules say, counsel. I'll have to allow it."

Ben scanned the gallery and saw Scout's father sitting two rows back, looking uncomfortable and angry. It had taken some doing to persuade the man to allow his son to testify in the first place, especially given that he worked at Blaylock. It's a civic duty, Ben had argued. No harm will come of it. Now the man was no doubt wishing he'd never laid eyes on Ben, much less believed anything he'd said.

Colby continued questioning the boy. "Answer the question, son. You told that lie, didn't you?"

Scout twisted uncomfortably. "I guess I might've exaggerated a little."

"And on another occasion, you led your friends to believe that your mother lived at home with you and your father, that she packed your lunches and bought you cool presents. Didn't you say that?"

"Well . . ."

"Don't bother lying. I can call your teacher to the stand if necessary. She heard every word you said on the playground that day."

Scout sighed, resigned. "I guess I might've said that."

"But it isn't true, is it? In fact, your mother hasn't lived with you for some time, has she?"

Scout's voice was barely more than a whisper. "No."

"I don't think the jury got that," Colby said. "Would you repeat it?"

"No!" he shouted into the mike, so loud it reverberated through the courtroom.

"The truth is," Colby said, being almost as quiet as Scout had been loud, "that your mother left you and your father a long time ago, didn't she?"

"Your honor!" Ben said, jumping up. "This is uncalled-for harassment. It obviously doesn't relate to the substance of this witness's testimony."

"That is simply not true," Colby said calmly. "I am permitted to challenge the witness's veracity . . . and to explore any motives he might have for . . . telling falsehoods. Which is exactly what I'm doing."

"Very well," Judge Perry said. "You may proceed."

Damn this judge, anyway! Ben pounded the table on his way back to his chair, making sure the jury understood he was not happy about this ruling. Judge Perry's deference to his old pal, the great trial god Colby, had gone too far. If he wasn't willing to challenge Perry on this obvious impropriety, Colby could get away with anything.

Colby resumed. "How long has your mother been living . . . elsewhere, Scout?"

"Since January."

"She's living with some other person. Some man other than your father."

Scout's head burrowed down. "I don't know where she is."

"But you do get to spend some time with her, right? Every other weekend."

"I guess."

"And I guess in the midst of all this turmoil, you must feel rather left out. Neglected. Right? That's what your teacher told me." He paused, even though he didn't really expect an answer. "I suspect at this point in your life, you'd do about anything to get your parents' attention, wouldn't you?"

"No," the boy said petulantly.

"And this little story you've cooked up—it's gotten you all kinds of attention, hasn't it?"

"No."

"Attention not only from your parents, but other adults. Like Mr. Kincaid."

"No."

"Probably scored some big points with your father, since you're causing problems for the employer he no doubt resents."

"No! It isn't like that!"

Colby drew in his breath. "Tell us the truth now, Scout. Wouldn't you do just about anything to get your mother's attention? To get her back home again?"

"No!" Tears began to well up in his eyes.

"You'd say just about anything, wouldn't you? You'd do anything to make them proud of you. To make them want to be with you."

Scout remained silent. Which spoke volumes.

"I was told you subpoenaed our corporate financial records," Blaylock said slowly, gazing across his desk at Mike. "But I was also told the trail was covered. I had no idea you would be quite so . . ."

"Smart?" Mike suggested.

"Perceptive," Blaylock replied.

"Hard to miss a sixty-million-dollar disappearance."

"Not as hard as you might think. We are a half-a-billion-a-year corporation, after all. The loss was written off to various causes and events. We've been audited every year, and thus far no one's so much as raised an eyebrow."

"Well, down at the station, we're professional eyebrow-raisers. And we're very . . . perceptive." When Mike returned to said station, much as it pained him, he would have to thank Pfeiffer. Maybe even forgive him. It seemed he'd given Mike the silver bullet. "So what happened to all the moolah, Blaylock? D'you decide to build a summer home in France or something?"

Blaylock frowned, his first sign of visible irritation. "I had nothing to do with the loss of funds. The money was stolen."

"So Pfeiffer had been right. Someone stole sixty million bucks?"

"It's true."

"Is it? You see, sir, I've already checked the police records.

No loss remotely approaching that amount was reported that year. And no lawsuit was filed for recovery."

"We didn't report it to the police. Or file suit."

Mike's credulity was strained to the limit. "You took a sixty-million-dollar hit—and kept quiet about it?"

"We did." Blaylock leaned back, steepling his fingers. "We had no choice."

"I don't get it. Am I wrong, or is this a business for profit?"

"I'm very fond of profits," Blaylock said. "But when the money disappeared, we had no idea who took it. It simply vanished—from a numbered Swiss bank account—without a trace."

"That would be a reason for calling the police."

"We couldn't. That was the year we took the company public. We were on the verge of our first IPO—initial public offering of stock. The stock had been registered with the SEC. The prospectus had been written. The day for the offering was set. We couldn't turn back. Any hint of scandal, or misfeasance, or . . . incompetence would have destroyed us."

"Quite a coincidence that the theft occurred at such an inopportune time."

"It had nothing to do with coincidence. The thief intentionally took the money at a time when we couldn't afford a full-scale investigation. We had to stay quiet."

"But sixty million dollars—!"

"I stood to make a great deal more than that from the stock offering—and did."

Mike's lips parted. "So you just . . . did nothing?"

Blaylock's eyelids fluttered. "Hardly. We initiated our own investigation. Quietly. I used only those executives I felt certain I could trust. And at that point, there were damn few of them, believe me."

"So the corporate VPs became Junior G-men?"

"Something like that."

"Was Ronald Harris one of them?"

"As a matter of fact, yes."

"And you never reported the theft?"

"No. Never."

Mike wiped his brow. "Jesus Christ. No wonder you clowns never found your money."

Blaylock straightened a bit. "But we did, Lieutenant. It took months, but we eventually determined that only one man could possibly have committed the theft. Only one man—other than myself—had access to all the information—knowledge of the account, the account number, the password needed to withdraw funds—and was not in Oklahoma at the time the funds were withdrawn. We had the man nailed."

"Oh, yeah? So you hauled the guy's butt up and shook him?"

Blaylock paused. "There was one problem with taking any action against our suspect."

"What was that?"

Blaylock settled back in his chair. His eyes rose toward the ceiling. "He was dead."

Ben had spent most of the previous night preparing Archie Turnbull to take the stand. After all, he didn't want a repeat of what had happened to Mr. EPA. Thorndyke had been an ideal witness—aggressive, committed, well-spoken. And Colby had still managed to shut him down. Of course Ben had redirected, trying to bolster his witness as best he could, but the damage was done. Colby had effectively pointed out all the gaps, all the unanswered questions that riddled Ben's case. And he did it with Ben's own witness.

By contrast, Turnbull was not aggressive, well-spoken, or confident. But he had resisted all the pressure Colby and Blaylock could bring to bear and given an honest deposition. Ben could only hope that courage continued to serve him on the witness stand.

By some miracle, Turnbull was still employed at the Blaylock plant. Actually, it wasn't a miracle—it was probably a direct command from Colby. A retaliatory firing might appear to give Turnbull's testimony too much credence—like they were trying to hush up a whistle-blower. Better to appear to be gently tolerating him, perhaps even humoring him, sort of as one might do with a wacky uncle who was slightly tetched—but not dangerous.

On the stand, Ben did his best to draw out Turnbull's story—how he had dutifully worked in the machinery department, how he had supervised the waste disposal, how the company had established disposal procedures—but had periodically not followed them, in order to save money. He tried to reemphasize the most important parts—that Blaylock had systematically buried waste, creating a health hazard, either with full knowledge that they endangered lives, or with reckless disregard for others' lives.

At almost every turn, Colby was on his feet objecting. Some of the objections were so frivolous even Judge Perry had to overrule them.

"What's with Colby?" Ben whispered to Christina, during a break. "Has he lost his marbles?"

Christina shook her head. "Far from it. Don't you see? He's just trying to interrupt your flow. Turnbull is probably your best fact witness and he knows it."

"But his objections are stupid!"

"Stupid or not, they interrupt the testimony. Break it up. Keep you from gaining any momentum. Make the story less coherent. Make it harder for the jury to follow what's going on." She tossed her red hair behind her shoulders. "The jury should be shocked and appalled when they hear Turnbull explain what the company has been doing. Colby is trying to prevent that from happening. He doesn't care about his objections. He just wants as little of what Turnbull is saying to sink in as possible."

Ben resumed his direct—and Colby resumed the frivolous objections. Ben approached the bench and asked the judge to intervene. Judge Perry refused. "Opposing counsel has a right to object when he thinks it proper. As do you."

As a result, the direct examination that should have taken one hour ended up taking four, interrupted by lunch, two bathroom breaks, and a record seventy-nine objections. Ben had no idea whether the jury understood Turnbull's story. After that, he wasn't sure whether he understood it himself.

And then it was Colby's turn.

"First of all, let's talk about what you didn't say. You don't know specifically what was stored in the drums that were allegedly buried, do you?"

Turnbull licked his lips, mustering his strength. "I know we used TCE on a regular basis. And perc."

"Mr. Turnbull, I know you're determined to get back at your employer in any way possible, but I must ask you to simply answer the question. You don't know what was in those drums, do you?"

"I can't specifically tell you what was in each one, no."

"And you don't know if the buried waste leaked, if it traveled half a mile downstream to the aquifer, or if it polluted the water supply. And you certainly don't know if these chemicals—which may not have even been present—could cause cancer!"

"Objection," Ben said. "Compound, confusing, and"—his voice dropped a notch—"stupid."

"That's all right, your honor," Colby said hastily. "I'll withdraw the question. I think we're all aware of the gigantic gaps in the plaintiffs' case."

"Your honor!"

"I'll move on," Colby said, raising his hands. "Mr. Turnbull, are you aware that your testimony directly conflicts the testimony of every other Blaylock employee—including many who worked with you on a regular basis?"

"Yes."

"And yet you're asking this jury to believe that you're telling the truth—and that dozens of other people are lying?"

"What I said was true. I wouldn't lie."

"Well, now, that isn't exactly so, is it?" Colby leaned toward counsel table and retrieved two thick bound deposition transcripts. "You gave two depositions prior to trial, didn't you, sir?"

Turnbull squirmed. "Y-yes." Even a blind man could see Turnbull was becoming uncomfortable.

"And your testimony in the first is . . . well, rather different from your testimony in the second. Isn't it?"

"I . . . made some mistakes the first time. I wanted to correct them. I volunteered—"

"You did a great deal more than simply correct your previous testimony, didn't you? You directly contradicted it."

Turnbull pursed his lips. "I suppose. In some instances."

"Or to put it another way—you lied."

Turnbull's face stiffened. "I gave the company line. Like everyone else is still doing."

Colby leapt on that. "So now you admit you consciously lied."

"I said what you wanted to hear."

"And then you changed it."

"My conscience bothered me. I felt that someone ought to tell the truth."

"How noble. So you took it onto yourself to contradict . . . virtually everyone else."

"I told the truth."

"Eventually. But you admit you lied." Colby drew himself up to his full height. "The question is . . . which time?"

Turnbull's brow creased. "I don't follow you."

"It's obvious that you were lying at one of these depositions, but which one?"

"I told you—"

"You admitted to this jury that you lied. The only thing we don't know is when—and why. Or how much. Or how often." He snapped his folder shut. "That's all, your honor. I have no more use for this witness."

"Dead?" Mike said, leaning practically out of his chair. "You're telling me the man who stole the sixty million bucks was dead?"

"So it appeared." Blaylock's calm demeanor belied the bizarre nature of the story he was telling. "I assure you, we had researched it quite carefully. An employee named Tony Montague, a senior supervisor in the accounting department, was the only man who could have committed the crime."

"But for the minor inconvenience that he was dead."

"Or so we believed, anyway." Blaylock stood on his spindly legs and opened the shutters on the bay window behind his desk. "There had been an accident. A tragedy. Several of our employees were on a company outing. A trip to an amusement park in Oklahoma City. There was an accident on the drive home. The bus they were traveling in caught fire and . . . well, everyone was killed. Incinerated. It's been years now. But you may recall reading about it in the papers. I'm told there was something defective about the bus. I don't know all the details, but I know our lawyers were tied up with it for years, suing Ford on behalf of our employees' families. Seems Ford—then led by a young man named Iacocca—had decided to place the fuel tanks on this model of school bus's chassis on the outside of the frame, rather than the inside. They saved money—but the bus was much less safe, caught fire more easily. And there were inadequate emergency exits. No breakaway windows."

"I remember reading about it," Mike said. "What a nightmare."

"You may also remember that school bus in Kentucky that killed numerous children about the same time. Same model. Iacocca should be ashamed, reviled; instead, the masses act like he's a hero. Some people have no sense of corporate responsibility."

Mike bit his lip, trying not to laugh at the irony of hearing these sentiments from Myron Blaylock. "You said everyone was killed. . . ."

"So we believed. The officials counted bodies—what was left of them. The remains were far too charred to identify, even by dental records. But they did determine that the number of bodies was exactly the same as the number of passengers who went on the trip, plus the driver. So everyone had died." He paused. "Or so we assumed."

"But if everyone died—"

"Do you want the short version, Lieutenant? Or all the details?"

Mike thought for a moment. "I guess I'll start with the short. You can fill in the details later."

"Montague wasn't dead. He managed to escape by breaking open a window at the last possible moment. He was the only passenger who survived. What we didn't know was that he had picked up a young woman at the amusement park, and that she was riding home with him."

Mike was beginning to follow. "So there was an extra body."

Blaylock nodded. "And after he escaped, the number of bodies was exactly what we expected it to be."

"But surely when he turned up—"

"He didn't turn up. He disappeared. I don't know how long

he'd been planning this theft, but he took this as his golden opportunity to implement his plan. From his standpoint, it was perfect. The imminent IPO would restrict our ability to investigate. And even in the best of circumstances, how could we catch a ghost?"

Mike marveled. It was just about perfect. "So Montague kept out of sight, and when the time was right, swiped the loot. And no one the wiser."

"Exactly."

"How did you finally find all this out?"

Blaylock's brow knitted. "Don't you know?" He smiled slightly. "It seems you're not as ... perceptive as you thought, Lieutenant. Once I became certain Montague was the only man who could've committed the theft, I spared no expense having him tracked down. By that time, he'd burrowed himself in but good. He was practically a hermit. But we still found him. Eventually."

Mike was almost disappointed. It was such a perfect crime, even a law enforcement officer hated to see it go sour. "But not the money?"

"To the contrary. We recovered the money. Almost every penny. He'd stashed it in a noninterest-bearing savings account. He was afraid we'd catch him if he started spending big money. He'd only spent what was absolutely necessary to survive—less than a hundred thousand dollars. Can you imagine? The man had sixty million—and he was living like a pauper."

"But if you recovered the money—"

"It was reintroduced into the corporate books just as subtly as it had been removed. Even more so, I suppose—since you didn't catch that one."

Mike frowned. On second thought, forgiving Pfeiffer was premature. "But you didn't file charges against Montague?"

"No. Under the circumstances, we couldn't."

"How did you get Montague to turn over the cash?"

"We made a deal. If he returned the money, we'd leave him alone."

"You couldn't prosecute him anyway—not without admitting you'd committed a fraud on your shareholders by not reporting the loss."

"I don't like the word 'fraud,' " Blaylock replied, "but your understanding of the situation is essentially correct. We couldn't go after him. So we made a deal. And recovered our money."

"Wow," Mike said, rubbing his brow. "That's some story. Where's Montague now?"

"He's dead. For real this time."

"What happened?"

"He had a stroke, not three months after we found him. Seems life on the run had been too hard on him. His heart eventually gave out. His body was found in a fishing cabin in south Texas. He was alone." Blaylock gazed out the window. "The man had possessed the riches of Midas. And it hadn't done him the slightest bit of good. Probably killed him."

"There must be a moral in there somewhere," Mike murmured.

"There is. The moral is: Don't steal from Myron Blaylock." He walked around his desk. "So, Lieutenant, now you know all our darkest secrets. But I'm afraid it has nothing to do with the murders. Montague is dead and gone. And our money has been returned."

They exchanged brief pleasantries, and Mike left the office.

He supposed Blaylock was correct; the theft seemed to be over and done with. Still, it was so extraordinary. He couldn't help but think there was some connection. Some link to all the killing.

Or perhaps, as Blaylock had suggested before, that was just because he wanted there to be a connection. Because he didn't have anything else.

* 33 *

Trying a lawsuit, Ben mused, not for the first time, was a lot like having a baby. Not that he would know personally. But women always said that childbirth was followed by a biological forgetfulness, an erasing of the memory of how painful it was, so that women could conceivably want to have children again. It was much the same for trial lawyers. Trying a case was mercilessly demanding, tiring, debilitating, and typically unrewarding. Every time Ben was immersed in a trial, he swore he would never repeat the agony. And yet, like most trial lawyers, a month or so later, he became bored and restless, itching to go back before the jury.

A trial lawyer's life, when the trial was on, was really no life at all. Once it began, there was no time for anything but that, nothing but attending to the needs of the court and the client. The days might seem interminable to the jury, but to Ben, they were never long enough. Each day swept past in a mind-reeling frenzy, one must-do task followed quickly by another.

He rarely slept well during a trial. He'd rise at five to prepare for the day's witnesses, arguments, whatever. He'd pore over the exhibits, charts, documents. He'd review deposition transcripts. There was always too much data, too much information to be absorbed and recalled, more than could possibly be fed into a single human memory bank. At eight fifteen, he'd trudge over to the courthouse, mounds of information in tow. And then he'd be in court all day.

While the trial was on, there was no time for random thoughts, daydreaming, a life outside. Total acuity was essential. His full attention had to be focused on the proceedings.

Any moment his mind wandered would be a moment opposing counsel would try to slip in something objectionable. He'd rarely go out for lunch; he'd have Christina bring him back a candy bar or a bag of Doritos while he reviewed the afternoon's witness examinations. At the end of the day, he'd go back to the office to strategize with the client, replay the day's events, assess damage, consider options, plan tactics, consider settlement offers. And once the client had gone home, he could start doing the real work. And if he was lucky he'd be asleep by midnight—but one or two or three in the morning was more common. More than likely, given how little time there was, he'd sleep on the sofa in his office. And all too soon, five A.M. would roll around again. . . .

Actually, most nights, Ben would awaken about four A.M. in a blind panic, dripping with sweat. What have I forgotten? What did I miss? These anxiety attacks were inevitable. Modern trials were simply too complex; no one could remember everything, no matter how good they were. Sometimes he would be able to get back to sleep, after running through a mental checklist of the next day's witnesses. More often he would not. He would try running around the block, or listening to soothing music or playing the piano. Or he would simply give it up and start preparing for the next day's work early.

Sometimes he would close his eyes and try to remember the forest behind the house his grandmother had lived in when he was growing up, deep in the rolling green hills of Arkansas. He would recall the crisp, clean air; the blissful silence; the occasional deer or squirrel darting about; the tall trees; the sense of peace. Sometimes that would help calm his anxiety and get him back to sleep.

But not this time. Not this trial. Grandmother's house was too far away and the forest had been clear-cut. Instead, all he saw was Cecily Elkins's tear-stained face. In his mind's eye, she was leaning toward Ben, keening with the pain of the bereaved mother, shaking Ben back and forth, pleading. Tell me it was not all for nothing, she would say. Tell me it was not all in vain.

* * *

By the third week, the trial was wearing everyone down. Some of the jurors seemed dazed or glassy-eyed; both lawyers occasionally had to resort to cheap tricks to make sure some important piece of testimony was heard.

The lawyers themselves began to tire. Ben noticed a substantive decline in the enthusiasm levels in Colby's entourage, not to mention other signs of stress—shirts that needed to go to the dry cleaners, suit coats creased around the seat. Tempers flared more often. Foolish mistakes were made. Sometimes the snipping and squabbling between lawyers became so strident that Judge Perry called a recess, "so you can get a grip on yourselves." It was no one's fault, really. But mental exhaustion, relentless pressure, and sleep deprivation will take their toll. This, Ben often reflected, is why this thing is called a *trial*.

By the middle of the fourth week, Ben was ready to put on his medical witnesses. This, as he well realized, was probably the most important part of his case. He had evidence that the Blaylock plant used TCE and perc and that those chemicals made their way to the aquifer. Colby could dispute and argue and rebut all he wanted; the evidence was there. But there was one more necessary step in the causation chain that led to liability. Ben had to show that those chemicals Blaylock disseminated caused the children's cancers. It was the causation problem Judge Perry had warned him about from the outset of the case. Without this essential element of proof, Ben had no case at all.

He started with the man who became known as the "cluster expert," Dr. Jonathan Daimler. He'd been recommended to Ben by the Centers for Disease Control in Atlanta. He was a tall man, lean, with a thin nose and a seemingly permanent intense expression.

"According to the CDC," Ben said, as he introduced the witness to the jury, "you're the world's foremost expert on leukemia clusters."

Daimler grinned sheepishly. "Well, in truth—I'm probably the world's only expert on leukemia clusters."

That's good, Ben thought. Be modest. The jury likes modest. Especially from someone whose resume is longer than most novels. "Could you tell the jury how you got involved in this line of work?"

"Of course. About twenty years ago, I was interning at the CDC. I received information about what appeared to be an epidemic of leukemia cases in a small town in Illinois. Six children died in a two-year period—in a town about a square mile in size."

"Why did that trigger your interest?"

"Leukemia is a rare disease—or it's supposed to be, anyway. Statistically, there should be only one case per one hundred thousand children. This could've just been a statistical anomaly . . . but it was still extraordinary. I thought it merited further investigation."

"So what did you do?"

"I went to Illinois. I was allowed to conduct detailed examinations of the medical records and the families of the victims. I examined bone-marrow samples, blood, written documents. I checked radiation levels. Family histories. I found no evidence of any hereditary illnesses or predispositions that might be contributing to the outbreak."

"So what, if anything, did you conclude?"

Daimler's gaze intensified. "I became convinced that there must be some infectious agent, a virus, perhaps, that was causing the disease outbreak. This is not, admittedly, the traditional medical view of leukemia. But previous researchers have discovered leukemia viruses transmitted among animals—birds and mice, for instance. And I noted that these cases were principally striking victims preteen or younger—when children are most susceptible to infectious diseases." He paused, gazing earnestly at the jury. "I simply couldn't believe this concentration of cases could be random. I couldn't isolate a causal agent. But I felt certain there was one."

Ben caught a quick glance of the jury. He had worried that this medical testimony might soar over their heads, particularly in their current torporous state. But as far as he could tell, they seemed to be following along. "So what did you do next?"

"I began combing the CDC files, looking for other leukemia clusters."

"And did you find them?"

"In spades. A small town in Texas, with nine cases in nine months. A village in New York, population less than a thousand, with three cases in a year. Six children in New Jersey, all attending the same elementary school. A 'leukemia house' in Georgia, where three residents and a visitor all developed leukemia in a single year. All extraordinary events. Too extraordinary for me to write off as coincidental. I was convinced that something was causing these microepidemics."

"Did the rest of the medical community share your views?"

"To be honest, sir, some did and some didn't. After I published my first paper in the *New England Journal of Medicine*, I got a lot of comment. Some researchers thought I had been misled by statistical aberrations. Some agreed there must be a cause—but what was it?"

"I have a question," Ben said, "and I'm sure this has occurred to some of the jurors as well. If there is something—a virus or . . . whatever—causing these leukemia cases—why doesn't everyone get it?"

"In my opinion, the causal agent must be a low-potency pathogen—something that would only affect the most susceptible victims. Like children, for instance. Of course, that very low potency makes it all the more difficult to discover."

"Have you made any effort to learn what that pathogen might be?"

"Of course I have. I have and others"—he nodded toward a familiar face in the gallery—"like Dr. Rimland have. But it's an extremely difficult process. A low-level pathogen might be too subtle to evidence itself in tests with lab animals. For all our supposed scientific sophistication, our current testing techniques are crude, and the incidence of the disease is too infrequent to readily establish a connection between cause and effect."

"But you don't rule out the possibility?"

"No. Theoretically, it can be done. And as I said, we are working on it."

"Thank you, sir. No more questions."

Ben sat down pleased. Not a home run—in fact, Daimler's testimony could've been omitted altogether. But he hoped it would lay the groundwork and establish credibility for the critical testimony from Dr. Rimland that would establish the link between the poisons in the water and the children's deaths.

Colby rose for cross eagerly. "Let's establish one thing up front," Colby said, his voice loud and confident. "You don't know the slightest thing about what happened in Blackwood, do you?"

Daimler drew in his breath and sighed. He'd been cross-examined before. "I would hardly say I don't know the slightest thing—"

"You have not investigated the deaths which form the gravamen of the present case."

"No. I have not been asked to do so."

"You didn't think that was important."

"Not to what I had to say. I was only asked to give an opinion regarding leukemic clusters. I did so."

"So you don't care what actually caused those deaths in Blackwood."

Daimler rolled his eyes, visibly irritated. "It's not that I don't care—"

"You just didn't think it mattered."

"Not to what I had to say—no."

"So your testimony cannot in any way be said to go toward the question of what killed those boys and girls in Blackwood."

Ben got the impression Daimler's academic temperament was about to spill out and explode. "That was not the subject of my testimony."

"Good. I just wanted to make sure the jury was clear on that. You have no idea what killed those kids." He flipped a page in his notebook. "So let's talk about what little you actually did say. You believe leukemia clusters exist."

"I think it's undeniable."

"And they aren't just statistical anomalies."

"Not in my opinion."

"So you said. But you don't know what causes the clusters, right?"

"That's correct."

"And if you don't know what causes them—you can't rule out the possibility that they may just be coincidental. It could be coincidental, couldn't it?"

"That's not my opinion."

"But it's a lot of other people's opinion. Right?"

"I . . . suppose."

"Your opinions haven't exactly been embraced by the medical community, have they?"

Daimler's face flushed. Colby had hit a delicate spot. "As I already indicated, some agree, some disagree. That's in the nature of developing research."

"Didn't the *Journal of Cancer Epidemiology* say"—Colby glanced down at his pad—"and I quote, 'Daimler has taken inevitable statistical anomalies and converted them into proof of a contagion no one can detect.' "

Daimler's lips pursed. "That was the opinion expressed by the author of that particular article, yes. One man."

"But he's hardly alone in that opinion, is he?" Colby glanced at a stack of medical journals perched on his desk, as if ready and willing to pull out one embarrassing example after another, if necessary.

"No," Daimler said, acquiescing. "He is not."

"Tell us the truth, Doctor. It could all be just a horrible co-incidence, couldn't it?"

"In my opinion—"

"That's not what I asked for," Colby said, cutting him off. "You heard the question. You've been looking for years without success for a causal agent for these clusters. You haven't found one. So long as that's true—isn't it possible that these outbreaks are simply coincidental?"

"I don't think—"

"Answer the question, Doctor! Isn't it possible?"

Daimler drew in his breath. "I suppose, until a causal agent is verified, that is possible. But—"

"Thank you, Doctor. That's what I wanted to know. That's what we all wanted to know." Colby started back to his table, then stopped. "Oh, yes. One more thing."

Ben sat upright. When Colby went into his Columbo act, it was time to beware.

"You don't have a very high opinion of the plaintiffs' leukemia expert, do you?"

Damn. Ben clenched his fists under the table. How did Colby find out?

"I'm talking about Dr. Abbott Rimland," Colby continued. "You don't think much of his work, do you?"

Daimler glanced at Ben. "I respect Dr. Rimland as I would any other colleague."

"You wrote in the *Stanford Journal of Medicine* that—"

"I have disagreed with his conclusions on occasion."

"You called him a quack!"

Daimler's ire was no longer masked. "I did nothing of the sort."

"You said the controls in his studies were flawed. You said he rushed to judgment."

"That's quite another thing. Peer review is an important part of the research process."

"And speaking as his peer," Colby said, drowning him out, "you totally disagree with everything he's about to tell the jury."

"I can't predict what he might say. I have disagreed with him on occasion."

"Well then," Colby said, spreading his arms, "if such a distinguished personage as Dr. Daimler can disagree"—he turned toward the jury—"I'm sure we can all feel free to do the same."

Ben was furious with himself. He knew about Daimler's article in the *Stanford* journal. But he wanted Daimler on the stand, and he had no choice but to use Rimland. He had gambled that Colby wouldn't find that short article in an obscure academic journal.

He had gambled, and lost.

Nonetheless, despite having the worst possible introduction, he had to call Rimland to the stand next. His case depended on it.

Rimland looked well-groomed and tanned, no doubt from several days out on the golf course, or the driving range at the very least. He'd let his beard grow since Ben saw him last. Normally, Ben preferred that his witnesses not have facial hair; Oklahoma juries sometimes distrusted facial hair. But he made an exception for expert witnesses; the more professorial, the better.

After Rimland was sworn in, Ben took painstaking care

to walk Rimland through a litany of all his achievements, awards, accolades, degrees, memberships and other such resume lines. The man was a pioneer in his field; he wanted the jury to know he wasn't just some crank he'd paid to testify—since that was undoubtedly how Colby would attempt to portray him.

After the expert credentials were established, Ben drew him to the subject of cancer agents. "How did you become involved in this line of research?"

"I first started while I was still a teaching assistant at Stanford. In part, I was inspired by your previous witness, Dr. Daimler. I read one of his early articles hypothesizing the existence of cancer clusters. It seemed to me that if such clusters occur, something must be causing them. Something external."

"Was that the common view of cancer at the time?"

"No." Rimland turned his head toward the jury, making occasional eye contact, but not overdoing it. "Typically, scientists have assumed that cancer, and in particular leukemia, is genetic—that is, it just happens. But throughout the twentieth century, it has become abundantly clear that some cancers are caused by external factors. No one doubts anymore that smoking causes lung cancer—well, except maybe the executives in certain tobacco companies. Many other substances are now generally considered carcinogens. Artificial sweeteners, for example. If so, I reasoned, why couldn't something be causing these outbreaks of childhood leukemia?"

"So what did you do?"

"Well, I had a theory. Now I needed a way to prove it. At the end of the year, I applied for a small research grant. I figured the best place to search for a causal agent was at the site of one of those clusters, so I traveled to the New Jersey neighborhood Dr. Daimler mentioned—the one where six children died in a square mile radius in one year. The families were most cooperative. After interviewing them, I began to suspect that there must be something common to the neighborhood causing the problem. But even after extensive investigation, I could find only two things all of the families in question shared—their air supply, and their water supply."

Rimland then described his extensive testing procedure. He

tried to isolate hundreds of possible factors. He used blinds and double-blinds. He used children who had been diagnosed with cancer and children who were perfectly healthy. He spent more than two years at it, applying for additional grants whenever the money ran out.

"But I still didn't find what I was looking for," Rimland said. "Until a friend told me that the EPA was in the neighborhood testing the water supply. They didn't know about the leukemia cases; they were just responding to complaints about the taste and texture of the water. But I talked with them and managed to secure a copy of their preliminary results. Needless to say, the results just about blew the top of my head off."

"What were those results?" Ben asked. Like any good trial lawyer, he checked the jury out the corner of his eye. They seemed to be interested, following what was said.

"Objection," Colby said, rising to his feet. "Dr. Rimland did not conduct the study in question. If we are to hear about this EPA study, we should hear about it from the people who did it."

Which began a twenty-minute argument at the bench, while the jurors sat quietly in their chairs, bored and annoyed. Ultimately, Ben won, but he suspected that Colby had never expected to win. His goal, once again, was to interrupt the flow of testimony, break it up, make the jury forget what they were hearing, undermine its dramatic impact. By the time Ben was able to resume questioning, he wasn't sure anyone still remembered the topic.

"The results of the study," Rimland answered at last, "were that the water had abnormally high concentrations of chemical contaminants, particularly TCE and perc."

"TCE and perc," Ben repeated quietly. "The same contaminants found in the Blackwood well. What a coincidence."

"Objection," Colby barked. "Move to strike."

"So stricken," Perry replied instantly. "Counsel, watch yourself."

"Yes, your honor," Ben said. "Sorry." His face was something less than the picture of contrition. "Dr. Rimland, what did you do next?"

"Well, nothing immediately. My money had run out, and it took me two years to get financing to continue my studies. I can't tell you how frustrating that was. Here I was, on the verge of something that could conceivably save thousands of young lives, and I couldn't go forward because I didn't have the money."

"But you did eventually obtain financing?"

"Yes, and I began a series of tests with both TCE and perc, using laboratory animals. Principally rats." Again, Rimland described his methodology in painstaking detail. He outlined how he established sufficient controls to isolate a result, how he compared rats with the same genetic backgrounds, how he gave half of them tainted water and half not, how he measured the responses. "I followed the procedures I established for over three years. My results were published in the *New England Journal of Medicine*."

"I have the article here," Ben said, holding it high. "Could you perhaps summarize the results for the jury?"

"Sure." He scooted forward a bit, inching closer to the jury. "My conclusion was this: The tainted water caused cancer. Leukemia, to be specific. Not every time, but often. The rats that drank the infected water developed cancer almost forty times more frequently than those who did not. In effect, I created my own cancer cluster. And the only distinguishing factor between the two groups of animals was the tainted water."

Ben paused to let the jury soak in what he had said. "Dr. Rimland, based upon your experiences, do you have an opinion as to the possible effect of TCE and perc in a water supply?"

"Yes, I do. In my opinion, these chemicals in water, which is then brought into contact with young people, either by drinking or by immersion, say in the shower or bath, can cause leukemia. When young people are exposed to these chemicals, their chances of developing cancer increase dramatically."

Ben cast a sober glance at the jury, making sure they understood the importance of those words. "Thank you, Doctor. I have no more questions."

*   *   *

Ben tried to remain acutely attentive during Colby's cross—even more so than usual. He remembered how much Rimland dreaded being crossed; it was the principal reason he had not wanted to testify in the first place. Ben had promised he would do his best to protect him; he meant to live up to that promise.

"For starters, *Doctor*,"—Colby overemphasized the word as if it was some kind of joke—"tell the jury how much you're being paid to testify today."

Rimland stroked his beard. "Well, I'm not exactly being paid to testify—"

Colby pounced. "Oh, you're just up here out of the goodness of your heart?"

Ben jumped up. "Objection, your honor. Mr. Colby's sarcasm is unnecessary."

Judge Perry shrugged. "This is cross-examination, counsel."

"I personally have not accepted any money in connection with this case," Rimland explained. "A fee has been paid to an organization I direct for the purpose of financing my continued research."

"Oh, well then." Colby winked toward the jury box. "That's completely different, isn't it?"

"Well, yes, actually. It is."

"Either way, the money goes into your pocket."

"No, it funds my research."

"Including your salary?"

Rimland slowed. "I can assure you my salary is about the least significant item in the research budget."

"But you do take a salary?"

"I have to eat, just like everyone else."

"And that salary comes out of the research funds?"

"I charge an hourly rate. Just as I imagine you do."

"So in fact, you are being paid to testify today."

Rimland exhaled heavily, resigned. "I guess you could say that."

"Thank you, Doctor. I knew we'd get to the truth eventually." Colby dramatically flipped a page in his notebook. "So how much did the defense pay you and your corporation?"

"Fifty thousand dollars."

The jurors registered shock. Colby did a nice job of

appearing shocked also, although he already knew from the depositions exactly what amount had been paid. "Fifty thousand dollars?" Colby leaned toward the jury. "I'm going to have to have a talk with Mr. Kincaid about the way he spends money. I know some bums down at the bus station who'll tell him anything he wants to hear for five bucks."

"Your honor!" Ben rose to his feet amid tittering from the jury box.

Judge Perry nodded. "The jury will disregard the last remark."

But no admonishment. It seemed those were just for the plaintiffs.

Colby continued. "By the way, *Doctor*—you aren't actually a medical doctor, are you?"

Ben rolled his eyes. Now Colby would play on the common person's feeling that the only "real" doctors were physicians—since those were the only doctors most people saw.

"No. Nor did I ever claim to be."

"You're . . . some kind of Ph.D.?"

"I got my degree in hematology, yes."

"You're not even qualified to diagnose a case of leukemia, are you?"

Rimland glared at Ben. This was exactly the sort of thing he had wanted to avoid. "I'm not a medical doctor, as I said."

"You can't see patients."

"No."

"Your work is more . . . theoretical, right?" Again Colby's face took on a sarcastic cast.

"I don't know what that means. I'm a scientist."

"But you can't actually treat diseases. You're not that kind of doctor. It means—"

"It means I spend my day slaving over test tubes and rats, trying to find cures, instead of hanging out at the country club or putting a swimming pool in my backyard. A medical doctor is not going to find a cure for leukemia."

"But you can?"

"I'm trying, yes."

"Are you trying to find a cure, or trying to find someone to blame?"

"First things come first. I have to discover the causal agent before I can formulate a means to prevent it."

"And you haven't been able to do that, have you?"

"I think I—"

"Dr. Rimland, can you look this jury in the eye and tell them you have absolute proof that those two chemicals cause cancer?"

"I've already told them my conclusions. I told them how I reached them—"

"Ah, now you're being defensive, Doctor." Was he? Ben wondered. He didn't detect it. But he supposed that was beside the point. By saying it, Colby suggested to the jury that Rimland was being defensive—and had something to be defensive about. "You have no absolute proof."

"I have seen the cancers develop in hundreds of laboratory rats—"

"But what about people, Doctor? We're interested in people."

"Don't be absurd. I can't experiment on people."

"Oh, well, that's convenient, isn't it? The truth is, you have no proof that these chemicals have any adverse effects on people."

"I have scientific evidence—"

"Proof, Doctor. We want proof."

Rimland was becoming so agitated he almost rose out of his chair. "Tainted water clearly caused a higher incidence of disease in laboratory animals. Obviously—"

"If it's so obvious, sir, why does Dr. Daimler disagree with you? Or, for that matter, the rest of the medical community?"

That stung. "I don't believe Dr. Daimler agrees or disagrees. He thinks we need to do more testing—and I agree. His criticism is that he believes I published too soon."

"And why did you do that?" Another knowing glance at the jury. "Maybe to help raise funds for your 'organization'?"

"I did it because I thought it might help people. There's no reason for children to go on dying because of tainted water."

"So you rushed to get your name into print."

"If I were a parent of a child with leukemia, I'd want to know everything there was to know, as soon as I could know it!"

"Even if you can't prove your outlandish accusations?"

"Common sense tells me—"

"We don't want common sense, sir. We want proof. Concrete legal proof. And you don't have any."

"Don't have any proof! I've been studying this for almost a decade! You've seen my results! It's clear—"

"The problem with your results, Doctor, is that they have nothing to do with this case."

"What?"

"We're not here to talk about some poor unfortunates in New Jersey, and we certainly don't care about lab rats. We care about the eleven children in Blackwood who died. And you don't know anything about them, do you?"

"I think I do. I—"

"You weren't their doctor."

"No, of course not, but—"

"Did you ever meet any of them?"

"No, but—"

"Did you examine their bodies?"

"You know that would be impossible."

"Did you test the water in Blackwood?"

"No, it—"

"Then how can you possibly sit there and try to tell the jury what caused these deaths? You don't know what killed those poor children. You're just guessing! Speculating! Saying what you've been paid to say!"

"Your honor," Ben said, "I object!"

Perry shrugged. "The man has been paid. He's admitted that."

"But this goes beyond—"

Perry cut him off. "Unless you have an objection, counsel, pipe down."

"Look," Rimland said, "this is science, not a traffic accident. Science moves forward by small steps—"

"You're making excuses, Doctor," Colby said.

"I'm not. I'm trying to explain. What you're asking is absurd."

"Asking for proof is absurd?"

"This isn't a game we're playing!" His face flushed. "You're asking all these questions to obfuscate the truth, not to elicit it. We're talking about something that kills children!"

Colby made a show of not being impressed. "When the witness has no proof, he resorts to dramatics."

"If you want to get right down to it, no study has ever *proven* that smoking causes lung cancer. But everyone in this courtroom knows perfectly well that it does. By the same token, I can't work backward and prove with absolute certainty what caused a specific incidence of childhood leukemia. But when the water is tainted with chemicals, and you know those chemicals cause cancer, common sense tells you—"

"Your honor," Colby said, cutting him off, "the witness is not being responsive."

"Answer the question," Judge Perry growled.

"And I move that the witness's rant be stricken."

"So stricken."

"No!" Ben jumped to his feet. "Your honor! He *was* answering the question. You can't tell the jury to ignore the most important—"

"I've ruled, counsel. Sit down." Perry's face was lined with anger. "Don't you ever tell me what I may or may not do in my courtroom. And be grateful I don't strike everything this witness has said. I find his testimony speculative and unconvincing in the extreme."

Ben almost exploded. What was the judge doing? He was practically ordering the jury to ignore Rimland. That was grossly improper—and devastating.

Colby held up his hands. "I'm finished, your honor."

"Good. The witness may step down."

Ben bounced back to his feet. "Your honor, I have some redirect—"

"Forget it. I've had enough of this . . . 'expert.' "

"I'll be brief, your honor, but—"

"This witness has wasted too much of our time already, counsel. I'm going to very seriously reconsider Mr. Colby's *Daubert* motion tonight, because I do not think you have met the standards that this case requires. So don't push your luck." He grabbed the papers on his desk, scooped them up, and walked briskly toward his chambers door. "This court is in recess. Everybody go home!"

* 34 *

Jones and Loving were waiting at the office door when the trial party, Ben, Christina, and Professor Matthews, returned.

"Well?" Jones asked anxiously. "How did the medical experts do? How is the trial going?"

Ben didn't answer. Matthews tried to fill the gap. "Like any trial," he said professorially, "it has its ups and downs. It's not nearly over yet."

Jones's eyes crinkled. "What does that mean?"

Ben slammed his briefcase down on a desk. "It means we're getting our butts served to us on a platter."

"Now, Ben," Matthews said, "it isn't that bad."

"We're getting whipped. And you know it."

"What about the medical experts?" Jones asked. "How did they do?"

"They sucked gas." Ben threw himself down in the nearest chair. "It was embarrassing."

"Embarrassing? We paid fifty thousand dollars for embarrassing?"

"It wasn't their fault. Colby ripped them apart. There was nothing they could do. He was ready for everything. He undermined their testimony, made them look like snake-oil salesmen."

"I don't know," Christina said. "I think some of the jurors liked Dr. Rimland. And believed him."

"It won't be enough," Ben moaned. "Not against Colby."

Christina gave Ben a sharp look but said nothing.

Jones decided to change the subject. "What took you so long to get back? I thought the courthouse closed over an hour ago."

"We stopped at the hospital," Ben explained. "Wanted to check on Mrs. Marmelstein."

Jones declined to ask the obvious follow-up question. This new subject seemed to depress Ben even more than the first.

"Loving?" Ben asked.

"Yeah, Skipper?"

"How goes the search? For Paulie."

Loving was visibly less comfortable. "I've made some progress. I've confirmed that there is such a person, and he is her son. He was born in New York State, which made the search all the harder. He should be about fifty-two now."

"But have you found him?"

"No. I'm still lookin', though. Takes a while to comb records in every state, even with Jones helpin' on the computer. 'Specially when you don't have a social security number. Still, it can't take more than a month or—"

"I don't think we have a month," Ben said somberly. "I'm not sure we have two weeks. According to the doctors, she could go . . ." His voice trailed off. He never managed to complete the sentence, not that it was necessary.

"Can I bring up one more incredibly depressing subject?" Jones said. "We're broke."

"We've been broke for months. Since we started this case."

"Which I told you not to take. But of course, I'm not the type to say I told you so." Jones sniffed. "But we're more than just broke now. We're deep in debt, hocked to the hilt, they're-coming-to-take-us-away broke."

"They've got my car," Ben said. "What else can they take?"

"Well, all this mediocre office furniture, for starters. And then the equipment. And then the office itself. And how are we going to continue this endless trial without an office?"

"The bank won't do that. They have a stake in this trial, too."

"Don't be so sure. The Brain's taking some major criticism for giving us that last loan, which you squandered on today's suck-o witness. I'll think he'd do just about anything right now to collect some of the debt."

"There must be something else we can do. Some option . . ."

"Then you tell me what it is." Jones dropped a tall stack of credit cards on his desk. "These are all maxed out to the hilt, and I can promise you no one's going to give us another one. I've been transferring funds between accounts and kiting checks like some kind of mob money launderer."

"Take the money in petty cash and—"

"There is no petty cash, Ben. There hasn't been for weeks." Jones folded his arms angrily. "Hell, we don't even have money in the coffee kitty. We can't even afford lunch!"

"I'll make our lunches," Christina chimed in. "I'll fix sandwiches and bring them with me in the morning."

"Still—"

"And we can all pitch in on the coffee."

"Says you," Jones sniffed. "I haven't had a paycheck for a month."

"None of us have, Jones. But we have to stick together."

"The supplies company has cut us off. That means no legal pads. No typing paper. No toner cartridges."

"We'll have to make do. Eliminate everything that's unnecessary. Cancel all the newspaper and magazine subscriptions. Stop paying the membership dues. Turn off the heat—"

"I did all that long ago."

Christina jumped back in. "Maybe if we made some kind of appeal to the press—"

"Who are you kidding? The press lost interest in this case weeks ago. They were hot for a day or so, when it was fresh and new. But they soon moved on to other, more important subjects. Like the mayor's sex life."

"There has to be something we can do," Christina insisted. "Something we haven't thought of."

"There isn't." Jones was resolute. "This is serious. We can't continue like this."

"We have no choice. We can't abandon everything in the middle of the trial."

"We can't go on when we can't pay the bills! Maybe if we accept Colby's settlement offer—"

"That was an insult!" Christina said. "Peanuts!"

"We need peanuts!" Jones insisted. "We need something!"

"Would you two please stop it!" Ben's voice boomed out of nowhere, startling them. "I've had as much of this crap as I can take!" His jaw clenched, he marched off. He made a bee-line for his private office, then closed the door behind him.

All four of the others watched as he disappeared from sight.

"Does this mean there's no team meeting tonight?" Professor Matthews asked.

Ben was sitting at his desk, not looking at the outline in front of him, when Christina floated into his office.

"Did you knock?" Ben asked. "Because I didn't hear a knock."

"No, I didn't knock. Because you're so busy feeling sorry for yourself you'd probably have told me to go away."

"Now listen—"

"No, you listen, buster, and listen up good. I know we're deep in a major-league mess. But that's no excuse for shouting at everyone and holing up in your office when we should be preparing."

"What is there to prepare? We played our best card. And we lost."

"Our best card, for your information, will be when we put our clients, the bereaved parents, on the stand. In case you've forgotten, that starts tomorrow. You have to be ready for it."

"I'm ready. Not that it will matter."

Christina leaned into his face. "What's wrong with you? This isn't the Ben Kincaid I know."

"Christina, I'm not in the mood for this—"

"As if I give a damn. Look, I know this trial has been long and hard. I know we're in an uphill struggle. But you can't give up. You've got to keep trying."

"I have been trying. I've been doing everything I can."

"Have you?" She continued glaring at him. "Look, I wasn't going to bring this up now, but since you broached the subject—" She pushed him back by the shoulders. "What the hell was wrong with you in the courtroom today?"

"Nothing was wrong with me."

"Nothing personal, Ben—but you sucked."

Ben drew his head back. "Excuse me?"

"Sorry, pal. I call 'em like I see 'em. Colby was using you for a doormat."

Ben averted his eyes. "Colby is a very experienced litigator."

"So what? I've seen you go toe-to-toe with the best, and you've always held your own. But for some reason—in this case—it's like . . ." She thought for a moment. "It's like you've been walking on eggshells from the get-go. Even at the very start, you were playing it cool, trying to hold down the emotion."

"I'm just trying to be smart. Not do anything improper. There's a lot at stake here."

Christina's head began to nod. "That's what it is, isn't it? It's because there's so much at stake. I should've seen it before. Eleven sets of parents who've lost their children. And they come to you. I should've known that would knock your heart for a loop."

"Christina, it isn't—"

"You're afraid of letting them down, aren't you? That's what's going on here."

"This isn't just . . . another lawsuit."

"No, it isn't. So you're trying to play it safe. Not do anything stupid. Nothing that might embarrass them, or dishonor their cause. But the ironic thing is, by playing it safe, staying low-key—you're giving Colby the opening he needs to stomp all over you."

"I think you're exaggerating."

"Am I? Colby was making objections right and left, delivering little speeches to the jury. Why weren't you protesting?"

"He has the judge in his back pocket."

"And what about that speech Judge Perry made at the end of the day, discrediting your witness? That was grossly prejudicial. Why didn't you move for a mistrial?"

"He would've denied it."

"Of course he would've denied it. But at least you would've registered your displeasure. Might've made him think twice about doing it again."

"Or it might've made him toss me out of the courtroom on my butt. And then where would the plaintiffs be? Don't you see? I can't take the risk."

"I see this. Your current approach is not working." Christina leaned in closer, till they were practically nose-to-nose. "If you're going to win this thing, Ben, you're going to have to get mad."

Mike strolled about the interior of Ronald Harris's corner office, drinking in the chairs, the carpet, the so-so SAM's Club office furniture. There was a bookshelf lined with legal volumes, although the layer of dust atop them told Mike none of them had been consulted in ages. There was a potted tree in the corner, looking even worse than it had the last time Mike was in this office. But for the secretary, Mike suspected it would've been dead long ago. The office did have a window with a view, unlike most at Blaylock, although the view was principally of the plant parking lot.

All in all, Mike was not impressed.

"This is the best they can do for you?" Mike asked.

Harris shrugged. "I'm just one of many executives in the Blaylock firm."

"You're the man who recovered sixty million missing buckeroos."

"I guess you've talked with Mr. Blaylock."

"I certainly have. Why didn't you mention that the last time I talked with you?"

"I didn't see that it had anything to do with the murders. I still don't."

"If I found sixty million bucks for Blaylock, I'd expect a lot better office than this. A penthouse, at the very least."

"There aren't any. And I felt amply rewarded at the time."

Given the size of the lump sum payment he received, Mike would have to agree. "How did you ever tumble onto Montague?"

"It was pure process of elimination. I'd been working on it for months. Trying to figure out who had all the information required to make off with the loot. The account number, the password, the credentials. I knew the money had been picked up in person; I learned that from the bank. Once I excluded all the people I knew good and well weren't in Switzerland on the fateful day, there were few remaining possibilities. I became convinced it was Montague." He paused. "I just couldn't figure out how a dead man could rob a bank."

"That must've been a hell of a meeting. When you waltzed into the boardroom and informed everyone that a corpse had cleaned out the cashbox."

"It was . . . memorable." Harris glanced at the open door, as if making sure no one was listening in. "Blaylock about had a fit. He ranted and raved. Called me names. Told me I was crazy. Frankly, I thought I was going to be fired. Probably would've been, too."

"If you hadn't been right."

"Exactly. If I hadn't been right. I hired private detectives—a platoon of them. It was expensive, but eventually they started to turn up traces. Indications that Montague wasn't dead. We figured his mother—his only living relative—would be in on the secret. So they staked her out. Sure enough, she didn't seem particularly grieved about the loss of her only son. Hadn't even paid for a memorial marker."

"She knew he was alive."

"She did. We staked out her house—and several other places we thought Montague might return to. Unfortunately, he had the sense not to go to any of them. We did eventually track him down, though. Took forever. But we nabbed him."

"Where was he?"

"Holed up in a fishing cabin, somewhere in Texas. One sunny Tuesday morning, five of my men rushed in on him, grabbed him, and drove him up to Oklahoma. He never knew what hit him."

"And that's when the negotiations began?"

"Right. And I guess you know how it came out. He gave back the money—everything that was left, which was almost all of it. We agreed to keep quiet about what happened. That really ticked off Blaylock. He wanted the man to pay. Pay bad."

"Sounds like he did, as it turned out."

"Yeah. Montague died just a few months later—this time for real. Stress had just been too much for him, I guess. Pathetic thing is, he never got any benefit out of all the money he stole. Mind you, I don't approve of theft or anything. But after pulling off such an ingenious robbery, it seemed like he was at least entitled to a shopping spree at the mall or something."

"At least."

"Has this been helpful?"

"Not especially. But I needed to fill in the gaps. Learn as much as I could. Can you think of anything else notable about the robbery? Anything you haven't told me yet?"

Harris shrugged. "I don't think so. There's not much more to tell."

Mike pushed out of his chair. "Well, I appreciate your cooperation. Can you think of anyone else who might know more about Montague? Or the robbery?"

"We kept this thing very hush-hush, for obvious reasons. I can count all the people who know about it on one hand. I don't think you'll have much luck in that direction."

"What about people who knew Montague? Before he died—the first time. Friends. Coworkers."

"From what I hear, Montague pretty much kept to himself. He was a bit strange. Dreamy. You know the type. Not content with his lot in life."

"He went on the company outing. To Frontier City."

"Yeah, he did. And picked up a woman there, apparently, which was what caused all the confusion on the body count. But as far as actual friends . . ." His head turned. "I just remembered. There was one guy people said he hung with sometimes. But you're not going to be able to interview him, either."

"Let me guess. Dead."

"Yeah. 'Fraid so."

Mike stepped forward; his interest level was taking a sharp upward turn. "One of the three employees recently murdered?"

"Oh, no. Is that what you thought? No—this guy was dead a good while before that. James David Fenton."

"James Fenton? Not the lunatic who held all those law students hostage?"

"The very same. I'm impressed. You recognize the name of every criminal?"

"No, just the ones who create major hostage scenes. Especially when my best friend is one of the hostages."

"Really? Wow. Small world. You knew the hostage. And Montague knew Fenton. Birds of a feather flock together, huh? Weirdness attracts weirdness. Crazies attract crazies."

Mike probably should've taken offense, but his mind was elsewhere, plowing through his memory banks. "Montague wasn't crazy. And for that matter, neither was Fenton, at least not totally. There was something he kept saying, throughout the hostage siege." He snapped his fingers. " 'Where's the merchandise?' That's what it was. 'Is the merchandise secure?' "

"What's the merchandise?"

"I don't know," Mike said. His eyes seemed to turn inward, lost in thought. "But whatever it is, Fenton wanted it bad. And I'll bet my killer is looking for the same damn thing."

* 35 *

Whether he cared to admit it or not, today was the day Ben had dreaded most since this whole trial had begun. Not that life as a litigator was ever a piece of cake. He'd put small children on the stand, mentally retarded defendants, even murderers. He'd cross-exed victims of horrible crimes, innocent bystanders. But this morning was something else again. This morning he would put on his plaintiffs, starting with Cecily Elkins, to talk about the one subject on earth they would least like to discuss.

Ben had wanted to put a representative of all eleven families on the stand. Colby had wanted him to put on none, arguing that the details of the parents' bereavement "weren't relevant." The compromise they'd reached was that Ben would select three of the parents to represent the whole group. It hadn't been easy, but he'd managed to select his three—including Cecily, the woman who'd gotten him into this mess in the first place.

As he watched the spectators flood into the courtroom at

the start of this fateful day, it occurred to Ben that being in trial was like being on the crew of a submarine, buried deep in the ocean, for weeks at a time. The real world, its sights, sounds, and happenings, become little more than a faint echo. Colors dim; food becomes tasteless. The world becomes a textureless blur. Governments could crumble, economies could fall, but the litigator would barely notice. It wouldn't matter. When you are in trial, the trial is all-encompassing, all-devouring. The case invades your every waking thought, even your dreams. Nothing else seems to matter. Worst of all, every second is marked by unrelenting pressure, like the weight of thousands of tons of water bearing down on you. Breathing becomes difficult. You wonder if your life will ever be normal again.

Except in those rare moments when some startling event brings the real world back into focus with shattering clarity. Like this morning, on the way to the office, when Ben had stopped to pick up his suit—and the dry cleaners wouldn't let him have it. Because he hadn't paid his bill. In months. And the exactly two dollars and forty-seven cents he had in his pocket wasn't going to do the trick.

So he'd had to race back to his apartment and pick up this ugly gray pinstripe he hadn't worn since law school, which was at least fifteen pounds ago. It barely fit and was extremely uncomfortable. The jacket hampered his breathing, and he felt as if the seat of the pants might rip at any moment. Now that would be the perfect topper for this miserable day, wouldn't it?

At last the time came. The jury was reassembled, Judge Perry raced through the preliminaries, and Ben called Cecily Elkins to the witness stand.

She looked good, all things considered. Ben had told her not to go overboard; this was court, not a society ball. Still, she should look neat and groomed, and not wear anything that indicated disrespect for the court. She'd chosen a simple blue denim dress over a red blouse. Her hair was combed and tied in the back. She looked good, but not too good.

Ben had barely established who she was and where she lived before Colby was on his feet.

"Objection," he said. "Lack of relevance."

He's starting, Ben thought silently. Already. "Your honor, I have a right to introduce my witness to the jury. They need to know who they're hearing from."

The judge actually seemed to be pondering whether this was true. "I'll allow it. For a bit longer, anyway."

Ben proceeded. But barely a minute later, Colby was objecting again.

"Your honor," he complained. "You said you'd allow a bit more of this. We've had more than a bit."

Ben clenched his jaw together. These objections were garbage in the extreme. Colby was just interrupting for interruption's sake, to disrupt the flow. If he kept this up, it would seriously undermine the dramatic impact of Cecily's story. "Your honor, this is still preliminary material."

"I understand," the judge said. "Still, this has already been a long trial. Let's not go too far with this."

Ben tried to restart, but he had trouble remembering where he was. And if he couldn't remember what they'd been talking about, what were the chances that the jury would?

At last, preliminaries finished, Ben brought Cecily around to the topic of her son Billy. "When was Billy first diagnosed with cancer, Cecily?"

"Objection!" Colby said.

Ben glared. If there'd been an Uzi in the courtroom, Colby would be a dead man.

"I must protest," Colby continued. "This is not relevant."

"She's a plaintiff," Ben said, his lips pressed tightly together. "She has a right to tell her story. We agreed—"

"That she would testify, yes. But not about matters that are not at issue." Colby stepped toward the bench. "There's no dispute about the fact that this woman's son died of leukemia. The dispute is about what, if anything, caused the disease. And this witness knows nothing about that."

"They may not dispute it," Ben said, "but they haven't stipulated to it, either. Besides, she can testify to matters relating to causation. The use of tap water in their home, for instance."

Judge Perry nodded. "I'll allow it. But let's not dwell on matters that aren't contested."

Once again, Ben tried to resume his questioning, but every

time it was harder. He was losing his train of thought, plus, his irritation at Colby was undermining his concentration.

"What measures did you take to try to save your son?"

"Objection!" Colby said.

Ben clenched his teeth together. What was it Christina had told him? *If you're going to win this case, you're going to have to get mad.*

She was right.

"Your honor!" Ben boomed across the courtroom. "How much longer are we going to put up with these frivolous objections?"

Judge Perry shook his head. "Opposing counsel has a right to make objections. . . ."

"Valid objections, yes. But these objections are garbage and he knows it. He's just doing it to interrupt the flow of testimony. To make it harder for the jury to follow the witness's story."

"I must protest," Colby said. "That simply isn't so."

"Do you have any proof, Mr. Kincaid?"

"Proof? How could I have proof? Why would I need proof? Everyone in this courtroom knows it's true!"

Judge Perry's face grew stony. "Now, counsel, I warn you—"

"This is an abusive trial tactic, unethical in the extreme, and I want a stop put to it immediately."

Perry raised his gavel. "Counsel, you're about to be in contempt."

Mad, Ben told himself. *Get mad. Stay mad.* "For what? Protecting my clients from unethical defense tactics?"

"Counsel, this is your last chance—"

"I won't tolerate this, your honor. If you won't put an end to it, I'll take an immediate interlocutory appeal."

"Citing what? Too many objections?"

"Abusive conduct. I'll attach a copy of the transcript. A blind man could see what Mr. Colby's trying to do here. It won't be a problem for three appeal judges."

"Mr. Kincaid—"

"Your honor, I'm sick of these tiresome, inane interruptions. And I think the jury is, too."

Without even thinking about it, the combatants turned to

look at the jury. Ben saw that three of them were slowly nodding their heads—thank God. They knew what he was saying. They were tired of it, too.

"Counsel, approach the bench."

Ben and Colby approached. Judge Perry covered the microphone with his hand. "Mr. Kincaid, this is my courtroom. I will not tolerate this insubordination."

"But your honor—"

"Don't give me any excuses. You will treat the court with respect, or I'll toss you in the clink." He took several deep breaths, almost hyperventilating, then turned to Colby. "And as for you, Mr. Colby, I would appreciate it if you would restrict your interruptions to those that actually have some merit. You've been practicing long enough to know the difference."

Ben's lips parted. Were his ears deceiving him? Had the judge actually scolded the great Charlton Colby?

Ben returned to the podium, doing all he could to suppress his smile. As always, Christina was right. He should've done this a long time ago.

And now that he'd gotten himself mad, he planned to stay that way.

After the big blowout at the bench, Colby's objections became few and far between. What objections he did make had some basis in law, however tenuous. Ben could live with that. At least they weren't so frequent that they prevented Cecily from telling her story.

Which she did. Better than Ben could've dreamed.

Cecily described the tragedy of her son's death with calm and dignity. She focused her large doe eyes on the jury and never let them escape. Although she did not skimp on the horrific details, at the same time, she never gave the impression that she was exaggerating or melodramatizing.

She took the jury through every stage of Billy's disease, from the initial diagnosis, through the painful bouts with chemotherapy, the invasive drugs, the hospital visits. She told them about his remissions, when everything seemed to be fine, only to have the disease reappear again, like some malevolent unconquerable specter. She told them of all the time devoted, all the money spent, all the immeasurable heartaches.

She concluded by telling them how Billy, who had seemed reasonably healthy again, suddenly took ill and couldn't breathe, how she had raced him to the hospital but never got there.

"You can't imagine what it was like," Cecily said, and for the first time, her voice betrayed the faintest hint of a tremor. "One day, your boy seems healthy, hardy, energetic. He likes to read books. He likes to play soccer and bowl. He's popular. He's beautiful in every way." She paused, catching her breath. "He's normal. In every possible way." The light in her eyes seemed to fade. "And the next day, he's dead."

She paused, pressing her fingertips against the bridge of her nose. "I did everything I could. Everything I could think of, everything I could imagine. Anything to save my boy. But it wasn't enough." Tears began to flow from her eyes. "No matter what I tried. It wasn't enough."

Colby did not cross-examine.

After the third of the designated parents had finished testifying, Ben rested his case.

Fred the Feeb was trying to withdraw his pension.

He couldn't believe it at first, even given the inevitability of it all. Fred the Feeb? True, Fred was the only remaining suspect—the only one he hadn't killed yet. But Fred? The utterly incompetent, thoroughly geeklike Fred? He couldn't steal rocks from a quarry, much less make off with the merchandise. *Could he?*

And yet, there he was, big as life and twice as ugly. It had only been a coincidence that he'd managed to see it. This was simply a preliminary run, scoping out his quarry in preparation for the fun and games to come. And there Fred was, in Stacey's office, trying to pry some money out of his pension fund.

He'd already heard about Fred's new alarm system, of course, and the guard dog. That was understandable enough. Fred knew he was on the list, whether he really deserved to be or not. But trying to get his pension money now? There could only be one possible explanation.

He was planning to run. Run far away, where no one could

ever find him, least of all his old buddy old chum with the bright green eyes.

Of course, that was what Tony had thought, too. He thought he would just disappear for a while, take up permanent residence in the fishing cabin. But the Blaylock goons had caught him.

Just as he would catch Fred, no matter where he went. But there was no denying that it would be easier to take care of business before Fred hightailed it. Which meant he would have to accelerate his plan.

He was a little worried about that goddamn unrelenting cop, Morelli. He'd been up at the plant almost every day, asking a whole new series of questions, acting like he was actually getting somewhere. He would've thought that after the shockeroo he'd given the fool he'd have backed off. If anything, though, it seemed to have made the man even more doggedly determined. He should've killed the chump while he had the chance, or fried his brains at the very least. This was his punishment, he supposed, for showing a bit of mercy. Although in truth, there was more to it than that. He'd had George to deal with, and it was always possible the cop had called for backup. He'd decided it was smartest to make tracks, to haul off George, finish the operation, and deliver him to his final destination.

So the cop had lived. For now, anyway. If he continued to get in his way . . . well, anything could happen. One good swipe with a ball-peen hammer could cure a multitude of problems.

For now, though, he had to concentrate on Fred. If Fred did have the merchandise, he wanted it now, before he left town, before he initiated a chase that could prolong this thing even more. It was time to bring this to an end.

Which meant bringing Fred the Feeb to an end. And maybe the cop, too.

* 36 *

Judge Perry denied Colby's Motion for a Directed Verdict.

For Ben, this was equivalent to hearing that the stalker who'd been trailing him for months with a blood-soaked axe was finally laid to rest. For months now, he'd worried about the possibility of losing the case before the defense put on a single witness. Colby had been threatening from the get-go, and the judge had repeatedly expressed his concerns about the plaintiffs' causation problems. If Perry had granted the motion, all his time would have been wasted—worse, all that money would be gone, with no hope of recovering it.

But he didn't. The judge denied the motion, although he expressed not a little regret as he did it. "Mind you," Perry said, as the lawyers faced him in his private chambers, "I'm not happy about the approach Mr. Kincaid has taken to establish causation. I think your so-called scientist was little more than a hired gun. Professor Matthews tells me he passes the *Daubert* standard, so I have to accept that—but if he does, it's just barely. Still, as a trial judge, it goes against the grain to take the case out of the hands of the jury. I hate to do that—and will only do that in the most extreme circumstances. No, I'm going to let this one go to the jury—and I'll just hope they do the right thing."

"Thank you, your honor," Ben said. His fists were clenched so tightly his hands were white. He released them, at last, and felt a surge of relief sweeping through his entire body.

"I'm afraid this is likely to be an appeal issue for me," Colby said. His tone was informative and matter-of-fact, not threatening. "Should I need one."

Judge Perry nodded. "Let's hope it doesn't come to that."

*　*　*

As he began putting the defense case before the jury, Colby's strategy seemed apparent. He wasn't going to risk alienating the jury by attacking the plaintiff parents, denying their loss, or suggesting any fault on their part. He wasn't going to deny that chemicals had been dumped behind the Blaylock plant, either. He probably could; Ben imagined he could have a parade of loyal employees take the stand and deny that any chemicals were ever dumped or stored in an improper fashion. But that would sound like exactly what it was—the defense being defensive.

Instead, Colby chose to focus on the weak link in Ben's armor, the one essential aspect of the case he could most easily win—causation. He would deny that there was any proof that TCE or perc, even if they were present, caused the leukemia outbreak. That was all he had to do. Because the burden of proof was on the plaintiffs. If Colby demonstrated that they had not met that burden of proof, the jurors would be forced to find for the defendant, regardless of what they privately thought, where their sympathies lay, or what "common sense" told them.

The first witness Colby called was a medical researcher from Boston, Dr. Gene Crenshaw. Crenshaw was in effect Rimland's opposite number; he was there to deny everything Rimland had advocated.

After Colby established the man's typically exhaustive credentials, he led him to the heart of the controversy. "Doctor, you've heard Dr. Rimland's testimony. Do you agree with his conclusions?"

Crenshaw was a short, moon-faced man with a bald head that he had a habit of scratching as he formulated an answer. "No, I do not."

"And why not?"

"Because he has no proof. His conclusions are unsubstantiated."

"So it's possible that he's right—he just hasn't proven it."

"No, I can't agree with that. I think he has made fundamental methodological errors that have led him in the wrong direction altogether."

"Please explain."

That was Crenshaw's cue to turn and face the jury. "Dr. Rimland's work proceeds from an initial belief in the existence of cancer clusters—pockets of leukemia that could only arise from some experiential or environmental source. But clusters aren't real. They're a myth. Therefore, all conclusions drawn from a belief in them are flawed."

Colby was playing the devil's advocate, although just as a means of leading Crenshaw in his attack on Rimland. "But we've been told about areas where there have been unusually high numbers of these cases. Including in Blackwood."

"But that's entirely consistent with the random distribution of cases over a large population. You have to bear in mind— we have over four hundred million people in this country. Even with a disease as rare as leukemia, it's inevitable that some cases are going to occur close to one another. That doesn't mean there's been some tremendous outbreak. It's just inherent in the nature of random distribution."

"It doesn't prove that the disease has been caused by some external agent?"

"No. Far from it. Think about it—if leukemia really was caused by something like the air or the water, wouldn't you see a lot more cases than we do? Particularly in the contaminated areas? We keep hearing about the eleven cases of leukemia in Blackwood—what about the literally hundreds and thousands of people who drank the same water but did not get leukemia?"

Colby nodded, obviously pleased. "Well, Doctor, if it isn't the water—what does cause leukemia?"

"Nobody knows. That's the truth of the matter. We just don't know. But we know this—it existed a long time before TCE or perc did. We don't know what brings it to the surface, any more than we understand what causes other cancers— although most researchers are looking at genetic causes, rather than environmental ones."

"In other words—you're just born with it?"

"Born with it, or born with a genetic predisposition to develop it, yes."

"Whose position would you say has more support in the medical and scientific community—yours, or Dr. Rimland's?"

"Objection," Ben said. "The question calls for hearsay."

"No," Colby rejoined, "the question calls for an expert to give an expert opinion regarding the state of research in a field within his realm of expertise."

Judge Perry made a shrugging gesture. "I'll allow it."

Colby restated his question.

"The consensus of current medical opinion is dramatically in support of the position I just espoused—that we don't know what causes leukemia, but it's probably genetic, rather than environmental. Dr. Rimland's position is . . . well . . . on the fringe, to say the least."

Colby wouldn't let it go at that. "He's considered to be a nut, basically. Right?"

"Objection!" Ben said.

Perry nodded. "I'll have to sustain that one."

"I'll withdraw it," Colby said. "But Dr. Crenshaw, Rimland's position has not been generally accepted, has it?"

"No. It certainly has not. Mind you, we would jump at any real evidence regarding the causation of leukemia. If we could figure out what causes it, we might be able to develop a cure, even a vaccine. But these unsupported fringe theories don't help. To the contrary, they hurt, because they distract public opinion from the serious work that might potentially lead to a solution."

"Thank you," Colby said. "No more questions."

Ben raced up to the podium. Crenshaw had raked his expert over like wheat in a thresher. He had to try to rehabilitate Rimland's reputation if he hoped to prevail on the causation issue.

Get mad, he reminded himself. *Get mad, and stay mad.*

"Dr. Crenshaw, have you yourself performed any studies concerning the causes of leukemia?"

"No, I have not."

"Dr. Rimland has. He's been working on it for almost ten years."

"I'm aware of that."

"So he's been working on it for a decade, and you haven't worked on it at all. And yet, you want to tell this jury that you know more about it?"

"Sometimes it takes an outsider to reveal the flaws in scientific methodology. In this case, I think Dr. Rimland is much too close to his own work. He's invested too much time in cancer clusters and chemical leukemogenesis to admit that his work is basically a flawed premise leading to a flawed and unsubstantiated conclusion."

"Dr. Rimland's studies conclusively link TCE and perc to leukemic growths."

"In laboratory animals, even if you accept his methodology. Not humans."

"Are you suggesting he should have injected humans with this toxic waste?"

Crenshaw looked at Ben dismissively. "Of course not. But you have to understand—animals are not like us. Not entirely, anyway. There is evidence that some cases of leukemia, or leukemic-emulating diseases, are transmitted virally. Lab rats have very different immune systems, different ways of processing disease. There is no parallel evidence with regard to humans."

Was it Ben's imagination, or had Crenshaw's use of scientific jargon increased considerably now that he was being crossed? He was answering Ben's questions—but in a way that would be virtually incomprehensible to much of the jury.

"Dr. Rimland is hardly the first medical researcher to use lab rats."

"No."

"Weren't lab rats used extensively in tests of the new AIDS treatments?"

Crenshaw bowed his head slightly. "Yes, I believe that's so."

"And those treatments are now being used on humans, and have dramatically decreased the number of AIDS deaths."

"That's true. But the critical moment of discovery was when the treatments were used on humans. Until then, no one went around claiming they had solved the problem. And might I remind you—Dr. Rimland has not discovered a cure. All he has is a theory of causation—a theory he is entirely unable to prove with regard to *Homo sapiens*."

Ben drew in his breath. He would never get anywhere with Crenshaw on this point. He might as well try something else. "Dr. Crenshaw, can you look this jury in the eye and tell them with absolute certainty that the tainted water did not cause the Blackwood leukemia outbreak?"

He shrugged the question away. " 'Absolute certainty' is not a term used in the field of medical research."

"Don't duck my question, Doctor. The jury wants to know. Are you absolutely certain Dr. Rimland is wrong?"

"I find his conclusions entirely unsupported by convincing medical evidence."

"Once again, you fail to answer my question." Ben took a step forward. "Why is this so hard for you to answer, Doctor?"

"Because it's a foolish question. As a scientist, I only accept conclusions based upon available evidence. Here, the evidence doesn't exist."

"I'm going to ask the question one more time, Doctor. Are you absolutely sure Dr. Rimland is wrong?"

Crenshaw was beginning to look a bit uncomfortable. He folded his arms across his chest. "I've already answered that question."

"But you haven't."

His voice rose. "I've said what I have to say."

Colby tried to bail his witness out. "Your honor, I object. Asked and answered."

"But he hasn't answered," Ben replied. "And if he doesn't, I think I know what conclusion the jury can draw from his silence."

"Your honor!" Colby said. "That's grossly improper."

Perry nodded hastily. "Mr. Kincaid's last remark will be stricken. I instruct the jury to ignore it." He peered down at Ben. "Counsel, let's move on to something else."

"Fine. Let me ask you this, Dr. Crenshaw. What if he's right?"

Crenshaw's discomfort appeared to increase. "I don't know what you mean."

"What if he's right? What if these poisons do cause cancer—and did in Blackwood?"

Colby jumped up. "Objection."

Ben ignored him. "What if they do cause cancer and we don't do anything about it—because you and others like you are more interested in collecting a corporate paycheck than in discovering the truth?"

"Your honor!" Colby repeated.

Judge Perry banged his gavel. "Mr. Kincaid!"

Ben plowed on ahead. "What if the guilty parties aren't punished? What if this corporation—and others like it—go on taking the most profitable course—the one that kills children?"

Judge Perry continued banging. "I'm terminating this examination right now, Mr. Kincaid. Sit down!"

Mad, Ben told himself silently. *Get mad and stay mad.* "Because I think the truth is, you just don't know, Dr. Crenshaw. You don't have the answers, so you're willing to say what the big corporation wants you to say. But if you're wrong, you've done a gross injustice to this jury—and those eleven families."

"Your honor!" Colby was practically screaming now.

Judge Perry pointed to the back of the courtroom. "Bailiff!"

"If you're wrong, Dr. Crenshaw," Ben continued, "then those eleven deaths—and all the others that might well follow—are on your head."

The bailiff came up behind Ben, ready for bear.

"I'm done," Ben said, throwing up his hands. "No more questions."

"Sorry to bother you, ma'am," Mike said awkwardly, as he lowered himself into an armchair. "I know you've been through a lot already."

What was with this woman, anyway? he wondered. He'd called ahead; she knew he was coming. And yet there she was, in a shimmery pink nightgown with puffball sleeves, her hair a mess, yesterday's mascara still smeared under her eyes. She looked more like a cathouse madam than someone who expected to be interrogated by a homicide detective.

"I knew you'd be back," the woman said. "You, or someone like you." There was a pronounced slurring to her words. Her eyes seemed to roam about, detached from what her mouth was saying. "They always say this is the last time. But it never is."

"Again, I'm sorry for the intrusion. Believe me, no one was more surprised than me when there turned out to be a connection between this latest spate of murders and, uh, your . . . late husband."

"Ex-husband," she corrected. "We hadn't been married for more than a year, when Jim went ballistic. Hadn't lived together for longer than that. And hadn't . . . you know. Lived as man and wife. For even longer than that."

"I'm sorry." During that long speech, Mike managed to catch a whiff of strong liquor on her breath, whiskey or something like it. Pamela Fenton was drunk. Which could explain a great deal, including the slurred speech and unsightly appearance. "Did you have any . . . indication of your husband's violent tendencies?"

"Not in the least." She leaned back against the sofa, spreading her bare legs in a manner that Mike wished she wouldn't. "He was always timid. A pip-squeak. Didn't have the balls to get what he wanted. That was the problem."

Her problem? Mike wondered. Or his? "So he didn't . . . beat you?"

"No. Never." She hiccuped. "More the other way around."

"And he didn't have any guns?"

"Not till the day he decided to shoot up the law school. And he'd bought that shotgun at a pawnshop that very day. Who'd'a thought? No one's safe anymore."

No, Mike mused, not as long as any crazy with twenty bucks in his pocket can stroll into a pawnshop and walk out with a deadly weapon. "I know you've been asked this before, but—do you have any idea why he went to the law school that day?"

"I'm as clueless as you, sonny boy. All I know is what I read in the paper. That he said he was looking for some professor or another. The Cobra."

"The Tiger," Mike corrected. "Professor Joseph Canino. Did you know him?"

"Never heard of him. Much less seen him."

"Then why was your husband after him?"

"Beats the hell outta me. Musta been somethin' he worked up after I dumped him." Her speech was worsening.

"They've never found Professor Canino. He was gone the day your ex stormed the law school. Hasn't been seen since."

"That's what I hear."

"I don't suppose you know where he is."

"I told you—I never seen the man in my life!" Her voice was becoming strident. Her drugged state probably caused her to talk louder than she realized. "I got no clue!"

"All right. I'm sorry." Mike had to placate her, he sensed, or this already mostly worthless interview would come to a screeching halt. "I don't suppose you know what your husband was after? What he was looking for?" Mike had spent the morning reviewing the file on the case. "He said he wanted something he called 'the merchandise.' "

The woman lurched forward. "I told you already! He was my ex-husband. And I don't have the slightest goddamn idea what he was looking for!"

"All right, all right." Mike held up his hands. "Stay calm." It was definitely time for a switch in subjects. "Let's talk about something you do know about. Why did you leave your husband?"

"Who wouldn't leave him? He was worthless!"

Worthless being a relative term, Mike thought, as he gazed at the unappealing hulk on the sofa. "He was employed, at the time. Had a decent job at the Blaylock plant."

"He had a peon job, fit for a peon. Hadn't had a promotion in twelve years."

"Still, he was employed."

"He was a loser, would you get that through your head already!" Spittle flew from her lips as she spoke. "A creep. Couldn't do anything right! Couldn't even get it up!"

Which was far more information than Mike actually needed. Or wanted. "So what made you finally decide to leave him?"

"Why not? I'd had enough."

"Was there . . . someone else?"

She whipped her head around. "What the hell business is it of yours?"

Mike shrugged. "I have to follow all possible avenues—"

"Look, a woman's marriage vows can only go so far, you understand me? If a husband can't do his duty, than she's entitled to—to—try to do somethin' to remedy the situation. You know what I'm sayin'?"

All too well. "What happened to your relationship? With the . . . other man, I mean?"

"He dumped me, the son of a bitch. Couldn't handle the pressure."

"The pressure?"

"From assholes like you! After Jim held up the law school and got himself killed. The police were all over us, every bleedin' second. And the press was even worse. Reporters sticking microphones in our faces every time we went outside. They wouldn't leave us alone. Everyone wanted a piece of us! He couldn't take it anymore. So he split."

"I see," Mike said, although, as he gazed across the room at her, he could contemplate other possible explanations for the lover's departure. "What was your husband doing? Ex-husband, that is. During the year or so after you left him, but before he died?"

"How the hell would I know? I never spoke to him. Never once. He called a few times, but I always hung up on him."

"Did he have any friends?"

"Oh, maybe a few other losers from the plant. Don't bother asking their names. I didn't know them."

"Was Harvey Pendergast one of them?"

She cocked her head to one side. "Now that you mention it, that does sound familiar."

"What about Tony Montague?"

"Montague? No. I'd remember a crazy-ass name like that."

"You're sure?"

"Positive."

Mike frowned. That screwed up the theory that was forming in his brain. "What about favorite places? Somewhere he liked to go. Other than work."

"I'm tellin' you, I don't know."

"Did he have anything he liked to do? A hobby? Something for his spare time?"

"Who cares?"

"He had to do something during that year."

"Yeah, but I don't know what it was. Can't you get that through your thick head? I don't know!"

Mike drew back, for both their sakes. She was about to terminate the interview, and he was about to terminate her.

To his surprise, Pamela Fenton was the one who broke the silence. "He did like to fish," she said, out of the blue.

"Fish? Where did he go?"

"I dunno. Out of state, usually. I think he thought it was more fun if he had to drive a ways to get there. More like an adventure. But I don't know where exactly he went."

"Did he fish alone?"

"Nah. He'd go with some other losers, most times."

Some other losers. The wheels inside Mike's head started spinning. Like Harvey?

His mind raced back to the first crime scene. The closet, where Harvey had hidden.

There was fishing gear there.

And Margaret, the second victim, had a fishing license in her purse. And George, the third victim, the one whose body still hadn't turned up, had told Mike during their interview that he wanted to get away to fish. And Tony Montague was found dead in a fishing cabin.

They were all fishers. That was the connection. That was the link for which he'd been searching so long.

"Are you sure you don't know where your ex-husband used to go to fish?" Mike asked.

"I'm positive."

"Maybe someone at the plant will know. Thanks you for your help, ma'am."

"You mean that's it?"

"Yup. And with any luck, you won't be bothered again." Mike was already out the front door when he heard his cell phone beep. "Morelli."

It was Tomlinson.

"What've you got for me, buddy?"

"What you probably want least," Tomlinson replied. "Another corpse."

Mike felt as if his heart had stopped beating. "From the same murderer?"

"We think so, yeah."

It would be George Philby, no doubt. The man Mike had failed to save. When he let the killer slip through his fingers.

"You still there, Mike?"

"Yeah," he said bitterly. "I'm on my way." He snapped the

cell phone shut, furious at himself, at the killer, at the whole wide world.

Fred the Feeb stood in line at Tulsa International Airport, waiting to get his ticket. Jesus and Mary, Mother of God! How could such a podunk airport make you wait so long just to get a plane ticket?

He'd finally decided—he was making a break for it. He had no choice. He couldn't put it off any longer. He couldn't go on kidding himself that alarms and big dogs were going to make a difference. Not if he wanted to live long enough to see another sunrise.

He had spotted his old buddy, currently employed as a mass murderer, at the Blaylock plant. There was no question about it this time; he'd seen him clear as day, twice as ugly. He was there, even though he didn't work at Blaylock anymore.

He was looking for Fred.

That was enough to spur Fred into action. He had managed to think of one place he could go, after giving it some thought. It was not a secret place—the killer knew all about it. But it was free. He could live there a good long time at little or no expense. And once he had realized the merchandise— nothing could be denied him.

If he could just stay alive that long. When it became clear that Fred was the man with the merchandise—because all the others were dead—and it became clear that Fred had flown the coop—because he wasn't coming in to work anymore—

Fred took a deep breath. One problem at a time. First, he had to get out of town.

He made it to the front of the line and told the airline teller his chosen destination.

She smiled and typed at light speed on her computer keyboard. "Will this be business or pleasure?"

"Neither," Fred said, sweat dripping down the sides of his face. "Survival."

* 37 *

Colby naturally made a motion for mistrial, based on Ben's rant against Dr. Crenshaw, but Judge Perry denied it. Ben wasn't sure why. Probably because of his great certainty that the jury would find against Ben anyway. If he granted the motion for mistrial, he'd have to hear this case again in a few months. If he let the jury rule in favor of the defendant, it would all be over.

Crenshaw was just the first of a parade of medical witnesses Colby put on the stand. Over the next few days, the jury heard from two cancer specialists, a leukemia researcher from Children's Medical in Oklahoma City, and the president of the state AMA. They were all top-notch witnesses, and they all said essentially the same thing: No one knows what causes cancer. The man from Children's Medical was able to update the jury on all the potential causes currently being investigated by the mainstream medical community—none of which involved TCE or perc, or for that matter any other environmental catalysts. All of the witnesses used different code phrases to describe Rimland and his work, such as "fringe" or "unorthodox," but they all amounted to the same thing. The man's a quack, they said. But nicely.

On Friday morning, Colby called a man named Alan Witherspoon to the witness box. Ben was so deeply mired in Colby's medical witnesses he couldn't even remember who the man was, until Christina slid the file to him. Witherspoon was a hydrologist, a field researcher and a professor at Yale. He had spent more than fifteen years investigating claims of chemically tainted water and its possible connection to disease.

After sharing his credentials with the jury, which took over half an hour, Colby started him in on Rimland.

"You're familiar with the present case, aren't you, Professor?"

"Yes. I've had a chance to review all the data, the reports and analyses."

"Is the Blackwood case similar to anything you've done in the past?"

"Oh, yes. This is directly within my area of expertise. I've been handling these kinds of cases for more than a decade now."

"And you had a chance to listen to the testimony of Dr. Rimland, did you not?"

"I did." Although the rule of sequestration allowed Ben to keep fact witnesses out of the courtroom during the testimony of others, expert witnesses could not be excluded.

"Were you persuaded by Dr. Rimland's conclusions?"

Witherspoon smiled. "Of course not." Of course not? Ben wondered. Had it come to that? His ace witness had passed from being challenged to being humored. "I think he's been misled, from premise to conclusion."

"How so?"

"The first problem is, he proceeded from data collected by the EPA. That always leads to skewed conclusions." He glanced at the jury. "I worked for the EPA for six years. Believe me, I know what I'm talking about." His smile was gentle, not presupposing. He seemed a likeable, casual, but very knowledgeable man. He had even managed to survive that endless litany of his accomplishments without seeming egotistical—no small feat, as Ben well knew.

"The problem with the EPA is, they go in assuming there's a problem. They don't go in at all unless they get a complaint; from that time forward, they're looking for a solution to the complaint."

Colby played the disinterested questioner. "Does that affect their results?"

"Sure. If you're looking for a problem, you're going to find one—even if it doesn't really exist. Especially if your job security depends on results. Say someone tells the researcher the water in their town smells funny. So he goes out and learns that the water has one one-millionth part per hundred more TCE than the water in surrounding wells. You wouldn't think that was a big deal. But if that's the only difference he discovers, sure as the world he'll write a report that says the contamination in the water is due to TCE."

"But that doesn't necessarily mean it's true?"

"Of course not." Witherspoon spread wide his hands, speaking in a calm, relaxed manner. "It could've been any one of a hundred things. Who knows? Maybe the complainant's pipes are tainting the water. Maybe the complainant is smelling her own perfume. The fact that TCE is in the water doesn't mean it caused every effect detected. It doesn't mean it caused anything."

"Have you ever known EPA data to lead to flawed conclusions?"

"Oh, sure." It was almost like he wasn't testifying; more like they were all sitting around at a party, shooting the breeze. "Please realize—the EPA is by definition a reactionary organization. They do not take a balanced perspective. To be fair, that's not their job. But because they operate with a single-minded perspective, their data often leads to errors. They perpetuate a logical fallacy."

"Could you explain what you mean?"

"Certainly. In the present case, we have two abnormalities—slightly higher levels of certain chemicals in the water, and elevated incidences of childhood leukemia. It's not surprising that people would try to link the two together; indeed, as the plaintiffs' lawyer has said repeatedly, common sense suggests that the two are connected. But of course, if common sense ruled, then the earth would be flat, heavy objects would fall faster than lighter ones, and I would make a lot more money than I do."

The jury laughed. They seemed be enjoying Witherspoon's lighter tone, by contrast to the last sixty or so witnesses. Damn all, Ben thought to himself. The last thing he needed now was a defense expert with charisma.

"As a previous witness established," Witherspoon continued, "outbreak clumps of diseases—even rare diseases—

will occur. They aren't too coincidental to be random—to the contrary, they are mathematically to be expected. Similarly, I don't think it's all that unusual that trace elements of certain chemicals sometimes trickle into the water supply. But does that mean that the two naturally occurring events are linked? That one caused the other? No. The connection simply isn't there."

"And when you say the connection isn't there . . ."

"I'm saying, based on my extensive experience in this field, that there's no proof that increased levels of TCE or perc lead to leukemia outbreaks. Not in this case, or any other."

"Thank you, Professor Witherspoon," Colby said with a slight bow. "Your witness, Mr. Kincaid."

That hurt, to put it bluntly. Sure, Colby's medical witnesses hadn't exactly been good for the plaintiffs' case. But Ben had expected that, and to some extent, so did the jury. Medical testimony sometimes conflicted; everyone was used to that. But to have the top dude from Yale, a man who'd been working with tainted water wells for fifteen years, shoot holes in their case so effectively—that was both unexpected and devastating.

Ben understood now why Colby had saved this man for last. He said what Colby wanted said and did it in a way that had jury appeal. Assuming Judge Perry didn't allow Ben any rebuttal witnesses, which seemed likely, Witherspoon would be the last witness heard before the jury retired. He would leave all the doubters wondering if he wasn't right—and provide ample fuel for those who were already convinced.

Ben had to knock some holes in him on cross. The problem was—he was well-spoken and smart. He wouldn't sit around limply while Ben turned him into a slice of Swiss cheese. He would fight Ben all the way. And Ben had to be careful about what he said to the man. After all, the jury liked him.

After Ben established that Witherspoon, like all the other experts, was being paid generously by the Blaylock corporation for his "cooperation," he launched into Witherspoon's analysis of the Blackwood water problem. "You say you're familiar with Dr. Rimland's work?"

"I am indeed."

"But you overlooked a great deal of what he did."

Witherspoon blinked. "I don't know what you mean," he said disingenuously, and in that second, Ben realized this distinguished Yale fellow was simply in it for the money. For all his vaunted degrees and credentials, he was saying what he got paid to say, using facts that helped and ignoring those that didn't.

All of a sudden, Ben didn't care whether the jury liked the man or not. He was going to tear him apart.

"Don't play coy, Professor. You dismissed Rimland's work without even mentioning his most important experiments."

"I saw no reason to bore the jury with unconvincing details."

"What about the extensive tests Dr. Rimland has performed with lab rats?"

Witherspoon waved his hands in the air. "Lab rats are not people."

"I think we're all clear on that point already, Professor. But if something kills rats, we could reasonably conclude that it might also kill humans, couldn't we?"

Witherspoon would not give Ben what he wanted. "The two are entirely different species."

"Then experiments with lab rats can't be used to predict results with humans?"

"Not reliably, no."

Ben smiled. "Then why do you use them, Professor?"

He looked up abruptly. "Excuse me?"

Ben patted the report in his file. God bless Christina. She always came up with the gold. "Two years ago, you were hired to test a new antiperspirant by a large corporation in Maine. In order to determine whether there might be any harmful side effects, you performed tests on lab rats. Didn't you?"

"Well . . ."

"Didn't you? I have a copy of your final report right here, if you're having trouble remembering what you did."

"All right, counsel, call off the dogs. I did use lab rats. But that was an entirely different situation."

"I don't see any difference."

"In that instance, I used rats in a preliminary test to screen out possible side effects, not to establish a link between cause and effect."

"Nonetheless, you used rats to determine the safety of the product. You wouldn't have done that unless you thought the effects on rats would bear some similarity to the effects on humans. It would be pointless."

"As I said, the tests with the rats were just preliminary. I later performed tests on human subjects."

"But only because the tests with rats had proved negative."

"Well, that's not exactly—"

"Professor. Are you telling this jury you would've gone ahead with the tests on humans if the tests with the lab rats had produced negative results?"

"Well . . . no."

"Then by the same token, I submit that since TCE and perc produced negative results on lab rats, they should not be tested on humans. And because they were, and children died—of the same disease that killed the rats—the parties that caused the deaths should be held responsible!"

"Your honor," Colby said, rising, "he's making speeches again."

"You're up there to ask questions, Mr. Kincaid," Judge Perry remonstrated. "Either ask them, or sit down."

"Yes, your honor." Ben returned to counsel table and retrieved a tall glass of water. "Do you know what this is, Professor?"

Witherspoon arched an eyebrow suspiciously. "A glass of water?"

"Correct. But a very special glass of water. I've tainted this water with trace portions of TCE and perc."

Witherspoon frowned. "Why on earth would you do that?"

"Why not? After all, it's harmless, right?" He approached the witness stand. "Here, have a big swallow."

Colby rose again. "Your honor . . ."

Ben cut him off. "Professor Witherspoon has asserted that water contaminated with TCE and perc is harmless. So now I'm giving him a chance to prove to the jury that he really believes that." He held out the glass. "Here, Professor. Drink up."

Witherspoon sat up straight. "This is ridiculous."

"It is not. It's a simple test. Put your mouth where your money is, so to speak." Once again, Ben pushed the glass forward. "Drink up, Professor. Drink big."

"I will not have any part of this," Witherspoon said indignantly. "This is absurd."

Ben smiled. "You're afraid of this water."

"I am not afraid of it!" He began to perspire. "I just think this is a demeaning waste of time."

Colby tried again to intervene. "Your honor—"

Ben ignored him. "Professor, either this water is harmless, and you'll happily drink the whole thing down, or it isn't, and you've just told the jury a pack of lies. Which is it?"

Witherspoon was finding it harder to sit still. He was kneading his hands, squirming in his seat. "I am not scared of your water! I just won't participate in a—a farce!"

Judge Perry leaned forward. "Mr. Kincaid—"

Before the judge had a chance to say another word, Ben lurched forward—with the glass. His arm holding the glass jutted straight toward Witherspoon's face—

But did not spill out. Because, as Ben then demonstrated to the jury, he had covered the glass with a near-invisible layer of transparent Saran Wrap. But that wasn't what was important.

What was important was—when he thought the water would come flying at him—Witherspoon ducked. He crouched down, covering his face with his hands.

It was more than just not wanting to get wet. He was afraid.

Colby ran up to the bench. "Your honor, I must protest. This is courtroom chicanery at its worst. I want this entire outrageous demonstration stricken from the record."

"It doesn't matter," Ben said quietly, looking directly at the jury. "They saw. They know. Don't you?"

"Your honor!" Colby continued. "This violates all conventions of courtroom decorum! This is a shabby attempt to persuade the jury with trickery rather than evidence."

"I agree," Judge Perry said. "The whole business will be stricken from the record. I instruct the jury to disregard it and to give it no weight during their deliberations."

"It doesn't matter," Ben said, even more quietly than before. "They saw. They know. Don't you?"

Amid the clamor and argument, Ben retook his seat at counsel table. None of the jurors had responded when he spoke to them—not even a nod of the head. But surely they got it—didn't they? Surely they understood.

He would never know, not till the jury returned with a completed verdict form in their hands.

Mike spotted Tomlinson in the distance as he pushed his way through the brush and densely packed trees. Tomlinson was waving his arms in the air, frantically trying to flag him down. As if Mike could possibly miss ten crime technicians, swirling red lights, and an ocean of yellow tape.

"Did you enjoy your hike?" Tomlinson asked, trying to be amiable.

"No," Mike said. He was feeling grumpy and he saw no reason to hide the fact. "I hate hiking."

"I thought you'd appreciate the chance to get out of the office and get some fresh air."

"I'd rather be at home reading Dickens." Mike glanced across the restrictive tape to the tall pile of red dirt that seemed to be the center of the crime scene. "So what've we got?"

Tomlinson led his boss back to the heart of the action. They were in a thick, undeveloped section of Tulsa just north of Seventy-first, between Harvard and Yale. Although in the heart of the most rapidly growing section of the city, several acres were still undeveloped. All around, all Mike could see was forest and thicket.

The crime scene technicians buzzed around like bumblebees going about their appointed specialized tasks. How many times had he been to a scene like this? Too damn many.

"How on earth did you ever find a body out here?" Mike asked.

"Well, I'd like to take credit for finding it, preferably at the conclusion of an ingenious series of deductions, but the truth is—we didn't find it at all. Some kids did."

"Kids?"

Tomlinson nodded. "See that apartment complex over there?"

Mike glanced in the direction he was pointing. He could just barely make out a high, shingled roof beyond the tallest of the trees.

"They live there. Not a very prosperous location. The kids come here to play."

"To play in the dirt?"

"They were on a treasure hunt, it seems." He jerked his thumb to the left, where two boys about elevenish were standing with a female police officer. "You can talk to them later, hear their story for yourself. They were out looking for pirate booty, and they saw a large pit where the dirt had obviously been turned. So they started digging."

"And found something a hell of a lot more interesting than booty."

"That would be one way of putting it." Tomlinson glanced at the boys. "They got the shock of their lives. I have a hunch those two are going to be in therapy for a good long time."

"Where's the body?"

Tomlinson pointed. "Over there. On the gurney. The coroners couldn't get their van back here, so they went back for more hands." Mike started toward the sheet-covered corpse. "I should warn you, though—it isn't pretty."

"Is it ever?" Mike growled. "Certainly not on this case." He crouched down beside the gurney. "I just want to see what that sick bastard did to his victim this time. Find out what merciless tortures he was able to inflict after I let him get the drop on me."

Tomlinson stuttered, just as Mike reached for the drape. "Oh—you think—oh no—"

Mike whipped his head around. "What? What is it?"

"I think you misunderstand." He slapped himself on the forehead. "I guess I didn't make it clear on the phone."

"You said you found another one of the killer's victims."

"True. But it isn't George Philby."

Mike's eyes bugged. "It isn't?"

"No. The body's in bad shape—but I'm sure of that. It isn't him."

"You mean the killer's gotten someone else since then?"

"Actually—I think this corpse may predate all of the others."

Mike had had enough. He pulled back the sheet covering the corpse.

The face was familiar, what was left of it. He'd definitely seen it before. But he couldn't place it.

"All right, Tomlinson. I admit it. I'm stumped. Who is this poor chump?"

"The distinguished and honorable professor Joseph Canino, civil procedure expert at the TU College of Law."

Mike's lips parted. "Of course. The Tiger."

"The one and the same. Although at the moment, his growl isn't what it used to be."

Mike ignored his second's poor humor. "This is the guy Ben substituted for the day James Fenton showed up with a sawed-off shotgun and took the whole class hostage. We speculated at the time that he might have been looking for Canino. But we never found him."

"And with good reason. He was pushing up dirt on the other side of town."

"You think he's been dead that long?" The gears were whirring inside Mike's head. "Since the hostage incident?"

"I do. I don't have anything official from the coroners yet . . . but look at the signs of decomposition, all over the body. Look at the color of the skin, the protruding skull. Look how the worms and other insects have burrowed into the body." Mike looked, although he didn't enjoy it. "He could've been here for six months. Or more."

"James Fenton knew at least one of the killer's other victims. And now it seems Canino was a member of their little club, too. Whatever the hell it was. The Fishermen of Evil."

Tomlinson did a doubletake. "What?"

"Never mind. I'm just babbling." Mike pushed himself to his feet. "I guess I'll go talk to those two kids. Have their parents been notified?"

"Moms are standing guard nearby. They're not too happy about this, either."

"I can imagine. Probably pissed that their kids were out here in the first place. What if they'd gotten lost?"

"They were following a trail," Tomlinson said. "That's what they say, anyway. Tracking the dangerous pirates. Following spoor, broken branches, trampled leaves. That sort of thing."

"They were following a trail—today?"

"So they say."

"A recent trail?"

Tomlinson's brows knitted. "I guess." He pointed. "See for yourself. But . . ."

Mike walked several paces down the trail. It wasn't long before he found another place where the soil had been turned—not recently, but turned, just the same. "Did anyone dig in here?"

Tomlinson shrugged. "Well . . . no. We didn't have any reason. . . ."

Mike grabbed a nearby shovel and started digging. Some of the other men at the crime scene gave him a strange look, but no one interfered.

Less than five minutes later, Mike felt the blade of his shovel lock into something soft but unyielding. Something that wasn't dirt.

After strapping on his plastic gloves, Tomlinson bent over and started pushing away dirt from the surface. Soon the general outlines of a body began to appear.

"The face," Mike said, staring intently. "Uncover the face."

With the stain of red dirt, the translucent skin, the pockmarks eaten away by small insects, the face was much changed. But it didn't matter. Mike had no trouble identifying it.

It was George Philby, the killer's fifth victim—or sixth, if you counted Professor Canino. *The one I could've saved,* Mike thought silently. *But didn't.*

* 38 *

After two months of trial, Ben was no longer able to distinguish one day from another. They all seemed to blur together, like a hazy montage from a dull and much-too-long movie. He had grown used to the fuzzy fluorescent lighting that made everyone in the courtroom appear a sickly dull gray color. He was accustomed to seeing mounds of paper piled up on his table, day after day, so high that he couldn't tell what was what without consulting Christina. He was used to the tacky bankers boxes they used to transport exhibits, the tan London Fog–type overcoats every lawyer seemed to wear. He had stopped noticing the doleful horn of the train passing the courthouse every morning at nine ten. He was no longer aware of sirens speeding by, sonic booms overhead. All were reminders that there was a world outside the courtroom, but that world seemed distant, muted, far far away.

Some of the days had been packed with suspense and excitement, marked by a pain in Ben's gut or a fear in his spine that kept him functioning with adrenaline-based enthusiasm. But as in any lengthy trial, most days were ordinary, perhaps even dull, riddled with interruptions and procedures and exhibits and all the rigamarole that so infused the modern trial as to insure that it never became too interesting. One day, Ben had noticed one of Colby's many assistants dozing at counsel table. And he hadn't been appalled. He had been jealous.

At the conclusion of the evidence, as expected, Colby made yet another Motion for Directed Verdict. Ben didn't even attempt to reply; he was much too exhausted to speak intelligently about complex legal issues. This was what he'd hired Matthews for; let the man go earn his salary.

Colby and Matthews went back and forth for more than an hour, out of the presence of the jury. Once again, Judge Perry announced that he was troubled by the "extraordinary causation problems" in the plaintiffs' case. Matthews tried to address each concern point by point, citing reams of relevant authority, spewing out case names at the speed of light. Ben only followed half of it, but he was clear on one point—hiring Matthews was the brightest move he'd made this whole trial. The man was seriously smart; he knew what he was talking about. He had an answer for every rabbit Colby pulled out of his hat.

"I am appalled by what has taken place in this courtroom," Colby said, turning his moral outrage up full throttle. "My client has been subjected to reams of bad publicity, has been accused in open court of the most monstrous crimes, and there is still not a shred of reliable evidence to prove that Blaylock's actions caused those kids' leukemia!"

"All very dramatic," Matthews replied calmly. "But it does not in any way get him around the lenient standard for the admission of developing or experimental scientific evidence established by the Supreme Court in the *Daubert* case. . . ."

When all was said and done, Judge Perry was unwilling to rule that the plaintiff had presented insufficient evidence to submit the case to the jury. "Although many aspects of this case still trouble me," he said, "it still goes against the grain to take the case away from the jury. I'm going to deny your motion, Mr. Colby. Let's get to work on jury instructions."

Ben didn't know whether to be relieved or disappointed. Well, he was relieved, of course—but this meant the case would proceed. The ordeal would continue.

The only remaining legal matter before closings was the finalization of the jury instructions. Preparing jury instructions for this case had been particularly arduous. Ostensibly, the purpose of jury instructions was to advise jurors on legal issues so that they could reach a verdict. As a practical matter, it was one last opportunity for each attorney to try to push the jury in their direction. As Ben had learned, a good jury instruction could win a case—particularly when the issues were as complex as they were here.

Christina had been working on the jury instructions for weeks, aided by Professor Matthews's research; Ben pitched in whenever he had time, which hadn't been often. All of them did their best to slant the law in the plaintiffs' favor, but for the most part—it wasn't. The burden of proof was always on them, the odds were always against them, and it was difficult to craft instructions that didn't make that painfully obvious.

The other problem was dealing with the vast complexity of the issues raised. On the whole, Ben thought juries deserved more credit than they got. In his experience, most jurors worked hard and tried to do the right thing. But you couldn't expect them all to be experts in hematology or cancer epidemiology. Colby, of course, had tried to exploit this to the max. The jury instructions he had submitted were so dense and complicated a Ph.D. in semantics couldn't have deciphered them. Ben and Christina had spent hours reworking the instructions, trying to boil them down and make them comprehensible, without rendering them so simple that they misrepresented the often subtle nuances of the law.

And they had failed. It was shamefully clear to Ben, as he listened to Judge Perry reading the final draft instructions aloud to the jury. They had failed. The instructions were still too complex—and they still favored the defendant. In the extreme.

"The fact that you may have determined that the defendant acted negligently or with careless disregard does not necessarily prove that its actions caused harm to the plaintiffs. In order to find in favor of the plaintiffs, you must find that it has been proven by a preponderance of the evidence that the defendant's wrongful actions did in fact cause the injuries to the plaintiffs. . . ."

Ben listened silently as the judge laid it all out, plank by plank. He was making a valid legal point, of course. Causation cannot be assumed; it must be proven. But to Ben, and to any juror, it just sounded like a lot of hoops that had to be jumped through before they could find in favor of the plaintiffs—a litany of reasons to vote for the defendant.

"Even if you find that the defendant did act recklessly, and that its actions caused harm to the plaintiffs, it does not mean that you have to make an award of actual damages or punitive damages to the plaintiffs. Punitive damages should be awarded only in the most extreme circumstances, where a party's actions have shown wanton or willful disregard for another party's rights. If you find that an award of punitive damages is appropriate, the amount awarded cannot be arbitrary. The punitive damages award must bear some rational relationship to the evidence presented in the case. . . ."

Now this was a matter of critical importance to the plaintiffs. Punitive damages. What every defendant feared most. Ben could only assume a big portion of both sides' closing arguments would be devoted to this subject. But now the judge was getting his two cents in, outlining in detail how difficult and complex it could be to make such an award to the plaintiffs, an award that was absolutely critical to compensating the plaintiffs—not to mention keeping Ben out of bankruptcy court.

"If you find that the corporate decision makers did not authorize or approve the wrongful conduct, you may consider this factor in mitigation of any award you might otherwise make. Other mitigating factors that may be considered include . . ."

Ben's eyes began to roll up into his head. He couldn't follow it anymore; trying just made his head throb. To their credit, he noticed the jurors were not falling asleep. On the contrary, they were listening closely, attentively. Perhaps for the first time ever, they were realizing how difficult the task set before them really was.

Well, it didn't matter. There was nothing he could do about it now. He had one last chance, he told himself as he approached the jury to deliver his closing. One last chance to make a difference for his clients.

After that, it would all be over.

"It is George Philby," Mike said as he compared the fingerprint on his record chart to the ones just taken from the corpse he had unearthed. "No question about it."

Bob Barkley, the medical examiner, forced a bristly smile.

"Wonderful. May I please take possession of the body now?"

"Sure," Mike said, but he didn't move away. "Care to give me a hint on the cause of death?"

Barkley tried to push past him. "You'll see the report."

"No doubt. But every moment I wait is a moment the killer can go on killing."

"Give me a break, Mike. You know I'll get crucified if I give you any half-baked preliminary conclusions."

"Off the record, then." Mike pointed to the black patches all over the naked body. "He was electrocuted, right?"

Barkley glanced over his shoulder both ways, as if someone might be eavesdropping here in an undeveloped lot a hundred feet from the nearest road. "Just between you and me?"

"Right, right."

"He got some juice, sure. Probably from that gruesome setup you discovered at his house."

"That's what I—"

"But he wasn't electrocuted. I mean, that didn't kill him."

"It didn't?"

"Nah. I'm pretty sure. See the color of the skin?" He pointed a few places Mike really didn't care to look. "You wouldn't see that if he'd been fried. The burning would be far more extensive. Smell would be different, too."

Mike was amazed, in a repulsive sort of way. To him, the body's smell was just something he tried to block out of his mind. To Barkley, it was a clue. "Then what did kill him?"

"Now this really is pure speculation, but . . ." Barkley twisted the corpse's head around and pointed again. Mike detected a small red puncture mark at the base of his neck.

"What the hell caused that?"

"I could only speculate. Ice pick, maybe. I can't guarantee that's what killed him. But it corresponds better to the available visual evidence. I think it's likely."

Mike thought for a long moment. "Why would the killer start out electrocuting him—then veer off into a sudden execution-style murder?"

"Maybe he already learned what he wanted to know. Maybe he got in a hurry."

Mike shook his head. "Maybe he got careless." His hands balled up. "Same reason he let me live. He thinks he's invincible. He thinks he can't be caught."

"I guess he's done pretty well so far."

"That's going to change. He doesn't know it yet, but I'm onto him. I've figured out the connection. And maybe, just maybe, I can follow that trail backward to the killer himself. And then I'll be all over his ass like ants on an apple."

As attorney for the plaintiffs, Ben would get to speak not only first but last, in rebuttal to whatever Colby had to say. Since he knew he would be back, he tried to keep his first appearance relatively short and to the point.

Ben stood squarely in front of the jury, trying to exude a confidence he did not feel.

"People have the craziest expectations of what's going to happen during closing argument. I don't know where they get them all. Perry Mason, I guess."

Ben smiled slightly, and to his great relief, some of the jurors smiled back at him. It seemed they weren't too tired to appreciate a little humor.

"I'm not going to do any of that melodramatic stuff you may be expecting. I'm not going to shout at you like a Baptist preacher. I'm not going to rant and rave. I'm not going to rehash all the evidence. You've already heard it—probably heard more of it than you wanted. All I'm going to do is point out the things that I think are most important. Then I'm going to tell you what I think you should do, what I hope you'll do. Then I'm going to sit down. And it will be in your hands."

Ben crossed over to the north end of the jury box, keeping his eyes locked on the jurors at all times. "Can there be any doubt that Blaylock polluted the Blackwood water supply? I don't think so. Hard as they tried to suppress the truth—it still emerged. Their own employees have admitted that waste was dumped on the ground, buried in the ground. Trace elements, chemicals, things that could have come from nowhere else, were found in the aquifer and Well B. We know where they came from." Ben turned to face them directly. "*You* know where it came from.

"The unresolved question is whether that pollution caused the deaths of my clients' children. We know that the leukemia rate in Blackwood spiked well above the national average—at about the same time that the pollution began seeping into the water well. We know the plaintiffs' children used the water, drank it, bathed in it. And we know the EPA has said the water is harmful—because those chemicals can cause cancer."

Ben glanced up at the judge. "I know you all listened attentively when Judge Perry read the jury instructions, so you undoubtedly heard the one that established the burden of proof. The burden of proof is on us, the plaintiffs. We admit that. But what is that burden? Some of you—the ones who watch Perry Mason a lot—probably remember him saying that guilt had to be proved 'beyond a reasonable doubt.' Well—that isn't the standard in this case—thank goodness."

Again, a few of the jurors chuckled. What did it mean? Were they with him?

"Here, as the judge instructed you, liability must be proved 'by a preponderance of the evidence.' In other words, we must prove that it is more likely than not that Blaylock is responsible for the plaintiffs' injuries. So I ask you, ladies and gentlemen of the jury—which is most likely? You can forget the evidence, forget the testimony" —an easy thing for Ben to say, since his medical testimony had come off so badly— "forget it all. Just close your eyes and look inside your heart."

To Ben's surprise, many of the jurors did in fact shut their eyes. "Close your eyes and answer this simple question. Which is more likely? That those children died because of the carcinogenic contaminants released into their water supply by the defendant? Or that this is all just an unfortunate coincidence? Which is more likely?

"Now open your eyes." They complied, and Ben felt the heat of twenty-eight eyes bearing down on him. "Which is more likely? I think you know the answer. I know you do. So please, please—listen to that voice in your heart. And do the right thing. That's all I ask."

Colby's approach was, to say the least, very different from Ben's. He took full advantage of the two hours Judge Perry had allocated for closing argument. He rehashed each and every witness who had taken the stand during the entire two-month ordeal. He spent extensive amounts of time detailing all the medical testimony, which he knew would be the crux of the jury's deliberations. He reminded them of every medical witness Ben had called—and how he had destroyed and humiliated each of them on the witness stand. He also reminded them of the parade of medical experts he had called, with their distinguished and impressive litany of credentials and accomplishments. He cast subtlety to the wind as he reminded them that his experts were respected members of the "mainstream" medical community, while Ben's experts were "on the fringe" at best—and paid quacks at worst.

Finally, when Colby had finished rehashing the case, he moved to the more rhetorical portion of his closing. He clasped his hands in front of him and gazed at the jury solemnly. "Please believe me when I say that I have nothing but sympathy for the parents of those children who died before their time. I mean that sincerely. My heart weeps for them. I'm sure you feel the same way."

He took a step toward a rail. "But as a jury, you have a duty to perform, and that duty must be fulfilled strenuously. This is not a court of sympathy. It is a court of law. And therefore, in your deliberations, you must be guided not by your heart, but by the law. According to the law, as set out in the jury instructions Judge Perry read to you, you can only render a verdict in favor of the plaintiffs if you find they have proven that their loss was caused by the defendant—by the defendant's acts of reckless disregard. Has that been proven in this court, according to the standard set forth by the court? By any standard?"

He leaned against the rail that divided them, leaving the jury no space to escape his gaze. "Now, Mr. Kincaid would have you believe that the H. P. Blaylock corporation is evil. That we deliberately set out to harm those children. Well, let me tell you something. The H. P. Blaylock company is not evil. It was founded over eighty years ago, by a born-and-raised Oklahoman, the salt of the earth. It has been employing Oklahomans ever since. Over ten thousand Oklahomans have been employed by this company since its inception; over five thousand are currently employed. Millions of dollars have been pumped into the local economy, thanks to H. P. Blaylock. Blaylock virtually single-handedly supports the Blackwood school system. Blaylock products are used and respected—all across the globe. Is that evil? Is that the hallmark of a company that wants to hurt people?"

He paused, letting the questions roam about in the jurors' brains. "I don't think so," he said, finally. "And I don't think you do, either. You're smart people; you know better. We may have made some mistakes, but we never did anything that would hurt children. We never did. We never would. That's not what the H. P. Blaylock company is all about.

"Mr. Kincaid talks a lot about common sense, which in his world, is just a code phrase meaning 'ignore all the evidence.' Well, I'll give you some common sense. Do you think H. P. Blaylock would be as successful as it is today if it did the things the plaintiffs accuse it of doing? Do you think this company could get where it is if it allowed things like this to happen? Of course not. We didn't get to the Fortune 500 by hurting people. You know better."

He took a step back, reclasping his hands, almost in an attitude of prayer. "What these parents have been through is quite possibly the most traumatic loss anyone can suffer. It is only right that they should be searching for answers, only natural that they should be looking for someone to blame. It's the natural protective instinct of a parent, and perhaps, in some cases, a way of dealing with guilt. But every tragedy does not have a simple solution. Every wrong is not someone's fault. Sometimes, bad things just happen—even to good people. We don't know why. The Good Lord sometimes moves in strange and inexplicable ways."

His voice quieted. "That's what we have here, ladies and gentlemen. An inexplicable tragedy. We don't know why it happened, and just as every credible medical witness has told you, we don't know what causes leukemia. It is a great cause for despair. It is an undeniable tragedy." He paused, looking each juror in the eye. "But it is not H. P. Blaylock's fault."

* * *

Ben didn't even wait for the judge to invite him back to the front. He wanted to hit the jury fast, before they had a lot of time to dwell on what Colby had said.

"Let me clear up one matter right at the start. I don't think the Blaylock corporation is evil. I don't think they did this because they intentionally wanted to harm children. I think they just didn't care. I think they acted carelessly, because they didn't think it was important. Or perhaps more accurately, because they thought it was more important to save and make money than to protect the community. I think they acted out of carelessness—and greed.

"They could've prevented their waste, the TCE and perc, from entering the groundwater. Wouldn't've even been that hard. But it was cheaper to dump it on the ground, or bury it in flimsy cardboard drums. So that's what they did, at least some of the time. They decided to save money, rather than to save lives. So the poison entered the water, the children drank the water—and the children died.

"I've said just about everything I could possibly say about the medical testimony. Let me just add this: the only person you've heard from who has actually performed detailed studies regarding TCE-contaminated water and its effects on living creatures is Dr. Rimland. He has seen what TCE-tainted water does to lab rats. He has visited cancer-cluster communities. And he believes, to the bottom of his heart, that the contaminated water caused my clients' children to die. Who can possibly know more about it than him?"

Ben uncovered a chart he had prepared the night before. Talking about numbers always made him uncomfortable, but it had to be done, so he had prepared a spreadsheet to help the jury comprehend the injuries and damages suffered.

"We've talked about all the monetary losses my clients have incurred as a result of what Blaylock has done. Cumulatively, they've lost just over a million dollars, money lost to medical bills, lost work, and so forth. Of course, I hope you will compensate them for their loss. But there is another element of damages in a case like this: punitive damages. Damages awarded not to compensate the plaintiffs—but to punish the defendant.

"There's been a lot of talk about punitive damages lately. Some people think they're a good thing; some people don't. You may dislike the whole idea of punitive damages. You may be thinking, 'Well, sure, Blaylock shouldn't have done that, but why should the plaintiffs get all that money? Maybe it should go to charity, some kind of cancer-treatment fund.' And you know what? You may be right. But that isn't the law right now. Maybe it will be someday, but at this time, the only provision the law makes for punishing bad actors is punitive damages. It's this—or nothing."

Ben checked the eyes of the jurors. So far, he didn't seem to have lost anyone. But were they truly with him? Did they agree? There was no way of knowing.

"Should Blaylock be punished? Should they be fined? Let's remember—the only reason they did this in the first place was to save money. They thought it would be cheaper to handle waste the wrong way than to spend money protecting the community. And you know what? They were right. It was cheaper—and still is. Even a verdict for full compensatory damages won't change that. There is only one way you can prove that they were wrong. Only one way to insure that this kind of wrongful conduct will not be tolerated. By awarding punitive damages. To prove that committing wrongful acts is not profitable.

"How much should you award? That's entirely up to you. There's no minimum and no maximum. But let me tell you one thing. If the number isn't big—it isn't going to mean anything. They can shrug off sums that would support you and me for the rest of our lives." He pointed to the figures on his chart. "This corporation makes half a billion dollars a year! That's over a million dollars a day. So here's my recommendation—fine them one week's profit. Just one workweek. Five million dollars. It seems huge to us, but it's not going to bankrupt them. But it is enough to make them take notice. It is enough to send this message: Next time you're thinking about saving money by doing something that will endanger the community—don't.

"When all is said and done, this case is very simple. It all comes down to something you probably learned back in kindergarten. When you make a mess—you're supposed to clean it up. Well, Blaylock made a huge mess in Blackwood, but they won't clean it up. They could've and they should've—but they won't. So you make them clean it up. Please. Make them take responsibility for what they've done."

Ben drew in a deep breath, then stepped away from the rail. "I've said everything I have to say. Maybe I've said too much. This case is so important, in so many ways . . ." He didn't finish the sentence. "But now it's in your hands. Please—I urge you—be bold. Don't shy away from doing what you know is right. When you return from the deliberation room, send not one but two messages with your verdict. Tell the Blaylock Corporation that this kind of conduct is unacceptable. And tell my clients, tell the parents who lost their children, that their loss was not in vain."

Ben allowed himself a small smile. "Thank you for your time. We'll wait around till you get back."

* **39** *

Christina confronted Jones in the hallway outside the office kitchenette.

"Excuse me, Mr. Office Manager."

Jones whirled around. "Yes?"

"I've just been to the refrigerator. There are no Cokes. None. Nada."

"I'm well aware of that. There are no Cokes and, for that matter, no exotic blended teas, no Chivas Regal, and no Bollinger 1953."

Christina's right hand went to her hip, the sure sign that her Nordic temper was rising. "Jones, Ben has had a hard day. He needs a Coke."

"If you'll recall, I was instructed to cancel or eliminate all unnecessary expenditures."

"Emphasis on *unnecessary*, Jones. Ben wants a Coke."

Jones made a sniffing noise. "He should learn to drink water. Soft drinks are bad for your health."

"Let's cut him some slack, Mr. Jones. He doesn't drink, he doesn't smoke, he doesn't do drugs. He doesn't even eat powdered doughnuts, unlike a certain office manager I know."

"In case you've forgotten, Ms. McCall, this office is massively in debt. I have a fiscal responsibility—"

Christina grabbed him by the collar and yanked him right under her nose. "This trial isn't over yet, Jones. We don't know what's going to happen next. The only thing we know for sure is—we need Ben. So get him a Coke, understand?"

Jones swallowed, then yanked a dollar bill out of his pants pocket. "There's a soda machine on the second floor."

She pushed him away, her eyes still narrowed. "Go."

When Jones returned with the Coke, Ben was deep in a strategizing session with Christina and Professor Matthews.

"Did you see the expression on juror number twelve's face as she left the courtroom?" Ben asked as he took the Coke from Jones. He drank half the can in a single swallow. "I don't think she liked me."

"Of course she liked you," Christina reassured him. "She just had a lot on her mind. This is a very complex case. They all know that."

"Colby doesn't," Ben replied. "He thinks it's all very simple. We represent quacks; he represents the forces of goodness and light."

"That guy makes me insane." Jones inflated his chest and emulated Colby's slightly swaybacked posture. "Please believe me when I say I have nothing but sympathy for the parents of those children," Jones said, in a dead-on impersonation of Colby's voice. "My heart weeps for them. See? It's weeping now. Really. Boo-hoo. Boo-hoo-hoo."

Everyone in the room burst out laughing. It was a release they had long needed.

"Colby called over here about an hour ago," Ben informed them. "Made another settlement offer."

Jones's eyes lit. "Generous?"

Ben shook his head. "Barely more than last time. Not even enough to pay our clients' medical bills. He's hoping to exploit the fact that the jury is still out."

Jones raised an eyebrow. "So? . . . "

"I told him to go to hell." Ben's eyes seemed almost hooded. "I haven't come this far to sell our clients short now. I just hope . . ." His voice drifted off.

"I think you should relax, Ben," Matthews said, after a bit. "You put on the best case possible. We won the legal arguments—"

"Thanks to you," Ben interjected.

"And you did great on the questions of fact," he continued. "It was just a tough case, bottom line. And you can't always win the tough cases. No matter what you do."

"We have to win this one," Ben said. His eyes wandered over to the picture of Cecily's little boy, Billy, which had been mounted over his desk since the first day Cecily walked into his office. "We have to."

"Ben," Matthews said, "you need some major stress relief. I've got a little yacht down south, near Corpus Christi. When this is all over, I want you to come be my guest. That goes for you, too, Christina."

Ben looked up. "Now that's a deal."

Loving stepped inside from the outer hallway. As always, his shoulders were so broad he barely fit through the doorframe. "Skipper? I got news."

"Good news, or bad?"

"Some of both. I found Mrs. Marmelstein's son."

Ben leapt out of his chair. "You did? Where is he? Here in Tulsa?"

"Not by a long shot. He lives in Manhattan. Got a crummy little one-room apartment on the Lower East Side. I don't know how people live like that. Do you realize those people don't even have garbage disposals?"

Ben wasn't interested in a discussion of the relative merits of urban living. "Did you talk to him?"

"Oh, yeah. And then some. That's the problem."

"What? What's the problem?"

"Seems there's a major-league dispute between the older generation and the younger. I can't get all the details. I gather Paulie's dad didn't approve of Paulie's choice of wife. Mrs. Marmelstein stood by her husband. There was a big row. Paulie got mad and split town—and never came back. The sad thing is—Paulie split with that wife more than twenty years ago. But he and his parents still never made it up."

"Did you tell him what's happening?" Ben asked. "Did you tell him she's asking for him?"

"I did. And he refused to come see her. Absolutely refused. Said they told him he wasn't welcome in their house, a million or so years ago, so he's never coming back."

"But surely if you tell him his mother is dying—"

"Believe me, I played every card in my deck. It made no diff to this schmuck. Talk about carrying a grudge."

Ben fell back into his chair. "I'm sure he's hurt. Still angry about what happened in the past. But I stopped by the hospital this afternoon and—" He shook his head. "We don't have much time left. If Paulie doesn't come now—it's going to be too late."

Loving frowned. As Ben well knew, he didn't like to disappoint. "I'll keep working on him, Skipper."

"Please do." Ben glanced at his watch. "I'm going out to Blackwood and talk to Cecily and some of the other parents. I think they had some hope that the jury would be so outraged they would render a unanimous verdict for the plaintiffs on the first vote. They must be even more nervous now than we are." He pushed himself to his feet. "Then I'm going to go over to the courthouse."

"Why?" Christina asked. "The judge's clerk will call when the jury is ready."

"I want to be there," Ben replied. "I can't concentrate on anything else anyway. The jury is still working; I should be, too. I want them to see me. I want them to know I haven't forgotten about them."

"But what will you do?"

Ben grabbed his briefcase and jacket and headed for the door. "The only thing there is to do. Wait."

*　　*　　*

Carl Peabody, the farmer from Catoosa, sat at the head of the single long conference table in the jury deliberation room. His frustration was evident. He had been chosen to serve as the jury foreman, and was currently walking his charges through the jury instructions, not for the first time.

"I just can't make head nor tail outta some of these instructions," Carl groaned. "I like to think of myself as a reasonably smart fella, but they're just too complicated, with all their parts and subparts and ten-dollar words."

"I don't know how that attorney could let this happen," said Mrs. Cartwright, the housewife from Broken Arrow.

"Which attorney?" asked Mary Ann Althorp, the TU college student. "The big fancy one?"

"No," Mrs. Cartwright answered. "He probably wanted the instructions to be confusing. I meant the other one. The little cute one. With the tiny bald spot on the back of his head."

"The plaintiffs' attorney," Foreman Peabody clarified. "Kincaid."

"Right," Mrs. Cartwright agreed. "He was always so good about explaining things during the trial. I don't know why he allowed these awful instructions."

"Probably didn't have any choice," grumped Evan Marshall, the black self-employed body shop owner. "I got the distinct impression the judge was none too fond of Mr. Kincaid."

"You know, I thought that, too," Mary Ann said. "Why do you think that is?"

"Who knows?" Marshall replied. "Colby probably contributed to the judge's reelection campaign."

"I don't think federal judges are elected," Foreman Peabody said. "Though I'm not totally sure about that."

"Whatever." Marshall waved a hand in the air. "Colby and the judge are tight. You could see that. And Kincaid wasn't in the club."

"I liked him, though," Mary Ann said. She looked down shyly. "I believed him. I don't think he'd lie to us."

"You know, I had the same feeling," Mrs. Cartwright said. "He seemed like a good boy. He reminded me of my sister Clara's boy, Rudy. He was killed in Vietnam, you know."

"Could we just cool it with the jury instructions?" Marshall said. "They're not getting us anywhere. Let's take another vote."

Foreman Peabody tilted his head to one side. "I don't have any reason to think this one will come out any differently."

"We can but hope," Marshall said. "Let's do it."

Peabody tore a piece of paper into twelve strips and distributed them around the table. Each of the jurors scribbled down their vote. A moment later, Peabody collected them.

"No change," Peabody said grimly. "Eleven votes in favor of awarding damages to the plaintiffs. One against."

"I'm tried of this anonymity crap," Marshall said, banging on the conference table. "We could be here forever at this rate. I've got a business to run."

Peabody shrugged. "I don't know what else we can do."

"I sure as hell do. I want to know who the holdout is. I want to know now."

"Now, Evan," Peabody started, "we agreed—"

"I don't care what we agreed. This has gone on long enough. I want to know who it is."

"Evan—"

"It's all right." The quiet, high-pitched voice came from the other end of the table. "I don't mind. He's probably right. You deserve to know."

The woman straightened, minutely adjusting her dress. "I'm the holdout," said Carol Johnson, the middle-aged housewife married to the stockbroker. Juror number twelve. "I'm sorry for what happened to those parents, but I just can't believe those kids got cancer from tap water—no matter what was in it. They didn't prove it to me. So I'm voting for the defendant. And I'll never change my mind."

On the executive office floor of H. P. Blaylock headquarters, the mood was subdued but undeniably tense. No one in any position of responsibility with the company could be unaware that the jury was still out in the largest class action lawsuit ever lodged against the company. Nor could they be unaware that their CEO, old man Blaylock himself, was taking the lawsuit as an affront to his personal integrity. Since the trial had begun and the accusations had become public, he had been in an uninterrupted foul mood, ranting at employees he didn't even know, raving with the energy of a man half his age.

One executive, a junior leaguer named Frank Chadwick, had been reassigned. Currently, his duty was to do nothing more than stay in touch with the courthouse and to report anything—anything at all—to the top brass, starting with Blaylock. Frank had an in with Judge Perry's clerk, so he was able to get information that would otherwise be off-limits. He reported everything—the expressions on the jurors' faces as they walked into the deliberation room, notes scribbled on scraps of paper found in the trash, offhand remarks overheard in the men's room. Anything.

Meanwhile, in Blaylock's office, a familiar group was assembled—Blaylock himself, trial attorney Charlton Colby, and his young up-and-coming associate Mark Austin. They had met together every day since the jury had begun deliberating. Even on weekends.

"Still no news?" Blaylock asked, his fingers drumming the desktop.

"Nothing concrete," Colby replied. "Nothing worth repeating."

"We can't let this go on," Blaylock said. "Do you know what this is doing to the stock?"

"Unfortunately, we don't have any choice," Colby said. "I have no way of coercing the jury to return faster. Unless you want to settle and pay the plaintiffs everything they want."

"I'd sooner choke on a porcupine and die." Blaylock pushed out of his chair and began pacing. "What a waste of time and energy this has been. Profits are down. Productivity is down. While you legal bloodsuckers play your games, people's livelihoods are at stake."

"Relax," Colby reassured him. "Those aggrieved parents aren't going to hurt your company. I won't let that happen. Judge Perry won't let that happen. It's not going to happen. We've spun Mr. Kincaid and his friends six different ways to Sunday, haven't we, Mark?"

His associate, Mark, had been strangely silent through the majority of the conversation. "We certainly have, sir."

"Charlton," Colby reminded him, not for the first time. "Call me Charlton."

"Right. Sorry."

"At any rate," Colby continued, "no matter what this jury does, we've scored one major victory." He leaned forward and tapped a report bound in a blue folder. "This didn't get out."

Blaylock whipped around. His agitation had increased, rather than diminished. "I'm still worried about that, Charlton. Are you sure—"

"It's privileged," Colby said, his hands raised. "You have nothing to fear. The report was distributed on a strict 'need to know' basis. You've made it perfectly clear that loose lips sink ships—and careers. And my name is all over it, so it's protected by the attorney-client privilege."

"Still, I worry that some judge might take a different view—"

"Don't worry about Judge Perry. He wants to be considered one of the big boys so bad he can taste it. Hell, I can taste it. He'll never cross Raven, Tucker & Tubb. He's probably hoping we'll hire him when he retires and give him a nice fat salary for doing nothing." Colby leaned back in his chair. "I've got him eating out of my hands. Don't I, Mark?"

Mark pulled himself up in his chair. "It certainly seemed that way. During the trial, I mean, s—er, Charlton."

Colby smiled. "So don't worry yourself into an early grave, Myron. Take it easy and wait for the jury to return. You won't be disappointed. That's a promise."

"You'd better be right, Charlton," Blaylock said, his lips pressed tightly together. "That's all I can say."

"I always am," Colby said. He leaned over toward Mark and winked. "Isn't that right?"

It was Fred. It was really, truly, believe-it-or-not Fred.

All along, he had considered Fred the least likely suspect— virtually the impossible suspect. But he had been wrong. It had been Fred all along.

He wiped his hand across his forehead, briefly covering his vivid green eyes. To think of all the time he'd wasted. All the

time he'd spent killing Harvey and Margaret and George. Not
to mention The Tiger, way back when. He'd exterminated the
whole club, except for Fenton. That poor schmuck had exterminated himself.

It seemed he had underestimated good ol' Fred the Feeb.
They all had. That, of course, was what had allowed Fred to
get away with it. Much easier, he supposed, to get away with a
brazen act of betrayal when no one in their wildest dreams
would suspect you.

He still couldn't quite make himself believe it, but there
was no other possibility, no one else left. Fred had the
merchandise.

And he wanted it.

And he would get it, too. No matter what it took. No matter
how long it took. No matter what torture he was required to
exact on Fred's body. He would do it. He would do it in a
heartbeat. He would do it with great pleasure.

And he would do it to anyone else who got in his way, too.

* 40 *

As Christina stepped off the elevator on her way to work,
she was almost flattened by a sofa.

"Whoa!" she said, ducking out of harm's way. "Remember
your elevator etiquette, boys. Unload first, reload second."

One of the workmen carrying the sofa tipped his hat.
"Sorry about that, ma'am. Didn't see you."

"That's all right. This sort of thing happens, when you're
only five foot one." She started walking down the hallway,
then froze. "Wait a minute."

She whirled around. "That looks like the sofa in my office." She blinked. "That *is* the sofa in my office!"

She ran in front of the workmen, blocking their access to the elevators. "What're you doing? You can't take my sofa! I love my sofa!"

The same workman looked at her sheepishly. "Sorry, ma'am. We've got orders."

"Orders? Orders from whom?"

"The bank."

Christina ran down the hallway and into the office. The place was crawling with workmen, all wearing the same blue coveralls and matching baseball caps. They were taking everything—the desks, the tables, the lamps, the lampshades.

Jones was standing in the center of the deconstruction, his hand covering his face.

Christina raced up to him. "Jones! What's going on here?"

"What does it look like? They're hauling off all our stuff. They've foreclosed on our loans."

"They can't do that."

"They certainly can. They were only supposed to be short-term loans, and they're way past due."

"Didn't they say they'd ride it out till the end of the trial?"

"As far as they're concerned, they did. They didn't expect jury deliberation to go on forever."

"It's only been a week."

"That's an eternity, in jury time. You know as well as I do that when a jury is out that long, there's a good chance they're hung. If that happens, we won't get a penny. And we won't be able to pay back our loans—any of them. So the bank decided they'd better get something now while the getting was good."

"Isn't there anything you can do?"

"Like what? The bank filed a valid foreclosure lien with the sheriff. He's required by state law to seize any assets he can to make good the debt. I tried to talk to the man, but I got nowhere."

"There must be something you could do. You're the office manager."

Jones's face steamed up. "Which is why, if you'll recall, I advised everyone not to take this case in the first place. But did anyone listen to me? Nooooo."

"Don't say 'I told you so,' Jones. It's so unbecoming."

"Everyone wanted to do the sweet, kind, heroic thing. Represent the parents no one else will represent." He gestured toward the men hauling away everything that wasn't nailed down. "And see what it got us?"

Christina stepped back, narrowly avoiding four men who were hauling her desk out the door. "Does Ben know?"

Jones shook his head. "Not yet."

"Where is he?"

"Where do you think?"

Ben sat on a bench in the hallway, staring at the closed door of the jury deliberation room. What were they saying in there? he wondered. He would give almost anything to know. The door was firmly shut, and every time he started to get close to it, the judge's bailiff gave him a harsh warning glare. He would just have to wait. And he had been waiting for so long now.

What was this—Day Seven of the courthouse vigil? He had lost count. He knew it was stupid to just sit here waiting, but he couldn't help himself. He had to know. The first day, he had tried to go back to the office and work on something else, but his mind inevitably drifted back to this case, this trial, his ever-diminishing hopes. It was clear he was not going to get any other work done until this deliberation was over, so he stopped trying.

On the second day, he'd started bringing a book to the courthouse with him, but now, so many days later, he was barely out of the first chapter. He couldn't focus. Everything he read reminded him of the trial. Did he do enough? Did he do it right? Did he do honor to the rights and expectations of those bereaved parents? The potential for second-guessing himself, for Monday morning quarterbacking the trial now that it was over, was endless. Did he muster all the evidence possible? Did he show it in the most favorable light? Did he do everything he could? Everything he had promised he would do?

He heard movement behind the closed door. Someone in the jury room was moving. Barely a moment later, the door opened. One of the male jurors appeared, and Ben could glimpse the others behind him. Was this it? His heart leapt into his throat; his pulse began to race. Was it finally over?

No. Only the one man left, and he went straight for the men's room. Just a false alarm. Like so many others he had suffered through these past few days.

He had been so intent on the juror leaving the room that he didn't even notice the woman who had sidled onto the bench beside him. "Any news?"

Ben turned. It was Cecily Elkins. She looked good in the cerulean blue jacket with matching brooch, although her eyes suggested she had not had much sleep of late. "What are you doing here?"

"I brought lunch." She lifted her hand, revealing a large bag from Taco Bell. "Hungry?"

"Not yet. Maybe later."

She nodded. "Any change?"

"Sorry. No."

"Won't they call you at your office? I mean—if something breaks?"

"Yeah. I just—I don't know. I want to be here. I want to see the jurors walk in and out of the room every day. I want them to see me."

Cecily nodded again. "Mind if I wait with you?"

"Oh, Cecily—there's really no need. This isn't your problem."

"Excuse me?" She drew herself up. "I'm the one who started this mess, remember? I'm the one who brought it to you and dropped it in your lap."

"I just meant—" He stopped. How selfish he had been–acting as if this was *his* case, as if he was the only one who cared about the outcome. She was Billy's mother, not he. She was the one who saw her son die in her arms, as she desperately tried to revive him. She was the one who had devoted years of her life to the boy, only to see that all come to naught, all due to the greed of a corporation that cared more about its bottom line than about people.

It was her case. It always had been.

"Actually," Ben said, "I could do with some company."

"Thanks. I should warn you, though—I'm not much for small talk."

Ben smiled. "Thank goodness."

*   *   *

"How many times are we going to rehash the same damn arguments?" Marshall bellowed. "We've been over all this before."

"I know that," Foreman Peabody said, trying to remain cool. "We've been over it before and we'll go over it again until we reach an agreement."

The bailiff had brought all the evidence into the deliberation room—which took several trips—and they had pored over it, piece by piece. They had asked the judge for transcripts of the testimony of all the witnesses. They had asked for a magnifying glass, so they could scrutinize the aerial photographs of the dumpsite and ravine. They even asked for a medical encyclopedia, to help them decode some of the expert testimony.

But they were still unable to reach a consensus. A week later, the vote was still eleven to one. And Mrs. Johnson would not budge.

"How can you deny what's right there in front of our faces?" Marshall asked. He had had enough of this case, enough of the deliberation, and most of all, enough of her intransigence. "The Blackwood water killed those kids!"

"No one can prove that," Mrs. Johnson said, folding her hands.

"Who needs proof? It's obvious!"

"Not to me."

"What do you think made those kids get cancer?"

"I don't know. And nobody else does either, except the Good Lord."

"Is that the same Good Lord who gave the kids cancer?" Mary Ann Althorp asked. "Those families have been hurt. They need our help."

"If they need help," Mrs. Johnson rejoined, "we can pass the hat. But I'm not going to give them millions of dollars of someone else's money."

Marshall threw himself back in his chair. "Isn't there some way we can get rid of this old bat?" he asked the foreman. "What were those alternates for?"

"They can't join the deliberations unless something happens to one of us," Peabody explained.

"Maybe I should strangle her," Marshall said under his breath. "That might speed things along."

"I heard that," Mrs. Johnson proclaimed. "And I am not amused."

"There's no need for unkindness," Mrs. Cartwright said. "I'm sure we can work through this without sinking to that level."

"Easy for you to say," Marshall grumped. "I think you're enjoying this. But I've got a business to run."

"Let me see if I can get us back on track," Peabody said. In fact, he was as tired of this as everyone else, but as the duly elected foreman, he felt an obligation to try to resolve the dispute. "Let's focus on the medical testimony. Let's see what evidence there is that the water caused those kids' cancers. I myself was very persuaded by that fella—what was his name?—Rimland, I think."

Mrs. Johnson groaned. "Mr. Colby called him a quack."

"Well, he would, wouldn't he?" Marshall rolled his eyes.

"Let's look at the published report from Dr. Rimland's study. I thought those results with the lab rats were kinda interesting." Peabody had no real confidence that reviewing the report—or anything else—would ever change Mrs. Johnson's mind. But he had to try something. He was the foreman, damn it. This was his watch. He had a responsibility. It wouldn't be easy—but he was a farmer. He was used to things not being easy.

He wasn't going to throw in the towel yet. Not without putting up one hell of a fight.

* 41 *

When Ben stepped out of the judge's chambers, Cecily was so excited she could barely restrain herself. She jumped off the bench that had been their home base for the past two weeks and met him halfway down the corridor.

"So? What did the judge want?"

Ben hesitated before answering. "The jury sent a note back."

Why was she having to drag this out of him? "Yes? And?"

"They say they're deadlocked. They can't reach a verdict."

Cecily was unprepared for the hollow pain she felt when she heard those words. Of course, she had realized it might not be good news, but this? She would almost rather be told that the jury found for the defendant.

"Why? What's their problem?"

"I don't know. And I can't ask. But they say they can't work it out."

"So what did the judge do?"

"Basically, he told them to get their butts back in their chairs and work harder."

"So—he didn't let them declare a deadlock?"

"Not yet. But eventually . . ."

Cecily knew what he meant; they had discussed it often enough during the past two weeks. The judge couldn't let the jury deliberate forever; eventually he would have to declare a mistrial. Which meant all their work, all their expense, would be for nothing. Their only option would be to try again with a new jury—an option she knew Ben couldn't afford. And the chances of another lawyer taking the case—when it had already bankrupted the first lawyer—were nonexistent.

"Surely they'll work it out," Cecily said, but her voice sounded weak. "Surely they'll see things the way we do."

Ben laid his hand gently on her shoulder and guided her back to the bench. "I hope so."

In the jury deliberation room, the frustration levels had reached an all-time high. No one had been happy about sending the note to the judge saying they were deadlocked—but they had at least thought it would bring this misery to an end. But now they had the judge's reply, and not only were they not off the hook, the judge was basically scolding them and telling them the work would have to continue, perhaps for weeks.

"I just can't stand this any longer," Mrs. Cartwright said. "I'm tired of the pictures and the transcripts. I'm tired of the charts and graphs. And most of all, I'm tired of all this bickering."

"I'm tired of everything, too," Mary Ann Althorp added. "I've missed so much school I may have to retake the whole semester in summer school."

"Don't tell me your sob stories, girl," Marshall said. "I got my own business. And it's been goin' to hell in a handbasket since I got stuck with this trial."

"None of which gets us where we need to go," Foreman Peabody interjected. "I think we need to reconsider the evidence and see if we can get anyone to change their mind. Should we start with the medical evidence or the damages evidence?"

"Why don't you ask Mrs. Johnson?" Marshall huffed. "Since it's her mind you want to change."

Peabody smiled thinly. "What about it, Mrs. Johnson? Shall we rehash the medical evidence?"

The woman at the end of the table looked up from the papers she had been reading. For the first time, at least in several days, Peabody realized how frail she was, how delicate. And yet she had stood up to the lot of them for two weeks running. That took some serious fiber. He had to admire that, even if he did think she was dead wrong.

Mrs. Johnson cleared her throat. "Actually, I think that may not be necessary. I think ... maybe ... I've changed my mind."

Peabody leaned forward, his eyes bulging. "You mean it? You agree that Blaylock caused the cancers?"

"To be perfectly honest, I'm not sure. But I remember what that young attorney for the plaintiffs said, and I saw it again in the jury instructions. We don't have to say that we think that definitely did happen. We just have to find that it's more likely than not that it did happen. And—well, I think I can do that."

Peabody felt as if firecrackers were going off inside his head. "Then you'll join the rest of us in a plaintiffs' verdict?"

Mrs. Johnson licked her lips. "Yes. I will."

A cheer went up around the table. Several of them leaned forward and slapped the old lady on the back. "That's great. Great!"

"And that just leaves the matter of damages," Peabody said, hurriedly returning to the verdict forms. "How much shall we give the plaintiffs for their actual damages?"

Mrs. Johnson answered for all of them. "Everything. All their medical expenses."

Peabody could not have been more pleased. He scribbled the numbers onto the verdict form. "And for punitive damages?"

"No," Mrs. Johnson said quietly. "No punitive damages."

"Wait a minute," Marshall said. "These people are out a lot of money."

"That's not the point," Mary Ann said. "Punitive damages are for punishment. This corporation did a wrong thing. A negligent, greedy thing. They should be punished."

"I agree," Mrs. Cartwright added. "We have to give them something."

"Fine," Mrs. Johnson said. "Give them one dollar."

"One dollar!" Marshall practically exploded. For a moment, it had seemed as if they were close to finishing this thing once and for all. Now he realized they were still far, far apart. "That's like an insult. It needs to be something big! We gotta send a message to corporate America. Tell 'em we won't tolerate this sort of thing."

"I can't agree with that," Mrs. Johnson said. "I'm not

positive that this corporation did anything wrong—I just think it's more likely than not. I won't tax the defendant millions of dollars on a mere probability."

Marshall pounded his head against the table. "I don't believe this. I don't believe it."

Mary Ann's eyes widened like balloons. "We're gonna be here forever."

"No," Peabody said, "we're not." He'd been holding back so far. But by God, if he could make a living as a farmer in the state with the most unpredictable weather in the union, he could make this jury agree on a verdict. "Mrs. Johnson, I'm going to take you through the evidence one more time. In great detail."

The elderly woman leaned away. "I don't want to hear it again."

"Now stay with me here; this is absolutely the last time. I'm going to show you point by point exactly why we should award punitive damages. And when I'm done, if you're convinced, then I want you to join the rest of us."

"And if I'm not?"

"Then I'll join *you*. We all will. We'll award no punitives— or just render judgment for the defendant. Whatever you want." He drew himself up, placing his thumbs under the straps of his overalls. "But one way or the other, this trial is going to end. Today."

* 42 *

When Ben finally heard, it came as such a shock he didn't believe it at first. Didn't even understand it. The bailiff had to repeat it twice before it finally sank in.

The jury had returned. They had reached a verdict.

He stumbled back into the courtroom, feeling dazed. He'd waited for this so long it seemed unreal. Slowly but surely, the players were reassembled. Christina was the first to return, followed closely by Professor Matthews and the rest of Ben's office staff. Colby strolled in shortly thereafter, trying to look unconcerned, as did the rest of his entourage.

And finally, just before the judge called the trial back into session, Cecily Elkins slipped in the back. They made eye contact, if only briefly. Ben knew they were both too concerned about what would happen in the next five minutes to give any thought to social niceties.

Judge Perry called the courtroom to order and brought back the jury. Ben watched as they slowly filed out of the deliberation room, one by one, solemn and serious expressions on their faces. As Christina had predicted, Carl Peabody, the Catoosa farmer, had been made foreman. He held a small folded slip of paper in his hand—a paper Ben would've given anything to peruse.

Just behind Peabody was juror number twelve—Mrs. Johnson—the one he'd been so worried about. He tried to make eye contact with her; he'd learned a great deal could be predicted based on jurors' willingness to look at you when they returned. He couldn't catch her eye, though. Was she intentionally avoiding his gaze?

What did it mean?

"Mr. Foreman, have you reached a verdict?"

Carl Peabody rose. "We have, your honor."

"And is this the verdict of all twelve of you?"

"It is." Twelve heads in the jury box nodded.

"Bailiff." The bailiff took the verdict from the foreman and walked it over to the judge. Ben was moved by the ceremony of it all. It was as if they were all performers in a great passion play, going through their ritualistic motions, drawing out the suspense.

Judge Perry looked at the verdict form. Old pro that he was, his facial expression gave no hint of what it said. He passed it back to the bailiff, who returned it to the foreman.

"Mr. Foreman, please announce your verdict."

"Yes, your honor." Peabody glanced down at the form. "On

the plaintiffs' claim against the defendant based on the cause of action of wrongful death, we find in favor . . ."

Why did they always pause there? Ben wondered. Was it the influence of television? Or was it the underlying knowledge each foreman possessed of how important his next few words would be to the people in the courtroom? Perhaps it was to give everyone a last chance to prepare, rather like warning someone to buckle their seat belts.

Peabody cleared his throat, then continued. "we find in favor of . . . the plaintiffs."

Ben felt himself breathe, possibly for the first time since he entered the courtroom. Thank God. Thank you, God. Waves of anxiety tumbled off his shoulders like scales.

He heard a whooping sound behind him. He turned, thinking to admonish his staffers, but saw that the noise had come from the gallery. Cecily had company; most of the other parents had joined her. They were squeezing one another's hands, grinning with satisfaction.

"On this claim," Foreman Peabody continued, "we award actual damages in the amount of one hundred thousand dollars."

Ben stopped breathing just as quickly as he had started. A hundred thousand dollars? Split eleven ways? That was nothing. It wouldn't begin to pay his clients' outstanding medical bills. It wouldn't pay his legal expenses.

He didn't look behind him—he couldn't bear it—but he couldn't help but notice that the excited chatter from the gallery had been silenced.

"Furthermore," Foreman Peabody continued, still reading, "we award punitive damages to the plaintiffs in the amount of twenty-five million dollars."

Someone in the back screamed. The judge pounded his gavel, but it was useless. The courtroom dissolved into sheer pandemonium. All of the parents leapt to their feet. They threw their arms around one another, squeezing with all their might. Tears spilled from their eyes.

Christina rushed up behind Ben and wrapped him up in a huge bear hug. "You did it, Ben! I knew you would. I knew it!"

Over her shoulder, Ben caught a glimpse of Colby, who was understandably stoic. His eyes were going not to the jury—but to the bench. He and the judge were communicating, if only with their eyes.

Judge Perry continued pounding his gavel. "I will have order or I will have this courtroom cleared!"

Eventually the clamor quieted, although Ben could see the parents were so excited they could barely sit still.

Perry peered down at the jury. "So say you one, so say you all?"

The twelve heads in the jury box nodded. Even Mrs. Johnson's.

"Then I suppose we've reached the part of the trial where I'm supposed to thank you for doing such a fine service to the community and dismiss you. But I'm not going to do it."

Ben felt his blood turn cold. What was happening here?

"I'm not going to thank you, because you don't deserve to be thanked. You were instructed to reach a logical, fair verdict based on the evidence presented, without resort to sympathy or other emotional considerations. But you have failed to do that."

Colby, never one to miss an opening, rose. "Your honor, I move that this court enter a judgment notwithstanding the verdict."

Ben leapt up. "Your honor, there's no—"

"The motion will be granted," Perry said, before Ben could so much as finish a sentence. "I dislike taking a case away from the jury. I put it off as long as possible, hoping that when the time came the jury would take the appropriate action. But you didn't." He glared at the jury scornfully. "The fact is, the plaintiffs presented no credible scientific evidence to establish causation between their injuries and the alleged acts of the defendant. Despite that fact, you not only found for the plaintiffs, but awarded them a huge sum of money in punitive damages. Much as I dislike interfering, to allow a jury award of that magnitude to stand would be a gross miscarriage of justice. I therefore strike the jury's verdict and enter judgment for the defendant."

Christina appeared dumbstruck. "Can he do that?"

Ben didn't respond. He knew the answer all too well. He ran toward the bench. "Your honor, please don't do this—"

Judge Perry began stacking his papers. "Counsel, it is already done."

"But your honor," Ben said. "You're making a mistake. We did present sufficient evidence—"

"It's over, Mr. Kincaid." Judge Perry stood up and started toward the door. "If I've erred, then your appeal should be successful. But I very much doubt that, don't you?"

"Even if I was successful on appeal, they wouldn't reinstate the jury's verdict. They'd just give me a new trial. I can't afford a new trial!"

"Mr. Kincaid, I'm afraid that's simply not my concern." Perry passed into chambers, closing the door firmly behind him.

Ben whirled around to find Colby lurking. "Ben, that's a tough break. This is a hell of a game we play, isn't it? You have my condolences."

Ben's jaw was clenched. "Tell it to the parents."

"Now, Ben . . ."

"You knew he'd do this, didn't you? You knew all along."

Colby tilted his head to one side. "I felt confident the judge would do the right thing in the end, if it was required, yes. You tried to pull off a sneaky, Ben. You tried to do an end run around the evidence. I knew Judge Perry wouldn't allow that."

"And I suppose the fact that the soon-to-retire judge is desperate to get into your firm had nothing to do with it?"

Colby's smile increased slightly. "I don't think I'd go so far as to use the word 'nothing.' "

Ben was desperate to tell Colby how sick he made him, but he knew this wasn't the time. Reporters were filing into the back of the courtroom; they'd love nothing more than to report how the "sore loser" Kincaid raved like a maniac at the victorious Colby. The best thing he could do right now was get the hell out.

He grabbed his trial notebook and one of the exhibit boxes. "We're leaving," he told Christina.

She grabbed some of the rest of their stuff, but by that time all means of egress from the courtroom were solidly blocked. Ben felt a horrible hollowness inside as he realized he couldn't make it out of the courtroom without talking. But it wasn't the talk with reporters he dreaded most. That would be a piece of cake compared to . . .

Cecily was waiting for him. Her face was streaked with tears. Two of the other parents were helping her stand. But she was waiting for him.

THREE

* *

Home Is the Sailor,
Home from the Sea

* 43 *

Maybe Pfieffer wasn't the physical incarnation of evil after all, Mike mused, as he entered the third day of his stakeout. He had, after all, managed to ramrod through Mike's expense check so he could leave Tulsa. He could just imagine the reaction when his request passed through the top brass. Morelli wants to take indefinite leave to fly south and hang out around a fishing cabin. Yeah, right—will the good lieutenant be taking his tackle box, too?

Somehow, though, Pfieffer had managed to get this approved. It was funny; since Mike had gotten him involved, since he found the missing sixty million dollars that gave Mike his first real lead, he'd done everything he could to advance Mike's investigation, as if all at once he'd become a team player. He even asked to come along on this stakeout. Imagine that—Accountant by day; Danger Boy by night.

Not that Mike would mind a little company right about now. Once he'd pried out of Ronald Harris the location of the fishing cabin where Tony Montague died, he'd been determined to stake it out. Everyone involved in this case had been into fishing. Although the corporate records were incomplete, it was clear that at least some of the victims had come here on occasion—maybe all of them. It couldn't be just a coincidence. Mike felt certain that if he staked out the place long enough, he'd stumble across someone else who was involved in this little escapade. A potential victim—or maybe the killer himself.

The problem was the waiting. In the course of his career, he'd been on a wide variety of stakeouts, of all shapes and sizes, and they all had one thing in common: intense boredom.

Sure, once the perp made his move, the pace might pick up a bit. But until then, it was just one long tedious sit. And he hated sitting.

What could you do? Couldn't listen to your Walkman; someone might get the drop on you. Couldn't read a book, tempting though it was. His eyes had to stay on the door, and besides, it was dark outside, and the luminescent glow of an itty bitty book light would definitely attract attention. Couldn't play solitaire, couldn't recite poetry, couldn't watch a ball game. All you could do was sit. Sit like a rock until you felt the moss start to creep—

Wait a minute. A shadow moved, down on the other side of the dock. Someone was moving toward the cabin.

Slowly, Mike lifted himself out of his private spot in the shadows of the brush on the opposite end of the dock. Slowly, he reminded himself. God knows he didn't want to blow it now. Not when he'd come so far.

The silhouetted figure continued toward the cabin at top speed.

Mike crept along the dock as quietly as possible, trying not to attract any attention. His prey did not appear to have heard him; he was much too busy trying to get into the cabin. He was having trouble with the key; nervousness was making his fingers fumble. Which gave Mike just enough time to sneak up behind him. . . .

"Freeze, buddy."

The man screamed. He whirled around, his hands flailing in the air. "Don't kill me. Please! I'm begging you! Don't kill me!"

Just a hunch, but Mike suspected this man was not the killer. He effortlessly blocked the man's mostly wild and aimless blows.

"I don't know anything! I don't have it!" The man tried to run, but Mike grabbed him by the collar and swung him back by the door.

"Let me go! Someone call the police!"

Mike pulled out his badge. "I am the police, you nitwit. Now put your hands in the air and calm down." He grabbed the man's wrists and pinned them behind his back. "I'm not going to hurt you."

The man peered at Mike's face. "You're the guy who's been

quizzing everyone at Blaylock. Morelli, isn't that it? What're you doing way out here?"

"I might ask you the same question." Mike jerked his head toward the door. "Can you open that door?"

"Well . . . uh . . . yeah." His face was red and flushed. "I think so."

"Do it. Then we can have a nice chat."

He was so nervous it still took several minutes of fumbling to turn the lock and open the door, but he finally managed it. Mike shoved him inside and turned on the lights.

The interior decor was spartan, to put it mildly. A few rudimentary pieces of furniture, that was it. Everything was covered with a thick layer of dust.

"So what's your name?" Mike asked as he pushed the man into a wobbly wooden chair.

"Fred Henderson," the man replied.

"Nice to meet you, Fred. What brings you to the cabin?"

"Me? I—I just came to fish."

Mike smiled thinly. "Nice try. But I notice you aren't carrying any fishing gear. And I've also been reliably informed that the company no longer lets its employees come here. Apparently they're trying to sell the place."

"Really?" Fred said, trying a bit too hard. "I hadn't heard."

"Yeah, right. And why should you, since you seem to have your own key."

Fred thought for a moment. "I . . . accidentally forgot to return it. Last time I came out here. Come to think of it, I forgot my fishing pole, too."

Mike grabbed the nearest chair and sat himself down in front of Fred. "Look, Fred—I'm going to make this easy for you. You're not here for any officially authorized purpose. You're here to hide. From the killer."

Fred's eyebrows twitched. "How did you know?"

"That reception you gave me was a pretty dead giveaway. You obviously weren't expecting the Avon lady."

"Oh, yeah. Right. Well—there's been so much killing lately, you know, back in Oklahoma. A guy has to be careful."

"Especially a guy who knows the killer personally."

"You—" He stopped himself. "I don't know what you're talking about."

"Fred, don't make yourself look more pathetic than you already do."

"I am not pathetic!" he said indignantly. "That's what they all used to say. But I showed—" Once again he stopped, realizing his mouth had gotten the better of him.

"How about this, Fred? I'll tell you everything I already know, just to get you started. Then all you have to do is fill in the blanks."

"I'm telling you, I don't—"

Mike held his finger up to his lips. "Shhh. Listen." He pushed himself back up to his feet. "Many years ago, you and some of the other employees discovered you had a common passion. Fishing. Maybe you knew each other from the company cafeteria. Maybe you lived on the same block. Maybe you had some special kind or way of fishing you liked, I don't know."

Fred's head was bowed. "Deep-sea fishing."

"Ah. Which would explain why you came all the way out here. I'm guessing this went on for years, and a good time was had by all. A pleasant, mindless diversion. Until one day, you stumbled across Tony Montague."

Fred's resistance seemed to be fading. "Harvey was the one who got it started. He was the big organizer. Mr. Social Event. Blaylock's Hookers, that's what he liked to call us. He and Maggie had a thing going back then, before they both married other people. Even after they married, though, they still stayed friends. Fishing buddies. Thick and thin."

"Untiiiilll . . ."

"Right. Until a dead man interrupted our lives, for barely more than half an hour. But after that, everything changed."

It was after dark before Ben made it to the hospital, and visiting hours were almost over. He only had about twenty minutes with Mrs. Marmelstein before the nurses chased him out—twenty of the most unsatisfying minutes of his entire life. Mrs. Marmelstein was entirely blind now, and her hearing was far from perfect. Conversation was a chore, not a pleasure. Probably the only reason she put up with it was that she hoped he would have some news about her son. And he didn't.

He couldn't even get that right.

After Ben left her room, out in the hallway, he was met by Loving and Jones.

"Any word?" he asked Loving.

"No luck. Paulie won't budge. Asshole."

"Language," Jones said, making a tsking noise. "Language."

"When a guy won't go see his own mother on her deathbed, I say he's an asshole." Obviously, this was something Loving felt strongly about. "Language or not."

"Is there no chance?" Ben asked.

"Not unless you want me to go to New York and haul him back by force."

It was tempting, but Ben suspected Loving probably would be arrested before he made it back. "I guess that's it, then."

Jones cleared his throat. "About . . . what happened in the courtroom today."

"You're not going to say, 'I told you so,' are you?"

"No," Jones replied. "I'm not. I saw Cecily Elkins when she came back to the office and—" He pressed his lips together, plainly frustrated. "Look, Ben, I just wanted to say—I was wrong. Sure, maybe we lost and maybe we got cleaned out. But you did the right thing."

"It's nice of you to say that, Jones, but—"

"I mean it. Sure, I pinch pennies. That's my job. But I know I'm free to pinch pennies, because in the end, you'll do the right thing, whatever the cost."

"I appreciate this, Jones, but I know what I've done. I know what I've done to all of us." He drew in his breath. "Is there anything left, back at the office?"

"Not much. I tried to get the sheriff to give us an extension until the verdict came back, but—" He drew up his shoulders and adopted a pitch-perfect imitation of Sheriff Conway's voice. "Sorry, son, but the law is the law. For everyone."

Ben nodded. "I'll see you two later. Don't expect me in the office tomorrow. Maybe not . . . for some time."

"Ben." Jones grabbed his arm. "Don't beat yourself up like this. It isn't your fault. You did everything you could. You have no reason to be depressed."

"I lost, Jones. I lost, and I'm broke, and my landlady is dying. And I let down all those parents." He shrugged Jones's hand away. "They depended on me. And I let them down."

* 44 *

"A dead man entered your lives?" Mike asked.

"Yeah," Fred answered. He walked to the north side of the fishing cabin and fidgeted with the shabby drapes over the window. "A dead man named Tony Montague. A few of us, myself included, had known him before, but remember—we all thought he was dead. Even after Blaylock's goons finally managed to track him down, they kept their discovery to themselves. One of the advantages of not reporting the theft to the police was that they had no need to make a report when they found him. Believe me, when I walked into this cabin and saw him, I just about lost it."

"What was he doing here?"

"I think he just came to get away. He had to go somewhere, right? And there aren't that many places for a man who's officially dead to hang out. Didn't have much money, either. Maybe Blaylock made this place available to him. At any rate, we didn't know he'd be here—till we saw him."

"So you found him after the Blaylock boys had recovered their money?"

"Ye-eah . . ." For some reason, the question seemed to make Fred uncomfortable.

"What kind of shape was he in?"

"Bad. He was dying. And he knew it."

"Dying?"

"Yeah." Fred pushed aside the drapes and gazed absently onto the placid waters of the gulf. "Heart attack. Not his first. He'd been under some major strain—and I don't think he really wanted to live anymore. He could've called 911; he didn't.

When our little crew arrived, he was almost gone. He barely had enough time to tell us about the money."

"The money? I thought Blaylock got it all back."

A slow smile spread across Fred's face. "That's what he wanted them to think."

After he finished feeding his cat, Ben crawled into bed and tried to pretend that he was interested in something on the television. It was hard work. He channel surfed for more than ten minutes, but nothing caught his attention. *Xena* was a rerun; Lifetime had Markie Post in yet another life-affirming drama as a struggling something-or-other. Was it possible Pamela Anderson Lee had another series?

He switched the box off. It wouldn't have distracted him, anyway. No matter what he did, his mind kept coming back to the same thing. The Elkins trial. Which he'd lost.

The sad thing was, it really was his fault. This wasn't just errant martyrdom; he knew this with absolute certainty. After all the time, money, and effort he'd expended trying to win over the jury, he'd forgotten one important detail—you also have to win over the judge. He tried to teach that to his law students; he forgot to teach it to himself. And that was why his clients went down in flames.

He'd forced himself to go out to Blackwood, even though it was the last thing on earth he wanted to do. Could any experience of his life have been more unpleasant than facing that sea of bereaved, stricken faces? What happened? they kept asking, over and over. How could this happen? Can the judge do that? They feigned indignation, but in truth, Ben knew they were wounded, each and every one of them, wounded to the core by the suggestion that the smartest, most educated man in the courtroom did not believe in them. That he would interfere and interrupt the whole process rather than let them prevail.

Ben tried to calm their fears and assuage their insecurities. We'll appeal, he said—the eternal battle cry of the vanquished. That's what they all say, right? Never mind that their chances of success were virtually nil. Never mind that he couldn't afford a new trial even if he won it. He had to maintain some glimmer of hope. Even if his clients didn't really believe it.

Even if he didn't really believe it himself.

Ben's cat, Giselle, padded into his bedroom. Apparently she'd finished her Feline's Fancy; she had that slightly fishy cat food smell that initially had made Ben nearly vomit, but over time he'd sort of learned to like.

"C'mere, sweetie," he said, patting the sheets.

She thought it over carefully for a few moments, then consented to join him. She snuggled up close, pressing her head against his hand.

"You're easy enough, aren't you?" Ben said as he stroked her head. "I feed you grossly overpriced cat food twice a day, put out water, wash you on occasion, and take you in twice a year for your shots. And you're happy. I've done everything I'm supposed to do for you."

Giselle made a pleasant mewling sound.

"Thank goodness for you, anyway," Ben said as he pulled her close. "You're the only one I haven't let down."

Mark Austin sat alone on the veranda outside his room at the Riverside Apartments. It was a nice place, as apartments go. The view of the river was spectacular; he had to pay extra for it. The breeze was cool and the air was clean. No traces of carbon monoxide or refinery reek or other spoilers. He was nursing a tumbler of Courvoisier, his favorite overpriced indulgence. There had been a time when he couldn't afford things like Courvoisier. But now he could, at least occasionally. Because now he was an all-important associate at the all-important firm of Raven, Tucker & Tubb. He was a litigator. He worked with Charlton Colby, the best trial lawyer in the state. It was the job he'd always dreamed of having.

So why was he so miserable?

He was glad they'd won, of course. Sympathetic as he was for those poor parents, he was still a litigator, and litigators like to win.

It was how they won that bothered him. . . .

From the outset, the interaction between Colby and Blaylock had given him the creeps. He didn't know why, exactly. There was always a sense that there was more to their conversations than was immediately apparent, that there was a subtle subtext he didn't comprehend, unspoken knowledge hidden just beneath the surface. And he hadn't entirely approved of some of the tactics they'd used during the discovery period—threatening employees if they spoke out, rewarding them if they toed the company line. But they hadn't actually done anything improper, hadn't done anything hundreds of other lawyers haven't done on a regular basis.

What was troubling him, then? Was it just wanton guilt? An inability to experience pleasure? Some childish sense that justice—whatever the hell that was—was being silenced?

He had tried to balance the equities once before, when he anonymously told that cop to "follow the money." He didn't know what Colby and Blaylock had been hinting about, but he figured if it had any relevance to the investigation, the cop would figure it out.

So hadn't he done enough? Hadn't he proved he was on the side of the angels, albeit somewhat secretly? What was it that kept gnawing away at his conscience?

Whatever it was, it was all summed up for him by that damned blue report. It had been Blaylock's principal concern since the case began. Mark suspected he was more worried about the report getting out than he was about losing the case. What was in the thing? What evil truths lurked between those blue covers?

Mark had to know. It had been too hard to get to the thing without being caught while the trial was still going and their security measures were all in place. Too risky. But now that he had a copy . . .

Now that he had a copy, he'd read the whole thing, cover to cover. Twice.

And what he read made him sick. Made him want to vomit. Made him want to drop a bomb on top of Blaylock and Colby and his stinking law firm and send them all to oblivion.

But what could he do? If he leaked the report, it would be the end of his career. Undoubtedly. Even if he did it secretly, it would eventually be traced back to him. He'd lose his job. Probably lose his license. After all, he would be betraying a client trust. Never mind that the client didn't deserve his trust and the report hadn't been properly subject to privilege in the first place. He could be disbarred for this.

All his dreams, all his promise. Up in smoke. No dining at

the Tulsa Club. No hobnobbing with society debs. No majestic estate near Philbrook. Everything he had wanted, everything he had dreamt about—gone.

He couldn't do that to himself. Could he?

He remembered what the other lawyer, Kincaid, had said that day in chambers when Colby taunted him, telling Kincaid he was going to bankrupt himself for nothing. Kincaid had said, "I'd rather go broke doing the right thing than get rich doing the wrong."

You had to admire a guy like that.

Slowly, Mark reached for the Yellow Pages and started looking up courier services. He was probably making a tremendous mistake.

But he was feeling good about it. The best he'd felt in a long time.

* 45 *

Mike stared at Fred, trying to make sense out of his story. "I've talked to the attorneys at Blaylock, and they told me they recovered almost every dime of the sixty million he stole. I saw the entries on the corporate ledger where the money reentered the books. And you're telling me Montague still had the money?"

"Not the money. His money." Fred stepped away from the window and closed the drapes. "You see, he had the stolen funds for more than a year. Money makes money. Over that amount of time, even a fool like me ought to be able to increase the wad."

"I was told the loot was found in a noninterest-bearing account."

"It was found there, yes. But had it been there the whole

time? No." An admiring smile crossed Fred's face. "Tony got wind of the Blaylock boys before they caught him. He knew he couldn't evade them forever, now that they knew he was alive. So he took sixty million dollars out of his investment account and put it in a noninterest-bearing savings account for them to find. He bribed a bank official to alter the computer records, make it look like the money had been sitting there for much longer than it had. Then he secretly withdrew all the profit he'd made."

"Was it a lot?"

"Are you kidding? Think about it. Sixty million invested for more than a year? Even with conservative investments, you'd expect an eight or ten percent return. And Tony was an accountant; he knew better than most how to make his money make money. He placed big chunks of change into some of those hot Internet IPOs. By the time Blaylock found him— he'd made almost fifteen million bucks."

Mike's lips parted. "What did he do with it?"

"He converted it to government bonds—not the U.S. government, either. He knew that these days, in the computer age, if he put the money in a bank anywhere, it could eventually be tracked down. But he didn't want to carry all that cash around with him."

"So he converted it to bonds."

"Exactly. He thought it was safer."

"But I assume the bonds were negotiable. Anyone could spend them. So it wasn't any safer—"

"Anyone could spend them—eventually. You see, these bonds had fixed terms. Five-year terms. At the end of the term, they could be cashed in for full value plus a sizable bonus—almost four million additional dollars. But until the term ended, they weren't worth a dime." He laughed. "Muggers don't usually have that kind of patience."

"But you and your little fishing friends did?"

Fred held up his hands. "He gave them to us! Really! We didn't steal them."

"Why would he—"

"He knew he was dying. For all he'd been through, he'd never gotten any pleasure out of the millions he stole. He wanted someone to enjoy the fruits of his labors. So he told us where he'd hidden the bonds." Fred lowered his head. "And then he died."

"I don't recall hearing that there were any fisherpersons hanging about the cabin when his body was discovered."

"No. We lit out of here in a heartbeat—with the merchandise. What was wrong with that? Tony was dead. We couldn't help him. And if we were found on the scene, the Blaylock boys would undoubtedly have a lot of questions for us. Especially if we suddenly came into a lot of money. And if they found out about the money, they'd try to take it. So we blew town."

"What did you do with the bonds?"

"Stuck them in a safe-deposit box in Mexico City. Nothing sleazy—a reputable bank. But one that didn't ask too many questions—like where'd it come from. And one that didn't check ID."

"You took the box out under an assumed name?"

"We did. It seemed safer."

"Who got the keys to the box?"

"We all did. But we left strict instructions that the box could not be opened except in the presence of all of us. That way we could rest assured that the bonds would stay in the box until they could be cashed in."

Mike took a seat at the thin, wobbly, linoleum-topped table that had probably served as a surface for cleaning fish more often than as a dining table. This was a lot to take in all at once, but he thought he was beginning to get a clearer picture of what had happened—and why. It was a tall tale—but it made a crazy kind of sense.

"Sounds like you thought it all out carefully. Planned well."

"Yup. Sounds like it, doesn't it? But the best-laid plans . . ." He shook his head. "About six months ago, we all got together to recover the bonds. The term wasn't quite up yet, but Canino thought it might take a while to negotiate them, since they were foreign and all. Lots of procedural hurdles. Papers to be filed. So we all went out to get them. Last December fifteenth."

Mike thought back. "That was just before your buddy James shot up the law school."

"You're quick, aren't you?"

"I gather the timing isn't a coincidence."

"No. Jim was nuts—totally bonkers. But there was definitely a trigger. Something that set him off."

"Which was?"

Fred drew in his breath. "We all got together and took a little trip down to Mexico. We all went to the bank and opened the box."

"And?"

"And the bonds were gone. All of them. The Blaylock bonanza had disappeared—again."

When Ben didn't answer his apartment door after she'd been pounding on it for more than a minute, Christina had to assume he wanted to be left alone. Unfortunately for him, she had her own key.

She let herself in and marched straight back to his bedroom, where he was sitting up in his pajamas staring at the same page of a Trollope novel he'd been at when she'd dropped by two days ago.

"Excuse me?" Ben said, pulling the covers around him. "What are you doing here?"

"Well, since you haven't been to the office, I had to come to you."

"I don't think it's unreasonable to take some time off when you've been in trial for months."

"Wah, wah, wah." She glanced down at his book. "Must be a real page-turner." She grabbed it away from him and dropped it on the floor.

"Hey! I was reading that."

She dropped a thin, blue folder in his lap. "Read this instead."

Ben picked it up and fanned the pages. It was only about ten pages long. It appeared to be some kind of report. "Where did this come from?"

"I don't know. A courier brought it to our office this morning. From an anonymous sender who paid in cash."

Ben glanced at the first page. The author's name wasn't given, but the distribution list showed who got it—all the top Blaylock brass, including Myron Blaylock himself. And at the bottom of the list—Charlton Colby.

"Why haven't we seen this before?" he asked.

"I think the last name on the list is the answer to that question. Colby withheld it under a claim of attorney-client privilege."

"Because his name is on it? He didn't write it, and it wasn't written for him."

"I didn't say it was a good claim. I'm just trying to explain why we haven't seen it before."

"There's no way they can—"

Christina covered his mouth with her hand. "Ben, just be quiet for a moment and read."

Ben did as she bid. He wasn't halfway through the first page before he understood the enormous significance of the report—why Blaylock had wanted it hidden, why Christina had brought it to his immediate attention.

When he hit the bottom of the second page, though, he gasped. Literally gasped. "I can't believe it," he said breathlessly. "I mean, I always thought they were responsible for the deaths. But I never in my wildest dreams—"

"Yeah." Christina nodded appreciatively. "I thought the same thing."

Ben climbed out of bed. For the first time since the jury had returned, he felt his heart beating again. "I'm going over to see Colby."

"I already tried to get you an appointment. He refused. So I made you an appointment with Myron Blaylock. He didn't want to see you, either, but after I read a few choice bits from the report, he changed his mind." She smiled. "I have a hunch Colby will want to be there for this meeting, too, don't you?"

"No doubt." Ben pulled his least-wrinkled shirt out of the closet. "Good work, Christina. Would you excuse me?"

She looked at him blank-faced. "Why?"

He held up his clothes. "I need to get dressed."

"And?"

"And—you're in my bedroom!"

"Oh, that's all right. We're professionals."

"Christina!"

"Fine. I'll wait outside."

"Thank you so very much."

She stopped halfway out the door. "Did I tell you how cute

your pj's are? I've never seen the ones with candy canes and little teddy bears before."

"Christina!"

"I'm going, I'm going."

* 46 *

Mike didn't know how long he'd been sitting in this fishing cabin listening to Fred tell his story. Time seemed irrelevant now. This bizarre tale of greed and deception was positively addicting.

"Someone had stolen the bonds?"

"So it seemed. As you can imagine, our friendship deteriorated somewhat in the aftermath. Accusations were made. Names were called. Canino and James got into a fistfight. James was really over the edge. He'd never been the most stable person—mentally, I mean. And to make matters worse, he was drinking too much, he'd just lost his job, and his wife had left him. He was counting on this money to put his life back in order. And it was gone."

"That's why he went ballistic at the law school, isn't it?"

Fred nodded. "By that time, he was totally psychotic. Crazed. Didn't even realize that Canino wasn't teaching the class, at least not at first. All he knew was that he wanted the merchandise. That was the codeword we had developed for the bonds during the years we waited for the term to run. We had all kinds of cloak-and-dagger nonsense we invented, just so we could talk about it without talking about it."

"Why did James think The Tiger had the money?"

"I don't know. Shortly after we found the bonds, Canino left Blaylock Legal and started teaching. Developed quite a rep for himself. I think maybe James resented that; it only reminded him of his own failures. And in his addled, booze-soaked brain—"

"He decided to go after The Tiger."

"Yeah. Except The Tiger wasn't there that day. He got some other schmuck instead."

"That schmuck is my friend. And he almost got himself killed."

"I don't know why Canino wasn't there. I haven't seen him since that day."

"I have," Mike said somberly. "He's dead."

Fred nodded. "I figured as much. Hell, they're all dead, now. All but me. And him."

Mike peered at Fred with a sharp and steady eye. "You stole those bonds, didn't you, Fred?"

He didn't deny it. "Bribed a bank official, just as Tony had years before. Easy to bribe people when you're about to become a multimillionaire. Cleaned me out, though. Left me with no way to run. No means of—escape." He threw his head down. "Damn that accursed money, anyway. I wish I'd never taken it."

"Most people would be tempted."

"I was a fool. What the hell good is it? All that money ever did for Tony Montague was ruin his life and get him killed. And now the same thing's going to happen to me."

"Fred, when do the bonds come due? When can they be cashed in?"

Fred did not smile. "Tomorrow. If I live that long."

The moment Ben and Christina hit the front door of Blaylock headquarters in Blackwood, they were met by two burly security officers who detained them and forcibly confiscated Ben's briefcase—including the blue report inside.

Ben wasn't especially surprised.

The security officers were gruff and threatening and went through most of the permutations of a good cop/bad cop routine. They frisked them, barked into their walkie-talkies, played with their weapons, talked about calling the police. Ben and Christina sat through it quietly. When the show was finally over, the guards escorted them up the elevator to Myron Blaylock's private office.

Colby was waiting inside. "Kincaid, I always thought you were a lousy lawyer, but I never thought you were a criminal. Until now. Rest assured we plan to prosecute you to the full extent of the law."

Ben yawned. "I haven't committed a crime."

"You have stolen a confidential document from these offices."

"No. It was delivered to me."

"Then you are in receipt of stolen property. Also a crime."

"It's just paper. It has no intrinsic value."

"It contains confidential trade secrets of incalculable value."

"Bull. It contains dirty little secrets that you want kept under wraps."

Colby stiffened. "I warn you, Kincaid. If you try to exonerate yourself from your crime by making libelous accusations about me or this company, the law will come down on you hard."

Ben looked Colby straight in the eye. "There's no audience in the room, Charlton, so let's put an end to this charade right now. You two boys have gotten caught with your pants down, and now you're going to pay the price." Ben marched into the office, with Colby close behind.

"That so-called report is a pack of lies," Myron Blaylock said, behind his desk. His knobbly hands were trembling slightly. "Not a word of it is true."

"Then why didn't you produce it during the discovery period when you were supposed to?"

"It wasn't relevant," Blaylock sniffed. "Since none of it is true."

Ben rolled his eyes. "Wonderful. Colby, may I please be in the courtroom when you make that argument to the judge? Please?"

"There's no need for sarcasm, Kincaid."

"That's a matter of opinion. I sat in the same room while you promised the magistrate you would produce all Blaylock's internal studies. You didn't do it. You lied to a federal magistrate."

"I believed the report fell under the protection of the attorney-client privilege. I still do."

"That's a load of crap and we both know it. This document

has nothing to do with the giving or receiving of legal advice. You just had your name stuck on it to create a feeble basis for withholding it."

"That is not true."

"Then why didn't you submit the document to the magistrate in camera, like I suggested at the hearing? Let the magistrate decide if it was privileged or not."

Colby had no answer, so he changed the subject. "You don't know whether that report has the least grain of truth in—"

"Like hell I don't. It's all true. I know it is, because the proof is right there in the report, which by the way I made dozens of copies of before I came here. Your man documented his work to a fault."

"He was an unstable person," Blaylock said.

"He was your own employee. Your own corporate lawyer. He spent more than a year researching the alleged funny taste the water in Well B had acquired. And he came to the same conclusion I did. He found that TCE and perc from this plant had contaminated the groundwater, which flowed via the ravine into the aquifer that feeds Well B. He even noted that TCE and perc were dangerous and could lead to serious illnesses." Ben drew in his breath. "And he did it four years before I ever heard of this case!"

Blaylock folded his arms, his hands still fluttering. "He was a lunatic. Irrational. We fired him shortly after he filed the report."

"Killed the messenger, huh? Very logical." Ben leaned across Blaylock's desk. "You *knew*! You knew all along! You knew you were responsible for those kids' deaths—and you did nothing."

"That's not true," Blaylock said. His nervous twitching was increasing. "We tightened up our waste-disposal procedures. Increased the budget for removals."

"But you didn't tell anyone. And you didn't remove the buried drums that were polluting the groundwater."

"How could we? If we let this get out, shysters like you would be crawling all over us, filing a lawsuit every time some kid gets a hangnail."

"You might've saved lives!" Ben's voice reverberated

across the room. "Most of my clients lost their children in the last four years."

"The harm was already done. I knew it was just a matter of time before the EPA would become involved."

"So you kept your mouth shut. Took no responsibility for your actions."

"I still remain unconvinced that any contamination that might have occurred resulted in those leukemias."

"Yeah, keep telling yourself that, Blaylock. You don't believe it any more than I do." Ben leaned forward. "You killed those kids. You killed them because you wanted to save money, and you kept quiet about it because you wanted to save money." He whirled around and faced Colby. "And you helped him cover it up. Because you wanted some of his money."

Blaylock fell silent. He steepled his fingers, as if deep in thought. "What do you want?" he asked finally.

"Myron!" Colby said. "Don't give him—"

"Shut up, Charlton. Can't you see that it's over?" He turned his attention back to Ben. "What do you want?"

"You know damn well what I want."

He pursed his lips. "How much?"

"I will accept, as part of a settlement agreement and in return for our agreement to forgo an appeal, the amount which the jury determined the plaintiffs were entitled to receive."

Blaylock's eyes bugged. "Twenty-five million? You must be joking."

"I've never been more serious in my life. That's what a fair and impartial jury said we deserved, before Colby's buddy yanked the case away from them. So that's what we'll accept."

"I will not pay it."

"Fine. Then I'll proceed with my appeal—which will be based upon the defendant's unlawful withholding of a key piece of incriminating evidence during discovery. Of course, by the time my brief is filed, the judges will probably have read all about it in the newspaper."

Blaylock opened his bottom desk drawer and withdrew a large ledger-sized checkbook. "Fifteen million."

Ben shook his head. "Twenty-five."

"Twenty. That's as high as I go."

"Twenty-five. Or I file my appeal. Today."

Blaylock's teeth clenched. He put his pen to paper. "We'll structure it to be paid out over ten years, one point two five each six months. This will be the first installment. I'll postdate the check; it will have to be ratified by the board of directors. Funds will have to be transferred."

"I'm in no hurry. I'll give you forty-eight hours."

Blaylock ripped the check out of the book. Colby intervened. "In exchange for this settlement payment, I will require you to return all copies of the report and to agree that you will make no mention of it or disseminate it to any third persons."

"No."

"Excuse me?"

"No." Ben didn't blink. "I won't sit on the report."

"You have no choice. Listen to me, Kincaid—this is a deal-breaker. We must have a confidentiality agreement."

"I won't do it. I won't help you cover up your dirty secret. But I will forgo pursuing criminal charges or filing a bar complaint based upon your conspiracy to withhold subpoenaed documents, which might keep you, Charlton, from losing your bar license, and you, Myron, from going to prison."

Colby was incensed. "What is this, blackmail?"

"No," Ben replied. "This is justice. Now give me my check."

Blaylock wordlessly passed the check across his desk.

"Thank you. Let's go, Christina." Ben paused by the door. "May I make one recommendation? Draft up some formal statement of apology and regret. When word of this report hits, you two are going to be about the least popular men in the state. A lot of people will be accusing you, calling you names, asking uncomfortable questions." He paused. "And there are eleven families who will never forgive you."

47

Funny how you could go almost five years avoiding the cops, and then when the one who tracks you down finally leaves, you miss him. Life will have its little ironies, won't it?

Fred pulled back the tattered drapes and peered out the window. It was not quite half an hour since Lieutenant Morelli had left the fishing cabin. He'd gotten a message from head-quarters on his cell phone telling him there'd been another murder, so he went to the local PD to see what he could find out about it. Don't worry, he'd said—if the killer's in Okla-homa, then he isn't here.

He had warned Fred not to try to flee, but it wasn't much of a warning. He knew Fred wasn't going anywhere. The jig was up. They knew he had the merchandise, and he couldn't run forever. No matter where he went, they would eventually find him. Assuming his murderous friend didn't find him first, which, all things considered, Fred thought the more likely re-sult. Which was all the more reason to stay exactly where he was. And hope the cop returned. Soon.

Maybe this would be a good time to fix a sandwich, he told himself. He had brought a few provisions. A tall, multimeat Dagwood sandwich—that might be just the thing right now.

He strolled through the living area into the kitchen nook—which in this cabin took all of three steps. He opened the ice chest and started hauling out supplies and—

He froze. What was that?

He'd heard something, somewhere behind the cabin. Hadn't he? He was almost certain. Something was moving out in the bushes and trees.

He ran to the back window and peered out. Could be

anything, he rationalized to himself, even assuming he really had heard something moving. Could be a raccoon or possum. Maybe a badger. Could be a hunter or fisherman. Could be two lovers out for a moonlight stroll.

Except he didn't see any moon. Or anything else, for that matter.

Would a raccoon hide? Would a badger?

He felt beads of sweat trickling down his neck. He had come so far. So far. He could live with losing the merchandise, maybe even doing some prison time. But he really really didn't want to die. Especially not at the hands of the homicidal maniac who used to bait his hook for him.

Fred's palms were wet. Get a grip, he told himself. Don't blow it in the final inning.

He heard something else, some movement. There was no doubt about it now. He not only heard it—he saw it. Something was moving.

Someone. It had to be someone.

And it wouldn't be Lieutenant Morelli. He was in a car. Only one person would try to sneak up without being heard. . . .

Panicked, Fred ran back to the front door and slid the bolt into place. An instant later, he flicked off all the lights. And sat quietly. In the dark.

Was this better? It seemed worse. Now he heard creaks in every corner, saw movement in every flicker of light.

There wasn't even a decent hiding place in this miserable cabin. The furniture was all thin and fragile—no tables or dressers he could use to block the door. Not that any of that would stop the killer for long.

He ran from one end of the tiny shack to the other, unable to decide where to stay put. No place seemed safe. No place was safe.

He pressed his hands together, but they were so wet they slid off one another. His whole body was like that; he felt as if he'd been standing out in the rain. Except that his heart was pounding so hard he thought it might explode at any moment. And his brain was so fried he couldn't figure out what to do next.

He heard it again—the unmistakable sound of movement behind the shack. Damn this dark, anyway! He flicked the switch, illuminating the cabin. At least now they'd both be able to see one another. They'd be on equal ground. Except of course that his friend was already a multiple murderer. And he was . . .

Fred the Feeb?

No, goddamnit. Never again. He would get a grip on himself. He would take control.

He drank in several deep breaths, calming himself. Forcing himself to take deliberate, even, slow steps, he returned to the back window.

He heard it again, saw the leaves and bushes move. But this time, he observed that they all moved at once, in unison. And a whistling sound accompanied the movement. . . .

It was the wind. All this time—it was just the goddamn wind!

His hands pressed against his face, wiping the sweat away. You see what happens, he told himself. See the result of letting your imagination get the best of you, letting fear take control? You end up running in a blind panic. Like a fool. Like Fred the Feeb.

He grabbed a towel and dried off the rest of his sweat-soaked body. Jesus Christ, what an idiot he'd been. He was never cut out for this cloak-and-dagger crap. He might not be Fred the Feeb, but he wasn't James Bond, either. Leave the action-adventure stuff to someone else.

He laughed quietly. As he did, he heard a car pulling up outside. Thank goodness. Nothing was going to happen to him while the cop was here, that much was certain. Prison time might be a small price to pay for peace of mind, at this point. No wonder Tony had a heart attack. If Fred'd been alone much longer, he probably would've worried himself into an early grave, too.

He ran, not walked, to the front door and opened it.

It was not Lieutenant Morelli standing on the other side of the door.

"Hiya, Fred," his old fishing buddy said, grinning. "Miss me?"

* 48 *

"I never thought we'd actually make it here," Ben said as he gazed out the main viewport of Professor Matthews's magnificent yacht. "It still seems unreal."

"The yacht," Matthews asked, "or the fact that you're in it?"

"Both." He meant it, too. He was still amazed that he'd managed to bring the Elkins case to a positive conclusion. Ben had delivered the check to his clients—Blaylock's first payment on the structured ten-year settlement payout. Although Ben's share wasn't enough to pay off all his creditors, he was at least able to appease the most insistent ones and give everyone something. More important, the money, combined with the media release of the "blue report," had given each of the parents the satisfaction of knowing that their child had not died in vain.

Christina popped through the door into the main cabin. "Well, I've seen the bedrooms, the sundeck, and the boiler room. I assume there's also a parlor and conservatory somewhere on this monstrosity."

Matthews laughed. "That'll be in the next model. This one's only thirty-five feet."

"Oh, is that all," Christina said, winking. The main cabin, where they were presently, combined the "bridge"—with all the steering and navigational equipment—with a larger dining area. Up above, visible through a glass ceiling, was a spacious deck, ready-made for sunbathing and stargazing. Down below were the sleeping quarters and the boiler room, with the engine and most of the other mechanical equipment. It was all connected by wide metal decks and ladders. It was a boat of which the Onassis family could be proud.

"I don't even want to think about what this set you back," Ben said. "Obviously, Dean Kronfield is paying you a great deal more than he's paying me."

Matthews laughed. "I couldn't afford this in a million years. I told you already—I inherited it."

"Couldn't you dock it somewhere closer to home?"

"I could. But this is an oceangoing vessel. It seems a shame to waste it on Lake Tenkiller or some such. Here on the Gulf, all of the Atlantic Ocean is at our disposal."

"We're not going too far from shore, are we?" Ben asked. "I'm a lousy swimmer."

Matthews laughed again. "It won't matter, unless you decide to jump over the rail and go skinny-dipping."

Christina arched an eyebrow. "I think I can pretty well guarantee that's not going to happen."

Matthews cut the engine. "At any rate, this is far enough." He pointed toward the windshield. "We can still see home. And we can get there lickety-split, if we need to. Probably won't, but the weather advisory did say there was a possibility of a storm."

"Storm?" Ben said. "As in, gale-force winds? Big waves?"

"I doubt that will happen. But if it does, we'll return to dock lickety-split." He checked the gauge on the metal gas tank, just to the left of the wheel. "We've got plenty of fuel. We're perfectly safe." He opened the cabinet to his right. "Now, if you'll excuse me, I'm going to start dinner."

"What can I do to help?" Ben asked.

"Zip," Matthews answered. "Nada. You've been under the gun for months. Tonight you just relax."

"I'll feel guilty letting you serve me."

"I'll feel guilty if you have a heart attack. I want you to live long enough to bring me some more cases." He lit two tall candles and placed them on the tablecloth in the center of the dining table. Then he popped open a bottle of Cordon Negro and started pouring it into champagne flutes.

"Well, if you insist on doing everything—mind if I take a look around the boat?" Ben asked.

"Of course not. But be back in about twenty minutes."

"Deal. Any place I can get a drink of water?"

He pointed. "There's bottled water in the cooler."

"What, you mean you don't have a faucet on this barge?"

Matthews gave him a pointed look. "Are you kidding? After this case, I'll never drink tap water again in my life."

Mike knew something was wrong before he'd even stopped his car. The lights in the cabin were out, but the front door was wide open. And he had that nasty tingling at the base of his spine, the one that never presaged anything good. . . .

He jumped out, brandishing his Sig Sauer, ready for the worst. He should've known better than to leave Fred alone, even for a few minutes. But the message said there'd been another murder—he couldn't ignore that. Plus, if there'd been another murder, that meant the killer was up in Oklahoma, not anywhere around here—

Unless he'd been bluffed. Unless the killer had his cell phone number, which wouldn't be that hard to get. Unless he'd been lured away . . . leaving Fred at the killer's mercy.

He wanted to slap himself up the side of the head, but both hands were busy clutching his gun tightly. Where was he, damn it? One thing was certain—Mike was not going to let him get away again. He was not going to let him take another victim. Mike couldn't live with that.

He meant that both figuratively and literally—since it was a dead cert the murderer would not leave him alive again.

Slowly Mike crept toward the front of the cabin. He passed through the door, which was blowing back and forth in the wind. He reached inside and turned on the light. . . .

The cabin had been wrecked. Furniture was strewn all over the floor, most of it broken. Some kind of struggle had taken place here, some titanic contest of wills. But no trace of the players remained now.

Well, there was one trace. A pool of wet sticky blood on the floor.

Mike bent down and touched the blood. Fresh. Whatever happened had not happened that long ago.

Mike ran through the whole cabin, making sure no one was hiding or lying unconscious or dead. It didn't take long. No one was here.

Were they outside? What had happened? What was going on? He passed through the door again and stepped outside. . . .

He fell on top of Mike like a concrete slab, knocking him to the ground. Mike was dazed, but he knew that if he let unconsciousness take him, he was a dead man. He forced himself to stay awake, forced himself to stay alert.

He couldn't see his assailant. He tried to roll around, but the weight on top of him was too heavy. His arms were pinned beneath him and his gun had been knocked out of his hand.

And the concrete slab on top of him had started punching him in the gut.

Mike gritted his teeth and tried to rock his assailant off. No use. The next blow hit him on the side of the head. He felt blood trickling down his face, but there was nothing he could do about it. He was pinned like a bug in a science experiment.

"I'm not going to let you kill me like you did the others," his assailant muttered, followed by another sharp blow to the gut.

"Fred?" Mike pushed upward with all his might. "Fred, is that you?"

"You know it is, you sick son of a bitch!"

"Fred, you fool, it's Lieutenant Morelli!"

The blows stopped. Hesitant at first, Fred pulled away, unpinning Mike from the ground.

Mike rolled around, wiping blood from his face. "You stupid idiot. Why don't you look before you punch? I'm not your killer."

"He was here," Fred said. His voice was small and scared. "He found me."

"And you're still alive?"

Fred seemed as surprised as Mike was. "We fought. Hell of a fight. You probably saw the mess inside. I did everything I could to defend myself—but I knew I was no match for him. He was toying with me, like a cat playing with a trapped mouse before eating it. He was just killing time."

"How did you get away?"

"I—I'm not sure I understand it, even now." His eyes seemed to drift as he tried to recall. "I got in a lucky shot, knocked him off his feet. I used that as my chance to blow past him, run to the door and escape into the forest. I shouted as I ran. I shouted, 'The bonds are in the ice chest. Take them.' And the strangest thing happened."

"Yes?"

"He did it. He didn't pursue me. He didn't wait around for me to return. He just took the merchandise and left."

Mike tried to make sense of it—the man who had taken so much pleasure in tormenting his former friends had let one escape. It didn't seem to fit the pattern. And yet . . .

"Maybe he doesn't want to kill me," Fred said. It was more a question than a statement. "Maybe now that he has the bonds, he'll leave me alone."

"Maybe," Mike murmured. "But I think this guy is a serious maniac, of the homicidal type, and you're a loose end who could put him behind bars."

"Then why—"

"You said the bonds come due tomorrow, right? He's probably got something set up, some means of converting them into cash quickly. He may be too busy to chase you around a forest right now. But that doesn't mean he won't get back to you later. You're a risk he doesn't need and can't afford."

"Oh." Fred's expression was so crestfallen Mike almost wished he hadn't been so honest. "I see."

"Don't worry. You'll be put under protective custody."

"Oh, whoop-de-doo."

"But the best thing that could happen to you is that we catch the killer. So starting right now, you're going to tell me every goddamn thing you know about this man." He led Fred back into the cabin and sat him down in the only chair that remained reasonably stable. "Start talking."

Fred shrugged. "What's to say? Jack worked at Blaylock like the rest of us. He liked to fish."

"How did you meet him?"

"As I recall, Harvey was the one who first got us together. We were all in queue to use one of the company fishing cabins—not this one, they didn't have it yet. A nicer place in Colorado. Harvey suggested that if we all joined together and went at the same time, we wouldn't have to wait so long."

"Made sense. How long ago was this?"

Fred cast his mind back. "A good, long while. Twenty years or more."

"And you all got along well?"

"Back then, yeah. We were compatible. James was a little

on edge; his life was always a wreck that would only get worse with time. But he was handling it, back then. Harvey and Maggie usually shacked up together, thus mutually cheating on their spouses. But who were we to judge?"

"And this Jack—the killer—he was a normal guy?"

"Sure. I mean, more or less. Nothing too strange. He did have a cruel streak; at least I thought so. Liked to torture small animals. Got off on setting small fires. One time he almost burned the cabin down."

Animal cruelty and arson, Mike thought silently. Two FBI profile hallmarks of the incipient serial killer. "When did the fishing jaunts stop?"

"After we discovered Tony Montague. And the bonds. We all still fished—but not together. I can't exactly explain it— but we really didn't want to see one another much after that. Maybe we were afraid we'd inadvertently spill the goods if we were together. Or maybe you just don't like looking at the guy who knows your guilty secret."

All very interesting, Mike thought, but it wouldn't help him track the killer down.

"Was he an accountant?"

"No, no. Worked in the legal department."

"I notice you say worked. He's no longer there?"

"No. He left a few years ago. There was some kind of trouble—I heard he wrote a report the upper management didn't like."

"And so they fired him?"

"Yeah, I think so."

"And you don't know where he went after that?"

"Sure I do. He went to Tulsa. To the law school."

All at once, Mike felt his blood run cold. "The law school?"

"Yeah. He became a professor. Like Canino. In fact, I think Canino helped him get in."

Mike grabbed the man by his shoulders. "What is this Jack's last name?"

"Matthews."

"Jack Matthews?"

"Yeah. Some kind of tort expert, I think. But I don't know where he is."

"I do." Mike jumped to his feet. His face was hard and set.

"He's somewhere here in Corpus, on his goddamn yacht. With my best friend."

Matthews and Christina clinked their champagne glasses together.

"A toast," Matthews said, "to a beautiful lady."

Christina giggled. "I haven't had champagne in ages. Certainly not since this case began."

Matthews rearranged the candles so he could lean across the middle of the table. "A lovely lady like you should have champagne every night. Champagne and bonbons."

Christina took another sip. "You're sweet." She glanced over her shoulder. "Isn't Ben overdue?"

Matthews took the hint. "So what is it with you two, anyway?"

"What do you mean?"

"Don't be coy. You're obviously very close."

"I should hope so. We've been working together for years. We've been through some pretty tight scrapes."

"C'mon. There must be more to it than that."

"If there is, he hasn't told me about it."

Matthews laughed. "Fine. I'll back off. Dinner's almost ready. I'll go find your colleague." He started through the steel door that led to the outside deck, then stopped. "But if you ever change your mind, and decide you'd like to try a new colleague—keep me in mind, okay?"

Christina smiled. "Promise."

Ben suspected that his twenty minutes was up, but he couldn't tear himself away from his self-guided tour of the yacht. He didn't know magnificence of this magnitude existed, except maybe in movies and comic books. You could live in a boat this size. In fact, if it were his boat, he would. Imagine living on the water, rocking gently back and forth with the tide. Maybe if he took more plaintiff's cases, maybe if he cut down on his expenses . . .

Who was he kidding? Every time he took a plaintiff case he ended up losing money—even when he won. And he didn't do much better with criminal work. He'd been practicing for years now, and at best he'd managed to survive.

Whatever the secret of making money practicing law was, he didn't know it.

The boiler room was the only part of the ship Ben hadn't already explored. Normally, mechanical things didn't interest him, but in this case, he was fascinated. He liked just listening to it—the swish-swish, pump-pump of the pistons, or whatever they were. The hum of the engine. Inhaling the faint but distinct odor of gasoline and oil.

He noticed the closed hatch at the far end of the room. Probably nothing there, but he couldn't resist looking. He was in his Curious George mode; a closed door was just an invitation.

He opened the hatch and found a small closet almost completely filled by a metal tank. Some kind of boiler, he guessed. But something else caught his attention.

There was a paper bag on the ground, large, and apparently filled. Odd, but he probably would've ignored it—if he hadn't noticed one word written on the side of the bag.

Blaylock.

Blaylock? Had Matthews brought some of his work along with him? That diehard. He couldn't quit working even when the case was won.

Ben picked up the bag and peeked inside. It was not legal work. Ben was no financial genius, but these appeared to be negotiable bonds, issued by some foreign government. Each one bore a face value of one hundred thousand dollars. And there were lots of them. Lots and lots.

Ben's eyes expanded. There must be millions of dollars in bonds here. How on earth did Matthews come by that kind of money? And why would it be tossed haphazardly in the boiler closet?

He turned—then jumped so high he almost hit the ceiling. Matthews was standing right behind him.

"I really wish you hadn't found those," Matthews said.

49

Mike blazed down the highway toward town, burning rubber every time he made a turn.

"Which dock is it?" he growled. "Think!"

Fred pressed his hands against his forehead. "I don't remember exactly. I've only been there once, and that was years ago."

"That's not good enough!"

"You're with the government. Can't you just ... call someone? See where it's registered?"

"In the morning, maybe. In the middle of the night, no. So I'm counting on you to tell me what I want to know. Think! Think hard!"

"I'm trying!" Fred turned and stared out the passenger-side window. "I think it started with an *M*."

"I need more!" Mike pulled the steering wheel around hard, screeching as he made a sharp right turn.

"If your friend doesn't know about the bonds, there's no reason to think he's in trouble."

"There is. Ben Kincaid is like a magnet for trouble. He has an unequalled knack for getting himself into it—and a near total inability to get himself out of it."

"Still, there's no proof that—"

"I not going to sit on my butt while my friend dines with a mass murderer!"

Fred withdrew into his seat. "Okay. . . ."

"So you're going to think, and think hard!" Mike bellowed. "I want the name of the dock where Matthews keeps his yacht. And I want it *now*!"

*   *   *

Even though he hadn't begun to fit all the pieces together, Ben instinctively understood that if he didn't get out of that boiler room fast, he never would. He rushed forward, tackling Matthews around the waist. Unfortunately, there was little room for either of them to move. Matthews slammed back against the opposite wall, still between Ben and the exit.

He grabbed Ben by the shoulders and thrust him back. For a professor, he was surprisingly strong. Ben slammed against the boiler closet, headfirst.

"I don't suppose you'd believe me if I told you I won the lottery," Matthews said dryly.

Ben wiped a trickle of blood from the back of his head. "That money came from the Blaylock company."

Matthews frowned. "I suppose technically that's correct."

"You stole it. Millions of dollars."

"I did not steal it." His face became rigid. "They owed me!"

"Owed you? But—"

"I used to work for them. In the legal department. I was on the fast track to a vice presidency. Till they fired me!"

Ben glanced at the exit, still blocked by Matthews. Since there didn't appear to be any way he could get out of here, he might as well stall for time. "Why did they fire you?"

"For telling the truth."

"There must be more to it than that!"

Matthews made a snorting noise. "I expected better from you, Kincaid. After all you've been through with Blaylock."

Ben's eyes crinkled around the edges. "Are you talking about the blue report?"

"Of course I'm talking about the blue report!" he shouted. "I wrote the blue report! And it cost me my job!"

"You," Ben whispered. "It was you."

"Damn straight it was me. I told you I did some work for Blaylock in the past, remember? Small wonder I was anxious to join your team and go after Blaylock. I knew damn well they poisoned the water supply. They knew it, too; they just didn't want to admit it."

"But why didn't you tell me?"

"I couldn't. I signed a confidentiality agreement when I left the company, in exchange for a measly severance package. If I had violated the agreement, the report would've been excluded. And I would've been kicked off the case. Maybe you, too."

"But you still had the report?"

"Yes. They thought they confiscated all the copies, but I still had one. And when it became clear we were hosed without it, I dug it up and sent it to Colby's associate. I'd watched him in the courtroom; I knew he was wrestling with his conscience. I sent it to him—anonymously—and he sent it to you, the same way. No one knew I was involved."

"So you were the source?"

"True. You owe your whole great success to me." He lowered his gaze. "Now give me that merchandise."

"Merchandise?" Something clicked in the back of Ben's brain, something he'd wondered about for many months, since that fateful day he'd agreed to fill in for The Tiger. . . .

"Give it to me," Matthews insisted.

"This is the merchandise?" Ben held tight to the bag. "You were in on it. With Fenton, and The Tiger."

"Don't be too smart for your own good, Kincaid."

Ben's lips parted as the horrifying truth set in. "You killed them. All those Blaylock employees. You killed them for the same reason James Fenton held us hostage. You were after the contents of this bag. The merchandise."

Matthews rushed him. Ben was knocked back against the metal tank. His head slammed back, making a harsh clanging sound.

"Why did you have to be so goddamn clever?" Matthews said, grabbing Ben by the collar. "Why couldn't you just drink your champagne and keep your nose out of other people's business? Do you think I want to kill you? Don't you know how tired of this I am?"

Ben tried to push him away, but he hadn't the strength.

Matthews brought back his fist and knocked Ben in the jaw, hard. "Stupid meddling son of a bitch." He stood up, then reached for something inside his coat.

A long, sharpened knife.

"I had expected to use this on dinner," he said, taking a deliberate step toward Ben. "Dinner will have to wait."

*   *   *

"Mermaid!" Fred said triumphantly. "Mermaid Lagoon. Or something like that."

Mike gritted his teeth. " 'Something like that,' isn't good enough."

"I'm sure that was it," Fred said. "Pretty sure, anyway. I remember they had a masthead with a redheaded mermaid. Cute, busty little thing."

Mike pulled over to the nearest convenience store and slammed on the brakes. Just outside, he saw a pay phone which, mercifully enough, still had its phone book intact. He flipped over to the *M*s, found what he wanted, and tore the sheet out.

He raced back to the car. "Could that possibly be Mermaid Cove?"

Fred's eyes brightened. "Yes. Exactly. Isn't that what I said?"

"It's on something called Pontoon Plaza. Got any idea where that is?"

"Jeez, it's been so long since I came out this way—"

Mike grabbed him by the shirt and shook him. "My friends are in the hands of a homicidal maniac. Do you think you can get me there?"

Fred swallowed. "Of course I can. Let's go."

Matthews was moving toward Ben, knife at the ready. Ben was still lying on the floor, pinned against the closet. He saw only one possible opening. Trite as it was, it was his only shot. He clenched both hands together and brought them up as hard as he could in Matthews's groin.

Matthews screamed. Ben scrambled forward on all fours, moving out of reach just seconds before the knife fell.

Ben crawled as fast as he could, but Matthews grabbed the heel of his foot. Ben fell forward, flat on his face. Matthews was still wincing with pain. Ben took advantage. He rammed his elbow back into Matthews's face. Matthews screamed again, and Ben got the half-second he needed to jump to his feet and run.

He raced through the bulkhead door, carrying the bag of bonds with him, and onto the metal deck, toward the gunnel. He knew Matthews had the edge. It was his ship, after all, he knew it much better than Ben. For all its spaciousness, there weren't that many places to go. And Ben couldn't leave the ship—they were parked somewhere in the middle of the ocean. He could try to swim to shore, but he knew the odds of making it were slim. Especially if Matthews started up the yacht and mowed him down.

No doubt about it—he was trapped but good.

Ben clambered up the ladder, moving so quickly he banged his head on a metal panel. The pain made his vision blur, but he ignored it. He had to figure some way out of this. Somewhere to go, something to do. . . .

"I'm coming after you, Kincaid!" He heard the voice below him and it chilled his blood. "There's nowhere you can go."

Ben threw open the door to the main cabin and ran inside. "Christina!"

She wasn't there, damn it. The two candles were still burning bright on the tabletop. A half-empty champagne flute indicated where she'd been.

"Christina!" He had to let her know what they were up against. Besides, she was the smart one in the team. Surely she could think of some way out.

"Christina!"

She was gone. Worse, his shouting would lead Matthews straight to him. There were few enough hiding places on this boat without him helping the killer locate him. He started back toward the door—

Just in time to see Matthews coming at him, barely five feet away. Ben tried to slam the metal door shut, but Matthews got his shoe wedged into it.

"Give it up, Ben," Matthews said, just outside the door. "There's nowhere you can go."

Ben strained with all his might, but he couldn't close the door. Desperate, he reached over to the table and grabbed one of the candles, still lit, and shoved it through.

"Ow!" Matthews's foot withdrew. His hand shot out, knocking the candle out of Ben's hand. Ben shoved the door closed, then tried to turn the friction handles to seal it. Before he could turn them, though, he felt the pressure on the other side remounting.

Matthews was slamming himself against the door.

Ben glanced over his shoulder. The candle had landed on the table. The tablecloth was burning.

"It's no use!" Matthews bellowed. "Give it up!"

"The cabin's on fire!" Ben cried back. "If you don't stop, your yacht will go up in flames!"

"I want those bonds!"

"If you don't put away the knife, I'll toss them into the fire!"

Matthews's only response was to pound against the metal door all the harder. Ben clenched his teeth and tried to hold firm, but he knew he couldn't keep this up forever. Eventually, Matthews would break through.

The fire was spreading. Ben wanted to put it out while there was still time, but he couldn't let up on the door.

An idea came to him. It was inevitable that Matthews would get in. Maybe he should bow to the inevitable—at least for a moment.

Ben gave it up. He released the pressure on his side of the door.

The door began to open. Ben waited until he saw Matthews's hand cautiously slip through the opening . . .

Then slammed the door shut, hard. Right on Matthews's hand.

Matthews screamed like a banshee. Which was fine with Ben. Besides the fact that it meant Matthews was in pain, which was good, Christina would surely hear it and know something was amiss.

"You'll pay for this, Kincaid!" On the other side, Ben heard the clanging of heavy footsteps on the metal floor.

Ben braced himself, waiting for the reprisal. But nothing came. The pressure on the other side of the door was gone.

What was the son of a bitch up to now?

After a long moment, he cracked the door open. Matthews was gone, both he and the knife. Why?

The answer hit him like an atom bomb.

He was going after Christina.

Where was she? He peered through the glass ceiling to the deck above. He couldn't see it all, but what he did see did not contain Christina.

He left the cabin and raced down the ladder. Most likely Christina had retreated to one of the private bedrooms. Maybe she had a headache, needed to lie down. He raced across the scaffold, opening every door and peering inside.

No Christina. And no Matthews, either.

Panic was setting in. He felt his heart pounding, practically beating its way out of his chest. What had he done? What had he done to Christina?

He smelled smoke; the fire in the main cabin must be spreading. Damn! As if they didn't have enough problems already.

He spotted the ladder that led to the upper deck. Maybe Christina was up there; maybe she wanted to stargaze or commune with her inner self or some such.

He clambered up the ladder, checking behind him with every other step. Still no sign of Matthews. But Ben knew he couldn't be far away.

He reached the top of the ladder and threw himself on top of the deck.

"Hello, Ben. Glad to see you."

It was Matthews. He was ahead of him. Just as he'd been all along.

He was holding Christina tight, one arm pinned behind her back.

And the knife pressed against her throat.

Mike pounded on the door. "Wake up! Police!"

Fred stood nervously behind him. "Maybe there's no one in there."

"There is someone in there," Mike growled. "He just doesn't want to come to the door."

"That might have something to do with the fact that it's the middle of the night."

"I don't give a damn if it's the middle of Armageddon." Mike pounded again, so hard the door almost splintered. "Wake up!"

A few moments later, an elderly man in a bathrobe hobbled to the door. "Yes?"

Mike didn't hold back an instant. "Are you in charge of this dock?"

The man's eyes, barely open to begin with, narrowed. "We're not open. Come back at eight."

"I can't wait till eight."

"We're not open!"

Mike whipped out his badge. "If I say you're open, you're open."

The man bristled. "What's this about? If this is about that goddamned Sam Bullfinch and his fishing license—"

"It isn't. Have you got a yacht owned by a man named Jack Matthews?"

"He docks here, yeah."

"Where's the boat? Show me."

"Can't. He took it out tonight."

Mike's head felt so tight he thought it might explode at any moment. "Where? Where did he go?"

"How the hell should I know? I'm just a dockmaster. They don't have to file a flight plan before they take off."

Mike laid his hand firmly on the man's shoulder. "Listen to me, sir. This is very important. I need to know where that boat is."

The man put his hands on his hips. "And I'm telling you, mister, I don't know where it is. And all the badges in the world ain't gonna change—" He paused, glancing over Mike's shoulder. "Well, hell, mister. Isn't that her?"

Mike whirled around. "What? Where?"

The man pointed past him, toward the ocean. "Over there. 'Bout a thousand yards out or so. See her?"

Mike squinted. The fog obscured his vision, but when he strained, he could see something in the moonlight. Some kind of ship. A big one.

"How do I get out there?"

"Well, I'm no expert," the old man said dryly. "But I think you probably need a boat."

"Where do I get a boat?"

"Beats me. The boat store?"

Mike leaned in to the man so close he had no room to hide, barely enough to breathe. "Listen to me, old man. This may be amusing the hell out of you, but I'm not laughing. I'm not laughing because my friends are on that boat and they're in danger. And so help me, you will get me out there, if I have to strap oars to your sides and row you like a boat!"

The old man drew his head back. "Well, jeez Louise," he muttered. "Why didn't you just say so?"

"I'm sorry it has to end like this," Matthews said, his knife still firmly pressed against Christina's throat. "I enjoyed working with you, and hoped we'd do it again. And I'm tired of killing. I admit, it was fun for a while. It was a release, a release of so much that had been pent up so long. But I thought it was over. I hoped never to do it again."

The bizarre thing was, the man actually sounded sincere. "Then don't," Ben said. "Don't kill anyone. Most especially, don't kill Christina."

"Second the motion," Christina murmured. She was being brave, but Ben knew she had to be terrified.

"I'm afraid I have no choice," Matthews answered. "You know too much."

"But I won't tell anyone. I'll be quiet as a church mouse."

"If only I could believe that."

"You can," Christina urged. "Ben is a man of his word. If he makes a promise, he keeps it. Even to—" She stopped short.

"Even to killers?" Matthews finished. "Sorry. I can't take that kind of chance."

Through the glass-bottomed portal on the deck, Ben could see into the cabin. The fire was spreading. The flames had consumed the tablecloth and started in on the table.

"The yacht is burning, Matthews. If you let it go any longer, there won't be much left."

Matthews pushed Christina's knees out, scooting her forward so he could get a closer look through the portal. "You're right," he said. "But with the money I stand to make, I could buy a dozen yachts. Give me those bonds! Now!"

"Shame to see a boat like this go up in smoke," Ben continued. "What happens if the flames reach one of those boilers? Or the fuel tank? We'll all go up in smoke."

"Damn you!" Matthews shouted. "Give me those bonds!"

Ben walked to the side of the boat. "You will release Christina this moment."

"Listen, you little—"

"You will release Christina, or I'll drop the bonds into the sea."

"No!"

"Think about it, Matthews. Millions of dollars turned into fish food. If they go in, you'll never be able to get them back. Never in a million years."

"If you do that," Matthews bellowed, "I'll slit your girlfriend's throat."

They were at an impasse, and Ben didn't know how to break it. They each had something the other wanted—and a threat that effectively prevented the other from getting it. But for how long? Matthews had killed before—many times. If this went on much longer, he would surely snap. He'd kill Christina, then hope he could get to the bonds before they sank to the bottom of the sea.

He had to think of something. There had to be a way out. But what was it? He couldn't think of anything.

Fortunately, Christina could. "Would you mind moving that blade farther from my face?" she asked Matthews. "It's awfully cold. I think I'm getting a chill."

Matthews smiled thinly. But he did not move the blade.

"But seriously, you don't want me coughing and sneezing all over you."

"Then tell your boss to give me the merchandise!"

"I would, but he never does anything I say."

"I'm not amused."

"See for yourself. 'Ben, give the man his merchandise.' See? He didn't do it."

Matthews's face twisted into a bitter snarl. "I'm going to count to ten, Kincaid. And if I don't have the bonds by the time I reach ten, I'll slit her throat."

"Don't do it, Matthews."

"One. Two."

"Matthews! Your boat is burning!"

"Three. Four."

"Matthews!"

"Five. Six."

"Ohmigosh." Christina's hands rose to her face. "I think I'm going to sneeze."

Christina cradled her face, as if to sneeze. Then, with a level of coordination at which Ben could only marvel, Christina managed to do three things at once. She faked a sneeze, knocked the knife away from her throat—and jabbed the spike end of her heel into his shin.

Matthews stumbled backward. His grip on her arm relaxed. Christina broke away and tried to run, but he managed to grab a piece of her dress. He jerked her backward, knocking her to the deck.

Ben dropped the bonds and ran for him. He tackled Matthews, trying to knock him over without success. He was too strong, plus he was still holding the knife. Ben tried to wrestle with him, but at the same time he had to stay out of reach of that blade.

"You haven't got a chance," Matthews sneered. He brought his fist around and hit Ben on the side of the face. Ben fell backward, reeling. Matthews followed up with a full-body block.

Ben tried to grab the steel ladder, but he just missed it. He fell backward, tumbling off the deck onto the metal scaffold below.

Matthews turned back toward Christina. "Now it's just you and me." He stood up, straddling her. "Nine, ten. Time's up." He lifted the knife into the air with both hands, then began bringing it down, hard and fast, straight toward Christina's throat.

A shot rang out, splitting the night air. Ben, still dazed, clambered up the ladder, trying to see what had happened. Matthews had been knocked backward; he was lying flat on the deck. The knife had fallen out of his hand. His arm was bleeding, limp and motionless.

Ben found the source of the shot on the starboard bow. A small motorboat was pulling up beside the yacht. He didn't know the older man at the helm, but the guy leaning across the prow with a gun in both hands was very familiar.

"Mike!" A flood of relief washed through him. "Where the hell did you come from?"

"Long story." As the other boat pulled in closer, Mike jumped onto the yacht. He came up the ladder behind Ben. He walked straight to Matthews, who was still conscious, although he appeared to be in considerable pain. "You're under arrest, you sorry, sick son of a bitch."

Ben ran to Christina's side. "Are you all right?"

She pushed herself up by her arms. "I'm okay. Just shaken up." She looked over at Mike. "Talk about your sight for sore eyes. Am I ever glad to see you."

"I aim to please."

She threw her arms around him and hugged him. "You did. Although next time, maybe, could you get here a little earlier? The last split-second thing is very dramatic, but once is enough."

Mike smiled wryly. "I'll work on that."

Matthews glared at Mike, his teeth clenched with rage and pain. "I should've killed you when I had the chance."

"You know what? You're right. But you didn't, you loser, so now I'm going to make you pay for what you did."

"I did nothing."

"You killed six people! After torturing them! You don't even deserve to live."

Ben peered through the glass bottom. "We have to get out of here, Mike. The yacht's on fire."

"There's a fire extinguisher in the cabin," Matthews said.

"Like I'm going to risk my life saving your stupid boat." Mike whipped out his handcuffs and snapped one end over Matthews's left wrist. "Come on."

He started to snap on the other cuff, but all at once Matthews lurched forward, knocking Mike's gun hand away. Mike fired, but the bullet went wide. It crashed through the glass portal and entered the main cabin.

"The bullet hit the gas tank!" Ben shouted. "The gas is leaking!"

"My God," Mike murmured. "Gas and fire. Now we really do need to haul ass."

Christina was already down the ladder and heading toward the motorboat. "Hurry!"

Mike jerked the loose handcuff on Matthews's arm. "Come on, asshole."

"I'm not going."

Mike shoved him hard. "You are going!"

Matthews barely moved. "I'm not letting you take me in.

Not now. Not after everything I've done. I know what will happen to me."

"I don't have time for this!" Mike bellowed. "This boat could blow at any moment!"

"I'm not going!"

"Fine!" Mike spat back. *"Stay!"* With a sudden twist, he hooked the other end of the handcuffs to the metal rail on the side of the boat.

Matthews's eyes widened. "Wait! You can't—"

"I already did." Mike raced back to the motorboat. Ben and Christina were already there, and the old man who owned the boat had the engine running. The second Mike hit the deck, it sped away.

They were barely halfway back to shore when the yacht exploded. It shot up into the black sky like a fireball. All at once, the pitch-dark night seemed brighter than day. An instant later the boom rattled their bones; the vibrations buffeted the boat.

"My God." Ben turned and watched as the yacht incinerated itself. Even from his distance, he could feel the heat. "I guess this means Matthews won't need a lawyer."

Christina nodded. "What a way to go."

Mike didn't look. "He got a lot better than his victims did. At least he won't suffer."

"Perhaps," Ben said quietly. He couldn't turn away. He was mesmerized by the intense orange blaze, the only point of light in the darkened sky. It was almost beautiful, in a way, as the flames reflected off the surface of the water and gave color to the colorless. He continued watching, all the way to shore, the last remains of what had once been Matthews's boat, and was now his funeral pyre.

FOUR

*   *

And the Hunter Home
from the Hill

✳ 50 ✳

Sunday was Mother's Day. It was also the first anniversary of Billy Elkins's death. A memorial service was being held in a Blackwood park, not just for Billy, but for all eleven of the Blackwood children who had died prematurely from leukemia.

Ben and Christina stood with Cecily and the other parents in a circle surrounding a blazing bonfire. The base of the fire was girded by eleven shrouded stones, one for each of the children.

"Thanks for your help with the bonfire," Cecily said quietly. "That's quite a blaze. What did you use for fuel?"

"All the documents from the lawsuit," Christina answered. "Almost two hundred bankers boxes filled with memos, evidence, and exhibits."

Ben nodded. "And in the end, it all came down to one ten-page report. A report written by a disgruntled lawyer who later became a multiple murderer."

"That's too strange," Cecily said, shaking her head. "Strange and . . . frightening."

"It is frightening," Ben agreed. "Because it means that at one time in his life, Jack Matthews was willing to take a stand, to stick his neck out for what he knew was right. And it cost him. Cost him so much that he eventually snapped. Became obsessed with tracking down his 'merchandise.' Making sure he didn't get cheated again." He paused. "We like to think of killers as being all bad, pure evil, but clearly that wasn't the case with Matthews, at least not originally. I suppose it proves the capacity for good and evil exists in all of us." He stared into the blazing bonfire. "That's why it's so frightening."

"Matthews is gone now," Christina said quietly. "Best not to think about it."

Cecily turned her head. "I read about that. He was killed when his yacht exploded?"

"Yes," Ben said, not looking at her. "He died in the explosion. Didn't get out in time."

"And the money?"

"The bonds must've burned up with everything else."

"So no one will ever have the benefit of all that wealth," Christina said. "Not Tony Montague, the first thief, and not any of the subsequent ones." She shook her head. "All that agony. All that death. For nothing."

A few of the parents who were in the Blackwood First Baptist Church began to sing softly—the "Air From County Derry," one of Ben's favorite requiem pieces. It started quietly, just on the threshold of audibility. It gave him shivers.

"I want to thank you both for coming," Cecily said. "You didn't have to."

"I did," Ben replied.

"Me too," Christina added. "I read that the EPA has allocated funds to clean up the Blackwood aquifer. Make Well B safe again."

"Yes," Cecily answered. "It's wonderful news."

"Of course, Blaylock still isn't admitting any responsibility," Ben noted. "But after the blue report hit the press, he agreed to contribute substantial sums to help with the cleanup."

"Do you realize that since Well B was closed down, there hasn't been another case of childhood leukemia in Blackwood? Not one. Eleven cases during Well B; none after. I think that says it all."

"Common sense may not count for much in the courtroom," Ben agreed. "But it certainly is useful in real life."

"The parents met last night," Cecily continued. "We've decided to create a fund with the settlement money."

"A fund?" Christina asked. "To do what?"

"To prevent this from happening again." She stared into the fire, which was now rising taller than their heads. "We'll start slow, then build as more of the money comes in. We want to train people to respond to complaints promptly, test water supplies effectively, identify potential carcinogens. Perhaps in time we can even afford to help with the cleanups."

"I think that's a great idea," Ben said.

"It wouldn't have been possible without you."

Ben shook his head. "It wouldn't have been possible without *you*."

Having finished the air, the choir began "Amazing Grace." Most of the parents joined in, some of them humming, some of them singing the words. "Amazing grace, how sweet the sound, that saved a wretch like me. . . ."

Ben felt goose pimples racing up his arms. "Looks like those trial exhibits are gone for good, Christina."

She shrugged. "It was a relief to get them out of the office. Although now, with all the furniture and equipment gone, too, there's not much left."

"I'm so sorry about what happened to you," Cecily said. "Perhaps we could give you some kind of loan. . . ."

Ben stopped her cold. "Absolutely not. We'll take our fair share and not a cent more. You have great plans for that money; stick with them. We'll be all right. We'll get our stuff back in time. We've paid off the most urgent bills."

"But you don't have anything to live on. And you still have debt."

"We'll get by. We always have."

Cecily did not appear satisfied, but she let the subject drop.

One by one, each of the parents stepped forward and removed the shroud from one of the stones. As they did so, they spoke their child's name out loud. "Emily Quatro." "Jason Bennet." "Jim Foley." Then they each said a few words about their child—describing his or her tastes, preferences, personality.

At last, it was Cecily's turn.

"My Billy loved books," she said. "He was a great reader. His hero was Robert Louis Stevenson. He even loved poetry. Can you imagine? A twelve-year-old boy who loved poetry."

She placed her hand on one of the shrouds. "This is the last part of his favorite poem; he knew it by heart: 'This be the verse you grave for me/Here he lies where he long'd to be/Home is the sailor, home from the sea . . .' " She paused,

her voice trembling. " 'And the hunter home from the hill.' "
She bent down and removed the shroud from the stone.

Ben turned and saw Christina had tears in her eyes. "This
is so sad."

Ben put his arm around her. "But a little less sad than it
was, I think." He stared into the flames. "A little less sad because, by standing firm and refusing to quit, these parents
were able, in their quiet way, to extract some tiny measure of
justice." He turned toward Cecily. "That's what this case was
all about."

In steady quietude, Cecily took a candle from a box and,
approaching the fire, lit it. She inserted it in a brass holder
and set it beside one of the uncovered stones. "This is for
Billy," she said. Her voice cracked slightly. "He's what this
case was all about."

* 51 *

Ben got the call at two in the morning, but despite the late-
ness of the hour, he dressed and raced to the hospital.

This was it, the nurse on the telephone had said. Mrs.
Marmelstein was dying. She didn't have much time left.

Ben drove to St. John's and raced up the stairs to the fifth
floor. In the main corridor, he found Jones and Loving hovering over a phone. The speaker was on and they were both
listening to an angry voice.

"How dare you wake me up at this time in the morning!"
the voice bellowed. "I told you I didn't want any part of this!
Now leave me alone!" The phone disconnected.

"Who was that?" Ben asked.

"Paulie," Loving said gravely. "Mrs. Marmelstein's son.

We told him she was dyin', but the creep still refuses to come. Won't even talk to her on the phone."

"I promised I'd bring him back to her." Ben felt an emptiness inside him he could hardly bear. "Has she been asking for him?"

"Constantly," Jones said. "It's all she thinks about. Seeing him again is her dying wish."

"We're just going to have to tell her the truth."

"I suppose," Jones replied quietly.

The threesome entered Mrs. Marmelstein's room; Christina was already there. Mrs. Marmelstein appeared to be awake.

"Mrs. Marmelstein? It's Ben."

"Benjamin?" She seemed lucid, although he could see from the monitor that her life signs were faint and fading. Her eyes were closed, but Ben supposed that was natural, since she was now entirely blind. "Is it really you?"

"It's me," he said, taking her hand. "I'm right here."

"Of course you are." A faint smile came over her face. "Aren't you always? You've always taken such good care of me."

"You've always taken care of me," Ben replied. He was trying to keep his voice from trembling, but it was almost impossible. "You gave me a home. When I didn't have one."

"Did you find Paulie?" she asked.

Ben closed his eyes. A stabbing pain split his stomach. "Mrs. Marmelstein, I'm very sorry, but—"

"I'm right here."

Ben whipped his head around. It was Jones speaking, but Jones, the perfect mimic, was speaking not in his own voice but in the voice they had just heard over the telephone.

Jones laid his hand on her shoulder. "I'm here, Mother. I came as soon as I heard."

Mrs. Marmelstein placed her shaking hand on his. "I'm so glad, Paulie. I've wanted to talk to you again so much."

"Mother," Jones continued, "I want you to know—I'm sorry about what happened."

She cut him off. "I'm the one who should be sorry, Paulie. I was wrong. I know that now. All this time, I've been hoping you'd return—so I could beg your forgiveness. A mother should stand by her son. Always. Can you forgive a foolish old woman?"

Jones squeezed tighter. "Of course," he said, barely above a whisper. "There's nothing to forgive."

"Paulie," she continued. "I want to explain something to you. About my will. I've left the house to Benjamin."

Ben's jaw dropped. She *what*?

"That may seem strange, but I know you never really loved it and probably don't want it. Ben needs it. He's always getting himself into money troubles, trying to save the world on a shoestring budget. He thinks I don't know how much difficulty he's had, just as he thinks I don't know how much money he's slipped into my petty cash box over the years. But I do know. I've known all along."

Ben felt an itching in his eyes he couldn't seem to scratch.

"That's all right," Jones reassured her. "You're doing the right thing."

"I know. I just wanted to explain it to you. I wanted you to understand that even though I'm giving Ben the house—I still love you. Very much."

"I love you too, Mother. And I always will."

Her voice seemed easier now, calmer, soothed by hearing her son's voice one last time. Jones never let the impersonation drop. He stayed with her for the rest of the night, as did they all, till early morning, when at last they saw the line on the monitor go flat, and the life-support console began to play its doleful one-note tune.

* Acknowledgments *

I would like to express my appreciation to all the attorneys and scientists who are working together to learn the truth about environmentally derived diseases. Of course, I want to thank Jan Schlictmann, whose courageous lawsuit based upon the contamination in Woburn, Massachusetts, was recounted in Jonathan Harr's masterly book *A Civil Action*. Unfortunately, that case was only the first, and Woburn is only one of many disease clusters that have arisen in recent years. All the outbreaks mentioned in chapter 33 are real. Too often it seems the diseases, ranging from cancer to autism and particularly targeting children, are linked to environmental contaminants. Readers wishing to learn the latest about this disturbing trend should visit the Web site: www.civilactive.com.

As before, I want to thank my friend and editor Joe Blades for his continued support and excellent work. I'm also keenly grateful to my literary agents, Robert Gottlieb and Matt Bialer at the William Morris Agency. I want to thank Arlene Joplin for reading my manuscript before publication and catching any number of foolish errors. I want to thank Robert Ginnish, Barbara Graham, and Hyla Glover for suggesting the title. And I want to thank my wife, the nicest person I've ever known.

My e-mail address is: wb@williambernhardt.com, and I welcome mail from readers. You can also visit my Web page at: www.williambernhardt.com

                                        —William Bernhardt

Acknowledgments

John Ferrand

MURDER ONE

WILLIAM BERNHARDT

Coming in hardcover in April 2001.
Published by
The Ballantine Publishing Group.

*Please turn the page
for a sneak peek. . . .*

* 1 *

"So what're we gonna do about it?"

Barry Dodds didn't want to encourage him. "We're gonna play cards, Arlen—that's what we're gonna do. So play already."

A toothpick darting out from between his teeth, Arlen Matthews tossed out a few chips. "Seems to me this isn't something we should take lying down. Seems to me we ought to do something about it."

Mark Callery called. "Do something? Like what?"

Dodds pressed his hand against Callery's arm. They were about the same age, but Dodds was a captain, and he knew that because of his senior rank, Callery, unlike Matthews, respected his opinion. "Don't encourage him."

"I just wanted to know."

"And I'm saying, don't ask."

"What's the matter with you, Barry?" Matthews asked. "Don't we still have freedom of speech in this country? Let the boy talk."

"No good can come of this discussion." Dodds was a short man with the beer belly that seemed like a mandatory stage in almost every police officer's career. "You boys would be better off if you just forgot about it."

"Is that right?" Matthews obviously didn't agree. He addressed himself to the fourth member of the group. "What do you think, Frank?"

Frank didn't respond immediately. He was an extremely large man; down at headquarters, they called him The Hulk. Given his enormous size, his colleagues imagined that it took longer for thoughts to make the trip from his brain to his mouth, sort of like the larger dinosaurs. "Can't say, really."

"That's what I like about you, Frank. You always know exactly where you stand." Matthews obviously wasn't satisfied. "I tell you what I think. I think this was a travesty of justice and I think we ought to do something about it."

"Hasn't this mess caused you enough trouble already?" Dodds was the youngest of the four and the most senior in rank, a fact which he knew caused some trouble, even if it was never directly mentioned. "The courts have spoken. You can't take the law into your own hands. That's not how the system works."

Matthews was not pleased. "Don't lecture me on the system, college boy."

Dodds grimaced. In truth, many of the police officers, and all of the younger ones, had college degrees. But because he had a graduate degree in criminology, because he had been promoted rapidly and he spoke the Queen's English, to Matthews he was always the "college boy."

"I think we should just let it alone."

"You'd feel different if it had been you up there on the witness stand." Matthews threw down his cards—which was no great loss since he was holding a pair of twos. "You'd feel different if that attorney had made you look like a lyin' jackass."

Dodds, the last player still holding his cards, scooped in the pot. "He was just doing his job."

Matthews jumped up on his feet. "Just doing his job? Just doing his job?"

"I didn't say I liked it, okay?" Dodds had been trying to calm Matthews down all night, and frankly, he was getting sick of it. "I just said there's no point in acting like it was some big surprise. You know what's gonna happen when you take the stand. The defense attorney's going to try to make you look like one of the Three Stooges. There's nothing new about it."

"This is different."

"It isn't."

"Like hell. This time it was one of our own. It was Joe. My partner. And if you had any loyalty to Joe—"

"Don't you dare lecture me about Joe." Dodds had had it,

all he could take. "Joe and I went to school together, all right? I've known him longer than any of you. I would've died for him, understand? *Died* for him!" He stood up to Matthews and jabbed him in the chest. "So don't you lecture me about loyalty. Don't you dare!"

The room fell quiet. Matthews and Dodds glared at one another, like two jungle beasts waiting to see who would make the first move. No one did.

Eventually, Frank cleared his throat. "So are we gonna play cards here?"

Matthews kept his eyes trained on Dodds. "I'm sick of cards."

"But it was my turn to deal."

"There ain't gonna be any more cards, got it?" Matthews pounded the table. "It's sick. Our buddy is dead, the lyin' whore that killed him is running free, and we're sitting here like a bunch of pansies playing cards!"

Callery's voice was quiet, and his eyes were trained on the table. "You know, Arlen, you weren't the only one who was up on the witness stand. I testified, too. I went first. You think I enjoyed it? I didn't. I didn't like that lawyer prying into every little thing. I didn't like him insinuating that we botched the investigation. But it's over now. We have to move on."

Matthews looked away. "It's different for you."

"It isn't, Arlen."

"It is. Goddamn it, can't you see? It is." To his companions' shock and horror, Matthews's small eyes began to well up. "It wasn't your fault, okay? I was the one who screwed up. I was the one who used Judge Bolen's crappy warrants. It's my fault that murdering bitch is still walking the streets."

Dodds gently placed his hand on his colleague's shoulder. "Give yourself a break, Arlen. You couldn't've known."

"I should've known, damn it. It's my job to know. I let Joe down. He was my partner. And I let him down." Tears began to stream down his face.

Even though it was obviously the last thing on earth he wanted to do, Frank broke his silence. "Arlen . . . it's none of my business, but . . . I think maybe you should get some help.

Maybe some counseling. Central Division's got that woman who comes in twice a week—"

Matthews's face swelled up with rage. "I don't want counseling, you idiot! I want the fucking little cunt who killed Joe!"

Another silence followed, this one even longer than the one before. No one knew what to say next.

"It's this simple," Matthews said, his chest heaving. "Are you Joe's friend, or not? 'Cause there's no way any friend of Joe's would let what happened happen and just walk away without doing anything about it." He leaned across the table. "So what about it, Frank? Are you Joe's friend?"

Frank took his usual eternity to reply. "You know I am, Arlen."

"What about you, Mark?"

Callery frowned. "Joe was my first supervisor, my first day on the job. He taught me practically everything I know."

"I'll take that as a yes." He turned toward Dodds. "And what about you? You claim Joe was your oldest friend. You claim you'd of died for him. Was that just talk? Or does it actually mean something?"

Dodds glared back at him, not answering.

It was Callery who broke the silence. "What did you have in mind, Arlen?"

"We're cops, aren't we?"

"Ye-es . . ."

"We're supposed to catch the bad guys, right?"

"Yes, but—"

"So I say that's what we do."

"But, Arlen, the case is over. Double jeopardy has—"

"There are ways around that."

Dodds stared at Matthews, stunned. "Arlen, stop right there. I don't know what you're thinking, but whatever it is—"

"What's the matter? Haven't got the guts for it, college boy?"

Dodds fell silent, biting back his own anger.

"I want that cheap piece of ass that killed our friend. And I want that cheap lying whore of a lawyer who got her off and made us look like fools."

"We all do," Callery replied. "But how are you gonna do it? There's no way."

"There is a way." Calmly, almost in control of himself now, Matthews fell back into his chair. "I've got three words for you, boys: The Blue Squeeze."

* 2 *

Ben stood beside the reception table sampling Dean Belsky's canapés. There were a wide variety of them, but they all seemed to involve cucumbers. Ben hated cucumbers. Actually, it wasn't so much that he hated them as it was that he didn't understand their purpose. After all, they didn't taste like anything. They weren't especially good for you. They didn't quell your appetite. What was the point? And yet, there they were, as far as the eye could see, rows and rows of sliced, diced, warm, and wilty cucumbers. All in all, it was about the most unappetizing display of appetizers he'd seen in his life.

"Paula, look! *Cucumbers!*" Jones, Ben's office manager, surged past him and bellied up to the table; his girlfriend, Paula, trailed in his wake. He slid his plate under half a dozen of the nearest selections. "I was starving." He glanced at Ben. "Aren't you having any?"

"I'd rather eat air. Actually, it's about the same."

"Nonsense. Cucumbers are great. So cool, so refreshing." He took a bite into one of them. The expression on his face rapidly changed. "Unless, of course, they've been out on the table a wee bit too long. When did this reception start?"

"Beats me. Seems like forever."

"Ah, don't be such a party pooper. This is a big day." Jones turned his attention to Paula. "Want some, sugar pie?"

"No thanks. I'll just savor the inside lining of my mouth."

Ben smiled. "A woman after my own heart." Paula was the head research librarian for the Tulsa City-County system. She and Jones had met on the Internet more than a year ago and been inseparable ever since. "Better watch out, Jones. I may steal her away from you."

"As if you stood a chance." He sniffed. "We're soul mates." He clasped her hand. "And hopefully we always will be."

"And I hope we always will be," she corrected. " 'Hopefully' is an adverb meaning full of hope."

"That's my cute little librarian gal. You'll always be my sweet thing, won't you, punkin?"

"You know it, huggy bear."

They rubbed noses.

Ben didn't know whether to be enchanted or repulsed. "All right, you two, calm down. We're in a public place, remember?"

Jones pulled away from Paula's face. "I remember, Boss. But it's easy to forget when you're around my hot little love bug."

"Uh-huh. So when are you going to make an honest woman of her?"

A touch of frost settled amongst their little group.

Paula laughed, a bit too heartily, trying to smooth over the awkwardness. "Bad question, Ben. Jones is still in his twenty-first century sensitive male mode."

"And that means?"

She winked and mouthed the words: "Can't commit."

"Anybody seen Christina?" Jones asked. "We're here for her, after all."

"Haven't seen her," Ben answered. "Probably searching for a robe short enough to fit. Haven't seen Loving, either."

"That's odd. He said he would be—" Jones stopped. "Wait—oh, my God! There he is."

"What's the big—" Ben swiveled around.

"Hey ya, Skipper," Loving said, with typical exuberance. "Am I late?"

"No, no," Ben said, trying not to laugh. "You're fine. A good fifteen minutes till the ceremony starts." He turned away, unable to suppress his mirth.

"What?" Loving said. "What is it? Did I do somethin'?"

"No. N-not at all," Jones stammered out. He was doing a considerably less capable job of containing himself. "You certainly look . . . dapper this morning."

"What is it? My clothes?" Loving, Ben's investigator, was about the size of a bear and built like a brick wall. But this morning, that admirable girth was encased in an ill-fitting tuxedo. With morning coat. "You told me this was a dress-up thing."

"Yes," Jones said. He was full-out laughing now. "Yes, I did . . ."

"And I wanted Christina to know how important I think this is. Wanted to treat her special day with respect." He hooked a thumb under his lapel. "When she sees this, she'll know how much I care about her."

"That," Ben said, "or she'll think you just came from a royal wedding."

"What a bunch of boobs," Paula said. She took Loving's arm and sidled up next to him. "I think you look dashing."

"Really?" Loving beamed. "I wasn't sure, you know?" He lowered his voice a notch. "I haven't actually worn this thing since high school."

"Ah. That would explain the fit."

"Ben!"

He twisted his neck in the direction of the voice and saw a familiar red-haired figure blazing a trail through the reception crowd. She was wearing a black gown and had a mortarboard tucked under her arm.

"Ben!" she said, bubbling. "You came! I'm so happy!"

"Well, of course I came," he said, standing there awkwardly. "I couldn't miss seeing my, um, you know, one's legal assistant graduating from law school."

Paula patted his arm. "Nice job, Ben. Very clinical." She gave Christina a hug. "We're so proud of you, Christina. All of us."

"Are you staying for the ceremony?"

Ben opened his mouth, but whatever he was planning to say, he never got the chance. "Of course we are," Paula said quickly. "All of us."

"That's wonderful!" Christina had always been on the exuberant side, but this morning, she was positively effervescent. "Can you believe I'm finally graduating?" She spun around, and the brick wall wearing a tuxedo caught her eye. "Loving, look at you! You look *extraordinaire!*"

Loving tugged on his bow tie. "Me? Nah . . ."

"You do! Very scrummy! If you wear that thing much longer, you're going to have to beat the girls off with a stick."

"Shucks. I wasn't tryin' to look good. I just wanted you to know what a big deal we think today is. And how proud we are of you."

She leaned forward and kissed him on the cheek. "You're very sweet." She turned back toward Ben. "Don't you think my gown has a certain je ne sais quoi? Don't you like it?"

"Better than most of your wardrobe."

"Wanna see what I have on under it?"

"No." Ben gave her a long look. "You do have something on under it, don't you?"

"Of course." She lifted the hem of the gown and gave him a fast flash of a pink poodle skirt lined with black fake fur, white socks, and saddle oxfords.

"You know," Ben said, "once you're a lawyer, you won't be able to dress so . . . eccentrically."

"Which is why I dressed up today. I have the whole rest of my life to be boring." She saw that the other graduates were beginning to file out the rear. "I have to go get in line now." She paused, this time looking at Ben. "See you after the ceremony?"

"Wouldn't miss it."

And then she was gone, like a strawberry blond poltergeist, three shakes and a cloud of dust.

It was well past time someone reinvented the graduation ceremony model, Ben mused, as he sat on one of the front rows of the First Baptist Church sanctuary, bored to tears. There were too many people crammed into too little space, none of them smiling. Even the graduates looked as if they might drop off at any moment. After "a few opening remarks" from the dean, it was time for the musical entertainment, which was neither.

And then, of course, the dreaded commencement address, delivered by a distinguished state senator. Why were these things so often delivered by politicians? Ben supposed it was because they were always ready to give a speech and didn't require an honorarium. This address went on for more than half an hour, and it seemed to Ben to have a lot more to do with getting the speaker reelected than offering words of wisdom to the graduates. As a part-time adjunct professor, Ben had tried to suggest a few innovative alterations to the dean—like skipping the whole ceremony. But for some strange reason, his proposal hadn't garnered much support.

At long last, it was time to award the diplomas.

"Here it is!" Loving said excitedly, jabbing Ben in the ribs. "It's almost time."

"Almost time? They're still in the As. Christina is an M."

"She'll be up before ya know it," Loving said, and he was almost right, because Ben managed to take a little eyes-open nap, a trick he had taught himself during Western Oklahoma motion dockets. By the time he knew what was going on again, they were finishing up the Ls.

"Steven Edward Lytton, PLA Vice President," the announcer said, and somewhere behind him, Ben heard a booming chorus of shouts and cheers.

"What boobs," Ben muttered, under his breath.

"They're not boobs," Loving said. "They're family. They're proud of him. It's what families do."

"Loving . . . you aren't planning . . ."

But there was no time. "Christina Ingrid McCall, National Moot Court, Law Review, Order of the Coif."

In the blink of an eye, Jones, Paula, and Loving were on their feet, whooping and hollering at the top of their lungs.

Ben wondered if the dean was watching. "Why are you doing this?" he growled under his breath.

"Don't you get it?" Loving hissed between hoots. "We're her family."

He was right, of course. Ben pushed to his feet and pounded his hands together. He even whooped a little.

After the ceremony, the group gathered at the office at Two Warren Place for a postceremony celebration. Jones had ordered champagne, chilled and ready when they arrived. Paula had made brownies and Loving picked up some exquisite bacon cheeseburgers from Goldie's.

"A toast," Jones said, hoisting his glass in the air.

"Another one?" Ben asked. By his count, they'd already had about three bottles of toasts, and they were all starting to wobble a bit.

Jones ignored him. "To our own Christina," he said. "She's been the world's best legal assistant for years. Now she'll be the world's best lawyer!" He hiccuped. "Excluding the Boss, of course."

"Of course," Ben said. Boy, she'd been a lawyer for what, an hour and a half? And already he was an afterthought.

"I think she should give a speech," Loving said. With his bow tie unstrung and dangling from his neck, he looked like a cross between a lounge singer and his bouncer. "Speech! Speech!"

Christina flushed, either with champagne or embarrassment. "I am not giving a speech."

"Hey, if you're gonna be a lawyer, you're gonna have to give some speeches."

"All the more reason not to give one now."

"Well then I will," Ben said. He raised his glass. "A short one, anyway. I've been delighted to work with you for some time now, Christina, but I've never been prouder of you than I am today."

Christina's eyes sparkled.

"Congratulations, kiddo—you're a lawyer now."

She shook her head. "No, not yet. I have to be tested by fire. In the courtroom."

"You'll get your chance."

"Hey, is this a private party, or can anyone guzzle your champagne?" Major Mike Morelli, Tulsa P.D.'s chief homicide detective, strolled into the office wearing his trademark trenchcoat. "Way to go, slugger." He gave Christina a hug.

"Thanks, Mike."

"You bet. Just don't get too many major criminals off the hook right away, okay? My job's hard enough as it is." He leaned over next to Ben. "Can I talk to you for a minute?"

Ben sat up. "Sure. You mean—?" He jerked a thumb.

Mike nodded. "Don't want to disturb the revelry."

Together, they made their way to Ben's interior office. He'd been at this location for more than a year now, but it was still as barren as the day he moved in—the result of a combination of tight finances and lack of interest. He had a desk and two chairs, a file cabinet, a framed diploma, and that was about it.

They each took one of the available seats. "So what's up?"

"Just wanted to warn you, Ben—I'm going to be gone for a little while."

"Gone? Why?"

"Got an undercover assignment. And I don't know how long it will take. So you'll have to find someone else to watch *Xena* with you and pretend that we admire it for its sophisticated scripts."

"Nothing dangerous, I hope."

Mike shrugged. "Who knows? Did you read about the murder last night?"

Ben nodded. A corpse found in a swing at LaFortune Park. Hard to overlook.

"We think we've got a line on the killer. Which took some doing, since we can't even ID the victim. It's a faint trail, but worth chasing. And will probably take a while. So I wanted to give you the heads-up."

"Thanks, I appreciate that," Ben said, but he sensed there was more to this than he'd gotten so far.

"You might also mention it to Julia. If you happen to see her. I mean, I don't know, she probably doesn't care. But still. I wouldn't want her to worry."

"Of course," Ben said, even though he knew there was no chance that his younger sister, Mike's ex-wife, would be inquiring after him.

"Who knows, she may finally realize she needs help with that kid of hers. Heard anything about Joey?"

Ben shook his head, and for about the millionth time wondered—Did Mike know? Was this just a game, or was he really oblivious to the fact that Joey was his son? Granted, Julia had never acknowledged the paternity to Mike or anyone else, but it was obvious to Ben every time he looked at the kid. Was it possible that Mike missed it?

"Something else, Ben." Mike squirmed, shifting his weight from one side of the chair to the other. Ben could tell he was more uncomfortable now than he had been talking about Julia. "About the Dalcanton case."

Ben waved his hand. "It's over, Mike. The court's ruled."

"It may be over for you, Ben, but for a lot of other people I know, it isn't. And never will be. Until someone pays the price for killing Joe McNaughton."

"I can't lose sleep over what some rednecks are stewing about."

"I'm not talking about rednecks here, Ben. Or country bumpkins or militia freaks. I'm talking about cops. Good cops."

"Mike, every time I win a case, I make some cop angry. That's just part of the job. I'm used to it."

"This is different, Ben. Way different. Joe McNaughton was a police officer. Moreover—he was well-loved, very popular with the rank and file. And the way he died"—Mike shuddered—"in public, and gruesome in the extreme—that really knocked some of the boys for a loop. Probably didn't help that he was killed by some cheap South Side stripper, either."

Ben sat up. "Mike, she was never convicted. And I don't think—"

"Yeah, yeah. But I can tell you this—there's not a guy on the force who isn't absolutely convinced that she's guilty. No one's happy about the way the trial turned out. And a lot of them just aren't willing to let it go."

"So what are you saying? You think Keri is in danger?"

"Maybe. But mainly I'm worried about you."

"Me? I'm just the lawyer."

" 'Just the lawyer' is not a phrase I hear much at head-quarters. Son-of-a-bitch lawyer, yes. Low-life ambulance-chasing scumbag mother—"

Ben held up his hands. "I get the picture."

"I wouldn't worry so much if I was going to be around. But I'm not. So watch your back, okay, kemo sabe?"

"Okay." Ben pushed himself out of his chair. "When are you leaving?"

"Immediately." He followed Ben back to the conference room where the rest of the group was still celebrating. "Well, as soon as I finish that last bottle of champagne."

* * *

Two hours later, Mike was gone, but the rest of them were still partying. The exuberance of the evening had not diminished with the last of the bubbly. In fact, if anything, Ben thought the rampant merriment had increased.

They were unwrapping presents now. Loving gave Christina a briefcase embossed with her initials, and Jones and Paula gave her a flowering plant for her new interior office. Christina was obviously pleased and touched.

"What about you, Skipper?" Loving asked, his voice loud and celebratory.

"I bet the Boss has something great for her," Jones said. "I think he's kind of soft on her, just between you and I."

"Between you and *me*, dear," Paula said. "So what's your present, Ben?"

Ben coughed uncomfortably. "Uh . . . yeah. Present. Right."

Loving looked aghast—and Christina looked shattered.

"Don't tell me," Loving said.

"Boss, you didn't—"

"No, no, I have something. Really." Ben scrambled awkwardly behind a desk. "I just wasn't expecting to present it so . . . publicly."

Loving winked at Christina. "Must be somethin' intimate."

Christina rolled her eyes. "From Ben? Yeah, right."

"Well, it's about time he gave her something intimate," Jones said. "How long has she been—" Loving jabbed him in the ribs, knocking the wind out of him.

"Here it is." Ben dragged out a large oversize package, long and thin like a poster, only somewhat thicker and more solid. It was wrapped in red and green paper—Christmas leftovers, obviously.

Christina's eyes brightened immediately. "You did get me something!" She wrapped her arms around his neck and pressed her cheek against his. "You old softie, you."

"Is she talking about the Boss?" Jones asked. Loving shushed him.

Christina tore into the package without hesitation. Barely a second passed before the interior was revealed, black and green and wobbly.

Christina's eyes crinkled. "Is it . . . a desk blotter?"

Jones looked up toward heaven. "He got her a desk blotter."

Loving pursed his lips. "Very intimate."

Paula nodded. "Sexy, even."

Ben appeared perplexed. "What? I just thought, she's going to have a new office, and she's going to want it to look all lawyerlike, so she needs a desk blotter."

"It's nice," Christina said, keeping her voice even. "I really like it."

Ben noted that the other three were glaring at him. "What's your problem?"

But there was no time to explain. Before anyone could even attempt it, they heard a harsh pounding at the outer doors. "Open up!"

Paula jumped. "Who the hell is that?"

The pounding continued. Christina moved closer to Ben. "Someone you forgot to invite to the party?"

Ben started toward the front doors, but before he could get there, they burst open.

The voice returned, this time amplified by the unmistakable sound of an electronic bullhorn. *"Police! Nobody moves!"*

MURDER ONE

WILLIAM BERNHARDT

Coming in spring 2001.
Published by The Ballantine Publishing Group.